Private Classes 2

By NatLJohns

This book is a work of fiction. Names, characters, and occurrences either are products of the author's creative imagination or are used fictitiously. Any similarities to actual happenings, settings, or individuals - alive or deceased - are totally coincidental.

ISBN: 978-0692594056

Cover design idea by NatLJohns

DEDICATIONS

To my family and my friends for their love and support

ACKNOWLDGMENTS

I would like to thank God for giving me so many gifts and talents. I really do believe in the saying "If you don't use what God has given you, He will take it away." If this isn't the truth, I don't know what is.

Secondly, there is my family. I appreciate the patience you have exhibited with me for not only getting the first book done and published, but for the second book to be done, preparing to be published, while I am working on the third book. I know there may have been some missed dinners, phone calls, interactions, and sports games (basketball, football, and track) … y'all have missed some too hanging out with friends lol. Some of you may have thought this was a hobby since I have had the love of writing for so long but as you see, it is not just a hobby. I love writing just as any other author, poet, storyteller, activist, speech teacher, blogger, etc. It is a passion of mine and I really do believe I should have started many years ago with publishing. Hey, maybe I'll publish some early writings. What do you think?

Thirdly, I would like to thank my friends for continuing to hang in there with me. From those who saw the very first draft of my creation when we were on that plane headed for Las Vegas, to those who have seen this particular draft come into its own. I repeat Jackie and Arlette, this is strictly from my creative imaginary house. I want to thank all of you. You know exactly who you are so I won't repeat names this time lol. All of you are very dear to my heart.

Fourthly, my loving pets. I finally got back to putting those special ingredients in your food. I apologize for it ever being missing. Again, your mama was on a mission and she made the first step in completing with the first installment. I might be almost done with Book 3 and I haven't skipped a beat have I? Mama still loves you!!

Here we go again "NL." Thank you so much for taking time out of your very busy and sometimes hectic life and schedule to help a sista out with this proofreading thing. I mean hey, it was about 303 pages for book one and now this one is over 390 pages. Don't worry about the third book. You get to see that one straight from me now that I'm an Indie writer!! As always, I have sooo much love for you.

Last but not least, but most importantly, my fans. Book 2 would not have been at all possible if it weren't for you purchasing my debut novel, wanting to read what I had to say, enjoying it, and looking for more. I stay in the Rank section of my author page and I was nervous several times as to where my craft was headed. However, to be listed in the Top 100 eight times within the first three weeks of Private Classes' birth, I most graciously thank you. I am an avid reader myself owning almost four hundred digital books. I know how the choosing and selection process goes. You encourage me to continue to write and extend this series.

As always, I love you Momma!!! Muah!!

Chapter One

1

"All right, all right Ladies, calm down. Listen to y'all. Everyone seems to be in a good mood today. That's what I'm talkin' 'bout. Come in here all revved up ready to GO!! How is everyone doing this evening?"

The Ladies begin to quiet down once they hear Kelly's voice in the room. They begin to make sure their outer garments are neatly placed on top of the stacked mats or on top of the chairs.

Kelly puts her bag down and takes off her outer garments. She is observing everyone trying to read their expressions. Most are ready but some appear a little uncomfortable. She is happy that BeLynda is not a part of that group.

Damn, her bag looks heavy as shit. What the hell she has in that thing, says Sandy to herself looking on inquisitively.

"What's the matter? What happened to all of that excitement and joy I heard when I walked in here," Kelly asks laughing. "Did everyone remember to bring what I asked you to bring to class?" Kelly looks around the class at the Ladies again to see who says "yes" and who says "no" and who says absolutely nothing.

Kelly walks over to the table she had set up an hour before class was to begin. With her back turn to the class, she begins taking out the items from her bag placing them on the table. Everyone looks on waiting for her to move out of the way so they can see what she has for them. When she finishes, she turns around facing the class to make a notation of what was going on behind her. Looking over to where their bags are placed she notices there aren't enough bags for the amount of people in the class.

"Oh, okay. Only a few of you forgot your goodies. Or did you not want to use the food for anything other than to fuel your body? Well, with your creative mind, you can surely provide fuel to your body in several ways." Kelly walks around the class talking to the Ladies always giving eye to eye contact to ensure they know she is serious and to ensure they are listening.

Colleen wants to see the fruits and vegetables everyone chose to bring to class. *Yea, pull them out so I can see just how freaky my classmates and friends are.* She starts looking around the room trying to imagine which fruit or vegetable each Lady would be. *Is she a cucumber woman? Ooh, I bet she is a zucchini woman. Oh, now with those lips, she is definitely a banana woman.* Colleen starts laughing to herself when she looks at one woman saying to herself, *Poor thing, you must be a carrot woman.* Colleen is really entertaining self right now.

Regina notices that Colleen is thinking about something that apparently is funny. She leans over to Colleen whispering in her ear, "Hey, what's so funny? Let me in on your laughter." That makes Colleen laugh harder. She makes sure she is quiet but it does nothing for the tears coming down her left cheek and her shoulders moving up and down. "What's so funny Lene?" Regina smiles wide knowing it is something nasty.

Colleen finally responds. "Girl I'm sitting here trying to imagine what types of fruits and vegetables everybody brought to class. If you only knew what has been going through my mind," she starts laughing again.

Regina just looks at her with a smile stretched across her lips yet they are open. "Oh no, you didn't just go there. Girl, you need to stop with your nasty ass. Well fill me in. What did you come up with?" Regina looks around at the women in the class waiting to hear what Colleen has to say about them.

Colleen straightens up saying, "Oh, don't worry, I will definitely tell you. But it must be later. I'd hate for both of us to get put out of class. We are too grown for that type of embarrassment. High school was over so long ago."

Sandy is trying to multi-task with her listening and thinking skills. She is partly listening to the instructor and partly listening to her friends, while Ray is on her mind. She is thinking back to her dinner date with Ray a few nights ago, which was actually last week. She hasn't had the opportunity to tell Colleen and Sandy that she went on a date with him. BeLynda knows but she doesn't know how it turned out. She is not sure if she wants to wait until Thursday at the Spa. That is too far away and she is already about to explode with the verbal portrayal of her experience.

BeLynda has no other choice but to listen to the instructor. She is already uncomfortable with bringing the food with her. She played with fruits last week with Khalil but not these kinds of foods. *Strawberries and raspberries are romantic and easily handled. Apples go great with wines so I understand those. But bananas, cucumbers, POTATOES?! What the fuck for? I am not sure what she wants us to do with these foods but I made sure mine are extra clean.*

Kelly is still talking while walking around the room, observing all of the faces throughout the class. Even though she is trying to be serious and in tune with her sensual side, some of the looks on their faces really have her wanting to laugh. That cramp in your side, with tears, and you can't breathe type of laugh. A few times she turns away from the Ladies so that they won't see her wide smile. When she regains her composure, she faces them and continues walking around them.

"All right Ladies. Those of you, who have brought your foods with you today, please retrieve them from your bag. I hope none of your foods got mashed on the way here." Everyone walks over to their bags opening them taking out the fruit or vegetable they brought with them. Some are enthusiastically ready to show off what they have. Others are hesitant, not really all that moved about presenting their props.

Kelly stands to the side of the room observing the Ladies as they return with their props to their original spots. She is paying close attention to what they have chosen and looking at each woman to see if the food actually fits the personality they have been showing the last couple of months in class. She isn't too sure about some of them. Kelly folds her left arm under her breast propping her right arm on it with her right hand under her chin. The Ladies are trying to figure out what she is thinking while she is looking at them. Colleen starts smiling looking at Regina.

"Mmm-hmm, I bet you she is trying to figure out why we chose the fruits and vegetables that we did. She told us to bring bananas and cucumbers or a large potato. As you see, some had the nerve to bring zucchinis, squash, eggplants and shit. They look like they came to class ready to cook and eat." Colleen and Regina giggle.

"I know. No one brought in a potato though. I wish they had because I really want to know what Kelly was going to say or show about that. Zucchinis … I can see that. Maybe they thought she was just telling us to bring in something longly shaped. You know she got some props up there on the table. You think she will let us come up there and take a peek?"

"I dunno. She might. Let's see what she says because she is looking very curious right now. I can guarantee you *whatever* it is she is thinking, she is going to tell us later. And I can't *wait*!"

Regina and Colleen return to completely paying attention. However, Regina decides to look around the room to see exactly what others have brought to class too. One particular piece of food catches her attention. She is not sure what it is but it looks like a dildo. Easing over to the Lady that is holding it, the Lady notices her advancing and begins to smile.

"Excuse me. I couldn't help but notice your prop. I'm sure you know why I am approaching you because you are smiling at me. From over there, I thought you had a light skin dildo with balls in your hand. Please enlighten me. What in the world do you have," Regina asks the Lady with a smile on her face.

"It is a deformed Fingerling potato," the Lady whispers to her laughing.

"Really? For real, a potato? A Fingerling potato at that, huh. That's usually a small potato. I have never seen one grow this big

… and so deformed. Oh my," Regina responds in astonishment at what she sees. "Where in the world did you find that?"

"I found it in my garden," the Lady says while looking at the potato, turning it around letting Regina get a complete look at it.

"Really?! In your garden, just growing? I am sure when you saw that, you immediately thought about class, didn't you?" Regina and the classmate laugh.

"Actually, I thought about how it had been awhile since I have had 'any' action," they both laugh quietly at her statement. "There I was out back, checking to see if my garden was doing okay since I planted potatoes in the wrong season. They were looking pretty good. And there it was. I kept looking at it and just had to laugh at where my mind was going when I saw it. Then it popped in my head that it would be a good conversational piece for class today." They both snicker trying not to be rude while Kelly is talking. Regina walks back over to where she was standing. Kelly had already noticed the Lady's odd shaped prop and decides she will speak on it later.

Kelly continues talking now standing in the front of the class. "Okay, now I see some have cucumbers, some have bananas, but some have decided to go with a different food. I see a few zucchinis and a few roots. Those of you that do not have anything, just be patient. I will get to you in a few minutes." The empty handed Ladies look worried.

"Now, let's start with the cucumbers. I would like for the cucumber Ladies to tell us why you chose the vegetable. Also let us know if you have a few others in mind that you would've brought with you." Everyone that doesn't have a cucumber is looking around to see who will be speaking. A slender Lady with natural curls walks towards the front of the class with her cucumber in tow.

"All right, let's give her our undivided attention. I'm sure everyone doesn't know your name, even though they may know your face. Please state it for us and gives us your explanation."

The Lady clears her throat. "Okay. Um, … hello everybody. My name is Tameka but they call me Tam or Tammy." Some Ladies speak back to her and smile. Colleen looks at her saying to herself, *Girl, you could've kept the ghetto self-references and get on with your declaration.* "I decided to bring the cucumber because I figured we were going to put our mouth and tongue exercises to use. I mean, this is the closest you can get to a penis, right," the Lady says while looking at her cucumber. She looks up at her classmates and saw everyone listening to her. She has nothing else to say, so she walks back away from the front of the class. Some of the Ladies nod their heads in agreement.

A very thick Lady with spiral curls walks up front to face the class with her cucumber. She smiles at the teacher, and then looks down at her cucumber for a few seconds as if to gather her thoughts. Then she looks up at the faces of her classmates, rubbing her forehead with her left hand fingertips and begins to speak. "Hello my fellow classmates how are you today?" Many of them reply with, "Fine." Colleen says in her mind, *Do we all have to ask how the class is doing when we get up there? After the teacher and the first chick, I'd think it is established that all of us are fine this evening. Maybe that is a way to buy some more time.* "Well, my name is Jamie. I enjoy coming to class on Mondays. I take pleasure in the camaraderie of other women. Okay, sooo … I have a cucumber with me today. I chose to bring the cucumber because I like this shape better than the banana. I think this would be a better prop for today's session. Since we are able to eat the skin on the cucumber, I figure it wouldn't hurt anything if we are going to be licking on it." When she finishes speaking, she begins leaving the front of the class. The Ladies in the class shake their heads supportive of her justification.

Kelly responds, "Okay, not bad. That makes sense. But, before you leave what is your other reason why you chose the cucumber?" Kelly smiles at Jamie. Jamie looks at her mystified. The class gets quiet waiting to hear more. "Class did you hear what she said?" Many nod their heads "yes." "In listening to Jamie, she kept it clean about the cucumber but she never really went into any details about the banana. Would you care to go a little deeper for us please?"

Returning to the front of the class, The Lady closes her eyes, takes a big deep breath and explains. "I know many have talked about women and bananas but I am not really sure why. It could be because it is curved like many penises. But what throws me off is that if you keep it in the skin, you have two rough ends and they won't be pleasant to insert into the vagina." Jamie begins to walk away again.

Kelly smiles folding her arms across her breasts and walking around the room listening. "Is there anything else?" Jamie pauses in her step turns and looks at Kelly as if to say, why are you picking on me. "I'm asking because I could tell by the way you were talking that it was really all about the banana as far as why you chose the cucumber. I've been teaching this class for quite a few years and I have heard all kinds of answers. But yours, I knew you could give a story. Don't be shy. But if you feel uncomfortable, I do understand. Please, remember, we are here to help."

Jamie faintly smiles at everyone in the class standing where she is and adds, "Well, also, the banana is too soft. If you take the skin off of it that just isn't something I would want to scoop out of my vagina. It's too fragile and I can it see it breaking off up in there feeling like two tampons. What if it all doesn't come out? Who would want to walk into the gynecologist examining room to tell that?" Jamie is serious but the entire class is in an uncontrollable laughter.

"Sounds like you have been there before Girl! Speaking from experience?" One of the Ladies in the class says and the class continues to laugh.

"Hide all scoops and spoons, please," Colleen says while laughing.

"Okay, okay, simmer down Ladies. Take back control of your emotions. Let's move on to the next," Kelly says slightly laughing at Jamie. Everyone straighten up and prepare to hear the next Lady.

The next Lady with bleach blonde hair and enough breasts and ass to share with everyone in class approaches the front of the class and begins to speak. "Hello, my name is Kamira. I don't have any nicknames, so you can call me Kamira." The Ladies laugh at her introduction. Looking at her cucumber, she says "Let's see … I chose the cucumber because … oh hell, I don't know. This is just my choice." Some of the Ladies giggle at her response.

Kelly smiles at the Lady, "*Okaaay.* I'm sure you can do better than that. You didn't have anything going around in your mind as to what we might do with it? Or what you would do with it?"

"Nope, I sure didn't," she says halfhearted.

"Oh, so you just went with the vegetable I said, huh? Is that what you're telling me Kamira," Kelly smiles looking at her side-eye.

"Yea, I did. What's wrong with that? You gave us three choices and I chose one of them to bring. I mean, well, you know …" the Ladies laughs.

"Aaah, here it comes. Let it out Girl. C'mon, we are in this together. Don't be shy. What can we do with your response? I'm sure you don't run into any of your classmates out in the streets." *With that color hair and the way you come in here dressed every week, I am one hundred percent sure that you don't hang out in the same places and circles as any of the other women in here. You don't even look like you belong in this class. You look like you should be training me to teach this class,* Kelly is saying to herself with a smile plastered on her face. *I wonder if any of them can ever read through my expressions.*

"Okay, look," she says rolling her neck with her eyes close, smacking her lips together, "I chose the cucumber because I actually have been practicing the mouth and tongue exercises using it. I mean, the ones I have used have been put in salads and vinegar already so they wouldn't go to waste. So I made sure I found one that was close to what I have been using. And then if you asked us to demonstrate, I'd be ready." The entire class erupts into laughter at her ghetto antics and honesty. With her hands on her hips, Kelly laughs too shaking her head at Kamira.

Colleen says, "I know that's right girlfriend. I don't even know why I didn't think of that. Hey, do your thang. I ain't mad at cha!!" *With your ghetto ass. I hope you are deep conditioning that hair every week or it's gonna fall out.*

BeLynda bashfully smiles at what Kamira and Colleen said. It was truthful and entertaining to her. She doesn't know if she is able to be that open with class. *Well, hell, I did bring two of them to class. Which one am I going to talk about? I don't know what I should say about either one. She told me to bring them and that's what I did. Maybe she didn't see what I have and I could put one back. Maybe I should have checked with the girls to see what they were bringing and gauge my decision off of theirs.* BeLynda can feel herself starting to unravel.

Looking over at Sandy, BeLynda whispers, "I didn't think she was going to ask us something this. I don't feel like getting in front of the class explaining a damn thing about my choices. What are you gonna say?"

"Well, just tell her that you brought them to class because she told you to. We have been attending these classes for several months now. I am sure Kelly knows how you are." Sandy already knew BeLynda was going to be uncomfortable. Just like she knew BeLynda was going to look at her like she is crazy after letting those words unintentionally flow from her mouth.

"Excuse me? She knows how I am? Hmmp, how am I Sandy? Let it out. Please tell me how I am." *What the fuck you mean Kelly knows how I am? What y'all be saying about me when I'm not around Dee Dee*," BeLynda says to herself while looking at Sandy. She is completely lost in Sandy's observation. What the other Ladies are saying about their cucumber is far from significant to BeLynda right now. She hears nothing they are saying, and doesn't give a fuck about what they brought to class.

Sandy looks at BeLynda as if to say, *"Damn, I shouldn't have said that. Fuck!!"* Trying hard to explicate her comment, she says, "Bee, that didn't come out right. You know I didn't mean any harm by what I said. But, I'm just sayin'. Kelly should know how you are by now. That's her job to feel us out, observe us … you know, like in psychology experiments. She can't help us if she ain't being observant. Hell, she should know how all of us are at this point. We've been in how many classes with her in the past few months so far." BeLynda is listening to Sandy with understanding, agreeing with her. She calms down.

To lift the melancholy cloud that is hovering over their conversation Sandy says, "Well, I'm not sure if she has drawn a conclusion about Colleen yet, but I am sure she will make an assessment soon." They both laugh looking over at Colleen, who has her arms folded with a facial expression of "Will they move the fuck on with this shit."

"Ooh, she is so not into this part right now at all," says BeLynda.

"Actually, she is in to it. She is irritated by the responses the Ladies are giving the instructor," Sandy laughs at her observation. BeLynda pays close attention to Colleen. Sandy continues embracing BeLynda's arm. "Look at her. She's probably saying to herself, 'That bitch is lying,' or 'Oh you gotta be kiddin' me,' or 'That heifer making that shit up.' They start snickering at Sandy's phrases about Colleen. Kelly notices them doing something else but listening.

"Hello Ladies. I see you like this evening's class, huh?" Some smile and others are looking around to see who she is talking to. "Ms. Giles and Ms. Robertson … how are you doin' today? Havin' a private moment that's just for two without sharing any with us? Shame on you two. We like to laugh just like you. I'm glad y'all are havin' fun in class today. I like that. Good, good. Now do either of you have a cucumber?"

Colleen looks over at her friends and smiles. *Mmm-hmm, I wonder who y'all were over there talkin' 'bout. Hell anything is better than these bullshit ass answers these chicks givin' right now. Just make sure y'all spill the beans when we get out of here.*

Sandy responds quickly, "Oh, I didn't bring that with me. But Bee did. As a matter of fact, she brought a banana *and* a cucumber with her today."

Kelly's eyes pop wide open. "Bee brought in a cucumber *and* a banana?" Sandy shakes her head "yes." "Wow! Isn't that great class? Bee made sure she was well prepared for today. Well, c'mon Bee let us hear all about your cucumber. I'm sure it has a story." Kelly as well as BeLynda's friends all smile at her as she wavers to move toward the front.

Before she takes a step, she looks at Sandy with an expression that seems to says, "I could kill you right now." Sandy softly responds to the look with, "Go 'head Bee. It won't take long. Just breathe. Love ya."

"I should stick this cucumber up your fuckin' ass," BeLynda responds through clenched teeth. Sandy jumps back a little in shock at what BeLynda said to her. *Damn!! I hope she gets up there and just let it out.*

BeLynda arrives at the front of the class. She looks around the room, trying to get rid of the huge lump in her throat. Taking a few slow deep breaths, holding up her cucumber to the class, she begins to speak. "Good evening Ladies. I hope everyone is feeling just fine today. I hope you're feeling more tranquil and comfortable than I am right now." A few giggle at BeLynda. She looks up to see who finds her amusing. This makes her a little less uneasy. Her heart slows down almost to a normal tempo.

"Hello, I am BeLynda but they call me Bee. Ummm, I have a cucumber." BeLynda shakes it in the air looking at it, carefully measuring her words. A few of the Ladies laugh again. "Let's see, I have a cucumber here with me today. I said that already didn't I? I chose to bring this because, well … for one, Kelly said to bring it. For two, it's shiny and I figured if she has us inserting this anywhere on us, I wouldn't have any problems with it sliding in. I mean, it's a simulation of a dick – I mean penis – right? What else could this be used for? These are sexual classes and I don't think any of us would consider the cucumber as a provocative food for when you're tryin' to be sexy or romantic. I mean, well if our man wants to see us using it on ourselves, then I guess it could be deemed as freaky but ..."

Everyone is floored at BeLynda's response. Colleen is smiling at BeLynda with her arms still folded across her chest. *That's my girl!! Let these bitches know you ain't as inhibited as you be tryin' to pretend. I knew you had it in you.*

Sandy is shocked and is immobile like a mannequin. *Well, I'll ... be ... damned. I thought she was gonna get up there and choke as usual. Hey, I told her to breathe ... and she did. Do that more often Sis. I'm proud of you.*

Regina is hunching Sandy but she can't seem to get Sandy's attention. "Do you hear Bee? Do you hear what she is saying? I can't believe it!! I think I need to be pinched. Is this actually happening right now? Did you tell her to say that?" Regina is still hunching Sandy, both are in disbelief.

Sandy turns her head towards Regina, still not moving her body and says, "Nope. I didn't tell her anything but to breathe."

"Breathe? That's all you said to her?" Sandy shakes her head in an up and down "yes" motion. "That must've been one of those 'Waiting to Exhale' breaths. Damn. Bee is going all out with her enlightenment for us isn't she?"

All Sandy has to say is, "Yeap, she sure is. Every now and then she does surprise me with what she says. And today is one of those times."

By the time BeLynda finishes her thorough rationalization to her classmates, everyone quietly watches her leave from her invisible platform to take her position once more by her friends. All the Ladies just stand there for a few seconds with all eyes on Kelly waiting to see what she is going to say.

Well, what do you know? Ms. Giles got very comfortable and into the session so far. I need to make plans to take her out for dinner soon. She's starting to come around. Kelly slightly turns to Sandy. Looking at her she bows her head with eyes close saying to herself, *Whatever you told her before she came up here, I thank you.*

Kelly starts off with a slow hand clap. Some of the Ladies join in with the slow clap. BeLynda is looking around at the applauding hands and then at the faces they belong to. In a few minutes, everyone in the class are clapping yet much faster, rooting for her.

"Now, *THAT'S* how you give an explanation!! That right there, that right there," Colleen says pointing at BeLynda, "will keep this class energetic and invigorating. Bee, keep that up at every class Girl. You were on your 'Keepin' It Real' game tonight!!"

"What? What did I say," she blushes and knows everyone is pleasantly surprised at how verbally open she had just been. *Don't get too comfortable with me doing that. This is a once in a lifetime thing Ladies. A once in a lifetime thing.* BeLynda is back to standing next to Sandy twiddling with her fingers. Sandy and Regina give her a big hug. Colleen gives her a high-five. She is pleasantly sated with the response from her classmates.

The instructor continues. "Well, I am in fact speechless. Bee that was excellent. That's an A+ for you for the *week!* Now, are there any others with cucumbers that haven't spoken yet? If so, let's keep it moving. We still have the other foods to get to."

"Girl, please. After Bee's response, who you think is gonna get up there and try to top that? I know I won't. Not that it's a competition but I'm sure her response can speak for the rest of the class. Some ain't gonna get up there and be that candid. Hell that includes those who brought in bananas, zucchinis, carrots … whatever they got with them." Colleen waves off Kelly.

Kelly and the other Ladies can't do anything but laugh. They know Colleen is right. However, Kelly still has to make sure that everyone gets to provide their reason. Laughing, she asks, "Does everyone agree with Colleen?" They nod their heads "yes." "Don't you wanna get up here and speak too?" They nod their heads "no."

"See? I told you. Just make a mental note of who didn't participate in this part of today's class and have something ready for them next week." They all look at Colleen as if to say, *Oh no she didn't just say that.*

"Ah, is that right Colleen? Because that would include you too, right? You haven't been up here yet either. Do you still want me to have something special planned for next week?"

Colleen covers her mouth with both hands and her eyes bugged out. *Damn!! I forgot all about that.* "Hell naw. Give me my something special right now. Let me take a look at those funny shaped vegetables you have up there on that table." Colleen points in the direction of the table and starts laughing.

Walking up to the table and picking up a few of the props examining them to see if they are real, she says, "Where did you get them from? Look at this carrot. Look at this y'all." Colleen places the carrot on the edge of the table. Kelly is a little perturbed but she hides it. "Now, what y'all think? Doesn't it look like a man sitting down with his dick – uh, I mean his penis, his stuff – hanging out?" The Ladies laugh at her description correction.

"Yes, you are so right," one of the classmates responds laughing.

Sandy picks up one asking, "Is this a potato? This looks like the ass of a woman bent over showing off her other set of lips." She shows it to the class.

"Ewww, it damn sure does," says one of the classmates. "How did these vegetables grow so deformed like this?"

Picking up another vegetable, Colleens says, "This pepper looks like an uncircumcised penis. Look y'all. What y'all think? Doesn't it look like that?" Some of the Ladies rush to the table to see what else is on it. They are laughing and taking pictures of the oddly shaped food that grew to resemble female and male genitals. Kelly is frustrated how Colleen took over her class with her own direction.

The Lady that was approached by Regina earlier says, "Hey that one looks just like my prop. The only difference is it's a Red potato and it's bigger," showing off her Fingerling potato. The Ladies turn to see what her potato looks like and starts laughing.

"Yours is about an average six inch. But Kelly's is what some of us have been wishing for at night," one of Ladies says and they all laugh harder than before. While they are laughing preoccupied with talk about the other crazy shaped vegetables, Colleen sneaks the instructor's red potato off of the table heading for her bag.

Hmmp, I'm sure she really doesn't need this. I'll take it off her hands. She won't miss this one," Colleen says while successfully getting the potato in her bag.

"All right Ladies. We've let the time escape us today. I am happy to have brought in a few conversational pieces. Everyone seemed to have enjoyed class today. Since we didn't get to the exercise, we'll pick up right here next week Ladies. So you will need to bring your props again to the next class." The Ladies aren't too happy about that. They thought she was going to move on the next class.

Kelly starts packing up her products and talking to some of the other ladies. Smiling at Colleen, she says to herself, *Oh I see you Miss Thang. When I get you alone, you will be explaining what you wanted it for. As if I don't already know.*

Chapter Two

2

"Ouch!! GIRL!! Hey!! You need to be payin' attention to what you're doing to my hair instead of listening to Shelley's gossiping ass. This is the second damn time you done touched one of my ears with that hot ass comb!! I can listen to her ass because I'm a sittin' *payin'* customer. Your expensive ass got work to do and I will not walk out of here looking like I was the guinea pig for the new stylist in the shop." Other clients and stylist laugh at Colleen's statement.

"Oooh, Colleen I am sooo sorry. I ain't even know I was dat close to yo ear. Now, you know I am payin' attention to what I am doin'. Don't play. Chantal don't mess around when it comes to whipping up her clients' hair. As long as I have been pressin' yo hair, I ain't never burnt you."

"Right … you mean you have never burned me more than once!! So don't *YOU* play!! I am not gonna be walking around worrying about my burnt ears being exposed for the world to see, when they shouldn't be burnt in the first place. You better remember Easter is coming in a few months. Don't let all these mothers see the job you did on my ears and take them 'chirren' somewhere else."

The entire shop explodes into laughter. Colleen laughs but she is actually serious about the blisters she feels popping up on the top of her ear lobes. Shelley is laughing cramming handfuls of French fries in her mouth twirling around in her empty client chair. Chantal laughs at what Colleen said but it really isn't funny to her either. She knows she is good at what she does as well as she knows Colleen all too well. Colleen is pissed.

"And Shelley, what are you laughin' at? You da reason why I burnt Colleen's ear in da first damn place, got me listenin' to dat shit. Maybe if you had a client in yo damn chair, you wouldn't be runnin' yo mouf. Dat seems to be da only time you ain't running yo mouf. Why don't you go entertain yoself by makin' appointments or washin' hair? Matter fact, go up to da break room 'n finish eatin'. You know you ain't supposed to be down here with dat anyway. Da first roach I see … I'm tellin' you ...." Shelley hurries to grab her purse and bag of food to head upstairs.

Damn I hate having to go to the hood to go to the best shop in the hood to get my hair done by the best hood chick. But I ain't gonna lie. I come out looking like I just walked out of Vidal Sassoon's Salon every time. I might have to sit down and have a few business lunches and dinners with Chantal's ass. She needs a plan to get out of this hole-in-the-wall she calls her business. And leave her bad speech and these hoochie mamas here.

Chantal puts a glob of pressing comb grease on the back of her left hand. Applying some of the grease on a small section of Colleen's hair she runs the hot comb through the section. The grease sizzles and pops, while she is blowing on the comb and hair making Colleen frown a little from the hot grease running down her scalp. Chantal starts a new conversation with Colleen.

"I'm really sorry 'bout dat. I know better dan to get caught up in her drama, especially while I'm workin'. I'm not into fuckin' up hair or ears. I be tryin' to be professional 'n shit but she catch me ervry time wit her 'man' stories. They be stupid as hell but unreal and sometimes dey do make my day. She can't be dat stupid, den again, some of dat shit I have witnessed." Chantal has Colleen facing the huge mirror on the wall. Styling her hair, she is looking at Colleen through the mirror as she speaks. Colleen's eyes meet hers through the mirror.

"Oh, don't worry about it but this is the last time girl, I'm serious. And you can't get caught up in her mess. This is your business Chantal and you need to tell her to chill. She's making you look bad tellin' that bullshit all loud so all of us can hear it. Half of that mess she shouldn't even want to tell alone in a dark room. If she has to release it from her heart and mind then she needs to do that in her bedroom closet. Hopefully what you have seen has been witnessed up in here. We gotta get you out the projects. There is more money to be made and you can make it."

"I know right? I've been savin' since the first time you told me dat. Debonair will be goin' to elementary school next year and I can't have him in dese schools 'round here pickin' up dat street shit like his fava. My baby gone be sumbody that a muva can be proud of, you watch. Mark my word Colleen. I'm serious." Colleen can see the tears welling up in Chantal's eyes.

"Don't get all emotional on me in here having people looking at us trying to figure out what we talking about. We will meet up soon and talk about a business plan for you. This will be our little secret okay? And work on your English. You are a Lady and we speak intelligently when we are working." Colleen gives her a humble smile to let her know she is serious.

"Okay. I'm not gone say nuffin'. Thank you so much Colleen. Sooo, what you got planned for today Ms. Jeffries? I meant to tell you earlier dat you lookin' really cute today. Who is da special man dis time?" Chantal is batting back her tears preventing them from falling.

"Okay, don't let me have to remind you to keep your mouth shut. Now, before I respond to what you just said, I want you to repeat what you just said but a little better. Yea, I am somewhat of a friend since I've been coming to you for years but treat me like a client you just met."

Chantal pauses and says, "Umm, okay. Let's see, I said, 'Okay. I'm not gonna say nothing. What you have planned for today Ms. Jeffries? I meant to tell you earlier that you are lookin' really cute today. Who is the special man this time?" Chantal and Colleen both smile.

"Now, that was better. You had a double negative in there, just don't make that mistake when speaking business. It wasn't that hard, was it? You don't have to sound like the hood just because you're in it. Well, I appreciate the complement but let's make this clear. I am a grown ass woman and I don't do 'cute.' I do 'nice,' … 'beautiful,' … 'bad,' … 'fierce.' 'Cute' is for children. And what you mean '*this time*'? You making it sound like I am a playa or a Ho or somethin'!! I have what I call *Options* missy. Choose your words careful boo-boo. However, you know I come in here, get my hair done, and listen to y'all's shit. Don't be trying to peep who drops me off or picks me up. I won't be up for discussion." They both laugh out loud a little. All eyes turn to them.

Chantel finishes up Colleen's hair, gives her a hand mirror so she can see her hair from all angles. Colleen smiles, looking at her hair through the wall mirror to see her hair from the front and the sides. She then looks through the small hand mirror to see how her hair looks in the back and top. She is pleased with Chantal's work, not that she wouldn't have been. She pays Chantel, tips the shampoo girl, and heads out towards the Subway to get a tuna salad to take with her.

Whew!! Chantel is sweet but she needs to get out of her surroundings. I got a headache listening to all that bad and broken language coming out of the mouth of a very beautiful woman. That cycle she's caught up in needs to be broken and I don't mind helping her make the start.

"Hey, Hey Ladies!! How's everybody doing?" Colleen speaks as she is approaching the table.

"Hey, hey to you too Ms. Jeffries. I'm great!! You look nice as always. How are you doing? Come struttin' in here with the fresh hairdo." BeLynda responds standing to give Colleen a hug and kiss on the cheek.

"Yeap, Chantal done whipped your hair … dyed, fried, and laid it to the side didn't she y'all? Did you forget you were meeting up with your girls and not a man?" Sandy responds standing to give Colleen the same as BeLynda.

"Well, hello Colleen. How are you doing?" Regina smiles and leans in for a kiss on the cheek as Colleen sits down at the table beside her.

"Hey, she gets paid good money for her services. Plus, it is still early. I figured since the Spa is closed today for their holiday party, I might as well take advantage of the free time." Colleen rubs her hands over her shiny flat wrap, making sure her sore ears aren't showing.

"Oh, so are you saying that you're leaving us early today? We normally have at least three hours together on Thursdays. Just because the Spa is close doesn't mean you alter your plans. So how long will you share yourself with us today? Don't be changing our together time for a man *neegrette*. None of us did it even with husbands, so don't try to change or adjust the rules," Regina says.

The waitress came to give them their waters and take all of their drink orders. She is surprised to see that they all wanted an apple martini. *Damn, I don't know if I should be asking for a martini after the Devin situation. Maybe I should get something else on the next round.* Colleen is looking deep in thought. She doesn't want one of her girls to have to drive her home tonight since she has other plans tonight. And she doesn't want to be sloppy for her date.

Colleen looks at Regina and she seems to be extremely quiet today even through her talking. She looks at her and she can tell that something is bothering her. *I will come over later and see what is up with her. I wonder if this has anything to do with that car the other night. You are not telling me everything Girlie. I better get the whole story when I come over. Be ready to talk Mrs. Wooten because I will be all ears.* Colleen doesn't like the mood that Regina is giving off this evening.

"That's right! We don't shorten our time with you and we don't expect you to start something new. So what you got planned? Don't be ditching us for dick either," Sandy gives Colleen the side-eye.

"Yea, yea, whateva!! I'm not doing any ditching of my friends. But today … I figured that I would meet up with Byron for a little bit of dinner, drinks, talk, and maybe something a little extra afterwards. We haven't seen each other for a minute and when he came over a few weeks ago, I was feeling what I was seeing before me. I mean, I'm sure y'all don't mind, right?" Colleen looks at all of her friends to make sure everything is still copasetic.

"Girl, you aiight. But you heard all of my words. I'm just sayin'," says Sandy. "You're the one that made the rule so long ago so don't be tryin to change it because you want to be filled up. We've adhered to your rule, now don't act like a politician and think the rule doesn't apply to you heifer." The Ladies start laughing at Sandy's statement.

"Sandy you hit the nail on the head Girlie. I like that. I'ma have to use that sometimes," BeLynda says. Colleen rolls her eyes at all of them.

"Whateva. I'm not going against the grain or the rule. I just thought that I can get a change of pace on a Thursday for a change. Hey, what can I say? Byron was looking real good the other day when he brought me lunch. I wanna catch up wit'em aiight?" She rubs her hair again.

"Oh, I hear you Girl. I know how that can be. Not trying to block your dick at all. Just want to make sure you didn't think that the rule only apply to everybody else but YOU!!" Sandy says staring at Colleen to make sure she understood.

"Oh, I don't think that. No, not at all. Sooo, what have y'all been up to since the 'vegetable' class? Has anybody been combining the mouth shit with the cucumbers? Or with the real thang?" Colleen smiles wide at her question, waiting for the juicy. "You know she said we need to be practicing and talking about it amongst each other outside of class."

"Don't be asking us. You got a story to tell us? Then spill it. Tell us what *you* been doing. I'm all ears," says BeLynda watching Colleen closely.

"Yea, what you got? You always want us to tell you first and then you hit us with a bomb. Let us have our explosion right now Lene. Then we will tell you what we got, that's *IF* we have something to give you." Sandy is looking at Colleen straight in the eyes to see if she starts showing signs of 'Oh-I-Got-A-Story-For-You' expression.

"Oh, I don't have anything to say today. Give me a minute. Actually, make it more like a few days since I am gonna see Byron when I leave here. He was looking real good, I can't stress that enough."

"Is that right Ms. Jeffries? We have heard so much about this Byron for so long and have never met him. Why is that? I mean, you ain't feeling him like that, right? That is what you said about a year ago. Now, you sound like things are about to change." Regina says looking down at her calamari and picking up one of the rings to put in her mouth crunching on the crispiness.

Colleen looks at her and the other two Ladies wondering what to say next. "Well, let's just say that I *am* feeling him and I don't want to speak too soon. I can't say that I am ready to give up my options just yet because he might have someone waving around in the wind. I'd hate to have to walk away right now. Hell, I'd hate to think prematurely about anything." Colleen is serious right now and her friends can see and feel what she is feeling. They don't know where to begin with the next question. It's unlike Colleen to be serious in the "man" department.

"Colleen, you ain't gettin' any younger. Don't you think it is time to get rid of the 'Options'? It's not like you have been married or had any children. Don't you want that one day? If so, it's about that time to be with just one man. Is there some sort of apprehension or fear lingering there that keeps you running?" BeLynda wants to know. She isn't sure why her friend wants to keep spreading herself so thin.

"Yea, that was okay for when we were in our twenties but we're in our thirties now. We don't want to revisit this conversation when we're in our forties. Every woman can't have children in their forties and we don't want your husband to be in his sixties … or his twenties. For you, one is too old and the other is too young. C'mon now, out of the men that you see, who do you see as a potential 'exclusive' man?" Sandy asks.

Colleen is trying to find the waitress because she doesn't want to get into this conversation right now. She wasn't expecting to get so deep into her dating preferences this evening. Especially, not before she meets up with Byron. *They are messing up my damn mood with all these damn questions. Just let me do me! Damn!*

"Well, I don't have any answers for any of y'all yet. But I tell you what … let me see how it goes this evening. Then one day soon Regina can invite us over for brunch and we can sit down and talk about everything. How's that? And for your information, I will say it again, YES, I am *feeling* Byron. Don't ask me why, but I am sure when I figure it out, I will be able to tell you." They can tell that she is disconcerted at this point and not knowing if they should press the issue.

"I came out to see my Girls since we won't be meeting up until next week. I know how old we are and yeah, I am tired of the young shit but it has been working for what I have been wanting. I just never thought about it. Relationships just seems too risky."

"Risky? What's risky about a committed relationship? I know you probably make him strap up but I'm just saying. You're too old to be catching something … or giving something." Regina is dumbfounded because that was a new one on her.

"Yes, it is risky and I don't want to get into my thoughts, okay. Yea, I can admit that I want a little more but I am not quite sure exactly what that is. I mean … Regina, you have your husband. You lucked up. Bee, you did experience the married life and I am sure it had its beautiful moments. Sandy, we are in the same boat … I think. But, hey, let me do me, okay? Let me figure all this shit out. But I can say one thing. Out of all of my 'Options,' Byron seems to be the one that is trying to make what we have a little more than what it is, whateva that is. I just don't want my heart broken and if this is how I deal with it, don't judge me."

"I don't know what to say to that. I can say that is the most honest and genuine that you have been in a long time. Are you tryin' to tell me that you are ready to be loved Colleen? Love is a very special thing. To me, you sound as if this Byron guy has somehow shown that he wants you to be his woman. Is that what you are feeling or saying to us," Sandy asks really concerned, dipping her cheese stick in the marinara sauce, taking a bite.

"Well, I can tell how he looks at me and all of the things he has done for me since I have met him. When he came over recently, I could feel it and he did something that made me think that he thinks of me as more than just 'somethin' to do.'"

"He did something like what? Stop being closed mouth about it. Ain't no strangers sitting at this table, you know everyone sitting here very well. Take a few gulps of your drink and let it out. You are amongst friends, for real." Regina wants to hear what she has to say.

"Well, I asked him to bring me lunch. He asked what did I want and I asked him to surprise me." Colleen held her head down. She is really showing vulnerability. "He brought me lunch from Georgia Browns." She raises her head to look at her friends with a look of help.

"Okaaay, that was nice of him. What am I missing?" BeLynda asks.

"The meal he brought to me was the exact meal that I ordered on our first date, which was at Georgia Browns." The Ladies get quiet absorbing what she has just said to them. Regina smiles thinking about Byron's gesture.

"So, did that make you uncomfortable? It sounds sweet to me. OH! OH! Okay, I get it." BeLynda says with a smile.

"You get what?" Sandy is somewhat baffled at what it is that BeLynda gets. Regina looks at her as if to say 'you can't be serious, right now Dee Dee.'

"She gets that he is in to her enough to remember what she ordered on their first date. Aww, Colleen, he really likes you." BeLynda is giddy. "Let me guess, you don't know how to process that. Am I right? If so, what are you scared of?" Everyone is playing around with their drinks and taking sips waiting for Colleen to respond.

"Colleen, you're holding on to something. Let it go, just like you tell Bee. Do you think he is in love with you?" Regina wants to know because Colleen has been a little reckless through her adulthood and Regina feels she needs to grow up A LOT.

"I can say that he is definitely into me. I can say that no matter what I ask of him, he always come through. And the sex is always more than I ask for. But *love?* I am not sure if he loves me or not and I am afraid that if he does, I may not be able to return that love." Colleen is rubbing on her hair, her hands feeling like she is someone else other than herself.

Everyone at the table gets quiet, pondering over their own thoughts about love and relationships. "Hey, get the attention of the waitress so we can order. Colleen, are you going to be able to eat with us? Or is that going to be reserved for Byron?" Sandy asks.

"Nah, I'm gonna have to pass on the meal. I'm gonna have dinner with Byron. I am not sure what I am in store for but with my nerves, I want it to linger. I don't want him to think that I'm all for dick today. Hey, I mean, even though I am … this love thing got me confused."

"Really? I am glad you are being honest with us today Colleen. I am glad to know that you are not just a nigga in a woman's body." Sandy and Regina laugh at BeLynda's comment. Colleen looks at her with the eyes of, 'I am still a woman and I can be vulnerable when I need to be.' BeLynda gives her a wink that insinuates, 'I know Girl … I know.'

"Hey, I'ma go 'head and leave to meet up with Byron. Y'all know I'ma let you know how it goes. Enjoy your Admiral's Feasts. Be easy on those Cheddar Bay Biscuits. You know where they end up on us and I ain't seen any of y'all in my Cardio class." They laugh and shake their heads 'okay.' Colleen gets up, gives them hugs and kisses and walks out of Red Lobster.

"I think she is getting tired of her 'Options.' What y'all think," BeLynda asks playing with the straw in her drink.

"Hell, who wouldn't be tired? *Shiit*, that is not for me. I am a one man woman and I expect who I am with to be a one woman man. Sharing the pussy with several can be draining, I am sure. I can't imagine and don't want to. That's too much attachment," Regina says.

"Hmmmp, been there before. And I might be there in a few. I got Larry and Ray. But I will be decreasing my choices down to one very soon. I just need to make sure I choose the right one," says Sandy as she watches Colleen walk out of the restaurant.

"I know what you mean," agrees BeLynda. Sandy and Regina look at her as if she has secrets. She does, BeLynda is not ready to tell anything just yet. *I need to make sure Paul is what I think he is. He just might be husband number two.*

"Hey!! Are you there already? I'm parkin' now."

"Hello, Candy. Yea, I'm here baby. I got a nice spot for us. It's been a minute and I want to enjoy this evening. Do you feel the same way?"

Uh-oh!! Damn!! What am I walking into? He sounds like he has something romantic planned for us ... for this evening. Colleen, are you ready for this girl? Colleen's heart is beating fast, not knowing what to expect from Byron or tonight. She parks her car, making sure it is in a safe place. Looking in the mirror, she makes sure she is not shining too much from nervousness. With purse in hand, hitting the alarm on her key, she turns to walk towards the elevator that leads to the restaurant to meet her "possible" lover … man … fiancé … husband … baby daddy.

Walking into the restaurant, smelling the menu through her nostrils, she walks up to the podium in Morton's Steakhouse. She looks around before saying anything to the woman waiting to greet her. She just wants to make sure she doesn't see Byron before she is greeted with the script and then have to interrupt her. She sees him sitting at a table for two and smiles at the woman saying, "I see who I am looking for." The lady smiles and allows her to walk off.

Walking up to the table, Colleen smiles at the man, that is her date for the evening. She has been checking him out and as usual, Byron is dressed expensively yet this time he is what *he* considers business casual. He is wearing a charcoal grey cashmere Prada deep ribbed v-neck sweater with deep ribbed cuffs. His initials are monogrammed on the left wrist cuff. Byron stands to accept her presence with a hug and a kiss on the cheek. She sees he has on Black Prada Houndstooth print wool pants topping it off with Prada No. 3 Cuir Amber cologne.

Colleen takes off her Shearling poncho and places it and her vintage Coach purse in the chair on her side while inhaling his smell. She is showing off her Ann Taylor burgundy tweed cuffed capris pants and Ann Taylor egg shell raw silk blouse, finishing the ensemble off with her Salvatore Farragamo black suede ankle boots. They both sit to begin their evening observing each other's overall appearance being satisfied with what they see sitting across the table from them.

"Well, well, well hello Ms. Jeffries. You are looking mighty inviting this evening. Is this all for me? Should I be saying 'thank you'?" Colleen looks at Byron enthralled by his gorgeous face and expensive clothing wondering why he hasn't been snatched up yet. Why is he hanging around waiting on her?

"Hey, good evening Byron, thank you for the compliment. I see you got the Prada thing going on this evening. You're looking rather enticing I might add. And this is your version of casual, huh?" Colleen asks as she squeezes antibacterial gel in her hands checking out his emerald cut canary diamond earring. *How many carats is that? Byron has some money somewhere. We have never had that conversation but everything about him says financially comfortable.*

"Enticing huh? Is that right? I'm really flattered Colleen." He leans back in his chair and folds his arms across his enormous chest smiling at her showing off his dimples. He notices she is looking at his earring. "I don't think I ever heard you describe me before. Even though it has been written on your face, you just never said anything." He turns his head pretending to look for the waiter but really to avoid her looks on his ear. He knows sooner or later what he does for a living is going to be asked.

"Well, I'm not sure if 'inviting' is the look I was going for today but it is good to know that you approve of my appearance. No need to say 'thank you.' You know me, I have to always represent wherever I go. It's not like I have to go to an office for my business. But I try to keep professional at all times. Not to mention I have to make sure I complement my date appropriately," she says winking at him taking a sip of her water.

"Is that right? Keeping it professional, huh? I will keep that in mind so I won't think that you are doing it for me." Byron gives her a sarcastic smile. Colleen catches it. "But you did say that you have to represent your date appropriately. So I guess I do have to thank you," he winks back at Colleen.

"Now, you know I don't mean the 'professional' thing the way you are taking it. I just met up with the girls for a few minutes to show off. We're normally together on Thursday evenings anyway. I didn't stay long and yea, they were wondering if I had a date. They knew I wasn't dressed for business." He smiles at her.

"I told them I was meeting you and they had a lot of questions that I wasn't ready to answer. Especially since they have never met you yet they have heard about you over the past few years."

"Oh, they have? *Really?* Like what? So they want to meet me, huh? Wow, you must've laid it on thick to make your friends curious." Byron wants to hear what she has to say. It's been two years since he has dropped that car off to her and they have been going strong ever since … or so he wants to think. There have been a few women just for "his needs" purposes since Colleen has a habit of disappearing from his life often. But he has kept himself relationship-free for her even though she seems to have nigga tendencies. Byron is lost for words because most women would be clinging, just a little bit. Colleen hasn't even gotten close outside of sex. He is wondering that maybe she doesn't read the signs, or doesn't want to. Maybe he isn't giving her enough signals but he's going to work on that.

"Oh, you know… the normal girlfriend questions. Like, 'How do I feel about you,' 'What do you do for a living,' 'Are you the one,' 'Am I ready to give up my options,' …" Colleen pauses because she knows that wasn't supposed to come out like that yet it rolled off her tongue with no reluctance.

"So you don't want to give up your options? Options, huh? What is that? I know we haven't hooked up in a minute due to our schedules but … do you have others that you see like *that*? Is that what your friends are talking about?" Byron raises an eyebrow at the mere thought that Colleen is being wined, dined, and dicked by another man … or other men.

"Like what?" Colleen isn't ready for that conversation with Byron. She is not ready to have that type of talk with him. *Hey, change the subject please. I want to enjoy this evening with you. I don't want to run away my potential. You have pissed off written all over your face.*

Leaning back in his chair putting his hands in the air, he responds, "Hey, I know you've been doing you. Is that what your friends call 'Options'? The men you've been seeing? Can you explain that for me? *Will* you explain that for me? If you don't care to go into details right now, I understand. I just don't want to cause any problems for you or me as well as between you and me, you feel me?" Byron is beyond annoyed and he is hoping that it doesn't show. However, it is hard to conceal the dissatisfaction on his face.

"Nah that is not what we call anything. I hope you didn't get the wrong idea when I said that. Byron, I don't have 'Options,' she lies. "Did you already order drinks?" Colleen is trying to avoid Byron's stare and skip the subject. For a second, she forgets she is on a date and not just hanging out with Devin. She and Devin are friends, which makes it okay to talk like that. She has only spoken seriously like this with Devin but not with someone she sees on an intimate level.

"No I haven't. I haven't been here too much longer than you. I was waiting for you to get here. When he comes back over I will order for us. You want the normal?" Looking around, he says, "Damn where did the waiter go? I would like a drink myself. Honestly speaking, a stiff one would be great. What is it that you want baby? I mean Colleen." Byron decides to keep it on name basis for the moment. He doesn't want to turn her away with giving her loving titles. Byron quickly sneaks a look at her cleavage. *Damn she looks good.*

Sandy feels embarrassed. She feels for Byron. Twenty minutes ago, she revealed to her friends she thinks he is into her and ends up saying something real crazy out of her mouth to him. She doesn't want him to think she is just sleeping with a bunch of men.

But each of her Options has something different to offer even though Byron seems to be the total package. He just never made a move for them to be more so she allowed him to do him while she did her. But something is different about them meeting up today. *Was I missing something every time we hooked up? I might have to reminisce over our times together and see what I actually overlooked. Could he really be looking at me as a relationship prospect? Did I somehow not know how to read the signs?*

The waiter comes over and takes their drink and appetizers order walking away to get them ready to bring back to the table. Byron is gaping at an uncomfortable Colleen. He can't figure it out and he really wants to know what has been the issue.

"Colleen, I know we haven't seen each other in a minute. That's not my fault. Well, it isn't either of our faults. Let's just say business and lives have gotten in the way. I don't want it to continue like that." Byron is looking at Colleen trying to read her but he is coming up with nothing.

She shakes her head in agreement taking a sip of her water. "I'm tired of this cat and mouse game we seem to have been playing for the past two years. It seems that we have been at first base in many categories yet we have hit a home run in the sex department. Wouldn't you agree?" Pure silence comes from across the table. Byron's left leg begins to shake from impatience.

Colleen doesn't respond. She just never thought about it. "Is it too much to ask if we can work towards being exclusive?" Colleen looks up at Byron stunned, taking a big gulp of her water almost choking. *Damn, where the fuck is that drink? I need it like yesterday.* She looks at him and takes another gulp. There is total silence and the look on Byron's face is worse than rejection.

"You seemed to have gotten aggravated when you heard the word 'options.' Are you telling me there haven't been any other women? I mean you are a man. A *manly* man. What have you been doing for sex in between us having sex? Surely you haven't been jerking off. I'm sure you wouldn't have to do that."

"They didn't mean anything to me. Not saying they were used. But you weren't making yourself available to me. What did you want me to do? What do you want me to do right now?" Byron grabs her hand and looks in her hazel eyes. She is uncomfortable with this gesticulation.

Removing her hand from his she says, "Byron … um, right now, I just want you to give me some good ass head and fuck my brains out … please." He leans back in his chair and just looks at her utterly flabbergasted. Yet he can tell that her eyes are yearning just for her request and her request only.

Wow!! She is really a nigga in a woman's body.

Chapter Three

3

"Hey babe, what are you doing in here so early? I rolled over to get me a few smooches and your side was empty and cold. That means you been in here awhile. Are we gonna have to put a bed in here for you?" Regina says in between yawns dragging her slipper covered feet across the chestnut wood floor.

"Hey you! Good morning … sleepy head. I'm just going over some paperwork. I got a few meetings this week that might be a little stressful if I don't have everything straight. Your man needs to make sure his shit is right, know what I'm sayin'?"

"Oh okay. Yea, I figured that was coming. You've been locked up in this office quite a bit lately doing a lot of yelling, cursing, and fussing at somebody. I'm just glad it's been over the phone and not face-to-face. Is everything all right with the businesses and clients? I don't want you to bust a blood vessel or something." She walks over to her husband and gives him a soft peck on the lips.

"Nah, I ain't been in here doing no 'cursing.' I been in here *cussing* some folks the fuck out! There's a difference. And you're right. Over the phone was the best for the situation. Face-to-face would have been merciless," Stan laughs. Regina doesn't find it funny. She knows Stan can go "there" if he is provoked.

"Oh really. Well, just don't be *cussing* them out too bad. Good working practices, remember? You need me to do anything? Maybe I can help lessen some of the stress." Regina walks around the desk to sit on her husband's lap. He rubs her back and butt firm yet soft and it feels good to Regina.

"Listen to you. You all ready to step in and help your man. My baby is always there for me. What you wanna help me with? Making a few phone calls? Setting up some meeting times … what? Actually, I have a few of some other types of ideas. You want me to move these papers out the way?" Regina laughs at his question and stands up from Stan's lap. He jumps up simulating that he is about to throw the paperwork on the floor. She shakes her head smiling.

"Now, there you go. Always with sex on the brain, why am I surprised? How is that going to help you with documents you getting together? You probably ain't brushed your teeth, had breakfast, or washed your ass yet this morning but you can *get* some ass, huh?" Regina and Stan laugh.

"Hey, as they say a man thinks about sex every twelve seconds of the day. I can vouch for that and as long as I am thinking about it being with my wife, she shouldn't be creating anything in her mind to worry about, right?" She looks at Stan as if to say, *you got a point there.*

"Every twelve seconds of the day? Yea, okay. Hmmmp, who is 'they' that said this? You know I'm gonna research that. It's probably just a handful of y'all that think about it like that and 'they' ran with the statistics. And if it is true, yes, you are right … as long as my husband is thinking about it being with me, I'm fine with that."

"Oh don't act like it gets on your nerves woman. You know you love that about me. Hell, I ain't the one who had a *subscription* to their favorite porn site." Stan laughs. He knows that would get Regina's attention. She looks at him and smacks him on his right shoulder. He ducks thinking she is going to smack him on his head and laughs harder.

"Oh, so we are bringin' up old shit now? I've not looked at that site in how many years? And I was only looking at it first to get some different ideas. Ain't anything wrong with sprucing up the bump 'n grind, right?" They have a good laugh out of this.

"Oh, it's been some years? So, you're telling me that you let the subscription expire? And you never renewed it? You could've fooled me. Every time I turn around you doing something new and exciting. Hey, a brotha ain't mad at all, I'm just saying." *That's riiight, something new and exciting from my private classes, Mr. Wooten. I found a new way to be a freak yet in a sexy way.*

Regina walks back over to Stan and gives him a hug around the neck and he responds by giving her a hug around the waist. Then she stands behind him and rubs his temples. She knows he is stressed and just happy that she can take his mind off of his bothersome clients. He closes his eyes as if it to say *that's just what I needed babe.*

"Hey Mrs. Wooten, how are the girls? I haven't seen or heard from any of them this week. What did y'all do the other day? I remember you said the Spa was closed for their holiday party. Is everybody doing all right?" He has his head resting on the back of his business chair sinking further into Regina's soft firm fingertips against his temples.

"Oh, we met up at Red Lobster for dinner. Yea, they all fine, nothing new. Sandy still hates her job and has two men to choose from. She said she is going to make a decision soon though. Colleen still expects to be the center of attention when she enters a room. She left us to go meet up with her friend Byron. And Bee is still Bee. She's just busy running her business and talking to Steve every other day. I think she has a young boy though. We've never met him."

"*Whaaat?*!" Stan turns around to look at her surprised. Then he turns back around to let her finish massaging his temples. "You are jokin' right? Bee and Steve still talk on the phone like that … every other day? Damn, it's been some years since they called it quits. Wow!! I bet you he's the one doing the calling too. Hmmmp, that nigga is feeling *real* guilty." Stan shakes his head. "Hell, they might as well give the marriage thing another shot. I mean, he can't be into no one else calling her like that. Or is he trying to make sure she's distracted from another dude? I hope not if he ain't tryin' to get back with her. *And* you say she might have a younger dude? Really? BeLynda is gettin' her 'Stella' on, huh? Wow! Yea, he's gonna go off because he is calling her for something! But hey, I know what he was out there doing. I got plenty of calls from him."

"I don't know what they're doing. At first I thought it was cute and that they were moving in the reuniting direction. Now … I don't know. Maybe he has attempted to but she said no or playing hard to get. Or maybe his ego won't let him make that step. Her being with a younger man just might make Steve wake up. I couldn't tell you. She doesn't talk about it and I don't ask. I know that's touchy for her. She really loved Steve and he devastated her. And what you mean you got plenty of his calls? He was calling you and telling you about his negative discretions? Wow! And you kept it to yourself, huh? Being a friend to a man you didn't meet until he got with Bee. You were supposed to be on her side." Stan ignores her comments. Sometimes men have to stick together. Besides he didn't need to help make it anymore messy than it already was by running his mouth to Regina. And he did know Steve before he met them.

"And, Sandy got two to choose from? Two men … who are still living and breathing? Is that right?" Regina looks at Stan like he is being ridiculous. Stan raises his arms. "Ay … hell, I can't tell. She still calls here like her time ain't being occupied by *one* dude yet you say there are *two*. That means she ain't spending that much time with either one of them, and that says there's a problem. Mmmp, I bet you her choice will be to leave both of them alone. I told you I can hook her up. You know she done caught the eyes of Patrick and Marco. I'm sure, whichever one she chooses will make her happy. They will treat her right, I'm serious babe." *Then she can stop calling here first thing in the morning like you're her man.*

Oh hell naw! We will pass on that suggestion! "Nah, she's all right with the two she has. She'll make a choice. I'm sure of it. Don't need her to start getting grey hair and migraines tryin' to juggle them like Colleen. She's a big girl." *And after your choice in trainers, no thank you. We might have to beat one of your boys' asses and leave him on the side of the road.*

"So Colleen left y'all to meet up with a man, huh? That's different. Who is this Byron cat? Have any of y'all met him yet? He ain't a shady type of nigga is he? If he is, I don't want you to be in that type of presence, you understand?" Stan is serious. The last thing he needs is for Regina to get caught up in some mess that one of her friends might bring her way. Especially if the friend goes by the name of Colleen.

"Nope, none of us have met him and she's been dealing with him for a few years now. She hadn't spoken about him for a few months here and there but I knew he was still around because she never said he wasn't. But I don't think it's anything serious. You know Colleen has to keep her options open." Regina and Stan laughs. "She kills me with that adjective. But one day she will meet the right guy and settle down." Stan looks up at Regina and laugh again. He gets up from his chair and walks over to the refrigerator for a bottle of water.

"Colleen? Settle down? Really? What 'Colleen' are you speaking of right now? You're definitely not talking about your *friend* Colleen Jeffries. Awww, my baby don't know her friends, I see. That's cute." Regina doesn't like what Stan just said.

"And what exactly are you saying? I am not naïve about my friends Stan. There is someone out there for her … hell, for everybody. She just hasn't met him yet. Then again, I don't know. She passed on her Admiral Feast to go meet this Byron guy. He just might be the one." *Or a good piece of dick. She did say she was expecting some action afterwards.*

"Okaaay, don't say I didn't offer to help. Patrick and Marco both got money … *long* money. Neither is bad looking, and the way the women keep stalking them, I know they laying it down like a real G." He puts the bottle of water up to his mouth and drinks half of it. *Damn he must've been in here drinking last night swallowing that water like he is dehydrated*, Regina says watching Stan.

"'Like a G'? I haven't heard that come out of your mouth in years. Don't start regressing on me. I don't care to go down memory lane with the street slang and all that comes with it. Let those terms and the 'Stan' I worked hard to help you bury stay where they are. Back there over on Livingston Road, southeast." Stan turns around looking over at Regina.

"You mean soufeast. That's how you say when you are that part of DC." He laughs. Regina doesn't find it funny. "You really are serious, huh? C'mon babe. I wasn't that bad. I did what I had to do to help my Moms out. We needed food, clothing, and shelter. She had two boys and two girls. That dry cleaners job she had wasn't worth shit but it kept her busy and her mind off of her struggle. You know the story with my Dad. He was a true rollin' stone, no doubt. As the oldest, I did what I needed to do since he wasn't. Hell, I don't even know where that man is. Don't even know if he is still living." Stan goes off into a place. Regina continues trying to bring him back.

"I know. I'm just saying. We had a few close calls here and there and I don't wanna have to deal with that again. It was too much stress on my heart at such a young age too. I have no grey hairs and I don't plan on sportin' any of those misbehaving strands anytime soon. You got that Mr. Wooten?" Regina is standing in front of Stan with her hands on her hips making sure he observes that she is serious.

"Hey! I hear you baby, loud and clear. He is buried deep … *deep*. I doubt if anything or anyone can bring him up. It ain't good for us or my business, and that's on the for real." Little does Stan and Regina know the old Stan is going to have to show his face in the near future.

"I know your boys are still lingering around somewhere. I'm not stupid. Yes, they are your friends but it doesn't mean you to still have to be associated with their mess. It's just sad that they didn't take the route you did. It was only supposed to be temporary but they seriously made a career out of it." Stan walks back over to his chair and sits at the desk. He is quiet listening to Regina. He knows she is ninety percent right about everything she is saying.

Changing the subject from the current topic, preventing the direction the morning can be steered in, Stan speaks up. "Hey baby. You mind doing me a favor? I mean since you all into rubbing temples and shit." Stan has that devilish smirk on his face.

"A favor, huh? What kind of favor? Hmmmp … what you want me to do Stanley Bernard Wooten? Don't write a check your ass can't cash, neegro," she retorts seriously giving him the squinted side-eye.

"Uh-oh, she addresses me by my full government name. All because I asked if you mind doing me a favor babe?" Stan is laughing real hard. "Dag. Why you treatin' a brotha like a step-child? What's up with that? You ain't got no more love for me baby? That's only momentary right," he laughs and Regina rolls her eyes.

"Oh, please. As if I didn't see that villainous sneer on your face a few minutes ago. You're up to something devious or nasty. Now, what is the favor? I can tell from your looks that it has nothing to do with either of the businesses." Regina has her hands on her hips tapping her left foot on the floor smiling. *He plays too much.*

Putting the devilish smile back on his face, Stan responds. "'Villainous sneer?' Oh my baby brought out the big words for this. But um, I want you to refresh my memory on what you used to watch porn for damn near every night. You think you can do that for me? All that talk earlier got your husband wanting to be in something warm, and wet with some slurping sounds." He undoes his belt and unzips his pants releasing his flaccid phallus from his drawers.

"Oh, okay. That's all? I'm sure I can do that favor for you. I thought you were gonna request something else. My hand was itching to slap your face. You know I'll play but there is a line I don't cross in playing. It was sounding like you were trying to cross it." She smiles yet her eyes look serious as she stands in front of him.

"Huh? Something else like what? What are you thinking Ms. Dirty Mind?" Stan is starting to get slightly hard just from the thought of Regina's mouth swallowing his dick. He knows Regina's head game is off the chain but his attention is focused on what Regina is saying. Whatever the insinuation is has her heated.

"I thought you were gonna ask me if you can bring a chick up in here. You know I don't play that shit. You were about to get slapped into next week."

"*Whoa, whoa ... WHOA*! A chick? Regina, really? You thought I was thinking about another chick? And bringing her up in here? WOW! How did that pop up in your mind?" Stan is rock hard now. He thought he was gonna get Regina's mouth to harden it for him but his mental visual did that for him while he's watching her lips. "That was the old Stan babe. He is buried, remember? Besides, you know damn well I was only playing back then. You know damn well, you ain't ever seen another woman up in here. I just used to like to see you get all worked up when I would ask. It was sexy. That feistiness used to get me going. But where the hell did that thought come from just now? As many times I have asked you to do me a favor, and now a 'chick' appears in your head?" Stan is really taken aback.

"Yea, well, I am just making sure. The subject of the old you did come up a few minutes ago, remember? Back in the day when we were just 'kickin' it' yea, I would get all worked up with you mentioning it but that was different. But once you said I was your woman and you were my man, then you said 'I do' to *me,* your *dick ... mouth* ... and *hands* became off limits to any other woman. There's nothing open about this marriage. I'm just making sure you still understood that hasn't changed."

"I hear you baby. *Preach!! Preach!! Preach* to the choir Gee Gee!! Let it be known whose dick this is!!" Stan grabs his concrete hardness pointing it at Regina saying in a whisper, "Now come over here and let your man know that it's really your dick. I wanna feel some warmth, wetness, tongue, jaws, and tonsils." Stan licks his lips.

Regina smiles shaking her head at Stan and laughs. "If you only knew what you look like sitting there holding your dick like it is a microphone or a hand weight. You are so nasty."

"Aaah, yes … I … am. And you love it don't you? Come over here and talk into this microphone sexy. Sing something to it while you're working your lips on it. L'il Stan will be overjoyed. Oh, and it is definitely heavy." *Wow, did he just ask me to talk to his dick? Is he keeping tabs on me pretending not to know what I have been doing? Did he see me practicing the other day? Nah, he would have suggested that I use the real dick instead of the dildo.*

Regina gets on her knees in front of Stan in between his legs and looks at the beautiful sight in front of her face. Getting close to it, Stan can feel the warm air from her mouth and nostrils sweep across his dick and hand creating a sound deep within his throat. She takes the head in her mouth and plays around with the frenulum with her tongue. Stan whimpers and grabs the bottom shaft of his dick. He's trying to hold back his nut.

"Damn! Hold up. Whew!! Woman what was that? What you tryin'a do?" He looks at her utterly amazed and releases himself from her mouth. Regina looks up at Stan wondering what the problem is. She's playing coy.

"What's the matter? What I do? Damn, all I did was put the head in my mouth. You normally love that." *Mmmm – hmm, the private class about those tongue exercises got your ass, doesn't it? You can't be greedy no more tiring my jaws out. Three minutes ...*

four at the max is your limit now. I know just what to do now. Regina is smiling inside. She knows she has Stan right where she wants him.

"*Shiit* ain't a damn thang wrong. That just felt too fuckin' good. I thought I was about to bust and you just put me in your mouth only a few seconds ago. Hell, lately, you've been having a nigga cryin' like a bitch with that head game of yours. Of course you didn't hear me say that." He and Regina laugh at the comment. "You got that shit on lock babe!! Hey, you know Maria is not off today. Don't have her listening at the door to me in here sounding all soft."

"Be quiet and let me get back to what I had started, please. You doing all that whining wasting all this delicious pre-cum. You know I like that." *I came in here to say good morning and see what you were doing. Now, you want some extracurricular activity? Oh, I gotchoo my husband. Watch your wife go to work on your ass.*

Regina puts her full lips around the head of Stan's dick. She holds it in her mouth for a few seconds before she starts moving her tongue alongside the frenulum. Stan closes his eyes and wrinkles his eye brows in ecstasy. Regina's mouth is feeling like a pussy. Inch by inch, she lets him in her mouth more and more wetting it up as she goes further down the shaft. Stan releases his hand from the bottom shaft and slide down in the seat giving Regina more access to his hardness.

She starts moving her head helping her mouth and tongue to form figure - eights loosely around Stan's dick. Intermittently, she moves in the normal up and down – in and out motions. She is giving his balls a massage when she slowly takes him deep into her throat, touching her tonsils on the way. Stan jerks forward at the move and opens his eyes fast to get a look at Regina doing her thing. Relaxing her throat muscles, she slowly puts him a little further in her mouth until she is able to lick the base of his shaft, letting lots of saliva drip from her mouth to methodically saturate. Stan is breathing faster now. He closes his eyes to prevent watching her, thinking this would slow down his eruption. She can tell by the slight vibration she feels on her tongue that his nut is building up.

She pulls him out of her throat slowly, giving him the memorable illustration she knows is going to send him over the top. Stan's breathing is rapid. His dick is expanding, getting thicker and larger. He feels as if he can knock a hole in the wall with it. He finally sees his entire wet shiny throbbing dick and swears it looks like it has been in her pussy. All of a sudden he gets lost in Regina's mouth again. She gives him the jack moves with the wet tight warm mouth being assisted by her hands.

Stan is about to blow and he needs to stand up. Once standing, he looks down at Regina and she begins the slurping noises he loves to hear. Regina starts humming deep in her throat intensifying Stan's build up. She moves her tongue fast, squeezing her jaws on the in and out motion. It is sloppy wet and he loves it. She slows it down looking up at him. "Damn, don't look at me like that babe." Five more slurps and he hoses her tonsils and throat down with his thick warm cream. Stan is growling, moaning and groaning with a little bit of whimpering, jerking his body forward almost to lose his balance. Regina continues to suck until the last of his nut has been collected. His eyes are closed and his lips are pursed tightly together, still frowning from the satisfaction his wife's mouth just gave him. She sucks him a little more and it's sensitive to her mouth. He whimpers stopping her.

After Regina stands, Stan flops down in his chair to recuperate. Still breathing heavily, he motions for Regina to sit on his lap. Sitting on his lap, she asks, "You all right?" He shakes his head up and down signaling "yes." "Did you enjoy your favor?" He shakes his head "yes" again. "I'm delighted that I could be of service. From the look on your face, I can tell that I have accomplished your request. I have done my good deed for the day," Regina says laughing. Stan peaks out of his right eye at her smiling.

Rubbing on her lower back and top of her derriere, Stan speaks. "Damn baby. Oh my God!! GEE GEE!! I haven't bussed one like that in a *minute*!! It felt like … it felt like … fuck I can't even describe how it felt. All I know is you had me wanting to buy you whatever you wanted and to marry you all over again." They both laugh out loud.

"You are so silly. Be quiet." Regina laughs shaking her head at Stan.

"Nah, I'm serious. And you be swallowing all of that like a champ, for real. My baby didn't miss a DROP! Gimme a kiss let me thank those lips for you." Regina leans down and kisses Stan on the lips. It is just a peck on the lips. She doesn't think he will take too kindly to receiving tongue that just had penis and sperm on it. Even though they both belong to him, it is just the principle of it.

"I'm glad you only talk like that to me. Or do you talk like that to your boys? I hope not. The day one of your business partners or friends slip up and say some slick shit, we gonna have a problem," Regina says shaking Stan's head back and forth.

"Oh really? Like Sandy does, slipping up when she's jokin' around with me when she calls here?" Regina's eyes look like they are about to pop out of her head. "Oh don't give me that look. I know you be talkin'. And she lets me know in her own little way that you do." They both laugh because Regina has been caught. "It's cool though. I know I be laying it down and you have to explain all those smiles on your face when you see them."

Regina taps him on his chest, he leans over laughing. "What … eva!! I'm about to go eat me some breakfast. You want something while I'm in the kitchen? I'm sure Maria has already fixed our plates and put them in the microwaves." She gets up from his lap and heads towards the office door.

"Nah, I'm ok. I'll get mine later. I really need to get back to this paperwork. My first meeting is tomorrow. You down here disturbing me, being all nasty causing distractions and shit," Stan smirks while moving his papers back in front of him.

Regina twirls around on her heels fast amused at what he just said, "*Me?! What?!* Oh no you didn't blame that session on me. You asked for the favor, remember? You are a trip," she smiles wide. Stan winks at her and blows her a kiss.

"Okay, if you say so Mrs. Nasty Wooten." They both just grin and Regina shakes her head. "But yea, I need to get this done. I can't just have on a thousand dollars suit and six hundred shoes. My shit has to be just as put together as my appearance. You know how it goes, baby. Represent to the fullest!!" Stan winks both eyes and blows two kisses to Regina. She catches them in the air and places them on her lips.

"Yea, I hear you boss man. Just make sure y'all ain't in there sizing up your penises through all that yelling. Be professional and keep the base out of your voice please. Don't scare off your clients. Which contract is this anyway?"

"You are so funny this morning. This is the two hundred and fifty thousand dollars contract, one of the small ones. So the only sizing up that will be going on is that check they better be ready to write out tomorrow so we can get started. You know what I'm sayin'?" Stan lifts up a few papers looking from one to the other.

"Oh okay. I hear you. Once contracts are signed when are y'all supposed to start? How long is it supposed to last?"

"Once everything is signed, we go to production in two weeks. It is suppose to last for three months. That will be good because that takes us into March and that means spring and rain. Rain will hold things up so we will be finishing up right before the rainy season starts.

"Okay. Well, get back to work. I'll see you around the house later. Love you."

"Aiight babe. Love you too. Hey!! That was a good but strange talk we had this morning. It was fun and interesting. I promise the old me will stay where he is but I might still go over the boss' head and work on something for Sandy." Regina looks at Stan with a smile on her face but shaking her head 'no' … he gives her a wink and gets back to his papers. Stan shouldn't have made that promise but Regina will thank him later for not holding up his end of the bargain.

Leaving out of the office, Regina heads to the kitchen to see what Maria has for her. Entering the kitchen, Maria is sitting down reading the paper and drinking a cup of coffee. Regina's slippers are so soft that her presence hasn't been noticed yet. She decides to speak as she walks over to the microwave.

"Good morning Maria. How are you today?" Maria almost jumps out of her seat startled by Regina's greeting.

"Oooh, my goodness. Senora Wooten, you scared me. I didn't hear you come in here. How long have you been standing there?" Maria folds up the newspaper, gets up and starts moving around the kitchen. Regina looks at her puzzled.

"Oh, I'm sorry Maria. I didn't mean to scare you. I've only been standing here long enough to know that you didn't hear me come in. My slippers must be very soft or you were immersed into something in the paper greatly. Is everything all right?"

"Oh yes, yes! I was just looking at a few recipes that I might cut out later. I was reading the ingredients. Did you need me to get you anything? I left your plate in the microwave over here. That one in there is Mr. Wooten's. I know you can't eat that much food. I fixed you a veggie omelet with turkey bacon on the side. Your fruit bowl is in the refrigerator. I didn't put any biscuits on your plate and I didn't think you wanted toast. I know how you watch your carbs. But if you want one of them, I can get that for you."

"Oh no, that's fine Maria. Thank you. What you prepare for me is more than enough. And you didn't have to jump up. Go ahead and sit down and finish doing what you were doing. Enjoy your coffee. It smells really good." Regina warms up her plate, grabs the fruit bowl from the all steel side-by-side refrigerator and leaves out heading for the sunroom.

She was acting strange for someone that was only reading recipes out of the newspaper. They must've been some delicious sounding dishes. Regina goes back in her mind to the envelope she saw in Maria's open nightstand drawer. *Damn I wanna know what was in it. Maybe it was nothing and I'm just jumpy from all the other weird shit that has been happening around me. I need to tell Stan but I just don't want all the mess that's gonna come with it. I know he's gonna flip when I start saying I think someone is following me. I will just wait.*

Regina sits down at the heavy oak wood table that sits twelve and begins to eat her breakfast. She is really enjoying her food, as always. She is reminiscing over the conversation she had with Stan in his office. Regina smiles faintly and shakes her head as she cuts into her omelet again. *That man is a nut case. But I love him.*

When she finishes, she gathers all of her dishes and heads back to the kitchen placing them in the sink. Maria always tells them to put their dishes in the sink. They have a very powerful dishwasher but Maria is old school and prefers to hand wash all the dishes. Regina doesn't mind washing the few dishes but Maria insists that she allow her to do that.

Walking around the corner heading for the stairs, she decides to take a detour towards the front door. It's December and she just wants to see how it looks and feel outside since the weather has been so nice. Opening the door, she steps out onto the massive front landing and looks around smelling the air and feeling the chill. Her plush robe is keeping her nice and cozy. She pulls it tighter to keep out the breezes while wiggling her toes around in her slippers.

Okay, it's not that bad out here. The sun is out and it's a pretty day. It's still fall and if I had to guess, it's probably about forty-eight to fifty degrees out here. It's so nice and quiet around here in the morning. Does everyone work from home? They probably get up to leave for work before I get up. She smiles at her thoughts.

Looking around at the well groomed lawn and flower beds admiring the landscape, Regina turns to head back in the house. As she is turning towards the door, she notices an envelope that is wedged in one of her flowering winter shrubs. Walking over to retrieve the envelope, she looks at it nervously. Opening it, she is checking her surroundings to see if anyone is waiting and watching her.

What is this? How did someone get up here to put this in my damn bushes? Pulling the note out of the envelope, she unfolds it. Her eyes get big when she reads the note:

Payback's a bitch

We will meet soon

BITCH

Regina's heart starts racing and she's trembling. She balls up the note and stuffs it - along with the envelope - in one of the pockets on her robe. Frantically looking around she hurries into the house slamming the door shut and leans on it with her eyes closed. Her heart is about to beat out of her chest. Stan runs out of the office and sees her leaning up against the door. He's walking fast towards her with a slight panicky look on his face.

"Babe, what the fuck happened? Are you all right? You look pale as a motherfucka. You scared the shit out of me slamming the door like that." Regina holds her chest heaving. "Why were you outside? What was out there? *Who* was out there? Say something! Please!" Stan grabs her holding her tight. She is trembling hard. He looks down at her and Regina just looks up at him still unable to speak.

Stan sees the fear in her eyes and realizes she still hasn't said anything. He can feel her heart beating as if it is his. Her words are stuck in her throat. Stan looks at her deeply with hurt in his eyes. They water but a tear doesn't fall. Stan releases Regina, turning around to go in the opposite direction down the steps on the left that leads to the west wing of the house.

Regina holds her hands out trying to speak. She wants to say, *Wait ... NO!! Don't do that Stan*, but nothing is coming out of her mouth. Her feet are glued to the floor and her legs feel like putty. Regina is about to fall trying to move. She has to prevent Stan from going down there. She knows from the look in Stan's eyes and with him taking the stairs towards the west wing, he is going into his office that is off limits to everyone. That means his sidekick persona is about to be revealed. Regina closes her eyes and a tear drops down her right cheek.

Chapter Four

4

"Yea, what's up Jo?!

"Jo, where you at man? We called you all night. We were tryin'a hang out 'n shit."

"Oh damn, my bad. I turned my phone off yesterday. I had somethin' to do. Where y'all go?"

"We went over to the Metro Club to see TCB. I thought you might've wanted to be up in that jont wit us. And you turned your phone off? For what?! Yo, where you at man?"

"*Man*, don't be asking me all those questions like you my bitch. I had plans nigga! Is that aiight with you? And I'm still with my 'plans.' What's up, did you want somethin'?"

"Nah, my nigga. It's good to know you aiight though. It ain't like you to not flip dat muhfucka open and answer it. Especially when you hear that it's *my* ringtone boomin' through your cell nigga. It's a good thing Mama hadn't been lookin' for your ass. But, you can at least tell your big bruh where you at."

Sigh! "Ay I'm with BeLynda right now. I'm at her house. You happy you know where I am now?! So I wasn't gonna be able to hang out witchall anyway. I was busy. And TCB … at the Metro Club?! Nah, I'm aight."

"Oh *word*?! You aiight, huh? Yea, okay bruh. I see you. Tryin' to do the grown up thang and impress the Lady. That pussy must've been *good!*" His brother lets out a deep animalistic laugh. Khalil's face bunches up into a scowl.

"Ay, watch your mouth Jamal. I got you on speaker phone. She is in the bathroom right now but that don't mean she can't hear you. Especially now that the she has turned the shower water off. You are trippin'. Did you want something? If not, we can talk later when I get home."

"Aiight Kha, I gotchoo. Oh snap!! This is the Lady that your boy be seeing comin' out of dat building across from the gym ain't it? He said she's a sexy older woman. Older as in, she was in high school when your ass was in elementary." Jamal laughs extremely loud through the phone. Khalil turns the volume down. He doesn't want BeLynda to hear his ignorance. "Man, you done got whipped on some *season* pussy?" Khalil hears his brother pull the phone away from his mouth, choking. That only means one thing. His brother is smoking Cush early in the morning. Khalil shakes his head.

"Yo, didn't I just say watch your mouth? And I ain't whipped on nothing. I'm diggin her. I really like her, aiight? So don't be thinking this is all about sex nigga. Respect what I'm doing with her. Maybe you should try it." Khalil is heated with his brother. For Jamal to be four years older than him, he has always acted younger than Khalil. Many have always been shocked to find out Khalil is the younger of the two.

"Try '*it*'? Try what? Try who … your woman?" Jamal finds it funny and when there is silence on the other end of the phone he knows he has taken it too far with his younger brother. "Aight, aiight, damn! I was just fuckin' witchoo. Do your thang bruh. I'll tell Mama you aight if she ask had I heard from you. Got a L'il Honey Dip comin' over in a few. I'll holla baby bruh."

"Aight, peace." **click**

Whew!! That was some good dick. It got the coochie box feeling a little sensitive this morning. Khalil worked my ass over last night. I don't think I ever had it like that before. Hell, I might need to invest in a multi-vitamin or something to keep up with his ass. But I am glad that he spent the night this time. Normally I feel like he is just coming over for some ass. BeLynda is smiling saying to herself while in the shower.

She is elated that Khalil has been spending a little more time with her lately. It seems that both of them are starting to come out of their shell to each other. Well, more like she is coming out of *her* shell. BeLynda is noticing that Khalil likes her a little more than he has been showing. She thinks it is cute and it helps her to feel younger than she is. Not a whole lot younger but younger than thirty-one, like somewhere in her late twenties. However, when it comes to sex, their experiences switches their ages. He is very much experienced and she is not surprised since the young women are out here doing all kinds of stunts to try and keep a man. BeLynda just never thought all of that extra stuff was necessary.

Getting out of the shower, she grabs her burgundy plush towel off of the rack and start drying off. She is smiling remembering last night. She somewhat let go and put her hip and belly rolling class exercises into motion. She had thought about the tongue and mouth exercise but decided to wait on doing those to Khalil since she has never been down that road.

BeLynda's thoughts are interrupted from hearing Khalil talking on the phone. *Oh, he answering his phone now after he cut it off last night. I should have known. He didn't want any of his chicks bussing him out last night. He must've checked his messages and had to call the main chick back.* She decides to listen to see who he is talking to. She hears that it is not a female at all and Khalil has it on speaker. She smiles as she continues to listen to the conversation, commenting as she listens.

Oh, you had something to do? Damn, I'm still a secret to his friends? Well at least one of them knows about me. The Metro Club ... TCB, really? So you still hang out at the go-go with the boys? Y'all can't find something else to do? Well, you are only twenty-three and I should have known. Hell, me and the girls used to follow Rare Essence everywhere with our best outfits on, so I guess I can understand. Bitch? Oh that's what you call your women? Or maybe it is a figure of speech between the boys. BeLynda is drying off her neck, back, and shoulders real slow listening. She is very much into what is being said between Khalil and the male with a deep voice on the phone.

You're still with your plans? Awww, that's cute. Mmmp, who is he talking to? That mouth sounds like the male version of Colleen without the bad enunciation. Oooh, shit, his brother?! Wow, did I know he had a brother? His family never really came up in any of our conversations. His Mama was looking for him? Does he have a curfew? Probably does since he still lives in her house. Is that why he hasn't spent the night before until recently? Khalil is really a youngin' and maybe I shouldn't be messing around with him. Fuck! BeLynda is still drying off her neck, back, and shoulders real slow. However, they all should be dry now.

Oooh ... he just said my name. Okay, he ain't really about hanging out at the go-go ... or is it the Metro Club he doesn't like? But he did tell his brother that he was with me!! Yea, that's what he said ... he's aight. Is there something wrong with him not wanting to be in those kinds of places or for him to try to impress me? She is now drying off her butt cheeks and the back of her thighs.

Oh no this motherfucka didn't!! But let me be quiet, let me see if he says how good my coochie is ... damn, he skipped that statement. Yeah watch your mouth Jamal. I can hear everything that is being said. Jamal, hmmm, okay ... someone in the family must be Muslim or of African descent for them to have names like that. She is still drying off her butt cheeks and the back of her thighs. Even though she should be done drying these parts, she realizes that she is still wet where the bottom cheeks meet the back of her thighs. She bends over a little to flatten out the crease to dry in the crevices.

Oh, he called you Kha? Is that your nickname? I like that. Damn! Was everybody around when your friend said he sees me on Monday nights? Sexy, huh? Okay, I'll take that but ... OLDER?! Fuck, he couldn't have found another adjective for me? Aight Jamal, I see how you rolling. Now she is drying her feet and ankles, skipping over the main parts.

Oh no this neegro didn't!! Yea, I was in high school and he was in elementary. Damn!! As a matter of fact, come to think of it, when I was a senior ... HE WAS IN FOURTH GRADE!! OH MY

GOD!! Shiiit!! How is he gonna act around my friends? I can't let Steve know, he will laugh at me. BeLynda has finally moved on to drying off her right leg alternating between it and her right arm and breast and side.

Um, did that motherfucka just say "seasoned pussy"? And listen to his immature ass, choking off of some weed probably. Uh-oh, Khalil you diggin' me baby? Awww, I'm digging you too. Can this be a real relationship? Damn, your brother hit a nerve with you didn't he? I've never heard you sound like that. You ready to whip somebody's ass!! That's right! Check his ass on that Boo. BeLynda has finally moved on to drying off her left leg alternating between it and her left arm and breast and side.

Oh, Jamal is off the chain! No ass-hole, you won't be trying anything with me. Oh, you better had been playing with him with that bullshit. Oops, did he just call the female he got coming over "Honey Dip"? Khalil how old is your brother? Fifteen? Granted immaturity doesn't have an age but damn!! Oh, he just got off the phone, let me hurry up and get out of this bathroom. BeLynda has been stuck on drying off her left leg alternating between it and her left arm and breast and side.

When she finally dries off completely, she hangs up her towel and grabs her thick Neiman Marcus bath robe and puts it on. She walks out the bathroom and is greeted with Khalil's eyes. They are smiling back at her. Her feet and toes sink into the thick carpet and she wiggles her toes for a few seconds against the carpet. She is smiling back at Khalil with her mouth closed. He is lying across the bed with his legs crossed at the ankles and his hands behind his head with this fingers intertwined. Surprisingly, he is still naked and BeLynda is pleased with what she sees laying across her king size bed. His chocolate skin contrast beautifully with her mustard colored eight hundred count sheets.

"Hey, what you looking at me like that for? What were you doing in there? You were in there for a minute. I guess, you didn't think I should be taking a shower too, huh? We could've taken one together," Khalil gives BeLynda one of his sexy smiles. *Boy!! Don't be looking at me with that sexy ass crooked smile showing those pearly whites,* BeLynda says to herself while smiling at Khalil.

"Oh, I am just surprised that you are still in the nude. I was cleansing my body, do you mind? And you could've come in there and join me. But I guess, you didn't want to, huh," BeLynda responds calling herself getting back at what he just said. *Yea, you're only twenty-three and that does imply a young man, but what I'm looking at right now and what you have been giving me the past few weeks says FULLY DEVELOPED GROWN ASS MAN!!*

"Baby, these sheets feel good as shit. I can stay in these all day. They feel like luxury and expensive. I'ma need to get me some of these. Where you get these from?" Khalil starts rubbing his hands and legs across the sheets enjoying the feel against his hands and feet with his eyes closed.

"They are Egyptian cotton and the thread count is high. They are expensive but I feel I worked hard enough to treat myself so I can sleep like a baby at night. And I'm happy that you rested nicely in them. I won't be broadcasting prices though."

"Oh damn!! They're *that* expensive and luxurious, huh Bee? *GOOD* quality shit. So you like nice things? That's all right babe. I see you Ms. Giles. Thank you for wanting to share this with me."

"Oh, you're welcome. But, you're just noticing the sheets? I guess you've never been here long enough to really enjoy them the right way, huh? Well, better late than never, right?" She is looking at him from head to toe in all of his nude perfection. *Damn this young man is fine. And he doesn't mind being seen with me. But the day someone thinks he is my son or brother, I'ma have a problem.*

"What's the matter Bee? What you thinking about? I see your mind working. You're smiling but something is off. Oh shit!" Khalil jumps up into a sitting position on the bed. His body is bulging with muscles everywhere. Abs, arms, chest, back, thighs twitching from sudden tension looking serious yet heartfelt. "Bee … did you hear my conversation with my brother? Honest, he didn't mean anything by those things. He doesn't know any better. Well, I mean he has never tried to know any better. He is older than me but he hangs out with youngins. I guess tryin' to keep his youth but it's the wrong crowd. He just never wanted to grow up. Please don't take it personal, I stood my ground with him. I'm into you Bee. No joke. Don't let him affect us …." Khalil is rambling on and Bee is paying his words no attention. His anatomy has her full attention and she is focused. She starts taking off her robe.

Once Khalil notices BeLynda is releasing her robe, his rambling slows down to a cessation and he watches her with a smile. "Woman, what are you doing? Oh, I see what you were thinking about. You saw something you wanted, didn't you?" Khalil lies back down, spreading his legs and BeLynda sees he is beginning to get hard. *Oh he is spread eagle like he wants me to put my mouth on that monster. I didn't even do that to my husband – even though I did think about it – so I won't be doing that on his ass. I don't know where his dick has been raw and he knows we use condoms. So he might as well get ready to mount me as usual.*

BeLynda is looking at him still smiling as she walks over to the bed. She gets on the bed and lays down beside Khalil on her back giving him the message that he needs to get to work. He looks over at her saying nervously, "Bee, you ain't ever put your lips on me. How come? What's the matter?" He thinks because she's older and has been married that she would be going all out with sex but for some reason he feels as if he is with a woman in her late teens to early twenties just starting out in the sex game.

"Huh? I have put my lips on you. What are you talking about?" He looks at her like she is crazy, not knowing what he should say next. However, she knows exactly what he is talking about and feels he is about to mess up the mood.

"Bee, don't. C'mon, you know what I am talking about. I do you all the time. This ain't supposed to be one-sided. It's just me and you. We've been kickin' it for how long now? What's the matter? Talk to me." Khalil is as serious as a man wanting head can be. Then he sees the look and he thinks he knows just what the problem is. He props up on his elbow and looks BeLynda straight in the eyes.

"Bee, I'm into you, seriously. There is no other woman. There hasn't been another woman since I met you. I know I haven't spent a lot of time with you in the beginning but I wasn't trying to crowd you. You got your business to run so I let you do that. Plus, it seemed like you had some other shit going on so I gave you your space. I know you've requested for me to use condoms every time but … well not the time we were on the top balcony. That was *real* nice too. But let's do something different." Khalil looks at BeLynda trying to read her face. He wants her to be open to him … with him. He wants to be with her without any restrictions and doubts. He has never had a problem with a woman giving him head until he met BeLynda.

Yea, yea, I hear the violins playing in the background of your speech. No other woman, huh? Men will say anything to get some pussy and head. But he does sound and look like he is telling the truth. How do I tell this boy ... young man ... a MAN that is eight years younger than me and he thinks I am more experienced but I'm not? Maybe I should be but at this moment I'm not. I don't know what I am supposed to say. I am taking these classes with the Girls but I just can't let loose completely to be free. Not all at once. I need to work my way up to that point, and I just have never gotten half way there. Sex feels good but I just think certain things are just too slutty. Or am I still hung up off of what my Grandmother used to say constantly? I don't want to turn into my mother. But my friends don't see anything wrong with expressing their sexuality. Maybe I need to start talking to them openly, especially about the things we learn in class. The instructors keep telling us that we are sexual beings. Sigh!!

Breaking her thoughts, she communicates to Khalil. "So there's no other female?" He shakes his head "no." "And you've only been sleeping with me all this time?" He shakes his head "yes." "You wanna do something different like what? I'm not all into that freaky shit Khalil. What is it that you want me to do?" He can tell she is uncomfortable. He wants to let the conversation go because now he is completely soft. But he prefers to get to the bottom of the matter now so he knows what he is dealing with. He doesn't want to have to revisit this.

Turning his entire body towards BeLynda, he grabs her around the waist allowing her breast to touch his chest, looking her in the eyes trying to read them and responds. "Bee, I'ma say it again. I am into you. *YOU*! There is no one else. I've always been into older women but they just thought I was a kid. But you gave me a chance. You're thirty-one and divorced. Are you telling me that you have never gone down on a man before? Even with the man you were married to and shared a bed with … your husband?" BeLynda looks away and that tells it all. His eyes pop open wide. He is completely flabbergasted by this new disclosure.

"Okaaay … wow!" Khalil releases her and lies back down on his back looking up into the ceiling. "A beautiful woman and yet you are so closed. I never knew. I thought you were just waiting for the right time to let loose with me. So on the balcony … you had never done anything like that before have you? The whole night with the set up, clothes, was your first and you did it for me?"

BeLynda shakes her head "yes" to the first question and "yes" to the second question.

Damn, he sounds like he is much older than twenty-three. I knew he was mature for his age. Am I the first older woman he has been with? It doesn't sound like it at this moment though. And he done had a young woman ... or women to turn him out and he thinks I am supposed to be doing the same things but better. I mean, he can eat the hell out of some pussy. He's had a very good teacher. And he is into me.

"Well, we can wait on that then. Have you ever been on top before?" *Damn, I feel like I'm talking to a virgin but she's not a virgin to sex. She's just a virgin to the entire experience. I guess we'll grow together. Who'd thought I'd be teaching her and not the other way around?*

BeLynda responds, "I have a few times but it hurt and I didn't feel comfortable. I don't know if it was because he was controlling it by holding my hips and ramming but …." Khalil puts his pointer finger to her lips and closes his eyes.

"Please spare me the details. I don't want the visual of you riding another nigga's dick. Say no more baby, I gotchoo. We'll take it slow okay? I want you to get on top. I promise I won't do any of that. Can we do it with you on top?" Khalil is looking like he wants to cry for this reserved woman that is lying beside him. But it makes him feel good at the same time. He likes knowing that she will be trying these new things with him. *I'm gonna have to put the boys on the back burner so she can get real comfortable with me. And she's worth it.*

BeLynda shakes her head "yes." She is feeling real embarrassed in front of this young man that just graduated from college earning a degree in Electrical Engineering. Khalil gives her a faint smile and starts stroking his dick to get it semi-hard. He didn't want to pressure her into doing that for him. He can tell her mind is racing and can feel she is already embarrassed by revealing her personal hang-ups about sex. *She comes out of that bathroom looking all sexy 'n shit disrobing for me and now she looks like she has gone into a huge shell. I have to make her feel comfortable enough with me to loosen up. Sigh!! I got my work cut out for me but I don't mind. I will have her molded for me in no time.*

Khalil is still stroking himself and BeLynda leans over and begins to kiss him deeply. Giving of her tongue, he accepts and gives his in return. She is exploring his mouth, running across his tongue, teeth, inner jaws, ending with a little bit of sucking on his tongue, then his upper lip, moving down to his bottom lip simultaneously. Khalil is moaning at her kissing action. *Damn, she can kiss me like that sucking all on my tongue and lips and ain't ever had a dick in her mouth? Note taken and I know what I will do later.*

With all the seductive kissing, Khalil becomes rock hard and he's ready. BeLynda is also nice and moist ready for entry. She can feel her stomach getting wet taps from his dick. His pre-cum is oozing and she wants to see it. Stopping the kissing, she looks down and touches him. He sighs saying softly like there are others in the house, "Don't be afraid to touch it. I like that. It can be all yours if you want it to be. I really want to be with you in all the ways there is to be with a woman." He sticks his tongue in her mouth and she accepts.

He gives BeLynda a signal with his body and hands saying that he is ready for her to mount him. She doesn't take the hint. He starts massaging her breast and she lets out a sweet moan. He lifts the left one to his mouth putting the entire areola in his mouth sucking like he wants something to come out of it. She lifts her left leg to wrap it around his left hip. He takes the opportunity to start fingering her clitoris. BeLynda lets out a gasp and starts kissing him deeper. *Aww shit she is wet as a motherfucka!!* He eases his fingers down and enters two of them inside her. BeLynda is grinding against his fingers. So he speaks in between her sucking on his tongue. "C'mon babe, we both are ready for me to put it in. Climb on top. The foreplay can wait until another day."

He lies down on his back in anticipation of what is about to come. Hesitantly, BeLynda begins to mount. She holds his dick in her hand and he request that she slide it up and down her wetness. She obliges and his body jerks up twice and he grabs her around the hips but quickly lets her go. He doesn't want her to be tense and dry up her juices. She finally positions it for entry and to her surprise, he slides in without hesitation. He fills her up entirely and she opens her eyes wide in shock. *Maybe I am still a little open from all that action he gave me last night. Damn he feels good.* It's as if he reads her mind and says to her, "Nah, you were just ready for me baby."

She sits there for a few minutes to get used to being on top. She looks down at him and he has his eyes closed enjoying being inside of her wet warmth. His body looks so damn beautiful, strong, and protective to her and she is afraid to let go. She is thinking about class and remembers the instructor said this position is great for the hip and belly movements and she can be in control. When she doesn't begin to move Khalil opens his eyes. He shakes his head "no." "Don't do it Bee. No thinking. Just do your thang. It's just you and me, remember? We're in your house, in your bed. Take control. Just don't hurt me," he gives her wink trying to help her relax. She blushes.

BeLynda comes out of her thoughts listening to him and she starts to move slowly up and down. She remembers Colleen saying something about riding like you are riding a horse and you're bouncing up and down. She begins to move and he grunts trying to figure out what to do with his hands. He really wants to put them on her hips. He can't hold onto to her breast because she is feeling so good, he just might squeeze them too hard. Khalil is sliding in and out of her slippery box. He still has his eyes closed. He figures if he doesn't watch her, she just might let go and go for it. She is still slowly moving up and down working on a rhythm, deciding on what feels right. Then she leans forward with her hands on his firm tight pecks tooting her ass out getting a different feeling and both of their bodies react. *Damn he feels good inside me.*

Khalil is enjoying her slow motion and starts to move with her a little bit. She is going up and down and he is going around in circles hitting her walls on all sides. It is feeling real good to both of them. His still has his eyes closed not wanting to make her feel uncomfortable watching her. Or watching them, joined between their legs. Khalil loves watching. *Damn she feels so good and her slow strokes have her long pussying me. Damn she is deep. Not too many females have been able to take all of me and she is swallowing all of me with no problem. What was your husband doing with your ass girl?*

After a few minutes, he places his hands on her hips and she tenses up. He looks at her assuring her that he won't hurt her. He moves her hips in a circular motion as if he is stirring the pot. BeLynda closes her eyes and moans with her mouth open. *Damn, she looks so beautiful right now. Enjoying the pleasure my dick is giving her. Yea, I'm churning like I'm making butter baby. Enjoy it.*

"That's right Bee, relish in it baby. Let yourself go, for me. I won't hurt you, I promise. I'm just helping with the moves that we both will enjoy. Now grind on it babe." He places her all the way down on him and he grinds against her to let her know what he is talking about. *Damn, I can feel him in my fucking ovaries but it feels sooo good. Oooh, his dick is hot and brick hard. I must be doing something right. I don't ever remember being this juicy.*

They've been going at it for about thirty minutes now. Sweat is everywhere. *Damn, he ain't come yet? Fuck, I'm feeling my shit build up. I didn't think I would be able to come in this position.* BeLynda is transparent with her thoughts. He is able to respond with, "I'm waiting on you babe. I'm holding out for you. Buck on it if you want to." *Buck on it? What does that mean?*

BeLynda starts getting extra wet from his talking and she goes back to riding with her horse movements. Khalil is moaning, groaning, massaging her breast and he is meeting her with strong thrusts of his own. "Shit! Baby, lean down and let me get one of those pretty titties. I wanna suck on them. She leans down and lets him put a nipple in his breast. That sends a jolt to her pussy and she is watching him. "Oh don't stop moving baby. I can feel you running down my dick and balls and you're throbbing. You ain't too far from coming on me. I feel it and I don't know how much longer I can hold out."

Damn, how does he know I'm about to cum? BeLynda starts moving faster and it is feeling so damn good to her. All of a sudden, she moves his mouth from her breast and goes to work. She sits up starting to do the up and down motion, grinding, rocking, and circular motions. Khalil holds on to her hips tightly jerking upwards every time she sits all the way down and grind on him. She can feel her butt is wet and before she can question herself, Khalil says in a whisper, "Damn, babe you are wet as shit. Your juices are runnin' all down on my balls and legs. You hear that smacking? Damn, keep going babe, don't stop." The talk turns BeLynda on more. She never knew she liked that. She is in control of this ride and enjoys the looks and noises Khalil can't seem to supervise coming out of his mouth. Focusing on words from class, she looks behind her at his feet. His toes are definitely curled tight. She smiles inwardly.

BeLynda feels her hot box throbbing like it's her heartbeat and Khalil grabs a hold of her hips and looks down towards the action. *Damn she got my dick covered in cream and juices and the pussy is talking. Oh shit! Oh shit! I'm about to buss off and she hasn't come yet. Slow down bruh. Let her get off so you can pull out.* Khalil is holding on for dear life. He looks up at BeLynda and she has her eyes closed, mouth open, and drool is running down the right corner of her mouth. *That's it baby. It feels good don't it? I know because I really want to ram up in your inferno. Damn it's hot.*

All of a sudden, BeLynda lets out a loud wail. Her body starts trembling and her walls are contracting all around Khalil's dick. Khalil can't take it anymore and he wants to really ram up in her but he promised he wouldn't. The next thing he knows a big splash of liquid gushes all over his dick, balls, thighs, and stomach and her inner thighs. He opens his eyes wide looking down to see what happened. *Did she just pee on me?* BeLynda is in another world. But he keeps right on stroking because he wants to "get his man." His deep long strokes are sending BeLynda over the edge. She is turning him on to the max. She looks down at him as if she doesn't know what is going on. He feels his explosion building and with four more deep hard thrusts he taps her on the ass to let her know she needs to get up. BeLynda releases him from her hot slippery box and he strokes his dick exploding strongly hitting her thigh before she could move it out the way. He aims himself at this stomach with three more explosions attacking his lower abdomen. He growls and his body jerks up three times. He eyes are closed now and he yells, "Aww, fuck!! Shit! Gotdamn!!" He raises his legs bending them at the knees.

BeLynda feels proud. Not ashamed anymore, she rubs her fingers across the white thick cream laying on his stomach. He is breathing heavy. Panting, looking over at her, he smiles saying, "Go 'head baby, play in it. You did that to me. It's yours." He really wanted to say, "You wanna taste it baby? Lick it up," but he knows that he is going to have to take it slow with her.

That was the best virgin ride he has ever had. The other women were just fucking him and weren't concentrating on cumming. He knows that BeLynda was making serious love to him. *I can marry her. All jokes aside. She gonna have my babies.* Khalil realizes BeLynda is who he really wants to be with. *I'm gonna have to bring her around the family. Hopefully moms don't have a problem with her only being ten years younger than her. But who gives a fuck? I don't and I'm falling for her for real. I need a joint after this.*

A few minutes later, looking at BeLynda, he asks, "So Bee, did you know you were a squirter? All jokes aside. I'm serious. We've been at this smash- … I mean lovemaking for a minute. This is only the second time you did that. That shit is like that. It really turns me on."

Embarrassed but feeling a little open with Khalil, she responds, "I had no idea. I had never done that before. I almost thought I pee'd on you but I thought that that bodily waste normally shuts down during sex. So I know it wasn't that." Khalil is listening attentively.

"No shit?! Really? I thought you had pee'd on me too but look at it. Look at me. I'm soaking wet on more than just my dick. It's real creamy too. So I hit a few G-spots, huh? Maybe it only happens in certain positions or with certain things. I don't know. I mean, you did squirt when I ate you from behind when we were on the balcony and just now with you riding me. And you were *riding* me too girl, damn it was good ass shit. I'm turned on like a motherfucka."

"I guess, I don't know. Just one more thing I have to research or ask my instructor." BeLynda cringed when she let out her secret. She didn't mean to say that.

"Ask your instructor? What instructor? What *kind* of instructor?" Khalil rises up looking at her with a smile on his face. "Why would you be asking your instructor about sex?" Khalil is sitting up on his elbows looking at BeLynda ready to hear what she has to say.

"Boy, I'm talking about the internet. What you sit up like that for? What did you think I was talking about?" BeLynda can't believe that she let that slip out.

"Oh okay. I didn't know what you were talking about. That's why I asked. You come out the mouth talking about an instructor. Hell, I was about to ask if I needed to be present. Let me be educated on the same shit," he laughs out loud and BeLynda hits him with a pillow a few times.

"What you hit me for? What did I do? What did I say? Hey, I just wanted to be enlightened on some shit. Don't leave a brotha out, ya know what I mean? I'm only twenty-three. There is always room for learning something new, right?" Khalil is cheesing hard trying to be funny.

BeLynda laughs and gets up from the bed walking towards the bathroom. Khalil is watching her ass do its own little dance with a mind of its own and decides to break out into a verse of some go-go:

Shake whatcha Mama gave ya!! Unh!!

To show him that she knows all about go-go, she drops down and puts the booty on the floor. Khalil covers his mouth in astonishment saying, "Aww shit now. Go Bee! Go Bee!! Hey, come here let me play the congas on that ass. They wanna be played." They both have a good laugh.

Chapter Five

5

"Did you get a good parking space?"

"It's aiight. Not too far. We just have to walk to side of the theatre. But we cool though. You are with me." He winks at Sandy. *Yea, you're a big buff brotha but sometimes I wonder.*

"Walk to the side of the building? Oh you must be going over there to get the car when it's over and pick me up right out front." Sandy looks at him as if to say, *this is not up for discussion.*

"Okay, I'm aiight with that. I don't mind showing these *boys* out here how it is done. You got the tickets already? You weren't waiting out here too long were you? I wouldn't want brown sugar to get too hard out here. It is a little chilly." Sandy smiles but wants to roll her eyes at Larry's corniness.

"No, I just walked over here to wait for you. We got about twenty minutes to get what we want and find our seats before the movie starts."

"Ok, let's get in this line. It's not that long. Then again, I'm not sure how these lines are going. Do you think we need to get our seats first? I can come back and get what you want."

"Oh, I can stand with you and help you carry the stuff. Plus, I have specific instructions for how I want my popcorn." Sandy smiles at Larry and he winks at her putting his hand in the small of her back. She tenses up a little not used to the public affection.

When they get to the front of line, the teenager asks what they want. Sandy goes right in on her request. "Yes, I would like medium popcorn and a medium blue icee, please. And can you put half of the popcorn in the bag, put butter on it and then put the rest of it in the bag with more butter?" The teenager shakes his head "yes" while keying her order into the register. "And I want the nachos grande with a red icee. Don't be chinchy on the toppings," Larry says. The teenager shakes his head stating that he understands what he means and leaves the register to prepare their snacks.

While the teenager is fixing their order, Sandy and Larry make small talk. He is close enough to her to make out with her in front of everyone. In the midst of their conversation, Sandy looks around at the other couples and families happily getting prepared to watch the movie they have paid for. Then she sees a young lady walking their way as if to get in line. But to her consternation, the lady is not approaching for that. She taps Larry on his shoulder to get his attention.

Larry turns around to see a woman he knows and from his expression, Sandy knew Larry knows this woman a little more than a neighbor, co-worker, or church member. Apprehensively, he responds calmly.

"Hey, Diana. So I see you're out tonight, huh? How are you?" He gives the female a hug that is a little too loving for Sandy. Sandy stands back waiting to see how the scene is going to unfold before she speaks up. Especially since technically he is not her man. *Let's see what her response is going to be because her facial expression isn't telling me much.*

"Oh, so we are being formal tonight? 'How are you'? When I was over your house the other night, you weren't being formal. What's up?" The lady says to Larry looking at Regina.

"What you mean 'what's up'? Nothing is up. I'm at the movies with this beautiful young lady. Sandy this is Devina, my sister. Devina, this is Sandy, my Lady." *Ah, his sister?!*

Devina bust out laughing. "Oh okay. How you doing Sandy? I was just checking to see how he was gonna brush me off. He tries to not claim me sometimes."

Sandy smiles with her lips closed. She is relieved. But just then Sandy sees another woman coming towards them and she had already notice that she was with Diana. *I wonder who she is and what she wants. Maybe she is his cousin or something. But she doesn't look too happy. Rolling her eyes at me and I don't even know her. Let's see if she is coming with the drama. I don't feel like having to beat a bitch's ass when I am supposed to be enjoying a night at the movies.*

"Heeey Larry. I'm surprised to be seeing you here at the movies." Sandy is about to vomit from the ghetto chick trying to be proper with not an ounce of class. *So this is what your sister hangs out with huh? Looking like an updated Sha-Nae-Nae.*

"Hi Sharon. What's up?" He doesn't give her a hug. He frowns irritatingly instead and Sandy notices. *Oh, he done slept with this bitch and she's trying to make her presence known*, Colleen says to herself watching the scene reveal more than Larry wants it to.

"What's up?" She stares angrily at Larry then looks Sandy up and down patting her braids with her extremely long nails. "Oh, so is this the reason I can't get any time? Is she your woman? Or is this y'all first time out?" Sandy is fuming and wants to slap the blue braids off the chick standing before her in the bama outfit. But she will wait to see how Larry handles this uncomfortable situation. She is gathering their munchies while listening.

"What do you mean '*this*'? She is a woman as you can see. Something you can't seem to be. She's a real one at that, so take a good look. You can't have any of my time because it's valuable so it's spent wisely on what and who I want to spend it on. Now, go on with that bull Sharon. Don't start some shit you can't finish." Waving Sharon off and turning to Sandy, he says, "Sandy this is my sista's friend Sharon. Sharon, this is my *woman* Sandy. Don't come over here trying to mess up my night. We've done been down this road how many times? The answer is still 'no.'"

With the neck rolling and the rolling of the eyes, she responds, "Oh so she is a woman to you huh?" She is looking Sandy up and down from behind now because Sandy is busy moving their food and drinks to the side so the next person can place their order. *I'ma give her ass a pass since we're in this damn theatre*, Sandy says really wanting to tell the little girl off. "Yea, ok. I got yo numba bruh. I guess I'm just good for suckin' yo dick, huh?" That ignited Sandy's attention and she turns around to look at the woman and then Larry. He feels the heat on the back of his neck. *Damn! This ghetto broad went there in front of Sandy and in public!*

Closing his eyes, rubbing his temples, he replies, "*Bi-* … okay, look, not here … not tonight, not ever. Me and my woman are about to go into the theatre and you can stand here with my sista and look stupid. Sandy you ready?" He grabs his nachos and icee looking at her waiting for a response. *I almost called her out of her damn name. I don't want Sandy to think that I disrespect women but this bitch is really pushing it. Of all nights to run into my sister and her ghetto fabulous crew, it had to be tonight.*

"Oh, babe, I was ready ten minutes ago. I was just letting you talk to your sister and her little friend here. It was nice meeting you Devina." Sandy heads towards theater number four and never say anything to Sharon. She adds an extra twist in her walk because she knows she is being watched. *Wow! That bitch got the game twisted. And Larry handled the situation like a diplomat. If the shoe was on the other foot, I would have cussed that nigga out trying to buss me out in front of my date. But I wouldn't have labeled Larry as my man though. I guess that would've been my mistake in the scene.*

But Sharon had to have the last word with both Sandy and Larry's back facing her as they walk away. "Play it off if you want to but when you call me to come over, I'm gonna ignore your call. C'mon Diana, I'm sick of your brotha!!" Devina stands there looking at her brother walk away with the beautiful Lady knowing damn well her friend can't match up to her. *I like her,* she says to herself.

Larry laughs and Sandy looks up at him trying to see what is funny. "Why you laugh?" Larry looks at Sandy saying, "A pressed bitch will never change. I have never led her on nor has she sucked me off yet she wants to try and give everybody the impression that she went there with me. I wasn't trying to diss her but she wanted to approach me and I'm out with my woman, she had it coming. She ain't my type and will never be. I know how she is and what she's about. Devina tells her big brotha all and I wouldn't let Sharon's mouth or pussy touch me, even if she was the last woman in DC."

Sandy has no other choice but to relax into her date. Rest assure, she was going to ask him about that head job Sharon insinuated but he just cleared all of that up for her. Then again he was sounding like he was doing too much clearing up.

Walking into the theatre for *Love Don't Cost a Thing* starring Nick Cannon, Steve Harvey, and Christina Milian, they start deciding on where they are going to sit. Sandy wants to sit in the middle section of the seats on the left. Larry wants to sit in the back in any of the sections.

"Why you want to sit in the middle over here?"

"Why you wanna sit in the back?"

"Hey, I surrender. You lead the way Ms. Robertson. This is your night." After all that bullshit they had just encountered, he is not going to argue with Sandy. He wants her to enjoy the movie and her snacks so he can fuck her brains out later.

About ten minutes later, Larry sees his sister and her crew walk into the theatre. *Shit!! They came to see the same fuckin movie? They better not be trying to see where we are sitting because we will be moving.* Larry watches them closely and can tell that at least Sharon is the only one trying to figure out where they are sitting. He knows she will start telling some shit that he doesn't want Sandy to know. Especially since it was just ten minutes ago that he tried playing it off by disrespecting Sharon in front of her. Sharon has never been his type but she did allow him to nut in her mouth a few times. He hasn't slept with her. Sandy is a woman and he doesn't want her to know that he has stooped so low that he would have encounters with any of his sister's friends.

They find a place to sit because the theatre is packed and they wanted to sit together. He and Sandy make note of Sharon looking around a few times as if she is looking for someone. *Mmm-hmm, that bitch trying to see where we are sitting. She may be young but I will beat that ass if she tries me. But a bitch that ain't done what she said she did wouldn't be acting like that. Larry lied somewhere. I'm not gonna worry about it because I do have another man I can spend time with if his ass is on some bullshit.* Sandy is saying to herself while throwing popcorn in her mouth getting really irritated with the whole night. *I'm too old for this shit right here and so is Larry. Men and their dicks, I tell you.*

Just then, Sandy sees a tall muscular body of a man walk into the theatre looking for somewhere to sit. His body frame looks familiar. She keeps watching him and then he turns to the left looking for a seat … or seats. Looking at his face, she sees that it is Ray. She starts to sink a little deeper in her seat towards Larry. *Fuck!! Can this night get any worse? What is he doing here? Who is he looking for? Oh he's on a date? Yea, okay, let me see what my competition looks like.*

"What's the matter? Are you cold? You want my jacket? Sandy doesn't respond to Larry. She continues popping corn in her mouth with her greasy fingers. The man starts walking over into their direction to take a seat behind her and Larry. Larry takes notice that she is watching someone and looks up at the man and then back at Sandy. He is becoming pissed. He is not sure what is going on but he has an idea it has something to do with this big ass man.

The man sits behind Sandy and Larry and she is starting to sweat a little. Larry's antenna goes up and he is trying to process Sandy's weird behavior. *She really must know this dude. Is this one of her niggas? Ah, you're about to be caught because he is who you been spending most of your time with huh? I'ma play this shit cool and see what happens. I'm not gonna get into it here. I will ask you later. Now ... we both have had a fucked up moment tonight.*

Just then another man walks into the theatre sipping on a soda looking around. Ray calls out to the man and he walks over and sits down. Sandy doesn't know what to do. She can't sink any further down into the seat. If she does, she will be attempting to give Larry some head.

The guys give each some dap, pulling in each other for hug and smack on the back. They begin talking and it sounds like business. *Why would they come to movies to conduct business?* She can hear them saying something about some women and some dates. One of the men has met a woman and then they mention that someone else they know has met a woman. She couldn't figure everything out because the movie was loud. However, the strangest thing happens. In the midst of the conversation, Sandy hears the second guy refer to Ray as Rick.

Rick? Why did he call him Rick? Sandy sits up in her seat at this point, fuming at her 'Ray' being called another name. *Hold up. That nigga called his ass Rick. Did he give me a bogus ass name? So he's on some game type of shit huh? Oh okay. Fine, be a motherfucka with games because I ain't playin'.* Sandy is ready to enjoy her movie with Larry now without any uneasiness. *Fuck him. He can lose my number and lose it fast. I'ma play too but my way. I won't be available for dinner Tuesday or Saturday. But I'll see what you talkin' about Wednesday. And I will be dressed to make his dick hard throughout dinner.*

"So did you like the movie," Larry asks standing up ready to leave out of the theatre. Sandy is so occupied with the two men behind her and barely responds.

"It was okay. I could've waited for it to come to Video On Demand though." As they walk out into the aisle she looks up at Ray, he smiles and keeps talking to the other man. *Oh, what, you just gonna smile and not speak? Oh okay. It's like that? That's what we doing Mr. Daniels? Okay. Peace motherfucka!!*

"Ay, what's going on? You are acting real strange. Do you know one of them or something? Or both, which one is it? They from one of the classes you take? Let me know what's up?" Larry has a scowl on his face. *Oh, he wants to get King Kong up in here? Nigga you show your ass and I will be catching a cab.*

Sandy is busy checking out Ray and then she sees it. The man she is looking at looks just like Ray but something is definitely different. He has ugly hands that look like he does a lot of hard work and she remembered that Ray has nice soft hands with no scars. This guy also has a mole by his left ear. Ray has a mole on the right side of his chin. *Oh my goodness he can pass for Ray's identical twin. Damn! It ain't him? I was almost sure it was him. Whew!! I just knew I was busted. Close call girl. But he did smile at me. Does he know me? Maybe he was just being polite.* Quickly, she responds to Larry playing it off, "What's wrong with you? I'm fine. Why you think I know those men? Are they in one of my classes? Hell naw! It was cold in here but once I warmed up, it was all good. That had nothing to do with anyone in here."

Larry looks at her saying to himself, *Oh no, something happened and it has nothing to do with you being cold. Yea well, hide it like you're doing. Hide it until it disappears. I really don't wanna know. But, you were checking those niggas out! Oh!! I see!! You like big buff niggas, huh? I gotchoo, I ain't buff enough for you. I guess I gotta start working out a little more. But I know what they say about those steroid dudes. It's cool, I'm about to be all in that pussy tonight to take your mind off of these pretty boys walking in front of us.* Larry doesn't know how much he is boiling right now but Sandy will know once he starts pounding against her uterus.

The drive to Sandy's house was quiet. Larry is driving with his mind on all the mess encountered tonight. He has never really been one for the movies and tonight just proved why. But he tried doing something different. Doing something different tonight with Sandy was almost a fiasco. It kept simmering and had Sandy said something, he is almost sure that it would have boiled over splashing on everybody like a pot of grits. *I guess I will try other things outside of the house. I just get tired of eating when we get together. I will ask her what other things she likes for entertainment.*

Sandy is looking out the window at nothing in particular. Watching the streets, sidewalks, trees, buildings, cars and people walking down the street as they drive by gives a scene of serenity. Tonight was very awkward and she doesn't know what to make of it. Was it trying to tell her something? She is not sure. For some reason, she reaches over and gently grabs Larry's hand. Larry jumps a little from being startled out of his thoughts. He grabs her hand back squeezing it softly and gives her a faint smile.

Arriving at Sandy's house, Larry asks if he can see her to the door. She accepts and they walk up her sidewalk to her front porch. Standing there for a few minutes looking around and at each other, Sandy breaks the discomfited silence. "Thank you for the movie Larry. I liked that we did something different. It was sweet." Sandy is playing around with her keys and looks down from Larry's eyes trying to evade his questionable stare.

"Oh, no problem. I was trying to think of something different to do since we always seem to eat whether it is at your place or mine. I thought I would get us out of the norm, you know? Take us out into the public a little bit around some civilization. Even though we chose the wrong night for 'different' and some 'civilization,' it was still cool." They laugh but Larry is serious.

"Oh don't worry about it. We can only control ourselves in order to control our moments, right?" I'm not affected by anything that happened tonight. Believe me. Really, I'm not." She begins to open her front door to walk in. Looking at Larry, she asks, "Would you like to come in? It is still early, right? I'm sure your sister won't be visiting you. She looked like she was going to the club."

"Oh all right! Yes, I will come in. I was hoping that you offered that anyway. I love spending time with you. We don't see each other often so since it is not quantity, I try to make it quality. You don't mind do you?" Larry walks over the threshold behind Sandy stopping in her living-room looking around as if he has never been there before. Boy, she has expensive taste. How does she afford her taste? Is there really another man that supplies these things for her? "Oh, and that's how my sister dresses all the time. She said she dresses like that so if someone calls about a party, she is ready." They uncontrollably laugh out loud.

"Make yourself comfortable while I grab a few bottles of wine and some glasses. Did you want something to munch on with your drink? I can whip up a little tray for us if you like," Sandy asks stepping out of the kitchen to look at Larry while she speaks. *I'm trying to smooth this over since I know it was obvious that I was acting crazy at the movies.*

"Sure, why not," he says walking into the kitchen where Sandy is. "What you got for us? Some quick snacks like some cheeses and fruits? You know … your specialty?" They both laugh.

"Yea, I have that and some cubes of ham and turkey that I cut up the other day." Going into the refrigerator, she pulls out a container saying, "I also made some stuffed jalapenos too. They go real nice with the Pinot Gris."

"Aah, we're drinking Pinot Gris and not Pinot Grigio, huh? That's it, or you got something else for us too?"

"Oh, now you know I have my Chardonnay and I have Gewurztraminer too. There is no red tonight. They are all gone." They both laugh.

"All righty then, let's take all of them with the munchies. You lead the way Ms. Robertson." Leaving out of the kitchen turning left to go upstairs Larry is watching Sandy's ass as she takes each step. *Damn, she is sexy. I don't know if I can take much more looking at her tonight. I need to slide in to something hot and wet.*

Arriving at the top of the stairs, turning right to walk down the hall towards Sandy's master bedroom, Larry is watching her hips and thighs swaying from left to right more pronounced than normal due to the five inch heels she has on.

Entering the room Larry looks around as if he is looking for something. A sign that says another man has been there. He has never known Sandy to be that woman but things change. But he is well aware of just a few weeks ago Sandy was showing signs of ending what they had. So he had to step his game in the sex department. He knows that's what bothering her. When he gave her the picnic in her living room a few weeks and he laid it on her a little bit, he saw a different side of Sandy. That at least earned him time outside of their homes with her. *I'm about to step my game some more. You're in for it tonight.*

"Get comfortable. Why you just standing there. You are not a stranger to my home or my bedroom. Even though the last time you were here, we didn't make it past downstairs." They both laugh. Larry blushes. He takes off his chocolate leather coat and chocolate leather Cole Haan shoes and sits at the table Sandy has by the window. Sandy looks over at him while she is getting comfortable and smiles. Opening up one of her drawers, she pulls out a pair of grey drawstring shorts and throws them at him. He catches them, looks at them then at her surprised. She responds.

"What, you left them over here. You thought they wouldn't still be here? They have been washed and dried. Now get comfortable." He wastes no time in doing just that.

They are having a good time talking, drinking, and munching on their appetizers. At least that is what Larry is hoping they are because he prefers his meal to be Sandy. An hour and a half later, Larry stands up to go into the bathroom. She hears the toilet flush and he washes his hands. But when he comes out of the bathroom, Larry is completely naked with a semi-hard on. Sandy is pleasantly surprised with a smile on her face looking at what is standing in front of her. A handsome toned hunk of a caramel man showing off the nice size tool he is working with.

"Mmmmp, mmmp, *mmmp*, look at you. I wasn't expecting to see Adonis walk out of my bathroom. What you got on your mind?" Sandy is liking what she sees and she is glad that he drunk most of the wine. Sometimes she can find herself a little dry from too much wine.

"So you like what you see? That is a good thing. Now, what I have in mind is some serious love making … with you. Are you up for that?"

"Serious huh?" *That sounds like he is about to lay it on me. His lovemaking be too damn sensitive for me but I can stand to feel some hardness up in my walls.* Sandy looks at him for a few more minutes, then stands and makes a request, "Why don't you undress me?" Larry wastes no time in meeting her request. He takes off her jeans first, then her socks and blouse pausing to look at her in her matching bra and panties. "Babe you look so damn good!" Hurrying to get her completely nude, they begin passionately kissing with their hands roaming all over each other's body. Larry starts guiding Sandy over to the bed. They both sit down continuing their kissing and exploring.

He lays her down and begins foreplay. Kissing on her neck, making wet circles with his tongue, Larry moves down to her chest and lingers on her breasts. Sandy lets out a moan and begins massaging his dick. He moves against her hand. Moving down to her stomach with the wet kisses pausing to play around in her navel, Sandy is breathing a little faster. He moves down to her hips and her inner thighs and she opens them slightly to give him access to what she wanted him to do next. Without further hesitation, he licks the outer lips of her vagina. With spreading her legs more releasing a sigh from her mouth, Larry begins licking inside of her lips. Her juices begin to flow and Larry is rock hard at the feel of this.

Moving her hips in enjoyment, he concentrates on her clitoris and inserts three fingers all at once. Letting out a sound of ecstasy, she grabs his head and Larry goes to work. *Damn she smells and tastes sweet as a motherfucka. I ain't had no pussy in a minute and I needed this.* Larry is making love to her pussy and she is about to cum from his slippery tongue. Sandy wraps her legs around his upper back and begins to shake and let out loud noises. Her cream releases and Larry laps it up in slow motion while moving his fingers around touching her walls. He continues a few seconds more. He wants her to do him next but right now, it is urgent that he enters her. *I want to keep hearing your screams baby. Give you something to remember who I am and not to be looking at other niggas.*

Larry rises up to crawl between her trembling legs. Sandy looks down at his extremely hard dick with a curve in it. Looking at Larry, she spread her legs wider inviting his body to meet hers. He puts the head at her wetness and shivers a little at what is about to happen. Trying to enter slowly, she is too hot and wet and he slides in with no problem but half way in he stops and looks at her trying to stall the nut that is building up fast.

"Damn you are so beautiful to me. I want to please you in every way I can. I know I have not made you happy in the past but I was trying to get in tune with my sensitive side. But I'm about to show you the real Larry." Sandy listens with the notion that Larry is about to go the next level but really wishing he would shut up. Kissing her on her neck, he slides the rest of his dick in her and she grabs his ass clinging with her fingernails. That turns Larry on with a passion. He just sits there in the pussy enjoying it wrapped around him.

Beginning to move slow and deep both are in another world. Sandy feels his hardness filling her up in width and length. Larry feels her hot, wet, and warmth surrounding him. Sandy's pussy begins to speak to him making all kinds of gushing and smacking noises. He loves the sounds and getting into it like never before with Sandy. He never wanted to bang her out because that was reserved for "nothing ass broads" that he wanted to fuck only. He felt Sandy deserved better than that. But right now, he is going to give her his lovemaking version of banging the woman he cares about.

Reaching as deep as he can go, Sandy wraps her legs around him and he jerks twice letting out a groan from the feeling of being engulfed in her softness. His movements are slow, deep, and beyond intense. His alternating moves of in and out, to the side, circles, and grinding, both are sweating and their sex boxes become sloppy wet. Sandy has had two more orgasm and Larry is right there at his moment. He begins giving it to her in a serious way grabbing her ass cheeks squeezing them while guiding her pussy up to his dick. He is giving her the business and she is making all kinds of noises, whimpering, and calling his name.

Whispering in her ear "Yes, baby. I'm here. I hear you. That's it, enjoy this dick. I know you feel all of me. What else what you want baby? I'm here to please." Larry keeps long dicking her and she is getting extremely wet. "What's up? You about to come again ain't you? C'mon babe. It feels good to you don't it? I'm about to buss off baby. Turn over for me. I need to get up in it." He pulls Sandy's left leg over to her right leg and he is still stroking her deep. Sandy is looking in pure ecstasy at this new Larry. This isn't actually new to Larry but he's new to her. The moves, talking, and control have caught her by surprise. She is on her stomach now and he moves his legs underneath moving the right one on the side of his right leg. *Damn, he stayed in me while he moved me from being on my back to me being on my knees.* Lifting her ass, he begins to bang her in a loving way and toots her ass up to give him more access. Sandy has her head back eyes close enjoying the sloppy wet strokes. She is moving her hips and butt in circular motions enjoying the slippery action she is receiving. She is moving like she is winding on a reggae dance floor. Larry is in admiration looking at the melon shaped cheeks in front of him bouncing firm with the right amount of wiggle. He is trying to hold out however with the imaginary visual of her ass representing humongous lips sucking his dick Larry loving rams ten more deep hard thrusts into Sandy's gushing pussy. He is growling like a werewolf and pulls out exploding all over the crack of her ass.

Entering her again, Larry lets Sandy get off one more time. He pounds and pounds making her butt and breasts jiggle and jerk. Looking over in the mirror, Larry and Sandy eye's meet. The looks in the mirror is a memory they will keep for a long time. Larry asks, "Let's turn a little babe. I wanna see my strokes from the mirror too." Adjusting on the bed a little, they both have a great view and sends Larry over the top. Spreading her butt cheeks, slamming in as hard as he can, Sandy is taking it. Larry is yelling louder than she is from the copulation being exchanged. The onset of her orgasm creates a puddle on the bed beneath them. Larry leans back to watch the cream ooze out of her swollen lips, down his balls, in a gob on the sheets. Laying her head on the pillow, trying to catch her breath, she slides her legs down and looks back at Larry. He is watching his semi-hard phallus slip out of her, covered in both of their juices, wondering if he could get her taste the mixture. He normally gives her a clean dry dick to swallow.

Where the fuck has all that been hiding? Don't be suppressing dick like that! She says to herself looking at him like he's crazy yet satisfied never noticing he isn't finished.

On to the next position.

Chapter Six

6

“Hey, hey, hey what’s up Ladies?! Colleen is in the *house*. Go, go, go, go, go, go, go shorty, it’s your birthday!! We gonna party like it’s your birthday!! Hey, hey!! How y’all Ladies doing?” Colleen comes in dancing singing *50 cent* like she just entered the club. Regina, Sandy, and BeLynda look at Colleen walk into the class always having to be the center of attention.

“She must’ve got some good ass dick after she left us to meet up with Byron the other day. I guess for her sake it was a good thing the Spa was closed, hunh,” Sandy says to BeLynda and Regina looking Colleen up and down.

"I don't know if that is it or not but she sure got a hold of something … or someone, come skipping into class like she's got a juicy secret," BeLynda says shaking her head still watching Colleen.

Colleen speaks to all of the Ladies in the class and finally makes her way over to her Girlfriends giving them the normal kisses on both cheeks and a peck on the lips. She takes off her coat and places her bag on top of it on one of the chairs. Facing her friends, she is smiling. They just look at her inquisitive trying to figure out what or who has her in this mood.

"All right, start moving your chops and spit it out Girlie. What are you so giddy about? What happened to you that has you coming in here all cised and shit? Give us the four-one-one. If it happened Thursday, you know you wrong to be holding it that long." Sandy says to Colleen with her hands on her hips.

Regina is standing there watching Colleen and listening to BeLynda and Sandy not commenting on anything. She is not feeling all that great after the other day but she is still trying to be herself and not have them asking her any questions. With Colleen's actions, that might just get them to not notice her quietness. She keeps looking over at the door wondering if this will be a repeat of the other evenings with seeing a shadow at the door. She is hoping that she doesn't see anything strange tonight because this will be the evening that she skips on class and goes back home where she feels safe.

Stan wasn't all that happy with knowing that she had held back the strange things she had been experiencing through her thoughts and observation. Now he is watchful and she knows that will bring out the old Stan. She still hasn't said anything to her friends and she's wondering if she should so that they can take notice of their surroundings.

Colleen responds, "Hey, what y'all talking about? I'm just in a good mood that's all. It's December, almost time for Christmas which means gifts will be coming. I'm just trying to get into the holiday spirit. Is there something wrong with that?" Colleen rubs her right hand across her right thigh and notices Sandy and BeLynda are looking at her as if she is lying. "Oops, my palm is itching. You know what the means. I guess some money will be coming my way soon."

They both laugh at her with Sandy saying, "Girl, you are a trip, for real! Quit stalling. You got some juicy and I want to hear all about it. Without all the exaggerations please. Just give it to us straight."

"Okay, okay, damn. GIRL!! I had a wonderful time with Byron. It was OFF … THE … MOTHERFUCKIN' … *CHAIN*!! I mean, it ain't like it's not 'on the one' all the time but the other *NIGHT*!! Girl!! He had me almost in tears!" Sandy is smiling at Colleen. BeLynda has her mouth ajar, while Regina has no expression at all. "Yes, girl. I told him that I wanted him to give me some head and fuck my brains out and he did just that. One thing I can say, he follows instructions very well. A sista ain't ever left hangin' when it comes to Mr. Byron! Yes Lawd!"

"Oh, okay. See?! I told y'all it was all about Byron. I'm not crazy. I knew what that skip in her walk meant. She only has it after she has spent time with Byron." BeLynda says proudly to be able to know her friend well enough to read her actions.

"Hell, it could've been Devin. You never know," responds Sandy. *Even though I have two "options" to make a decision from, it still wouldn't have been a bad thing to have tried a piece of Devin. That's before he had his fingers all up in Colleen though.*

"Unh-Unh … nope, she didn't have that much time to meet up with both. Plus, like I said, she is normally like this after she has seen Byron. That's her all-purpose man and it seems like he has graduated to becoming her multi-purpose man," BeLynda says and they laugh. Regina just smiles.

"Um, Bee, they mean the same thing don't they," Sandy asks.

"Not when it comes to the bedroom, they don't. He was all-purpose when he was providing services throughout many categories. *NOW*, he is providing a myriad of services *just* in the bedroom. That brotha laid it down more than he has ever just by watching Colleen. Oh he is a multi-purpose man for sure," BeLynda says.

Colleen looks at BeLynda surprised. "Listen to you. Do you hear yourself? Do y'all hear Bee? What you been up to Bee? Sounds like there has been some multi-purpose shit going on in your life too," Colleen gives her the side-eye smiling.

"Maybe … maybe not. But that's not what we are talking about right now. But I'll talk to y'all later about that. The topic is you," BeLynda says winking.

They all look at her with Sandy saying, "Aww shit!! Bee got some juicy y'all!! And you want us to wait? Oh you must got some serious juicy to tell us. Don't have us passing out," Sandy says.. BeLynda blushes and waves them off. Sandy breaks out with

♪I'll take you to the Candy Shop

I'll let you lick the lollipop

Girl go 'head don't you stop♪

Colleen starts laughing and Regina just smiles shaking her head.

"What is this, 50 cent night? I didn't get the memo. First it was Colleen now it's you. Damn. Don't start asking 21 questions," BeLynda says laughing at Sandy.

"Ay, he just so happen to have the perfect lyrics for the current events. I don't know why Colleen came in here with *In da Club* because it ain't anyone's birthday but, for you … tell us all about how you licked that pole Girlie!! Oh by the way, 21 questions, that was corny for you to say that." Sandy is smiling all excited that BeLynda has a story to tell for a change.

"Whateva! But um, well, it won't be none of that in my story," BeLynda says with a smile but instantly feel the eyes of her friends burning a hole in her. She is not about to look at any of them. "Anyway, as I said, this topic is about Colleen, not me." BeLynda is dodging the bullets fast.

"Well, it is Byron's birthday coming up soon. He's having a party and he wants me to bring my girls. I do expect all of y'all to be up in the place having some fun. Y'all can bring a date if you want to. We can talk about that later too. I will give all the logistics. He'll be celebrating his birthday and bringing in the new year at the same time." Then Colleen looks over at Regina and says, "But … no, the topic is Regina. What's up Gee Gee? You all quiet this evening. What's been going on with you," Colleen asks. She notices that Regina hasn't said much this evening and that is unusual.

"Oh, nothing much is going on with me Girl. I'm fine. Hey here she comes," Regina turns her concentration to the teacher as she enters the room.

Mmm – hmmm, and you are standing here not really participating in our conversation. Sandy may be your best friend but you can't fool this friend. Oh, we will talk later too. I need the update on that black on black Charger anyway. You are acting mighty funny. It looks like you have had a new situation to come up. I might have to meet you at your house later on tonight. Hell, I need to sit in your sauna room anyway. I think I just might do that.

"Good evening Ladies! How is everybody doing today? How was your weekend? Did anyone do any practicing? I know some, if not all of y'all have had some sex since the last time we met. Did you try any of the exercises we've gone over already?" Looking around the room, no one is responding. "Don't let your money be wasted Ladies. I try to keep your sex lives out of these sessions but I just might have y'all reporting back what you did and how did it work."

No one responds to Kelly. "Don't everyone speak at once. Geesh! Well, did you at least remember to bring your items back to class today? I don't want any excuses. Those who didn't bring your items the last time, I do expect you to have them with you today. Now let's get started. Go ahead and get your fruit and vegetables out while I get situated." Kelly watches the ladies walk over to their bags to retrieve their items. She smiles. Everyone came to class prepared. She only has to take one prop out of her bag and that will be for her to demonstrate.

Everyone goes to their bags taking out their bananas, zucchinis, or cucumbers waiting for Kelly to tell them what they are going to be doing today, as if they don't have an idea.

"All right ladies. I see everyone came prepared today. I am pleased. I don't have to share my fruits and vegetables with you this time." The class laughs. "Now, I hope none of you came in here with extremely large foods. I'm sure the majority had an idea what this class is all about when I mentioned to bring these items with you. So hopefully, you got something that you can wrap your mouth around. I don't want anyone to get lockjaw in here. I am not a doctor and I am sure you don't want to explain how you got that." Kelly and the entire class are laughing now.

"Okay, now … do you remember our mouth and tongue exercises from the oral stimulation class?" Everyone nods their head "yes." Kelly claps her hands to together once and continues. "Okay, well, today … we are gonna practice those exercises on our props. This helps you to get used to what you should be doing with your mouth when giving oral to your partner. Okay, first, everyone in here is heterosexual, right?" No one responds yet they look at her wondering in what direction she is going with the question.

"I'm asking because this here will not help you if you are giving a woman oral. That is another class using different techniques and other types of foods." *Damn, this bitch teaches all kinds of shit huh? She got something for everybody huh? Hey, make that money baby,* Colleen says to herself.

"So is everyone in here with a man … or men?" They all finally respond with a "yes" head nod. "All righty then, let's get started." Looking around the class at all the faces, she hesitates and responds. "Is everyone comfortable with what we are going to do? It seems as if once I walked in the class there was pure quietness. Let me know that everything is okay before I proceed. No one should be uncomfortable when it comes to sex in any form. Does anyone want to just sit and watch?" The ladies assure her that they are fine and to continue with the lesson.

"Now, I do have some flavored jellies up here on the table. The foods can be very dry and if you have been practicing, you have found that out already. Their dryness can make your mouth dryer. There is no pre-cum or wetness with this. You only have your saliva. Sometimes a little extra help works great but don't use this on your man. The mixture of your saliva and his pre-cum will be – or it should be – more than enough wetness for you to get the job done. No pun intended." There are some snickers heard around the class.

"What I want you to do is get a partner ...." There are groans of displeasure from her statement heard in the class. "Yes … get a partner Ladies. What? You don't want someone watching you give head to your prop? You will eventually get up in front of the class and show us, so why are there complaints? Your partner may be able to tell you something extra to do. Or help you in your sticky areas. And the class may be able to tell you something that your partner wasn't able to tell you. We are all here to help. It is not just on me. I know y'all don't want my sisters to come in here and assist do you? They are not as tamed as me in my classes as some of you may already know," she looks over at the Fantastic Four: Sandy, BeLynda, Regina, and Colleen, winking her eye at them. "So let's get started. Pair up with someone, please. We've already wasted ten minutes as well as this is the second class on this. Oh, and I hope everyone has given their foods a good washing." She looks at everyone and only a few have the face of *"I didn't think of that."*

"Okay, now that you have your partner, I want you to practice the 'moving the tongue up and down in fluttering motions' technique. Practice it first and then try it on your prop. You will see it is a big difference in doing it without something in your mouth. Once you have practice it a few times, insert your prop in your mouth and try it. Try it on the tip first which would be the head of your man's penis. Then gradually move down what would be the shaft and practice this. It may not feel as if you're doing anything, but this gets your jaws and throat moving and he will definitely feel more than you think. This gives the simulation of your vagina walls contracting right before an orgasm. This would be appropriate for when he is about to have an orgasm too. This will heighten the sensation he is feeling." This sparks everyone's attention. To be able to have your mouth feel like a pussy, they were intrigued with her education.

Kelly is walking around the class observing everyone. Those who need a little more assistance, she provides. Those who are doing rather well, she gives them a smile and a head nod insinuating to keep up the good work. However, there are a few that seem to be doing something other than what she has instructed them to do. She stops at their team and demonstrates on her cucumber for them. Then she waits to see them do it properly. Once they have shown her that they got the idea, and she approves, she leaves them to practice together without her.

"Okay, it seems that everyone has gotten the picture and the feel of what this technique does. Keep practicing when you get home in your spare time, of course. Hopefully, you are practicing the 'tongue to the nose' as well. We don't want your mate to look at you like you are crazy. Then again, it might turn him on. This exercises the tongue, making it limber enough to do some wonderful things with it. It will definitely help in the technique you just demonstrated to your partner. Now, moving on, what is another technique we did in class?"

One of the ladies raises her hand to respond saying, "We did the 'move your tongue in circles to the left and then to the right' technique." Kelly smiles and gives her a yes nod.

"Yes, very good. I see some of you have been paying attention in class. This is a good one. Does everyone remember how to do that? If not make sure you practice it with your partner first then demonstrate it on your prop. It does take some concentration if you are not used to making circles with your tongue. This is a lovely oral stimulation. It does give great pleasure.

Especially when playfully and seductively performed. Now, let's get started Ladies. I want to see you practicing this first so your partner can either help you or you help your partner by showing them. This one is better done with your prop because you get the idea of what you are supposed to do."

Walking around the class again, she is watching the teams meticulously. She walks pass Sandy and BeLynda and notices that BeLynda is having a little struggle producing this method with her mouth for her partner. Stopping to assist, she notices that BeLynda tenses up at her presence. "You okay BeLynda?" She closes her eyes and shakes her head "yes" to Kelly as if to signal to her to keep walking. Kelly ignores the signal and asks, "Do you need some help?" With eyes still closed she shakes her head "no" trying to signal to her more to keep walking. Kelly looks at Sandy asking, "Y'all all right Sandy? Do you want me to help with this?" Sandy smiles and shakes her head "no." She knows BeLynda is beyond uncomfortable and she would not want to torture her girl. Kelly responds, "All right, just let me know if you need me." Kelly moves on.

Noticing that quite a few are having little difficulties with this tongue motion, she walks to the head of the class and gets everyone's attention. "All right ladies. I see there are a few struggles here. Would you like for me to demonstrate this for you?" There are "yes" head nods from the majority. Since the majority rules, she proceeds with a visual for the ladies. *Yea, girlfriend, show us what you got. Let me see if you're better than me at this*, Colleen smiles and says in her mind.

Kelly begins, "Okay, this is how the technique is done with practicing." She starts to make slow circular movements with her tongue going to the left. She repeats the movements but going to the right. Then she speeds it up a little to show them how it should actually look when done right. Kelly decides to get a little extra with it by opening and closing her mouth like she is blowing smoke rings but still moving her tongue in circles. The ladies are really into what Kelly is showing them. While some are watching Kelly, they are moving their mouth like they are chewing but keeping it closed.

"Now this is how it looks when performing it with an object be it your prop, dildo, or the real thing." Kelly gets her cucumber and begins the circular motion around the tip of the cucumber. She first uses the tip of her tongue advancing slowly to the middle top and bottom of the cucumber, her tongue is circling the tip of the vegetable. Once they have a clear picture of what she is doing, she closes her mouth and continues to perform the procedure. After a few seconds, the ladies could see a few droplets of saliva drip from Kelly's mouth, she stops at this point.

"Now, do you get the idea? I am sure some of you saw that my mouth was getting real juicy doing that. Trust me, he will like that. The wetter, the better and if he is watching, you will send him over the top. Some of you may not like it because it can get a little juicy for you. Just have fun with it. It doesn't have to be all messy nor does it have to be so neat. Hey, get a little x-rated with it if you will. We are all adults in here, right? And what did I say about adults, Ladies?"

"As adults, we are all sexual beings," the class says in unison.

"That's right we are, and don't be afraid to express yourself. It's not just for making babies. We are allowed to enjoy it. Remember that." BeLynda is listening and saying to herself, *I think I am starting to realize this Kelly. Thank goodness I am only thirty-one. I wouldn't have wanted to find this out in my forties, which is when I'm supposed to hit my prime. I want to be well prepared and skilled by then.*

Walking pass Colleen and Regina, Kelly notices that they are talking and looking very serious. She can tell it has nothing to do with the class. Colleen appears to be carrying on a conversation with Regina even while the zucchini is in her mouth. *What in the world are they talking about? And she is trying to talk with a mouth full of zucchini. Let me go over here and see what is going on.* Stopping in front of the duo, Regina jumps and Colleen takes the zucchini out of her mouth.

"Oh, hey Kelly. How am I doing? I am not too sure if I'm doing this right? What you think?" Colleen says trying to pretend that she was actually doing the exercise by doing a little demonstration for Kelley. Colleen is not too sure she is convincing.

Kelly looks at her with her left hand on her left hip. Looking at Colleen she says to herself, *I'm sure of all the people in here, you know exactly how to do this. Don't play with me.* Colleen can read her mind. "I really don't know if you are or not. It looks like you were talking with a mouth full of zucchini. I know that is not part of this exercise. Do you need assistance?" *Which I know you don't but I'm gonna play your game just for a minute.*

"Oh naw we are cool. I was just asking Regina if I was doing it right. But since you came over here, I decided to ask you too. You want me to do it again so you can let me know? I want to make sure I am executing my moves just right." Regina never responds. She is just looking at Colleen and Kelly interact. Kelly then looks at Regina and notices the different deportment.

"Regina are you all right this evening? You look a little down?" Kelly seems real concerned yet Regina doesn't want her to be. She has never seen Regina look so meek and mild. Kelly can't put her finger on it but it seems like Regina is hiding something. She knows she is not close enough to Regina to find out but she at least wants her to know that she is there if she needs her for anything.

Regina really doesn't feel like talking to anyone but she responds to keep down the suspicion. "Oh, yes, I'm fine. I didn't realize I was looking down today. Maybe I need to see what I look like so I can see what you see. I mean, other than being a little tired, everything is okay." Regina walks away towards the mirrored covered wall to see her face and to avoid Kelly's inquisitiveness. She is definitely tired emotionally.

"Are you sure? I am here if you need me. Honestly, I am not just your teacher here in class. It will be confidential." Kelly is offering her time and ear to the back of Regina since she has already walked away. She just looks on as she sees Regina stand in front of the mirrors and play around with her face massaging her jaws as if to change your expression.

"Um, I believe she has ended the conversation a few minutes ago Kelly. Don't press it. That wouldn't be a good idea," Colleen says inserting the zucchini back in her mouth swirling her tongue around it. Kelly sort of gives her a "what is that suppose to mean" look and Colleen shoots back with an "I didn't stutter" look. Kelly takes the hint and walks on. *Woo!! These bitches keep trying me and I am trying to remain calm,* Colleen says to herself almost biting down on the zucchini forgetting she is to be circling her tongue on it and not biting on her prop.

"Okay, class, I see that the majority is doing quite well today. Good. Either you have been practicing or you've remembered. Now, moving right along, what would be our next oral stimulation to use?" Looking around the class, Kelly surprisingly notices BeLynda is raising her hand to answer. Pointing at BeLynda to answer, she says, "We demonstrated 'sticking out the tongue, move it left to right, and pull it back in' technique."

Kelly winks at her and smiles turning to face the class. "Did everyone hear BeLynda? We will be expressing the 'sticking out the tongue, move it left to right, and pull it back in' technique. That should be pretty easy especially after the two exercises that we performed. The jaws and tongue should be nicely relaxed now. This is a nice teasing move for the under shaft. Also, if oral is something that you don't do often, this gives the jaws a little break while still pleasing your partner."

"One thing is for sure, we know she can please her partner real good don't we?" Colleen says leaning over whispering to Regina.

"Uh, how do we know that? We ain't seen her do that and she has never said. I take it you're going off of assumptions based off her wide mouth and full lips?" Regina responds with one eyebrow raised.

"Ooh, now you said that, not me. I wasn't even going there but since you mentioned it she does have a mouth piece. I hadn't even thought about her mouth because with all those teeth, I'm almost positive that her inner mouth is rather small. But, what I was referring to was back in the oral stimulation class when she demonstrated the 'reaching your chin with your tongue' move. You remember how long her tongue was and how it actually touched her damn chin? That was *amazing.* The whole class was quiet just watching." Regina smiles at what Colleen is refreshing her memory on. "I was actually awestruck behind that shit. With a tongue like that, all she has to do is walk into a room full of men and flick it out. Every man in the room will feel their dick twitch and jerk. Then if she adds one of these demonstrations to it, there will be plenty of broken zippers all around the room."

This gives Regina a good laugh and slightly removes the grey cloud from above her. Colleen is happy to see her friend smiling and laughing. She continues. "I'm serious girl. Hecht's would have an increase in sales with men buying new pants. Or the dry cleaners would rack up in the seamstress department trying to repair all of those damn busted zippers. They would be trying to figure out what the hell happened in one night. And what the hell happened would be Kelly's long ass tongue came to the party." Regina is beside herself. She has forgotten that they are in class and the teacher just might call her out.

Looking over at Regina and Colleen, Kelly now knows for sure they are not talking about class. Whatever is going on with Regina, she is just glad that her friend was able to make her smile. She didn't like seeing Regina in a funk. She ignores it and keeps on going.

"All right ladies, have you gotten the feel of some techniques to use or to add to what you already do when performing fellatio?" They nod 'yes." "Good. You see, that wasn't very hard at all was it?" They nod "no." "Is there anyone that would feel uncomfortable performing these on your mate?" Some answered "no" but some didn't respond. That wasn't exactly the response she was expecting but she figures that many just didn't want to let on to the others in class. "It's all right if you don't want to give your answer in front of everyone. Just make sure you practice, and practice, and practice. You'll be a pro in no time."

"And that doesn't mean that you're not a lady. It just means you know how to please your partner well with your mouth. It is a part of intimacy. Sometimes that is all your partner wants and needs at the moment. And you should get great satisfaction from knowing that you made him happy. You can give yourself a personal A+ for that. Now, that is all for this evening. Enjoy the rest of your evening Ladies. Have a good weekend too. We'll resume back in here on Monday. Oh!! That's right. Some of you are going to be in the pole class. Be ready. Tina will be teaching that one."

Some of the ladies grumble at hearing Tina's name. Kelly looks around at everyone and smiles. "What's the matter Ladies? Tina too hard on you? Maybe you should enroll in her cardio class to lift some weights and do some push-ups to strengthen those arms and upper body along with the abs. Trust, you're gonna need it. But I will put a little bug in her ear to take it easy on you. Make sure your attire is flexible. Yoga gear works great for that class."

"Yea, that's what I told her in the sexercise class and she damn near killed us. It's apparent she has no idea what 'be easy' or 'don't kill us' means." Colleen says rolling her eyes. Everyone in the class laughs out loud.

"Yeap, that sounds like Tina. But I will remind her." Kelly laughs. "All right ladies, I gotta go. My next class starts in ten minutes. Be careful."

The last statement almost wrecks Regina's nerves. *Be careful? Shit, that's what I've been trying to do and fucked up shit keep happening. I'm gonna have to talk to my girls soon and tell Stan all the stuff that has been happening.*

"Whew, girl!! My jaws are tired. They feel like I need to let them hang to the floor. I don't even feel like talking. But I will rest my mouth once I get in the car. An hour of this is more than enough. It don't take this long to make a nigga buss off," Sandy says moving her face around like she is rinsing with mouthwash.

"Yea, mine too. I didn't know you had to do all of this to give oral stimulation. It seems like too much if you ask me. All that jaw and tongue action is ridiculous. I mean damn you gotta do all of that to make him feel good. *Shiit!*" BeLynda says. Sandy, Colleen, and Regina all look at her.

"What you mean Bee," asks Colleen.

"I'm just saying, it just seems like a lot. I know my jaws and neck would get tired fast. And he is just sitting back watching? Hell naw!! I would need to have my eyes closed through that." BeLynda is shaking her head "no." Her girls continue to look at her like she is unreal.

"Okay, hold up. Wait a minute. Stop the muthafuckin' press!!" Colleen says with her eyes closed scratching her head. She looks at BeLynda and continues. "Are you saying to us in so many words that you have never given oral before? Not even to Steve?" Colleen waits for the answer while Sandy and Regina look on. They want to know too.

"What?! Is that surprising?" BeLynda looks at her friends wondering. "Every woman doesn't get down like that Colleen. I just never felt the need to do that."

"Girl, what are you talking about? You are thirty-one and have had a husband once upon a time. You mean to tell me that you have never put your lips on Steve like that? I don't know a woman that hasn't. Hell, I don't think I know a female *period* that hasn't. Fuck being grown. That is a pre-requisite nowadays for these young men and boys." Sandy says. *I know damn well if she says no, that could be the reason why Steve was out there doing his thing without her ass. Damn Bee!!*

"Bee, what is the matter really? I'm honestly not understanding for real. I mean, you were married. If you were going to do that, it should have at least been with your husband. Did he ever ask you to?" Regina asks. She's been quiet most of the evening but she needs to know what is going on with her girl.

BeLynda holds her head down trying to get her things together to leave and responds. "I know Steve was my husband. And yes, he used to ask all the time. And yes, he used to get frustrated because I wouldn't. I just didn't feel like I should have had to do that, you know?" They all look at her quiet listening. They are completely stunned at what she is saying to them. Looking at their expressions, she continues. "Oh, so all of y'all have done this before?"

"What?!" They all yell in unison like the choir.

"Haven't you had a man to do you," Sandy really wants to know. BeLynda shakes her head "yes." "So you are a stingy lover? It's okay to do you because they want to but that doesn't necessarily mean that you should repay the favor huh?" BeLynda doesn't respond. Sandy looks at BeLynda with raised eyebrows waiting for an answer that she never gets.

"GIRL!! We have to have a class just the four of us at one of our houses because you are blowing me right now. You need some Sista Sex Talk 101 for real. But all I have say right now is *whenever* you decide to do it, keep your teeth out of the way," Colleen says frowning and shaking her head. Sandy and Regina laugh out loud. Sandy is holding her stomach and Regina has tears in her eyes. BeLynda just frowns at the thought and begins to walk out of the class.

"Whateva! You can keep your skanky ass 101 lessons to yourself. I'm aiight!"

Chapter Seven

7

"Yo! Who dis?" He asks because he doesn't recognize the number.

"Yo?! It's your brother nigga. What you mean 'who dis?' I done had this number for the longest. It's not stored in your phone?"

"Rone? Oh hey, what's up baby bruh? This is my business phone. You ain't ever called me on this one. I didn't know you had this number. Plus, I didn't recognize the number so I had to put my hood voice on." They both have a good laugh.

"Your hood voice, huh? Yea, well, I figured you have this phone with you wherever you are just in case. So I decided to call on this one. What's going on with you? How you been big bruh?"

"Yea, as you see I do have that phone with me but normally, I cut it off thirty minutes after I am done for the day. I am normally off the clock around three-thirty but I guess I forgot to do that. But nothing much is going on with me. Just the same old bullshit, you know? Tryin' to keep my head above water, away from the sharks and it's hard. You know how it goes. How is my sister-in-law?"

"Oh she aiight. She's in the family-room helping the children with their homework. I already gave them their dinner. In a few they are getting ready to go to bed. Then we both can relax. And if you had turned off your phone, you would've missed my call. But I'll make a note to call you on your personal phone after four from now on." The brothers laugh.

"I know that's right! Go 'head daddy. Do the damn thang. That's aiight. I like that about you bruh. That will be me one day." They both snicker at the statement. *Not if you keep fuckin' around with Rennie's dumb ass,* Rone says to himself.

"Yea, well, you know … you have to get you a 'possibility' or a 'definite' in the women's department. You do know that right? I know you're not still holding on to …. Well, you know what I mean?" Rone didn't finish the statement, trying to be sensitive to Ray's heart.

"Yea, I know what you mean, man. I got a 'possibility' or a 'definite,' I think. I just have to figure some things out."

"Oh, you do … really? So you've met someone? That's good Ray. I'm happy for you. But what you got to figure out big bruh?" *Now it's time for me to fish around for some information. He sounds like he wants to talk.* "What's been going on with you? I hear something in your voice."

"Yea, I met someone and I'm digging her alot too man. I've only been out with her a few times and I don't know what to do. I gotta figure something out fast before shit go all wrong." Ray sighs. This signals to Rone that he needs to keep him talking.

"Oh yea? What's getting in the way?" Rone hears silence from Ray. That's a sign that Rennie is involved somehow, he can feel it. So he speaks up. "Hey, listen, does this silence have anything to do with Rennie?"

"Rennie?! Why are you asking that?" Ray asks nervously.

Yeap, this has EVERYTHING to do with his rotten ass. "Ay, you just gave yourself away. You know you weren't ever too good at hiding shit when it's fuckin' with you. Talk my nigga. What bullshit is he on now?"

Ray pulls the phone back from his ear and looks at it. He is shocked at Rone and smiles before putting the cell back to his ear. "Hey, Rone … where you been man? When you start talkin' like that? Tryin'a sound like you are about that life and shit." They both let out a hardy laugh.

"Shiiit, my wife will kill me but you know I have to stay up on the lingo y'all use. I got tired of feelin' like I was in a room full of foreigners when y'all would kick the shit, you know? It felt like I was learning a new language too *dawg*!!" The brothers have a great laugh at Rone's new second language. "But anyway, hip me to Rennie's shit?"

Ray lets out a big sigh and begins spilling his guts. "You know that chick that he was training named Regina? The one whose husband that was paying Rennie mad loot for his services?"

"Um … oh … yea, I remember her. You're talkin' about the pretty sexy brown skin chick. What about her? Oh shit, what happened? What did he do?"

"Well, after a while, he started feeling her."

"Word? Feeling her how?"

"Yea, I mean *feeling* her, man. Apparently he came on to her but she wasn't budging or responding to his advances. So this nigga starts asking to take her out and shit. I told him that wasn't a good idea because she is married. But of course brick head didn't listen."

"You told his ass right!! She is married and not to mention she was a client. Go on. I'm listening."

"Well, you know like I said, he didn't listen. He was tellin' her that he wanted to take her out and shit like that. Sayin' that her husband didn't have to know. I told that nigga he was stupid. All of these available women out here … especially in his clientele and he chose the married one. So look, during one of their sessions, this nigga tries to grab her and kiss her and shit."

"*OOOH*!! Damn! Ray, what? Word?! He went that far bruh? Let me guess … she broke that nigga's ego didn't she?" Rone asks shaking his head.

"Boy!! Did she?! She slapped the hell out of his ass and ended his services. That dumb ass was walking around with a hand print on his face and heart for like two weeks. After that, some of his clientele stopped fuckin' with him …. Something about being connected to her through her husband."

"Which means he lost money and never got the girl," Rone asks interrupting him. He rubs his hands through his curls disappointed in Rennie's action.

"Damn sure did. So now he's on some revenge type shit."

"Oh snap!! Revenge, like what?! What is he up to now man?"

"I am not sure because he hasn't actually said but he wanted me to get next to one of her friends and act like I'm interested and start dating her. Thinking that this would give him an advantage of getting next to her." Ray hears silence on the other end of the phone. "Hello? Hello Rone, you still there?"

"Yea, man. I'm just absorbing what you just said. Sooo, let me get this straight. He wants you to pretend that you like one of her friends in order for him to get next to her?"

"You got it. And right about now, I'm not feelin' this shit. I told him that I wasn't gonna get caught up in his shit if he got some kidnapping or murder bull brewing. I got a business to run and too much shit to lose."

"Right, right I hear you! So what you gonna do? This doesn't sound safe bruh. That's why I don't even take his calls half of the time. He was calling me back to back about a month ago and I just let his ass leave messages. I ain't even call him back bruh."

"Oh yea? Damn! I should've done the same damn thing. But he also has Rufus in on this shit too. He got him hooking up with one of her other friends but only as Plan B just in case my shit don't work out. Talkin' about if it doesn't work out with me and 'ol girl that he will call on Rufus. Rufus done told that damn woman his name is 'Paul.' Rennie tried to get Twin to get involved but I told him that wasn't going to work since we are identical. "

Rone is just quiet. He is totally stunned by what Ray is telling him. He doesn't know what to say or where to begin. He looks over into the den observing his wife helping the children with their homework, smiling thanking God that he has them as a reason to no longer get caught up in Rennie's bullshit.

"Man, I don't know what to say. That is some serious bullshit that Rennie is on and he knows it. There's a possibility of murder or kidnapping? C'mon *man*! That nigga will be thirty-seven this year and he still doing boy shit? And you right. Of all the women for him to be sprung over – and he ain't even got none of the pussy – he goes after a damn married woman that ain't thinking about his ass. And Rufus going around with a pseudo name these days, huh? Them niggas crazy."

"Yea, they are. We both met the women at the Zanzibar last month. And you got that right. Rennie barely kissed her and she surely wasn't receptive. And her husband is loaded too."

"Oh yea? What kind of loaded are we talkin'?" Rone's eye pop out like a cartoon with curiosity wondering if this is more about the woman's husband.

"Man, they live in this big ass house, luxury cars and shit, a maid, Regina wearing the best of the best, and his ass is always in suits costing in the thousands. Man, this woman doesn't even work nor does it look like she has too!! His mother even has a driver man and she walks around in furs. I told his ass that he can't compete. He got all in his feelings and shit when I said that. I mean, she seems to be a nice beautiful woman dedicated to her man. Clearly she ain't gonna mess that up to be with his wishy-washy broke ass."

"If her husband has this type of money, do you think Rennie is on some ransom type of bullshit? I mean, kidnapping would involve that, right?"

"Or murder but I don't even know. I couldn't tell you. He seriously hasn't told me anything more and that's why for one I am not trying to get caught up."

"Okay, hold up. Let's back up a little bit. How do you know all of this about 'Ol Girl, her man, and their living arrangements? Are you scoping the chick out for him Ray?" There is a moment of silence. "Ray?! What the fuck?!"

Ray sighs and closes his eyes. "Yea, man, he got me following her and I think she knows something ain't right. She caught me a few times watching her in class."

"In class? Oh, she in college trying to get a degree? I guess that gives her something to do. That's all right, for real. It keeps her from having an idle mind and out of trouble."

"Nah man, 'ol girl is taking some kind of sex classes or 'get-in tune- with- your- sexuality type' of classes. And her little crew takes them too. So she is never alone. And the out of trouble statement … well as you see Rennie is trying to put her in some trouble."

Rone is taking a swallow of his Minute Maid fruit punch and chokes when he hears this. "Huh? Come again? Sex classes? And her girls go too? So you get to see her and her friends at the same time? What they be doing in them classes?" Rone laughs out loud at the visual.

"You heard me. But they don't seem to be that bad. I think it is just something they do as some type of bonding shit, you know? This is on Monday nights and then on Thursdays, they meet up at the Spa. They are a nice group of attractive, sexy, voluptuous women Jo. No joke. I don't even see why he didn't try for one of her friends. She is the only one that is married out of the crew."

"Oh, I see you have been *really* checking her out, huh?"

"Hey, it ain't like I wanted to and now I'ma have to tell him that I'm backing out of this fuckin' madness. I've been following her in my black Charger since I'm rarely seen in that. But sooner or later the shit is gonna hit the fan and I don't need to be caught."

"No bullshit! Tell that nigga to do this shit solo. But wait, you're telling me all of this and I still don't understand something. I know how you are feeling, but what is the major issue?"

"The girl that he has me getting next to … I'm digging her. Like I really wouldn't mind being with her on some for real type of shit Jo. She might be the one bruh. All jokes aside, she might be the one." Ray sounds depressed.

"Word?!" Rone is excited but feeling for his big brother right now. He knows it has been a minute since his brother has dated due to the tragic loss of his love.

"Yea, man. I even told Mama about her and she caught on to how I was acting and looking and started questioning. I already know what she is gonna do."

"Oh, you told Mama about her?" Rone is playing it off. "Wow!! That's serious Ray. Hey, go for it bro and fuck Rennie. Let his ass get locked up or six feet under fooling around with a man's wife. I know how I will be, for real!"

"Yea, Mama was at the house cooking up all this food for me. You know how she does. Thinking I'm still twelve years old. And I had gone out with Sandy that evening. So I told her that I didn't eat alone. She got all excited and shit. You know how she wants more grandbabies. But when she saw my face, she knew something wasn't right."

"Damn. That woman put a number on your ass didn't she? You got the Love Jones going on, huh? And her name is Sandy. I take it that's short for Sandra?" They start laughing.

"Yea, that's her name. I ain't gonna say all that, you feel me? But I will say that she did and said enough to make me rethink all this shit with Rennie. I'm not tryin' to mess this up if I have a chance to get something real with her, ya know what I mean?"

"Hey, I feel ya bruh. But look, check this out … what y'all know about Regina's husband? Who is this cat anyway? Do you know his name? Has anyone done any research?"

"Hey, I have no idea who he is, what's his name, if Rennie did any research … nothing. But the nigga looks like he may be connected, if you know what I mean."

"Oh word?! Connected?! Fuck that! Hey, I say do you and don't get involved with Rennie. But in the mean time, try to find out his name so we can see what kind of bells his name rings in the streets."

"Aiight, listen at little brotha giving big brotha advice." They laugh. Ray's eyes open wide. "Oh!! Wait … Mama called you didn't she? She wanted to see what was going on with me so she had you get in contact with me so you can report back to her. Your slick ass!"

"Hey, what can I say," Rone laughs. "You know how Mama is when it comes to her boys. Rennie is always plotting on something or somebody recruiting his damn brothas. It's fucked up that he is plotting on a woman … a married woman at that. Then to have you and Rufus mixed up in this shit with two of her friends? Not good at all. Oh, she is going to get his ass and get him good. You know Mama don't play. If Rennie wants to be taken down, that's fine but Mama ain't gonna allow *three* of her boys to go down," Rone laughs and Ray agrees.

"Yea, you right about that. I can see her now with the wheels spinning in her head trying to figure out what she is going to do with Rennie."

"Oh, I can assure you she is going to threaten to take back all of his money. I mean, he does nice with this training business, but to have those millions taken out of his account, I bet you this plan of his is going to disappear quickly. But, wait, you called Rennie broke. What happened to his money?"

"Compared to Regina's husband, he *is* broke. He's an irrational spender and I know he would empty his bank account to get in place the things Stan provides. That means he wouldn't be able to maintain. But, yea, that's a lot of money to miss. More than likely, she is going to make three calls, not including the one she made to your ass," they laugh.

"I can't help if I don't get involved with Rennie's crap. Plus, I'm the baby of the five of us and I'm her heart, don't forget that."

"Oh, you are huh? How are you the favorite? Let me hear your explanation."

"Well, there is one word for that. It is 'grandkids.'"

"Yea, I know. Don't worry, you and I will be running neck and neck for the 'favorite' spotlight because I am gonna give her some grandkids too."

"Oh, I hear you bruh. And you banking on this 'Sandy' woman being the mother? But to do that, you still have to have a possibility or a definite and you aren't sure about her yet. Messing around with Rennie's ass … you won't have a muthafuckin thing. Trust and believe. He is Spawn in the flesh." They laugh at Rone's last statement. "My advice is for you to leave him alone and live your life."

"Yea, I hear you. That is what I plan to do too. Damn, you call that nigga Spawn." Ray laughs at Rone. "Man, you watch too much damn TV."

"Hey! I got kids big bruh! But hey, check her husband out though bruh. That's what you should've done before jumping in bed with Hell himself."

"You right. Aiight Rone. Let me get off this phone. I need to go spar in this gym real quick."

"Aiight bruh. Yea, do that. Work off some of that frustration. Too bad Sandy ain't in that position yet for you to work it off on her. But due time, my nig … due time." Rone and Ray laugh.

"Talk to you later." **click**

Ring! Ring!

"Hello?"

"Hey Mama, how you doing?"

"Hey baby! I'm just fine. How are you?"

"I'm fine too. What you doing?"

"Oh, nothing much. Just eating me some dinner. I just sat down to eat. How did your day go?"

"My day was fine. What you cook? I might need to come over tomorrow and get me a plate," Rone grins.

"Something quick. Nothing special at all. Just some baked turkey wings, collards, and cornbread. Where my grandbabies?"

"Damn! That sounds good. But you know you about to have turkey in a few weeks for Christmas. Why you fix turkey wings? You won't be tired of turkey by then?"

"Because that is what I wanted. Is that all right with you?" They laugh. "And I don't have to have turkey for Christmas even though I will. I didn't have any bird for Thanksgiving. I know you and the family will be over. You better send that wife of yours to cooking classes or something. But duck can be my bird if I want it to be."

"Yea, we will be over there. But ay, if you all right with it, so am I. But the kids are fine. Salisha is in the family-room helping them with their homework."

"Oh, okay. Good. That's right." Rachel takes a pause to chew her food. "They must be educated and continue to be educated. There is more than enough ignorance going around. My grandbabies don't need to add to that statistic."

"Oh, you don't have to worry about that. That won't even happen on my watch. Education is a must."

"That's what I wanna hear. Now, you called me so I'm gonna let you lead this conversation. What can I do for you?"

"I was calling to say that I spoke with Ray a few minutes ago."

That caught Rachel's attention in mid chew. "Oh you did?! Well, I am going to bypass all of the formalities and jump right to what did you find out. My instincts were right weren't they?"

"Yeap, your instincts were right Mama. Rennie got some shi – I mean stuff going on and he got Ray helping him. He was down for it at first but now he … "

"This involves the young lady he just met doesn't it?"

"Yea, and Ray really likes her and wants to really date her, not just to pretend for Rennie and mess it up. He thinks he might have a good thing about to start with her. He said he thinks she is the one, Mama."

"Mmm-hmmm, I knew it. You should've seen how he was talking about her to me. Then I saw him talking on the phone to her and even though he sounded fine talking to her, he looked like he had a bad case of constipation going on. So he thinks she might be the one, huh?" Rachel asks and Rone laughs at his mother.

"Yea, that's what he says. He talking about children and everything. Ray doesn't know what the plan is exactly. All he knows is it is some type of revenge on one of his ex-clients. So he wants him and Rufus to get close to her friends in order for him to get next to her."

"What?! He is scheming on a female?! And trying to get Ray and Rufus along with two of her friends spun in his damn web of deceit?!" Rachel is furious.

"Yeap, that's what he said Ma. Ray said that she was one of his clients and Rennie started liking her. Then he started coming on to her and she wasn't biting. So he made an advance at her and she slapped him and fired him. Ray said he had a hand print on his face for a minute." Rone laughs at this part of the situation. "That was a ricochet effect because some of his other clients fired him too because they were her friends.

"So the dummy trying to mix business with pleasure. I figured that's what he had planned anyway when he started that damn training business. Thinking eventually one of them bimbos were gonna want to become involved with him. Or give up some ass." Rachel stuffs a piece of turkey in her mouth chewing like she is mad at the world.

"Yea, well, I guess that might not have been a bad idea if he wanted to meet someone or get some tail from one of the bimbos. But the problem is, he didn't go for one of the bimbos. The girl he's trying to get is married and her husband apparently has big money."

"Okay, okay, my son has lost his damn mind. She's *married*?! She should've slapped his ass and the mark should've been permanent. And her husband has big money, huh?" Rachel shakes her head and slams her fork down on her everyday china plate. "Are you sure Ray doesn't know the plan?! It sounds like a ransom to me and for what?! That turd has money and he doesn't know what to do with it, but I can take that away if he keeps this shit up. Does anyone know who her husband is?" Rachel is yelling all through the kitchen, her voice bouncing off the walls.

"Ray says he doesn't know who he is. But the woman doesn't work, he wears expensive suits and they have servants and drivers. I told him that he needed to have done his research on him before he agreed to participate in Rennie's foolishness. Oh and he said that Rennie be messing up his money, so he might be a little low."

Sigh. "Ray has been following this woman around sounds like. Where the hell was he when they were giving out common sense?!! He must've been in the 'Good Looks' line. Or did Rennie tell him all of this? Following her to her damn house?! And Rennie's ass can be totally broke if he keeps thinking I'm gonna accept his skullduggery. Going after a married woman like he's desperate. Kidnapping her ass surely isn't gonna get him any closer to a relationship with her that's for sure. Apparently she didn't want him to get into any trouble because it's obvious she didn't tell her husband. He needs to take that damn slap, suck it up, get some more clients and move the hell on."

"I know but you know his ego is crushed. But nah, Rennie ain't told Ray nothing. He has followed her a few places and he knows that she is usually with her friends on Mondays and Thursdays."

"Oh, this fool is already too caught up. What places are they going to every week on the same days?" Rachel only hears silence. Nothing but air can be heard through the phone. "Boy don't you play with me. I asked a damn question."

Damn!! I got too happy with talking. "They go to the Spa on Thursdays and some sex class on Mondays," Rone mumbles the latter part real fast to his mother hoping she doesn't ask him to be clearer. Mama Rachel bursts into loud laughter and gets choked a little on her cornbread. She takes a sip of her Pepsi with fresh limes squeezed in it.

Rachel continues to laugh asking, "Did you say the woman and her friends go to sex classes? They offer sex classes now? For adults, not high school shit? And y'all know of some girlfriends that actually attend these together? Where in the world does this take place?" *I have got to see for myself. Hell, I might join a few of them or just sit and watch. Mama may be older but she ain't in the ground yet.*

"Mama, what's so funny? Yea, they teach those types of classes. I don't know what they do in them though. Why you wanna know where the classes are? What are you gonna do? I know you ain't gonna try to walk up in there as a student!!" Rone is furious and can't believe his mother, even though she hasn't admitted to anything yet.

"Excuse me? Your mother is fifty-eight, not seventy-eight. You better hope Salisha is still spreading for you when she gets to be my age. As a matter of fact, I'm gonna drag her ass with me and she can tell you just what she saw." Rachel thinks it is funny messing with Rone knowing he is getting furious.

"The hell, um … the heck she will. Ma!! Don't do this!! Let us handle the foot work. You handle behind the scenes, aiight?!" Rone is pissed at his mother's insinuation of his wife being anywhere near those classes. Even though it might not be a bad idea.

"You need to tell me everybody's full name. Hers, her husband's, and her friends'. I need to give that information to somebody. I need to see what kind of crap Rennie might get himself into if I don't get to him fast enough to stop his ass."

Sigh, damn!! "Yea, okay Ma. I'm on that now." *She is getting too old for this shit!! Rennie is gonna send her to an early grave. But I guess this also keeps her young to an extent and gives her something to do. She needs to find some new shit to do.*

"All right, good. That's that I want to hear. You get on that like last week for me. Love you Last Born!"

"Yea, I love you too Mama." *Fuck!!*

click

"Hey baby, who were talking to that got you looking like that? You wanna talk about it?" Salisha is looking at the stress written all over her husband's face and she isn't liking it. *Probably one of his simple ass brothers.*

"Nah, I'm fine babe. I'm gonna go in the library for a little while."

Salisha's phone chimes indicating a text message came through on her phone. She flips it open to see who it is. She sees it is from her mother-in-law. *Mmm-hmm, he just got off the phone with her and she doesn't want him to know she is speaking to me.*

WHAT'S UP DAUGHTER-IN-LAW?

HEY MAMA RACHEL. HOW YOU?

I'M FINE. LOOK WHEN IS YOUR NEXT FREE TIME?

IN A FEW DAYS, Y? WHAT'S UP?

WE NEED TO MEET UP FOR LUNCH. DON'T TELL RONE.

K MAMA. JUST LET ME KNOW TIME N PLACE WHEN U DECIDE.

ALL RIGHT BABY. WE GOT SOME WORK TO DO TO KEEP THESE KNUCKLE-HEADS OUT OF TROUBLE.

AGAIN?! WHAT'S GOING ON?

I'LL LET YOU KNOW ALL OF THAT WHEN WE MEET.

K, MAMA.

GOODNIGHT BABY.

Mmmp, he won't tell me what that look is all about but his Mama will. More than likely if she is contacting me, Rennie is up to some no-good bullshit AGAIN and she is trying to save the others! That means, we're gonna be spending quite a bit of time together until this shit is over. At least it gets me out of the house on some exciting Inspector Gadget shit. Ha, ha, ha, Mama reminds me of Donna Mills' character on Knots Landing, the villainous Abby Cunningham, just an older version now. But when it comes to her boys, she is the mother from off of The Terminator. Salisha is smiling from her thoughts.

"Now, babe, what are you doing? You're supposed to helping Tannin and Tanner with their homework. Who you texting? And where is Talisha? What you up to Lish?" Rone is looking at her with narrow eyes leaning up against one of the amber painted walls in the family-room.

"Um, excuse you?! I thought you said you were going into the library. I *am* helping them with their homework and Talisha is done. She's upstairs getting ready for bed." She has a smirk on her face still responding. "Now, I asked you about three minutes ago what was wrong and you told me nothing was wrong. Meaning that you didn't want me to know or to get involved with whatever it is that got you so tense. So don't come in here being inquisitive Tyrone Daniels. Stop meddling, it isn't attractive." His brow flies up in astonishment and he walks away. She laughs to herself. *Two can play that game, hmmp.*

Ring! Ring!

"Yea, what did she say?" Ray knew for Rone to call him back tonight he had already spoken with their mother.

"Oh, she's hot bruh! Like an iron set on cotton/linen bruh! Like boiling grits!" Rone thinks it is funny yet Ray doesn't find anything funny at all. "As if you didn't know she was gonna be pissed off that Rennie hasn't grown up. Like she wasn't going to be pissed that he has once again recruited his loyal ass dumb brothas.

She talkin' about she wants me to give her everybody's full names. *And* she wants to know where their classes at too Ray. I didn't like that part because you know she is gonna try to go up in there and check it out."

"Fuck!! What she wanna know that for? She don't need to be up in those classes with those young chicks, man. You know she is taken those names to her police connect Rone. I don't want her doing that."

"Well, she ain't had no man since Dad, so we don't have to worry about her and them classes. She is just going there to check it out. Probably want to see what this Regina chick looks like. But did you not think she wasn't gonna call Detective McSwain? He's the perfect one to check out dude. Especially since you said he looks like he is connected. All that shit might have started from street money, which means he has had some run-ins at some point with the law. Now that will tell us whether Rennie needs to go sit his ass down and find a woman that is fuckin' available."

"I guess you right. But I don't need Sandy seeing her in those damn classes and they haven't even met yet. That's all I need is for some questions to be brought to me from Sandy. Not to mention, with Mama talkin' to McSwain, that might open up another can of worms."

"Maybe, maybe not. Let's deal with that later. But hopefully Sandy doesn't pay any attention if she does go up in there signifying. What her other friends look like and how many more is it?"

"There are two more. All of them are extremely beautiful. One seems a little timid but the other one was with her one night and they were scoping out my car in the parking lot after class. I think she saw me outside her house once too. I can't be too sure about that. But her friend that was with her … I don't know but there was something about her stance once Regina brought to her attention my car."

"Ah she got a beautiful bad bitch on her team, huh? A BBB?! That's sexy as shit! Yea, well I guess we will find out soon enough who they are all, won't we? You know Mama is probably gonna be on that shit like first thing tomorrow morning."

Sigh! "That's what worries me. And yea, that one friend just had a look like she was ready to go bruh. You should have seen her." Ray is wishing he can blink back into three months before he answered that call from Rennie.

"Nah what should worry you is when you finally speak to Mama. She is gonna lay into that ass!! And that will call for a family meeting. You know how those go! And if that BBB was ready to go, you need to be careful." Rone is laughing so hard, he doesn't hear Ray hang up.

Chapter Eight

8

"All right Girlies!! We are back on track!! I need my damn Spa time. This body is aching and tired." Colleen says giving the usual greeting to everyone.

"Yea, me too. I need to get rid of some of these toxins and impurities that probably have built up from us not being here last week." BeLynda is rubbing on her arms and stomach as if to rub off a few layers of dead skin.

"Impurities? Toxins? What are you talking about? Impurities as in what, film, crust … filth? Or getting rid of some of the dick juice that you might be holding onto from last night?" Colleen laughs at her own questions. Sandy smiles and shakes her head. BeLynda rolls her eyes. Regina says nothing.

"Girl, will you shut your nasty ass up? Everybody don't have dick on the brain all the time, unlike you. I *swear* we need to carry around a tape recorder so you can hear yourself, seriously. Maybe you will start thinking a little more before you just spit out your words." Sandy and Regina laugh at Colleen.

"Well, Stan told me that men think about sex every twelve seconds of the day. So if that's true, then I don't see why women wouldn't think about it just as much." Regina sits down and crosses her legs swinging her foot back and forth.

"Or close to it. Hell, or even more. Especially when she hits her prime. Hell, I mean all we have to do is come across a sexy ass man from his face, dress, shoes, smell, and body build and I am sure the majority of the women he walks past will be imagining being in bed with him. So you got a point there Gee Gee. You and Stan may be onto something." Colleen says agreeing with Regina.

"Well, that's not me. My thing is, there are other things to think about throughout the course of a day. Dick don't put any money into my account, pay my bills, feed me, or help me to survive. Nor does it pay for these damn Spa appointments." BeLynda responds.

"Hmmp, if you loosen up it just might do all that and more Ms. Giles." *Here we go with the killjoy comments*, Colleen says to herself rolling her eyes at BeLynda.

"What?! Loosen up? You think I'm uptight Colleen? How is that?" Sandy and Regina look at Colleen waiting for her to respond to BeLynda's questions, wondering if Colleen is going to be lovingly or crassly honest.

"*Think*," Colleen asks. "Girl, please, I *KNOW*! For as long as I have known you, whenever we talk about men or sex, you crawl into a shell in the form of the three monkeys. You don't wanna hear, speak, or see. Like your ears, mouth, and eyes are virgins to those types of conversations or something. Even though you surely be listening. Sometimes you will participate but most of the time, you act like we are saying something that is *taboo.* So yes, I think you are uptight. Do anyone of you want to add something to what I said?" Colleen looks at Regina and Sandy. They are just sitting there with eyes saying, *Really Colleen?*

"Okay, okay, don't start y'all, please. No Frick 'n Frack mess tonight. Colleen you could have said that better than that." Sandy opens her Dooney & Bourke handbag and pulls out her Chap Stick putting it on her lips.

"Oh, no you didn't go there." Regina is laughing hard at Sandy's response.

"What is she talking about Frick 'n Frack?" Colleen asks watching Sandy smear the Chap Stick across her lips five times rubbing them together. She is waiting for an answer.

"Well, does Tom and Jerry sound better to you Ms. Jeffries? It seems to me you're now in the same boat that you just put Bee in." Sandy looks at Colleen pissed at how she spoke opinion of the truth to BeLynda.

Regina is shaking her head signaling to not mention their inside joke as part of the conversation. Sandy ignores and is waiting for Colleen to respond.

"Neither of them sound better and I know exactly what those terms stand for. I wanted to hear why you said that. But that's cool. I got your Frick and your Frack heifer. Now give me a kiss. You sound a little jealous." Colleen stands up walking over to Sandy with her arms out and lips pursed trying to kiss Sandy. Sandy puts her fingers in the sign of a cross. Everyone laughs.

Regina is being sort of quiet but she is trying to be her normal self. Stan told her to go about her days as normal as if nothing is wrong. She is trying her best to do that but every now and then, she sees the black Charger when she is out. She still hasn't said anything to her friends and is really wondering if she should. The last thing Regina wants to do is alarm any of her friends and have them as paranoid as she is. She hasn't told Stan about the car either. He just knows about the note she found. However, Colleen knows a little bit since she has witnessed the car but they haven't had a sit down talk. She has seen a little change in Colleen but she can't put her finger on it. When they have their sit down talk, she will ask her what it is all about.

Just then, Lyla came to escort them upstairs to the locker room. Removing their shoes and clothing, there is silence as if everyone's mind is somewhere else. To pretend as if she is not pre-occupied, Regina breaks the quietness.

"So, what has everyone been up to since we last spoke or seen each other? Why is everyone so quiet? No talking or laughing. I just thought I'd break the silence in here. It was too quiet. Oh, I know … y'all trying to figure out how you're gonna start off the conversation once we get in the Tranquil Room, right? Ay, I'm all ears. I have nothing to tell. So I'm gonna sit back and enjoy y'all fight over the spotlight."

Colleen looks over at Regina giving her the expression, *Oh you don't have anything to tell us?* Colleen knows that if anything, Regina needs to speak on that car situation that has her circumspect.

Something had to have happen for her to think that the car is following her. I wonder if Stan is having her followed and she is paranoid that he might find out about our private classes that he is paying for. I can tell she is working hard to be her normal self but it isn't working for me. Maybe I need to stick a little closer to her. I might need to follow her home tonight to make sure she is okay and to see if there is anything I need to see. I wonder if she has told anything to Stan. Maybe I need to give him a call. Then again, I'll just wait. I know if there is anything to be aware of, Stan would definitely be calling us soon. More likely, it'll be me that he contacts first.

Regina notices that Colleen is looking at her closely. She isn't liking the feeling. She is burning huge holes into the side of Regina's face and body as if she knows something is wrong. Sandy and BeLynda are oblivious to what is transpiring between Regina and Colleen but Regina is locked on. Looking back at Colleen, she notices that the look Colleen has seems to say, *What's up? We need to talk and talk soon because I don't like being left in the dark.* Regina responds to her look with a look that says, *We will. Give me some time.* Colleen responds with raised eye brows that says, *Do we really have more time for you to be holding this in?* Regina looks away and continues to remove her clothing so she can get into her robe.

"Well, what the fuck is wrong with you two? Would one of you like to share with the rest of us?" BeLynda asks after catching the facial conversation between Regina and Colleen. *One of them or both are hiding something. Keeping secrets now, huh?*

"Nah, I have nothing to share. But Regina might. Do you have something you wanna share with us Gee Gee?" Colleen asks trying to get Regina to open up to everyone. Sandy looks at the scene between her friends perplexed.

Nervously looking at her friends, Regina replies, "Why would I have something to share? I just told y'all downstairs that I didn't." She gives Colleen the look of, *Bitch don't start no shit. I will say something when I am ready*, and rolls her eyes. *Stan is already asking me why I haven't said anything to my friends. Since I am seen with y'all a lot, whatever that might be going on could involve y'all too indirectly. I hope it doesn't.*

Colleen rolls her eyes saying, "I will be in the Tranquil Room waiting on y'all and to hear some juicy." She walks past Regina giving her the "*we need to talk as soon as possible*" look. Regina jumps a little bit from the cold look that Colleen gives her. She has never seen that look in Colleen's eyes before. It is almost as if she doesn't know her at this moment. *Damn, my friend has some hidden secrets. Yet she wants me to talk. Yea, okay Colleen.*

Walking into the Tranquil Room, BeLynda, Regina, and Sandy see Colleen sitting in her favorite chair with her legs hanging over one of the arms swinging her feet back and forth making flapping sounds with the massaging flip flops. Sandy and BeLynda look at her trying to figure out what is wrong but Regina has an idea what the mood is about.

Not skipping a beat Colleen speaks up. "All right, now … who has the juicy this week? Regardless of what Regina says, *somebody* has some juicy and I need to hear it. Relax my mind please."

"Oh, you do? You tensed from what? What happened Lene? You ran out of outlandish fables to tell us? I always look forward to your exaggerations." BeLynda says smirking.

"Oh, really," Colleen says smugly. "Outlandish, huh?"

"Yes, really. It gets me through my wait time for Marcus. That's why I do more listening than talking. You take up all of the damn time." BeLynda is purposely trying to get under Colleen's skin.

"Well, if you step up to the nigga, maybe you wouldn't have to wait on my stories. I've been dealing with clients mostly so I am sure none of y'all want to hear about them. Business is not a topic to speak about on Thursdays." Colleen gets up walking over to the table to get a few vanilla wafers.

"Hey what's wrong with you? You need to vent about something this evening? The last time we saw you, there was some juicy involving the infamous Byron. You know … the man we've not ever met. Y'all fell out already? Or does he even exists?" Sandy asks following behind Colleen to get some vanilla wafers too.

"Right!! How come we ain't ever seen him? How come you not talking? Oh, I get it. You wanna save the best for last, right? Or you think it is the best and that's why you want us to go first, huh Colleen?" Regina asks trying to get Colleen's mind off of her for a little while.

"Nooo, I want to hear somebody else speak for a change. I know damn well, I am not the only one getting some action. Or have some crazy shit going on." Regina knows Colleen is directing the last statement at her but she ignores it. She goes to grab a handful of sunflower seeds.

"Well, considering your action isn't always with the same man, that's why we wait to hear what you have to say." She turns to Regina with a look that could make compost out of all the plants in the room instantly. Regina takes that expression as if to mean she needs to sit her ass down. And she does, sitting at the table with her seeds not looking at Colleen.

"Okay, well, let me start then. Khalil spent the night." BeLynda is all smiles, excited that she has something to talk about.

"Khalil? Who is that?" Colleen asks raising her left eyebrow.

"C'mon Colleen. This is Bee talking now. You know it surely ain't a pet name for Steve. It has to be her young boy toy." Sandy is grinning from ear to ear ready to hear what BeLynda has to say.

"Oh *whaaat*? That's his name? Your little boy toy, huh? Bee got some juicy for us? I guess I was speaking too damn fast downstairs, huh? Oh okay. Well, hasn't he spent the night before? I know you done slept with the youngin already. So what's the news you have to tell us?" *Did you use any of your lessons on the young man*, Colleen says to herself smiling.

"Well, yes I have been intimate with him before. Not that many times but enough to know that he has always left by a certain time. He has never left when the sun came up, or noon the next day. Or even at night the next day."

"Really? Left early as in he had somewhere to go? Or he had to punch the clock? Or had to make sure some chick didn't blow his phone up wanting to know where he is?" Colleen asks popping a cookie in her mouth grinning.

"I've never asked him what or where he had to go. I never got into his business. I didn't want to know anything that was going to agitate me. I was just happy that he spent some time with me."

"So he stayed the entire night this time, huh," Regina asks shaking her seeds around in her hand popping a few in her mouth.

"Yea, and I did some new things too." This statement catches everyone's attention. Their eyes and ears are locked on to her mouth.

"Well, well, please do tell Ms. Giles. What kind of new things did you do? Something that he has learned and trying to teach you? Or something you used from class?" Sandy asks. All eyes are on BeLynda and she doesn't know where to start.

"Okay, don't look at me like I'm stupid or crazy but I was on top this time. I was in control." There is silence between the Ladies again. They are looking at her as if that is nothing new yet, Regina finally gets it and realizes this is something her Girl hasn't done before.

"On top of what?" Colleen is confused. Sandy is frowning trying to figure out what BeLynda is actually saying. "Okay, wait a minute. Let me sit up for this." Colleen sits up ready to ask all kinds of questions. "Are you telling me that you have never been on top of a man before? Exactly what are you used to when it comes to sex Bee? Missionary … *ONLY*?!"

"I'm used to the man being on top. Is there something wrong with that?" The three sets of eyes are burning holes into her like laser beams. She feels the heat. She gets up to prepare a few of the sesame crackers with port wine cheese.

"Missionary style? That's it? Nothing more, huh?" BeLynda nods her head "yes" to the first two questions and "no" to the last. "Oh my goodness!! No sitting on him in the chair? No, doggy-style? No shower action Bee? I mean, just to name a few. Those are the basics." BeLynda shakes her head "no" at all the questions. Sandy is scratching her head in total confusion looking at BeLynda as if they are back in high school just learning about sex.

"Not that it is right but I see why Steve was seeking elsewhere. Her ass hasn't venture into nothing but the plain shit. The straight up and down shit. Just black and white and no color to it. Damn Bee!!" Colleen gets up for more cookies. "Damn, I needed to be getting a Spa pedicure to have this conversation. They give wine over there."

"So, let me get this straight. Steve who was your husband was subjected to boring ass missionary sex Bee? Not that his actions were right but c'mon Bee … GIRL … what happen to exploring? That's what you do with your husband. Now, you're doing shit with the young nigga that had you done them with Steve, it might have saved your marriage? I'm not saying it is everything but it plays a very important role in a marriage." Sandy is in shock.

BeLynda is extremely quiet and starting to feel stupid. She thought she had something exciting to share. Yet, what she is revealing is something her friends are telling her is normal and should have already been experienced. She just always thought when her friends were talking, they were just doing some things that weren't necessarily a requirement or expected. She had no idea that they were considered the norm.

"Sooo, I'm not trying to get into your business but we do tell ours to you … have you ever given Steve – or any man – head? I'm just asking because you seem so closed." Regina really wants to know and she gets no response.

"Okay, we will get into that conversation some other time. I meant it when I said we need to seriously meet up on another day and see how we can help our sista here. Bee, you blowing me, no joke! I ain't condoning Steve's guttural actions but damn … you hear us and you do talk about sex with us at times. GIRL!! You basically told your man in no uncertain terms that he was gonna have to hit the streets for the freak he should have had in you. And what we are asking ain't even you being a freak! What the fuck!" Colleen is getting heated and Sandy is watching her. Regina wonders if some of the attitude stems from her not talking about her issue.

"Slow down Colleen. Don't do that. We are told that if it doesn't feel comfortable, we shouldn't do it." Looking at BeLynda,

Regina asks, "Did you not feel comfortable Bee? What's wrong? Did something happen in your past that made you so inhibited?" Looking at her with empathy, Regina really wants her friend to open up to them. "We are the only ones in this room. You can express yourself. I won't judge you. How can I?" Regina is hurting for her friend because it seems as if BeLynda has some hidden abuse and afraid to reveal it.

"I don't want to talk about that. I mean y'all know how my mother was when we were younger." BeLynda holds her head down trying not to look in their eyes. She is embarrassed of not being able to let go and of her mother.

"Yea, no offense Bee. Angel was out there. She made sure she didn't have to work a nine-to-five, that's for sure. She knew exactly what to do to be home with her kids. I have to admit she was a hands-on mother." All eyes are on Colleen stunned at her outspokenness.

"Come again? What do you mean my mother was 'out there'? How did you know anything about what my mother was doing? You were hanging with us?"

Damn!! I didn't mean to say that so easy. "Um, I mean … it was obvious Bee. The clothes, the walk, the men … did you think your mother was selling Avon like you?" *She was a door-to-door saleswoman though.* "She would have had to sell just about as much if not more than you to give y'all the life she provided. Back then, Avon didn't cost what it cost now. I mean unlike many over there on Mississippi Avenue where I was, y'all dressed y'all ass off." Mouths are open wide and eyes are about to bug out from Colleen's statement.

Regina is trying to get Colleen's attention to tell her to end it but she doesn't look at her. Interrupting she says, "All righty then, let's move on please? That is not a memory lane any of us want to go down this evening." Colleen looks at her and Regina is able to signal with her eyes, *let it go*.

Colleen keeps on talking. "I'm just saying out of love Bee. Maybe I said that wrong but … hell, none of us had it like you did, including Gee Gee. I'm serious." Regina looks at her wondering what she means by her statement. "Angel is your mother. We all know that and respect her. Are you trying not to be like her? We are grown women now. We have sex Bee. In multiple positions and we wrap our lips around dick once in a while … or often. And we put balls in our mouth too. Hell, some of us even swallow all their little babies. Especially if we done made the decision to meet a man at the altar in a gown before a Pastor and in front of our friends and family. What is it? What happen? Did some dirty ass Uncle try to force you when you were younger?" Colleen really wants to know what is up with her friend.

"Oh Lord. She's in her zone. Colleen not today, okay? We can't help her like that. You're being too blunt." Sandy interjects furiously.

"Maybe, maybe not but it's all a part of the act. The act of enjoying our sexuality. The act that shows the man we are into him. That he is ours and we are his. That we love him or care for him deeply. If we are not to do these things with our man … our husband, then who are we to do them with?" Colleen is serious and doesn't mean to ruffle anyone's feathers.

"Um, Colleen … are you into any of the men you do it with? Do they know you are theirs and they are yours? I'm just asking because you don't have a husband. That is what you said, right? I mean, since you are hitting below the belt." BeLynda is upset and Colleen has hurt her feelings several times this evening. It is time for payback. Colleen squint her eyes at BeLynda and doesn't respond.

"As for me, smart ass, it is me enjoying my sexuality. I am a sexual being. Haven't you heard that before Bee? I have no problem putting a beautiful dick in my mouth because it pleases me just as much as it pleases him. I can have an orgasm from giving head." Sandy and BeLynda look at Colleen overly stunned.

Trying to prevent her friends from not speaking for the next six months, Regina comments, "Hey, you got a point there Colleen. I give Stan head while he is in his office working. There is no one in there but me and him. And I enjoy it. I can't say that I have had an orgasm giving him mouthy pleasure but I can say that I have gotten quite moist. The fact that he's my husband, he knows this and he gets off knowing that I'm enjoying myself while I'm creaming." Regina looks at her friend who is playing with the lemon in her water and says, "Bee, if you can allow him to enter your vagina with it, then what is wrong with putting it in your mouth? Steve was a clean man, from what I recall. You used to talk about the high water bill from all those showers he used to take …"

"Now, that could've been because he was probably washing 'them' off his body. All in all, his neat freak ass was dead wrong. Bee you probably should have cut it off and put it in a damn jar as a reminder of all of his dirt. Lorena Bobbitt his ass." Sandy laughs at what she just said.

BeLynda is just sitting here listening to everything her friends have to say. She is getting a little disconcerted but she feels as if there is some truth to what Colleen has been saying. But she still wants to know what Colleen knew about her mother. *Who else knew back then what my mother was doing to support us and afford her being able to be home for her children?*

"Hey, I will say that all of you have valid points. I will say to each of you your points have been taken. I won't say my mother was a Ho." *Hmmp, even though she was. No need in denying it,* says Colleen and Sandy to themselves. Regina doesn't comment to herself. "However, whatever she was doing my Grandmother had a big issue with it and she had no problems expressing her feelings."

"Ah, the *Grandmother*. That's what the issue is. God rest her soul. But you have to let it go Bee. Free yourself of what she said and tried to instill in you. You didn't go down the same path as your mother. You know we know it was you in class that vomited all over the floor. That was a sign that you released all of that green shit. Or so I thought." Colleen frowns and shakes her head.

"Green shit," Sandy and Regina asks in unison.

"Yea, the green shit. Like in The Exorcist, Linda Blair started purging all that bullshit once that priest started praying over her. When Kelly was saying all that stuff she was saying in class, it had the same effect on Bee. It allowed Bee to experience a catharsis."

Damn I didn't think about it that way. I did feel much better and lighter but for some reason, I'm still holding on to something. I guess some of it came out but not all of it. BeLynda is deep into her thoughts while Colleen is talking and explaining what she went through in class.

"Hey, I can't argue with Lene on that. I did feel a little lighter but I'm not gonna compare it to no damn exorcist." All the Ladies laugh out loud uncontrollably.

"But Bee, you were so excited when you started off your juicy. What was exciting about being on top? We do have control of the strokes and rhythm that way but you looked like you had something else to say about your experience. What did you want to tell us?" Sandy wants BeLynda to get back to her story. She has had enough of Colleen's mouth at the moment.

Bashfully yet proudly speaking, BeLynda responds, “Well, I found out that I am a squirter. Who would have thought me of all women?” Everyone is quiet and trying to visualize the act of squirting.

“What?! A squirter? So you’re saying that you splashed the nigga with a cum bath, huh? My, my, my. You didn’t know this already,” Colleen asks smiling

“Nope.” BeLynda is excited that she has done something her friends haven’t. “That had only happened once before and that’s when he was giving me oral from behind on the top balcony.”

Regina and Sandy look at each other with a big Eureka smile on their face. Colleen spills her water and doesn’t flinch to catch the glass. Regina stands up and starts salsa dancing around the room. Sandy and Colleen give each other dap and ogle BeLynda.

“Sooo, this young tenderonie is turning your ass out and you squirting all over the place? Eating ‘it’ from behind? On the top balcony of your house? When did this all this happen closed-mouth heifer?” Regina asks full of excitement.

“Recent. And I have to admit, I did enjoy it.”

“Girl, I am speechless!! I ain’t ever done no shit like that. Bee is a squirter? I know young ass is in love now!” Colleen smiles wide.

“Yea, I’m speechless too! I’m with you on that Lene. I’ve never done that either!” Sandy is just staring at BeLynda happy for her.

“I’m not, I’ve been waiting for her to explore some other aspects of sex. It is not all about the dick and pussy connecting. There is foreplay too Bee. And the two times you tried something new made your ass squirt? Well how did it feel Bee? Don't keep us waiting on the details."

"It felt good, I must say. I wasn't all that keen on having my ass turned up outside but I guess we were up high enough for us not to be seen." They all laugh. "The second time, Khalil thought I pee'd on him. But it was too thick and white to be pee."

"I know what you mean girl!! Larry and I finally put those mirrors in my bedroom to some good use. We both were in there screaming. He said he had been holding back thinking he was making love to me."

"Oh, you got some juicy to tell too, huh? Well, right now, we are gonna focus on BG." Colleen gets a strange look. "What?! BG? BeLynda Giles. Y'all so caught up in the moment that you forgot her damn initials?" Laughter is heard throughout the room. "Continue Bee. Tell us all about Kareem hitting your G-spots."

"His name is Khalil, Lene. But, okay, well, he did want me to go down on him but in the midst of the conversation, he was confused as to how I had never done that yet I've been married." All the Ladies look at her saying with their eyes, *duh.* "I know, I know, y'all just told me. But he understood and didn't press the issue. He told me that he is into me and that he hasn't been with any other woman since he met me." Regina smiles.

Colleen interrupts looking at Regina, "Oh stop! You are such a hopeless fuckin' romantic. Sitting over there smiling. I'm sorry Bee, go head. So he's into you huh? No other woman?"

"I can say that he was a gentleman when I got on top. He was real patient. He let me control the movements, he didn't touch my hips trying to ram up into my throat. The two times I did that with Steve he would do that shit and nothing felt good about that. All that damn cramping for an hour afterwards didn't say good sex to me." BeLynda pauses for a moment thinking about how rough Steve used to be. "But I did have Khalil's toes curling Girls. He was jerking and yelling, telling me that it was my dick if I wanted it to be. Hell, I can do that again. When I splashed all over his stomach and thighs it was a sight to see. It sort of reminded of the story Lene was telling us about backed-up Devin." She smiles winking at Colleen who was smiling back at her. "But it was really a sight to see when I splashed all over his face. He didn't even flinch. I didn't know what the fuck was happening. I just know I was having an orgasm. I thought he was gonna curse me out." They all laugh out loud.

"Yea, I bet it was a sight to see. And he didn't flinch, huh? But he probably had to take a break to wash his face, before he gave you the 'business,' didn't he?" Sandy says still laughing.

"Actually, he didn't stop. He kept right on going. He was loving it as if he knew what was going on. Actually he did because he said, 'I didn't know you are a squirter.' But I guess he was enjoying my sweet smell all over his face. He might've been turned on. But it didn't look all that attractive after we were done because it had started drying up on his face."

"Ewww, now that's nasty. Now, *that's* too much information. It probably looked like he had damn eczema all over his entire face. That's fuckin' gross!! I don't want that visual, please," Colleen frowns sipping her water. Regina laughs so hard she falls on the floor. Sandy sprinkles some of her water on her silently giggling.

"For real. Can y'all imagine what that might've looked like? All dried up on his face. I hope he washed his face good before he left. Going around his Mama with a spot of dried up pussy juice on his face. Then get it on her lips from giving his ass a kiss on the cheek." Colleen is demonstrating the visual.

Regina can't control her laughter. "Girl, stop! Please. I can't take no more. You got my stomach hurting."

"I'm serious," Colleen is laughing. "But he probably didn't let his Mama kiss his cheek. He probably didn't go near her. She might have smelled Bee's 'sweetness' on his face and looked at him like he was crazy. Saying, 'Boy, I know you ain't come up in my house with your damn face smelling like you done been in between some winches legs. Go wash your face and put on some cologne.'" Colleen is scrunching her face up at the thought.

Sandy is laughing so hard at Colleen that her laugh gets stuck and she can't breathe. BeLynda has her hands over her face and her shoulders are trembling from laughing so hard.

"You better work on him getting his own place Bee. That will stop his humiliation. Just make sure he ain't eating it from behind on the days his Mama comes to visits. Hey where is Darla? I am ready for my body polishing. Bee got me feeling dry and ashy as a motherfucka with that ending."

BeLynda finds this extremely funny.

Just then, Darla comes into the Tranquil Room motioning for Colleen. "All right Ladies, that's my cue. Darla must've heard me from across the hall. I need to get out of here. Y'all are crazy up in here. As usual though, hold the fortress down until we meet back up, right here. And no talking about anything that needs to be shared with all of us." She is pointing at each of them making sure they know she is talking to all of them.

Sandy wipes the tears from her eyes looking at Colleen. "Say what?! *We* are crazy? I don't remember any of us having everybody on the floor laughing at their three minutes stand up," she is laughing and pointing at BeLynda, Regina and herself. "That would be you."

"Yea, well I did lighten up the once gloomy environment with it didn't I? Bee, I do apologize for earlier. Hey, look I'm out. But let's talk about our New Year's Resolutions later. Not today, though because we need to talk about Byron's holiday party. But we do need to talk soon. We only got a few more weeks before two thousand and four will be here. You know we start the new year off right!"

"Hmm, you right. I hadn't been paying any attention. Okay, we can do that," Regina says deep in thought pondering over the statement.

"Girl, will you go on already? You holding Darla up, which means you're holding me and Gee Gee up. Hunh, I got a New Year's Resolution for you. It is 'Work on not being so crass.'"

Colleen smiles at Sandy, giving her the middle finger, sashaying out of the room behind Darla.

Chapter Nine

9

Turning over, pulling back the covers getting a face full of sunshine, the mouth opens wide to yawn, arms lift up for a big stretch. With eyes still closed, rubbing the space to the left, there is no warm nude body with breasts, flat stomach, and thick thighs to touch. The bed is empty with a slight chill. The sun is too bright to open the eyes but something has awakened one of the other senses. Inhaling short audible breathes through the nostrils the delicious scent that floats into the room awakens different parts of the body slowly, ending with a dick salutation.

Sitting up, turning the legs over to the right side of the bed and places the feet on the floor. Standing naked with the semi-erect penis, taking another yawn and stretching his arms, the feet begin to pitter-patter across the floor mechanically towards the bathroom standing over the commode with one hand leaning on the wall for support.

Damn that food smells good. And I'm hungry as shit too. I ain't worked out like that in a long time. A brotha done burned some fat and calories last night. I hope she ain't one of those stingy cooks. She is always trying to feed me but I have always said, "No thank you." This morning will definitely be different. I welcome the grub this time. Flushing the toilet, washing his hands with the all natural liquid soap, he walks back through the bedroom to exit to the hallway blinking the eyes. He then decides to go back into the bathroom and wash his face of the sleep matter in his eyes. Grabbing his boxers to put them on, he heads back towards the hallway.

Walking down the hall towards the staircase the aroma coming from the kitchen gets stronger and his stomach begins to growl angrily. Walking down the stairs, he can hear sizzling, something being mixed in a bowl, a little bit of chopping, and a few doors opening and shutting. *It sounds like she is multi-tasking on a smorgasbord. Oh yeah, I am about to thrown down. Since she is always trying to feed me, she will get to see just how I keep this body fueled.* His stomach growls again loudly just in case he didn't hear it the first time, letting him know that it needs to be fed. *Those damn four bologna sandwiches I had for dinner didn't do much to hold me over.*

Entering the kitchen a few minutes later, BeLynda is humming to a soft jazz tune echoing through the kitchen. He looks around to see where the music is coming from but only sees kitchen gadgets and appliances. *She must have a built-in stereo system.* He smiles watching her from behind admiring her meticulousness. Leaning up against the wall with his arms folded across his built-up muscular chest, crossing his right ankle over his left he smiles and continues to watch her move around the kitchen never noticing

Khalil is behind her. After watching for another minute he clears his throat catching her attention showing his handsome smile yet still looking sleepy.

Startled from the noise, BeLynda turns around to see Khalil standing in the kitchen's entryway smiling at her in his boxers. "Ooh, boy you scared me. How long have you been standing there?" She walks over to Khalil planting a juicy kiss on his lips still beating the eggs in the bowl. Khalil is looking at BeLynda as if he is watching his wife-to-be.

"Good morning to you too babe. Didn't mean to scare you. I ain't been down here long. Only a few minutes. I was just watching you do your thang. The smell got me out the bed. Well, that and the fact that you weren't beside me."

Turning around to look at him again smiling, she asks, "Oh, I'm sorry, good morning sleepyhead. Thank you, I see my plan did the job. You're real comfortable, huh? Walking around with just about eighteen inches of cotton wrapped around you. I see you sexy." Khalil blushes at Colleen's words.

"You are getting down in here this morning Girl. You got a lot going on in here Bee. Is this buffet just for us? Or should I be dressing for company?" Khalil's eyes pop out and blink twice as if the scene is going to change.

"Dag, a buffet? You think this is too much food?" BeLynda looks around at the different dishes she has prepared and realizes that it just might be too much. She got a little carried away. "I was trying not to overdo it. I guess I failed at that, huh?" Khalil laughs giving her a "you think" look. "Well, I am almost finished." BeLynda turns around and goes into action. She flips the five buttermilk pancakes on the middle griddle, folds over the steak, onions, and cheese omelets in the pan on the front left burner and flips the smoked Applewood thick bacon slices on the front right burner.

Khalil sits on one of the counter chairs at the breakfast nook observing BeLynda maneuvering around the kitchen. *Damn, my baby can throw down for real.* The light inside the oven shows him grand size biscuits plumping and rising on the top rack and a pan of sausage patties keeping warm on the bottom rack. He just shakes his head propping the left side of his face with this hand. He is overwhelmed. *I'ma be happily miserable. I ain't ever seen this much food unless it was at a buffet when I am out with the niggas, for real. My Mama has never cooked for us like this. I guess she didn't want to mess up her freshly done nails or smell like she had been cooking for her kids. Her fresh outfit was more important.*

"I thought I was going to have to bring you breakfast in bed, but since you're up, I guess we can sit over there and enjoy the outdoor scenery. It's up to you though." BeLynda walks over to the fridge, opening the left door to take out the pitchers of juice and water preparing two glasses of each.

"Ay, do you babe. I will eat wherever you want us to. Where do you want us to eat? I'm not hard to please." Looking at the large spread around the kitchen smirking, he adds, "But wherever you decide for us to eat, there needs to be enough room for at least four plates. We're gonna need two plates a piece Bee." BeLynda looks at all the food then back at Khalil laughing. He gets up to grab one of the glasses of water, drinking all of it. *Damn that felt good going down.* BeLynda gives him a refill. "That's the freshest water I've ever tasted." BeLynda looks up at him smiling. She doesn't know what to say to that.

"Um, well, it just came off of the fridge. I just put it in the pitcher just in case you wanted it to be on the table. But, actually, we are going to need to add a bowl to this setting too." Khalil raises his eyebrows and slightly grins. "Yea, I uh … I sliced up some fruit for us to start off with," BeLynda says bashfully yet sounding a little bit like she is bragging. She knows she can cook.

"Goddamn Bee! What time did you get up? The bed didn't feel that cold. You got pancakes, omelets, bacon, sausage, biscuits, *and* fruit?" Khalil is feeling so thankful. There is no other woman that could take BeLynda's place in his heart right now. That includes his mother.

"Don't forget the cheese grits. They're over there in the pot keeping warm. Oh, and the homemade whipped cream too. I thought this would go nice with the fruit bowl." She doesn't look at Khalil this time. The silence was enough to know that he has never had a woman cook for him, especially not like this. *They can say what they wanna say. But I will forever say the way to a man's heart is through his stomach. That has nothing to do with what I do with his dick and what position I am in.*

"So really, what in the world is the occasion Bee? Did I miss something? Was I supposed to bring a gift or something? Is this like our anniversary?" She smiles and swats him on his shoulder with the oven mitt. "I mean, hell, I had said to myself that I was gonna thrown down but all this here," he makes wide circles with his arms motioning at the food, "you're gonna have to wheel me off in a barrel when I get done." Laughing he asks, "What happened to, you know, scrambled eggs with American cheese, brown 'n serve sausage patties and toast with grape jelly?"

Who the fuck cooks that? That is not cooking. A microwave and a toaster oven is all you need for that menu. Oh hell nah!! Hell, who eats that? Ooh shit, he does!! And he always told me "no thank you" when I'd tried to cook for him. How do I respond without hurting his feelings?

With a faint grin she carefully responds, "You trying to be funny? There is no occasion other than you are here. This is how I cook. I'm a city girl with southern roots. I never learned how to cook small, having to cook for me and my siblings while my mother worked. Plus, since I enjoy food, I never fell into the trap of doing quick and instant box stuff. Too much sodium and it just doesn't taste good to me." BeLynda notices a distant frown comes over his face like he is thinking. *That must be what he considers a satisfactory meal. Maybe I shouldn't have said the last part.* "I mean, after that workout you had last night, I thought you might've worked up an appetite. There will be no dehydration around me from wonderful yet excessive exercise and starvation. So I decided to help restore your electrolytes," she winks at him, adding items to their plates. Khalil is cheesing from ear to ear like a Cheshire cat.

"So you're saying that those are homemade biscuits in that oven I've been watching rise? They're not Pillsbury?"

"Pillsbury? I've never had one of those ever. Those are mine. You'd be surprised what flour, a stick of real butter and buttermilk will do for a biscuit." They both laugh.

"I hear you sexy. I'm gonna have to visit the gym a little more often now before I start looking like a couch potato and I don't even sit around like that. But all this good home-cooking is going to be sticking to my ribs real quick if you cook like this all the time." Raising his hands with palms facing BeLynda, he says, "Cook whatever you want to babe. Everything you know and everything you want me to try. I'll eat it." *Yea buddy ... I got a classy older woman. Jamal is gonna be pissed that he is stuck with hot dogs and pork 'n beans, and grilled cheese sandwiches since that's all his Girl seems to cook for him. That's the difference between a woman and a girl.*

BeLynda takes the biscuits out of the oven, buttering their tops and insides. She then scoops out of jars, grape and apple jellies placing them into bowls with spoons in them, walking towards the morning-room. *Oh, so he is saying that he will be around more often if he plans on eating my cooking. And I'm not complaining. That's a good response Khalil. I haven't cooked for a man since Steve and I broke up.* BeLynda is saying to herself smiling while she is still preparing their plates. "I hear you Kha. Do you want one biscuit or two? Or do you wanna wait to see if you have any room left?" She giggles.

"I will take two, thank you. I want everything you cooked. Did you just call me 'Kha,'" he asks as he smirks. She smiles and turns back around making sure all of the food fits on the plates. "I like that. Where did you get that from?" He is caught off guard but he likes it.

"I heard the conversation you had with your brother the other day. I thought that's what they call you. And since you call me Bee instead of BeLynda, I didn't think anything would be wrong with me calling you 'Kha' instead of 'Khalil.'" He shakes his head listening saying in his mind, *so she really was listening to me on the phone. My brother can be so fuckin' embarrassing.*

"Is that all you heard his simple ass say? He can be very annoying which actually turns into embarrassment for me. You will never believe he is four years older. Hanging around dudes younger than me, he will never grow up. Yet my family loves him to death."

Just as he finished talking, BeLynda picks up the linen napkins and silverware sets taking them to the morning-room. Entering the kitchen, she gathers and carries two of their plates into the morning-room, sitting them across from each other. Coming back into the kitchen she takes the last two plates off the island heading back into the morning-room. He grins watching the two bowling balls move around in the back of her gown. He smiles reminiscing on the night he just had palming them.

BeLynda yells behind her, “Well that’s how it is Kha. Or at least that’s how it should be, I guess I should say. Family shouldn’t judge. Unless there is some questionable behavior. Is there? And I know for some it is very trying when one can’t seem to stay out of trouble. Yet he is your brother so you are seeing things from a different perspective than maybe your Mom, Dad, Aunts and Uncles. You understand what I am saying?” Knowing she is being watched she smiles saying, “I hate to interrupt your nasty thoughts but may you grab those fruit bowls, juices, and waters off of the counter please? Thank you. And tell your little big friend to go back to sleep. We’re getting ready to eat breakfast. He can be brunch.” They both laugh relishing the morning.

Khalil is astounded by BeLynda’s words. *She is getting comfortable around me and really beginning to open up.* He sits there for a minute because she told him not to come in the morning-room with a stiff one. Currently he is beyond stiff. “I’m coming babe. Khalil is at your service. Just give me a minute while I tell ‘him’ to go back to sleep.” BeLynda knew what that meant. A few minutes later, jumping off of the counter stool semi-hard, he enters the kitchen to gather the items. “Ay, is there anything else you want me to grab while I’m in here?”

“Um … I think we got everything we need. If I’ve forgotten something, I will just go back and get it,” BeLynda says while placing the napkins and silverware on the right side of their large plates preparing to sit down and wait for Khalil. She stands back and admires the set up.

The phone begins to blare through the house. *Who can that be calling me early on a Saturday morning? Just when I am about to sit down and have breakfast with my handsome overnight guest?*

Surely it's not any Avon customers or the Girls. Walking over to the phone in the foyer, BeLynda sees it is none other than Steve. Hesitantly, she reaches for the phone then pauses for a moment. She decides to ignore the ringing phone returning to the morning-room to wait on Khalil. He already has peeped at the number on the Caller ID in the kitchen and sees that it is her ex-husband calling. *She didn't answer it. Is she used to him calling bright and early on Saturday mornings? I may have to stay over a little more often on Fridays to see what's up. I didn't even know they talk like that since there are no kids running around here.*

Entering the morning-room with a tray full of the rest of their meal Khalil places one of each of everything on the tray in front of BeLynda and then in front of him. He sits across from BeLynda and she grabs his hands to say grace. He wasn't sure what she was doing at first since he has never said grace before. Following BeLynda's lead, he bows his head, closing his eyes and BeLynda blesses their food. Khalil hears her but his mind is on the phone because it rings again two more times. BeLynda speaks a little louder during the blessing to drown out the annoying ringing phone. Khalil peeps at her through his right eye. "Now, let's eat. You want jelly on your biscuit?" Observing the nice spread on the table, BeLynda realizes some things are missing. "Ooh, I knew I forgot the jelly, syrup, and the whip cream. I'll be right back."

Jumping up she trots to the kitchen to get the condiments. Basically she wants to escape the phone call situation, knowing that Khalil probably saw the number on the caller ID when he was in the kitchen. She would've peeped at it too had the situation been reversed. She sits them in the center of the table setting. Khalil grabs the pecan praline syrup and pours it in between the layers of his three-stack pancakes. Picking up a strawberry, BeLynda dips it in the whipped cream biting it before asking, "Now, what were you saying while I was setting the table?" The phone stops ringing.

BeLynda doesn't miss a beat. The last man she is thinking about is Steve. He had his chance. The look on Khalil's face says he is wondering if the "chance" is over.

"Well, I was saying that I wouldn't necessarily say there's questionable behavior but he's a high school dropout and is always in some type of trouble, or has seen something, or is connected to some bullshit. Even though he somehow seems to always get off. He just seems to get all of the attention, and for the wrong shit, you know? Yet, when it comes to me, I guess I am supposed to always do right. So I am more criticized about small shit. The big things … big accomplishments go unnoticed." Khalil forks around with his cheese grits deep into the conversation. Someone is taking the time to listen to him.

"Why would you say that Kha? Sometimes when one is always into something, it doesn't mean he is getting the *right* attention. I can see how you feel he has taken the attention away from the good and proud things. But do you really think the way you are feeling is accurate? I am sure your family is proud of your accomplishments. What really makes you say that?" BeLynda puts her silverware down lifting her water glass to her lips. She is looking straight into his eyes and his family disconnect.

"What makes me say that? C'mon Bee. Are you really asking me that? You were there and what did you see?" BeLynda lowers her eyes to her glass to avoid the pain in his eyes. "What did you see? You saw that no one … and I do mean NO ONE except for you and my grandmother showed up to my graduation. No one cared enough to say congratulations when I got up that morning or when I came home. My mother wasn't even there with the tears, wanting to take a picture with me or even with my damn degree scroll like the other mothers. The flowers I had were for her and I gave them to my grandmother." BeLynda feels for Khalil. She hasn't experienced this and doesn't want to be in the place he is.

"So you live with your mother and not your grandmother?" Khalil gives BeLynda a "yes" head nod, getting up walking towards the kitchen. BeLynda continues. "Kha, you never told me that. Did you ever find out where she and Jamal were?"

"Hell, I have other siblings too." BeLynda looks surprised. "Jamal was out in the street of course. He told me she was over her friend's house too busy getting those pixies or micro braids … or whatever y'all call them, in her hair. Talkin' 'bout she was going to the Justin Timberlake and Christina Aguilera concert in Dallas with some dude. That meant the rest of the kids were gonna be left for me and Jamal to watch."

Damn, I don't have a comeback to that shit right there. I don't know how old his Mama is, but damn! That was more important?! My Mama may have been a lot of things but one thing for sure, she was a Mama and she was there for her children, whatever it was. Hell, she is still there for us today. "So how many siblings do you have?"

Khalil returns to the morning-room with a bottle of champagne and pours some in his orange juice. Gesturing the bottle towards BeLynda, she drinks some of her orange juice then extends her glass for him to pour some of the champagne in her glass. "There are five of us now. There used to be seven. The twins died in a fire with my father. They were the oldest of us."

BeLynda chokes on her drink giving her food on her plate a mimosa shower. *Dammit! I'm sure that's not the response he was expecting but … seven children? Twins died in a fire … WITH the FATHER? That had to have been a sad day for his family. This is not the type of conversation I had planned for this morning. I have to regroup this shit fast.*

Khalil jumps up to pat and rub BeLynda's back asking, "Are you all right Bee? I didn't mean to catch you off guard with that. I guess we'd been so preoccupied with each other's company that we never touched on the topic of 'Family.'" Laughing trying to pat her mouth with a napkin, he says, "Your choking is a sign that we should talk about something else. Maybe over lunch or dinner … or in bed we can finish the 'Family' conversation." He bends down and gives her a soft peck on the lips and goes back to his seat.

Unbeknownst to BeLynda, after Steve stopped calling he has been sitting in his car at the corner of the block, looking out the driver's side window at the premium white pearl Honda Prelude parked beside the Avalon in his ex-wife's driveway. He knows if it is there this time of morning, it has been there all night. *So you're having overnight company now Bee? Of all mornings, I come over here with breakfast and you are already serving up breakfast. You in there fucking while I'm calling? So you just gonna ignore me, huh? We'll see how long this bullshit lasts.*

Furiously shifting the floor mounted knob into first gear, Steve pulls away from the curb in his estate green Ford Explorer Sport XLS. He gets up to sixty miles by the time he shifts into third gear not paying attention to the revolutions per minute or the stripping sound of the gears. BeLynda and Khalil hear the speeding car. *I bet that was her ex-husband's ass speeding off. Mad as a muhfucka! So he was sitting outside her house all this time and saw my car in the driveway, huh? Good nigga. Take a good look at it. You'll be seeing it over here a lot.* Khalil finishes up his fruit bowl inwardly smiling with a slight mood change.

"So what do you have planned for today? Do you have to check on your siblings? You hanging out with the fellas?" BeLynda slices her pancakes putting some of them in her mouth.

"I have absolutely nothing to do today. It's Saturday. No work for the next two days. I plan to take advantage of every minute of these two days too. That has nothing to do with my sisters or the fellas. Did you have something in mind for me today? I'm already here and I have clothes. What you want me to do? Cut the grass or rub your back?" He gives her a mischievous grin.

"I hear you. It's always wonderful when you can just sit around and relax. Not working or thinking, just clear your mind and enjoy the day. I don't have anything for us to do just yet. I am sure I can think of something for you, or us to do. I love Saturdays and I see you enjoy them too. So cutting the grass will not be the answer." They giggle and BeLynda stuffs one of her pineapple chunks in Khalil's mouth. "So you have three sisters?"

Khalil nearly stuffs one-fourth of the pancake stack in his mouth taking a sip of his orange juice with the pineapple chunk while nodding his head "yes." "Mmmp, baby, these pancakes are delicious. This is not Aint Jemima, is it?" He stuffs another fourth of the stack in his mouth like someone might want some of it and he doesn't want to share. BeLynda watches on.

"Slow down please. Don't kill yourself babe. Breathe. Those are your plates. Mine are over here. I promise I won't sneak anything off either of your plates," BeLynda giggles softly. "But those are homemade, dear. I told you, no box shit here. Straight from scratch."

"Damn!! *Word*?! For real? Flour, eggs, and all, huh? Oh yea, I can see I need to definitely increase my days at the gym. I will not be caught with a gut. I guess that's why you're faithfully at the gym with your friends, hunh? All these southern, homemade, smorgasbord type of meals? So, what do you do? Cook like this over the weekend and then make sure you are in class first thing Monday?" Khalil grins taking a bite of his maple sausage, placing it back on the plate licking his fingers. Realizing he has a napkin in his lap, he quickly grabs it wiping his mouth. He has to remember he is not at home where manners have never been obligatory.

Lost in the moment, BeLynda doesn't realize what Khalil is asking her and answers too quickly. "Huh? What do you mean? Colleen is the only one that goes to the gym … faithfully anyway. I workout right downstairs. And lately when you're here … I get a good workout going in the bedroom." Snickering she continues, "What makes you think …." Then it hits her. *He is insinuating that my private classes with my friends are exercise classes, even though they are across the street from a gym. Oh that was good Khalil. Still fishing for answers, huh? Well, reel the rod back in so you can see that it is empty. I didn't take the bait.* Trying to back up and start over, she can't find the words to replace what has already been said.

Khalil puts the other half of his omelet between his jellied biscuit and takes a huge bite. "Oh, okay. So that's not a fitness class for females? Well, what is it that you do over there on Mondays with your friends?" Looking at BeLynda chewing and swallowing, he waits for her response. No words escape her mouth. He continues watching her for a sign, trusting she will say something. He lowers his head smiling to mask the awkwardness. *Damn! That private, huh?* He says to himself taking another bite of his sandwich.

"Let's talk about something else, please. It sounds like you are looking for something. What could you be looking for when I am merely out with my friends? When you leave here, I don't ask you anything. When you are with your friends, have I ever asked where y'all go or what y'all do? How about we go back to you adding more days to your gym time." She cuts her omelet and put a piece in her mouth irritated. She tries not to show it but it is too late. Khalil notices and is a little stunned by the off-putting.

"We *were* talking about that Bee. I was talking about all this good food we have here and how I am gonna have to maintain all this physique." He smiles and rubs his abs and shows off his arms.

"What's wrong with me asking what I asked? I was only talking about how your toned body isn't for a woman that cooks like this. Or at least I haven't seen one. Hell, babe this is 'grandma' cooking, for real. So why can't you answer the question Bee? It's like *that*?" Khalil laughs with one raised eyebrow looking at BeLynda thinking, *Are you serious right now? You got secrets?!*

"I just asked if we can go back to something else. Or something new. If that is not up for a suggestion, then how about we just sit right here, finish our food and get into something more pleasant? Sorry. I hope you don't think I'm being evasive, I'm not ok?"

Leaning back in his chair chewing, running his tongue across his teeth cleaning them of the steak and biscuit, Khalil looks at BeLynda. *She hasn't really open up to me, she hasn't really let herself go sexually, her husband sitting outside her house making phone calls, and now she has secrets? And what the hell is "evasive"?*

"What just happened here? What are you hiding Bee?" He laughs. "What is it about that place? I asked you before and you continued on as if I had said nothing to you. Remember? When we were going to Pentagon City so you can find an outfit to hang out with the Ladies. And here, this morning is a repeat. I mean, I don't want you to actually tell me to mind my business but if that's what I need to do, then say so. Never did I think me asking about that would cause such a shutdown from you. I really wasn't trying to be nosy but all the silence surrounding your Mondays make a person more curious. Don't you think?" Khalil drinks half of his water looking at BeLynda avoiding his eyes.

"I'm not hiding anything. Especially from you. You asked me about something I don't care to speak on. I'm out with my friends. Leave it at that. So what your friend sees me and my girls on Mondays. Hell, I have never noticed anyone so how am I sure he wasn't lying? You know, trying to stir frustration in you? I asked if you were having me watched and you said you weren't. So, what is all the curiosity about?"

"Okay, hey, babe. I'm not trying to argue with you. I don't wanna argue with you. I won't argue with you. Outside of my sisters, I have never had an argument with a woman. So, really … I just asked about your Mondays thinking they were exercise classes and it felt like I was put on the outside of the door trying to get back in. I apologize. I never want to make you uncomfortable. So let's just forget I asked, aiight? Can we agree to move on with another topic?" Khalil looks at her seriously. He really is into BeLynda and just thought he was asking an innocent question. Now he sees it wasn't innocent to BeLynda.

BeLynda doesn't respond. She plays around with her pancakes that are cut up and soaked in syrup. *Oh my! I expected his young ass to fly off the handle, have a tantrum, and storm out of my house prepared to not see me for a week or something. Of course I didn't want that but it just seems awkward right now because I really don't feel like talking to him. Especially after he tried to slide into our conversation about my Mondays ... my private classes ... my damn secret. It is none of his damn business what I do outside of him because for one, we have not exchanged or updated any titles. For two, I'm not at a place within myself that I can just sit here and tell him what my Mondays are all about. And for fuckin' three, he's not gonna start confronting me about anything his friend – someone I don't know and have ever seen – feels he needs to say about me. Oh we won't start that at all.*

"Hell-oooo? Will BeLynda Giles please come back to meet Khalil Smith at the table? I repeat, will BeLynda Giles please come back to meet Khalil Smith at the table? He is looking for you.

There's breakfast to be finished." Khalil is using his butter knife as a microphone.

BeLynda quietly smiles as she gets up with her plates. Her appetite is gone. The irritation swelled up in her stomach and made her full. Not necessarily looking at Khalil, she asks, "Are you finished with any of your dishes babe? I can take them in the kitchen with mine. Or do you need something from the kitchen?"

Khalil looks up at her and realizes she isn't giving him her eyes. She is avoiding his face and he feels awful about bringing up the subject. Scooting his chair back, he stands up taking two steps towards her. Looking at her, he can feel her breath on his bare chest. She still hasn't met his eyes. He grabs her wrists because her plates occupy her trembling hands.

"Bee, wait. So you lost your appetite, huh? Talk to me. Don't go back in your shell. I thought we were making progress. Maybe I misunderstood something. Can we please just move on from this scene? This moment? This tension … please? This is our first Saturday morning together. I really have been enjoying and appreciating the time. This goes down in my memory bank. You cooked this lovely breakfast for me … for us, and … yes, I put my foot in my mouth. I'm sorry and right now, I'm trying to take this size twelve out of my mouth." BeLynda finds the last part of the last sentence funny. She silently giggles, looking up at Khalil. His eyes are begging for her to sit down.

"I'm not going back into my shell Khalil. We both have done a great job in bringing me out. I thank you for that." *I thank my instructors for that too.* "I don't plan on going back in there. I actually didn't like it there. My friends talk about me enough. It's just that …"

"Ahhh, so we're back to full names now … BeLynda," Khalil asks interrupting her. "Damn, I done hit a nerve. Bee, I really didn't mean to …"

"No, wait, let me finish. We *are* making progress, just not as fast as you thought but you didn't misunderstand anything. Yes, we can move on because this scene, this moment, has definitely tensed me. I want to enjoy our first Saturday morning together too. As for as memories, I want this to be a day we remember on a positive level. It hits me deeply in my heart that you are appreciating the time you spend with me. It's really been a minute since another man has been in my life. No other man has even been in this house. It's just been me and my Girls. I'm taking baby steps but I can see that my steps may be too small for where you are going. But none of what we just said means that because I don't answer a question right now says I have something to hide."

"Okay, I can respect that. I have to understand that I am dealing with a mature woman … a real woman. Not one of these knuckleheads out here that's willing to tell everything, selling their soul, believing that means they are being open and honest. When in fact it only makes me judge them because a lot of the shit they expose is actually stupid. You not wanting to answer me almost took me there and I was wrong for that. Again I apologize." He takes the plates out of her hands and places them on the table where they were.

You damn right you were wrong and I am definitely not one of those knuckleheads ... never have been, and won't start now. I was always taught to not reveal too much too soon because "he" will judge you by it ... and I see that is exactly what he has been prone to do before me. My private classes with my friends need to just be enjoyed physically. If and when I decide to disclose that information, you will be smiling. Not looking at me like I'm crazy or need help.

They hug each other tightly and he gives her a kiss of endearment on the forehead. She loves it when he holds her. "You haven't said that you accept my apology."

She leans back looking up at him, smiling. "I accept all of your 'I'm sorry' and 'I apologize' … and you can take your size twelve foot out of your mouth now. I don't want your toes to get cramped in there."

He looks at her wide eye laughing and starts tickling her. She starts running around the table and he chases her wiggling his fingers at her insinuating that when he catches her, she is going to be tickled. He is pretending that he can't catch her but actually he is watching her ass jiggle in her gown.

Damn that ass looks good. She still doesn't have on any panties.

Chapter Ten

10

Ring! Ring!

Smiling she flips open her cell and answers it. "Well, hello Ray. What a nice surprise. How are you this morning?"

"Good morning beautiful. It sounds like you were already up. It is refreshing to hear your voice this time of day. My day just brightened a little more." *Damn she sounds good. I can imagine how she looks first thing in the morning too.*

"Is that right," blushing rubbing her hand across her hair walking into her master bathroom looking at her clean make-up free face. "It's pleasing to know that I can be of service to someone in that way. I am here to elevate at anytime you need me." *Hey, it might sound a little too heavy but that's how I am feeling talking to him right now.* She looks at herself in the mirror, checking out her perky breast in the grey bra shelf tank top. Turning to the side, she lifts the tank to check out her flat stomach and how it makes her ass look extremely large against the curve in her lower back. Smiling, she hops up on the double sink swinging her legs in the opposite direction of each other.

"You don't say? That sounds so welcoming Ms. Robertson and that's truly a plus for me. I care not to be where I am not requested. I thank you for the affirmation. Now, what are you doing right now? I am going to assume that you are lying in your bed enjoying a little relaxation." *It sure would be nice to be there beside you. I know that body is banging the way it looks in those outfits when we go out to dinner.*

"You are quite welcome. Well, right now, other than talking to you on the phone, I am sitting on my bathroom sink swinging my legs. I'm no longer in the bed. What do you have in mind Mr. Daniels on a Saturday morning?" *Well, one thing for sure neither of us have company and I'm glad. You would've gotten my voicemail. And you wouldn't be calling.*

Ray's mind swiftly moves into Lustland visualizing Sandy in one of her matching bra and panties sets blessing the sink with her plump ass while swinging her legs as if she is so in love … with him. Coming out of his thoughts, "Oh, I'm sorry I was feeding the dogs," he lies. "What is that you asked?"

"I asked what you have in mind on a Saturday morning. I figured you must have an idea about something to be asking me what am I doing. After being at work all day at a damn place I care not to be, I enjoy my home."

"Is that right? A place you don't like working at? Well, how would you like to come over for breakfast? You can tell me all about the dreadful office you hate going to." *Please say yes. And if everything works out, you might be telling that office to kiss your ass. I will take great care of you. I can promise you that.* Ray is saying this to himself waiting for her answer not realizing that he has a full erection until his pants feel like they are two sizes too small. He rubs it trying to calm it down but isn't working.

What?! Did he say breakfast? Breakfast at his house ... with him ... just the two of us? Oh my God! I can't think of a thing to put on this morning. Shit!!

"Hello? Sandy I know you're still there. I can hear you breathing." Quietness and it frightens him. "Hello? Sandy?! Do I need to provide CPR?" He's trying to lighten the situation working on making her laugh. Rubbing his hand across his curly mane he soothingly says, "Calm down, I don't bite, honestly. But if coming to my house is too soon for you, I understand. But that doesn't mean we can't still have breakfast. So what do ya say?" He smiles knowing that her silence isn't about her wanting to say "no." It's about shock, surprise, fear, excitement and his heart is melting in the moment. Sandy has turned Ray on and he is at another level still trying to calm his big little member in his pants down.

"Oh, I'm here Ray. I'm not running from you. You just caught me off guard, that's all. We've been meeting up three evenings a week. I am just shocked. Breakfast at your place is fine Ray. Is there special attire? What time? What's the address?" Sandy is shaking like a leaf, trying to perpetrate her nerves are not wrecked. Once her palms start sweating, she knew she needed to put the phone on speaker. She is used to inviting the man over to her place and here Ray is beating her at her own dating steps.

"Why are you shocked? We've been having such a great time during our dinners. Did you not think that the day would come that I'd invite you to my place?" *Uh-oh, going over a man's house must mean something.* "When a man invites you to his place … what does that mean to you?"

Sandy laughs nervously and stops swinging her feet. "Oh, it means that he is inviting me to his place. And for you, it means that you are inviting me over for breakfast. Did I make you think that I was thinking something more?" *This time of morning, it would probably mean you want some morning pussy but I'm going to hope you actually mean breakfast. And if I want to give something more, then it will be up to me. But after a little over a month worth of dinner dates, I won't be offering more than my company.* Sandy is looking at herself in one of the mirrors shaking her head saying in her mind, *He gets no coochie Sandy.*

"So, you're not running from me, huh? Good because my palms are over here sweating thinking you were going to say 'no' and then I'd have to eat alone."

Sandy eyes pop out like a Popeye Fish looking at herself in the mirror. *We both have sweaty palms? He must be looking at me from somewhere. Nah, I doubt it. But it just seems as if we have a lot in common from how we dress to the affect the opposite sex has on us when we are digging them. Way to go Sandy. He is into you.* She gives herself two thumbs up in the mirror.

Ray continues, "Well, attire is comfortable weekend wear. Nothing extravagant. It is breakfast at my home. I want you to be as comfortable as you can be. Let me see Ms. Robertson on a dressed down day," he's tickled that she asked what she should wear. "I would say breakfast will be in two hours which would be nine-thirty. Now as for the address, I was thinking that you would provide yours.

I would be cooking while you are getting ready and I can send a car for you."

Hold the fuck up? A car?! A fucking CAR?! This man is sending a car for me? And he said that he would be cooking breakfast? For me? Ordinary Sandra Robertson? Sandy is really blinking looking at herself in the mirror trying to see if she actually has been asleep all this time. She curls her toes trying to make sure she is not still sleep.

"Hello? You disappeared on me again Sandy. I thought you weren't running from me. What did I say that offended you?" Ray is serious walking around the kitchen, no smiling.

"Ray … um," her words are caught in her throat. Coughing from the sudden dry mouth she strains to say, "Ray? A car? Wait." She places her right hand on her chest trying to catch her breath.

"Yes, Pretty Lady, a car. What's the matter? He's my driver. He won't bite. He's cool. Has been working for me for the past ten years. Hello? *Sandeee* … are you there?" *Damn, I lost her. Shit! I've been living this way too long. This is all new to her.*

"Ray, you have that kind of money?" *Damn, his occupation affords all this? What the fuck am I doing here?* Jumping down off the bathroom sink, she grabs the cup turning on the faucet for cold water.

"What kind of money? What do you mean? To have a driver? Sandy …"

"The kind of money that affords you to have a Billiards Room in your home and it is not in your basement. Expensive cars and drivers if you don't feel like driving. *That* kind of money," Sandy interrupts him.

"Hey, I am not sure what you think or where your mind is going but it's just breakfast between two adults that I thought were working on spending more time together. Right? Isn't that what we agreed to? I mean, it is true that this morning is not one of the scheduled times but we don't have to stick to it all the time do we?" Silence. "I tell you what, I will come get you. Does that sound better? I don't want to scare you." *Damn, she really is one of a kind. Whereas most women that have crossed my path normally jumped at the opportunity to be up in my place and that's why they had been rejected. My wealth scares her. I like what it says about her but I don't want her to start avoiding me.*

"Oh, no the car can come get me, I'm fine. You caught me off guard, that's all. Some of the things you said had thrown me a little, but I'm honored that you want me to eat breakfast with you this morning. Besides, I want my breakfast cooked by Mr. Ray Daniels. Usually, the man is expecting to be invited over for the woman to be doing all the slaving in the kitchen."

Whew! That was close! "Okay, great, thank you Sandy. Now, you go get ready, the car will be there at nine-thirty, I will be in here slaving over the stoves, and you can ask me anything you want when you get here. I have nothing to hide." *Well, the Rennie bullshit, but that is not worth talking about and it's about to ....*

"Okay. Well then, I guess I will be seeing you in a few." Sandy pushes the "END" button on her cell phone. *Did he just say "stoves" as in plural? That house sounds huge. And he lives ALONE?! What would he need with that much house? What the hell?! Let me call my Mama to let her know who I am going to be with so if anything stupid happens ....*

Pulling up to the black thick iron gates to Ray's house in a brand new silver Rolls Royce Phantom, Sandy is smiling while basking in all of the top of the line treatment she is receiving. She notices the fancy "D" initial in gold at the top of the gates and smiles. The driver removes his tall hat, leaning out of the window, punches a code into the keypad, the gates open and he drives up the long winding road. The huge mansion is in the middle of nowhere. Sandy is in awe looking at the massive estate. The beautiful landscape and mini houses perfectly placed around the land as if they are a small development all trapped inside of the iron gates. Sandy can't believe what is surrounding her as she sits in the back of the luxury vehicle.

Finally reaching the front of the house, an older white man opens the heavy front doors with a struggle. The driver stops the car to get out. Walking around to the right side rear door, he opens it and offers his hand for Sandy to take it. She smiles nervously, taking his hand with her shaking hand and he helps her out of the car.

Damn! This nigga is loaded and he met me at the goddamn Zanzibar. Of all the women in there and I caught his eye. Just think if I had told my girls that I wasn't going to go with them that night. Hell, he might've been asking Colleen for a damn dance. Then again, we do attract different types of men. Looking down at her outfit, she wonders if she is appropriately dressed. *Hell, how do you dress to come to a place like this for breakfast with the owner? Ray is on some royalty type of shit with all this here. Well, it's too late to turn back now Sandy but I did bring a change of clothes just in case.*

Gathering herself and nicely packing her thoughts back in her head, Sandy slowly walks towards the door where the smiling man dressed in a butler outfit awaits her. Standing in front of the man, she smiles greeting him. "Good morning. How are you today?" He smiles and bows before her, then straightens his body motioning with his hand for her to step inside the house. Stepping into the house overwhelmed by the grand foyer, she looks back at the driver as he drives off towards the back of the massive land.

After shutting the door, Sandy stands there holding on to her handbag and her other bag waiting to be told what to do next. The hunched over man turns to her still smiling saying, "Right this way Ms. Robertson." She follows him through the grand foyer feeling like she wants to yell to see if she hears an echo. Looking around as she walks behind the man, she wants to take pictures for keepsakes and to show to her friends but her phone doesn't have the capabilities. *I need to upgrade my damn flip phone. Now I see what Colleen has been talking about.*

There are huge pieces of art on the walls that look expensive. So many decorated rooms she can't count and she is starting to wonder where the white man is leading her. All the way down at the other end of the end the hall she sees a large picture framed in gold with an off white matte finish that covers the entire wall. She sees Ray and four men surrounding a beautiful lady sitting in a chair in the picture. She doesn't get a good look at the all of the faces in the photo. *Damn, I've never seen a photo that big before. That must be him and his family. They all look like some fine ass men.*

Finally, they stop in front of a pair of beautiful hand-carved Italian nut wood doors. Sandy is still looking at the photo at the end of the hall. The man turns around still smiling, he asks, "Are you ready?" She turns her head looking at the man and laughs asking, "Is it a surprise or something? Go for it. Let's see what's behind doors number one and two." Sandy's heart is beating fast not knowing what to expect in this extravagant home.

The gentleman opens both doors at the same time pushing both of them inward. The scene was a sight for sore eyes. Sandy's mouth was open wide with her bottom lip hanging damn near on the floor and her eyes scan the beautiful room. Standing in one place, she scans the room. It has sage colored walls with a bisque shade trimming. There were ceiling to floor windows all professionally decorated in champagne tapestry valances with cloth-like shades lifted two-thirds up. Sandy is slowly turning like a mechanical mannequin looking at the beautiful room she has walked into. Ray smiles at her, knowing that she doesn't see him yet. He doesn't disturb her. He allows her to continue to mentally critique the room.

There is a long acid washed expensive looking wood table against the back wall with a beautiful spread laid out on it. There are fresh pansies in purple, white, and yellow decorated throughout the table. Sandy smiles. In the center of the room is a matching table that seats twelve with a huge vase of fresh yellow mahonia and white daphne flowers in the center of the table. The chairs match the table with burgundy brushed suede cushions looking as if only royalty is welcomed to sit at the table. Sandy rubs her hand across the top of the chairs and then feels the velvety soft seat cushions.

Turning around she sees two round acid wash wood tables that seat four with huge yet smaller versions of the floral arrangements on the center table as centerpieces. The chairs to these tables have cream color seat cushions. It is not until she walks further in the room that she sees Ray standing over in another corner smiling watching her with two champagne glasses in his hands. Something else catches her peripheral vision. Turning to her left, she sees four beautiful shiny coat Rottweilers. Two have red bows tied on them. The other two have blue handkerchiefs around their neck. She jumps a little and then smiles.

Extending his left hand to her offering one of the glasses, he speaks. "Good morning Ms. Robertson. You finally made it. I finished just in time. Would you care to join me in a glass of Mimosa? Or is it too early for you to have champagne? If so, let me know what you want and I will get it for you."

Sandy just stands there speechless looking at Ray as if he is someone out of a white woman's novel. All he needs is a long ponytail and a male poet shirt and she will swear she is in a Harlequin Romance novel. *Even the hood niggas with money wouldn't have this much poise and class*, she thinks to herself walking over to Ray accepting the glass and takes a sip.

"Wow, Ray. This is really beautiful. I really don't know what to say." Looking at the dogs, she asks, "And who are they?" They are sitting up watching her. Two of them appear to be smiling.

"Oh, those two with the red bows are females. They are Rain and Storm," he says pointing at them. When he says their name, they look at him twitch their ears and tilt their heads but never move from their sitting positions. Sandy laughs at them. "And these two are males. They are Black and Rocko." One of them starts scratching and the other one stands wagging his nub. "They all dressed for you this morning." Ray lifts his empty hand to his waist and lowers it which motions for the male dog to sit.

Sandy looks at them feeling very moved by the entire scene. Blinking twice, she asks turning around and around soaking in her surroundings, "Did I wake up and fall into a dream. Ray, this can't be happening." Looking at him she is waiting for an answer. He can see her eyes water and he wants to grab her face and give her the most intimate kiss he has given a woman in a very long time. But he doesn't move. He takes a sip of his mimosa instead. *Be cool Ray*, he says to himself.

"Why can't it be happening? Are we not supposed to have money? Fortune and wealth isn't just for other races Sandy. I'm just like you." She looks at him saying, *No we're not*, with her eyes. He catches the look and responds, "Yes, we are. This is all material and it has nothing to do with who I am and what's in my heart. Take the money away and I am a special ordinary man. My heart told me to share a breakfast with you on a Saturday. Tuesdays and Wednesdays, allow us to have dinner. Now Saturday, which is today, I just couldn't wait 'til dinner to see you. Was that greedy of me?" He takes another sip of his drink waiting for her to respond. *Damn, she's beautiful.*

Taking a sip of her drink as well, she says to herself, *Who is this man? Damn! He is fine, built, well groomed, smells good, can cook, has money I've never experienced, and he's interested in "Sandra Robertson." I guess I thought all men with all that he has to offer is looking for a woman with the same things.*

"No, not at all. That is not what I said or meant to imply. I guess you wouldn't understand where I am coming from. I am beyond pleased that you wanted to see me before this evening. So does that mean our dinner date is off?" Sandy takes a sip of her Mimosa, then a gulp waiting for his response.

A huge smile spreads across his lips and he responds, "That would be up to you Ms. Robertson. If you still want to have dinner with me that is no problem at all. I hope that you didn't think that because I wanted to have breakfast with you that I had something else to do this evening. We had a deal and I'm sticking to it. Now, where would you like to go? And would you need to go home and change?"

"Why don't you surprise me? I did bring a bag in here with me but the smiling man that lead me to this beautiful room took it with my handbag. It's not gonna get lost in all this house, is it?" She laughs. "But if what I have is not appropriate, then I can go home and change."

"Ah, she came prepared. I like that. Your things are always safe in this house. It's just me. And if anything gets missing, I will fire everybody, after I replace your things. Don't worry about going home. If what you brought isn't what you decide to wear, we can go get you something." Sandy looks at him with an expression of *DAMN,* plastered on her face.

"Are you ready to eat? I worked really hard on this spread. I've been sweating with flour on my nose and clothes since yesterday. I hope you enjoy everything I cooked. My heart was all in it." *Calm down Ray, you're acting like you're about to get down on one knee for her. Even though that's not a bad idea. She may not be into quick proposals.*

"Since yesterday, huh? So you really cooked all of this by yourself?" He winks at her smiling from ear to ear. "No one helped you?" He shakes his head "no." "Not the butler, your sister, aunt … or your Mom?" He smiles and shakes his head "no." "Okay Mr. Daniels. Now, what if I had said 'no' when you invited me this morning?" Sandy takes the last swallow of her Mimosa looking at his handsome face waiting for his response.

"Then I would have eaten something else and all of this would have been in the freezer until you said 'yes.' And let's hope that you would have said 'yes' at least within the next three weeks though. I would've hated to throw all of this hard work in the trash. Or have to share it with my mother and the workers." Sandy looks at him and they both laugh.

"Oh, so your 'workers' as you called them eat like this?" Sandy points at the spread at the table in the back of the room. "They must love you."

"Most definitely. Why wouldn't they? Yes, I am African-American and they are Caucasian but I don't run a plantation sweetheart. If I want them to continue to work for me and to be loyal to me, they have to be treated good. As for my mother, she enjoys my cooking even though she enjoys cooking for me. So she would have jumped at the chance to eat my cooking. She taught me well." He winks at her pouring more of the Mimosa in his glass.

"Oh so your mother likes cooking for her baby? Aww, how sweet. So, does your mother live here on the premises? I saw quite a few buildings surrounding this estate."

Ray smiles loving her observation. "Yes, she lives in the townhouse that you can see from here." They walk over to one of the back windows and notices a nice size all brick three level two car garage townhouse. At that moment, she sees a lady resembling the lady in the photo out in the hall walk out with a sun hat on sitting in one of the chairs on the porch. It looks like she is talking on her phone.

"Ah, speak of her and she appears." They watch her relaxing on her porch. *If she only knew that I have the infamous woman I told her about over here for breakfast, she just might run up here instead of having her driver bringing her. I will tell her later that I had her over for breakfast today. Then again, maybe I will wait because I know my mother will go too deep into her questions asking if I have had sex with her today. I already know that isn't going to happen. It hasn't happened yet and that tells me she is the "ninety day" woman. Or maybe she is the "sixty day" woman. Either way, I will wait for her.*

"Oh, and by the way, you look rather ravishing this morning Ms. Robertson in all your splendor, I must say." Sandy looks at him smiling with raised eyebrows as if he is a handsome alien. "Siiike, nah, babe, I'm just fuckin' with you. My mother *dreams* of the day that I talk like that. But um, for real … Sandy you are lookin' scrumptious as a mother - … you look nice," he says rubbing on his beard with a devilish smirk. They both laugh and Sandy swats him on the arm. "Ooh, was that a love tap you just gave me? Let me see." He rubs his arm saying, "Yeap, I think it was."

"You are crazy Ray. Hand me one of those blueberry muffins, please." He jogs over to put one of the plumpest muffins on a beautiful piece of china, walking it over to Sandy. "Thank you Ray. Oh, and you might as well fix me a plate, please." Sandy looks at the china saucer that is supporting her muffin rubbing her fingertips over the platinum edges walking over to the table to sit and eat it. "Ray this china is beautiful. It looks like it cost a small fortune."

"Ray Daniels is here to serve madam," he takes a bow and starts preparing her plate. Ray is too excited. "Actually, this set was handed down from my grandmother about three years ago. She felt out of all of us, I would take better care of the set. This is my first time using it. I'm glad that you were available to help me break in the set." Looking back at her, Ray notices she is blushing picking off chunks of the muffin putting them in her mouth. *I can really see her as Mrs. Daniels. Damn, I hope I am not moving too fast. I wonder if she will tell me about those classes she attends.*

I see I am gonna like him. And all of this surrounding me is just an added bonus. The girls are not gonna believe this. Especially Colleen, the way she was looking at him in the Zanzibar. Sandy stuffs a piece of the muffin in her mouth smiling.

Ray is smiling at Sandy watching her enjoy her muffin while he prepares plates for both of them. He is on cloud nine and loving the company of a woman in his home on a Saturday morning. He really wants to go outside and yell an announcement that she is there at his home having breakfast. *Sandy may think I am crazy for sure.*

Sandy is sitting at a corner spot at the table. Placing her plate on the linen placemat in front of her, he places his on the placemat diagonal from her which is the head of the table. *Hmmm, is she submissive to let me have the head and she sits near me at my side? She better not give me too much too soon because I will be buying a ring tomorrow.*

Sandy looks at all of the food he places on her plate. She notices that he hasn't given her everything and that's fine. What she has is perfect and if she wants more, she will get up and get it. Cutting into her stuffed French toast, putting the piece in her mouth, she closes her eyes enjoying it melting in her mouth. *Damn this tastes so good.* "Ray you have a lovely home. At least what I have seen of it so far is lovely. No one lives here with you?"

"Thank you Sandy. You are more than welcome to take a look around. As I said, I have nothing to hide. I am the only one here. I like it like that." He catches himself not trying to give her any negative ideas. "What I mean is, my mother is here but in her own place and one of my brothers is here also. But right here in this building, I am the only one. It might be enough for everybody to live here but I wouldn't want you to feel uncomfortable."

"Oh, okay. Have a few family members close but not close. I like that. Has a female ever lived here with you?" *Is he giving me signals that he wants me to live here? What does this mean so fast? So early? Is he lonely? Or is he really feeling me like that so soon?* Sandy is wondering as she eats her breakfast. "I saw the lovely picture at the end of the hall. I saw you were in it. Would I be correct to say that the lady we saw sitting on the porch out there is the lady in the photo? And she is surrounded by her sons?" Sandy bites a slice of bacon.

Damn, she doesn't waste any time I see. "Nope. It's been just me." *I will tell her later about her.* "Yes, the woman you see in the picture is mother and standing up around her are my brothers and me."

Sandy looks at him wondering why. "So, your occupation as a video game creator … or whatever it is you do with the video game industry … it allows you to live like this? I mean, this is really interesting. I see I've been in the wrong business all this time." Ray laughs are her comment.

Hell, you're in the right business. Anything more and you might not have looked my way when I stepped to you at the Zanzibar. "The video game industry pays very well. It's actually my business and I present my ideas to video game companies and if they like, they bite. If they don't, then I contact another company. I've just been lucky enough that the one company I approached bit, and they don't want any other company to compete with bite. But my family has had money for a long time."

"Ah, I see. So it's safe for me to say that you have old long money as well as new money?" Looking around the room she adds, "And together, you get to live quite well. Well enough to actually not work, right?"

Ray looks at her not really knowing how to answer that without her getting up from the table requesting to go home. "I'm going to say this safely. I don't have to work and never have had to but I chose to. I do want to have children someday and I want to make sure they all have something to look forward to. However, that also would leave me with the decision as to who would run the business. But if the business has to shut down, I wouldn't be upset with that."

Leaning back in her chair, Sandy chews the food in her mouth looking at Ray. "Okay, that was real safe. Safe enough to make me wonder more but I will let you talk."

"The business that I run was actually started by my father. When he died, he had in his will for me to run it. Of course my brothers were kind of upset but they also understood. I didn't want the headache but my mother refused for any of the others to take on the company. So, to make sure she was straight, I agreed to takeover."

"So do your other three brothers live like this? If they do, I mean hell, where are their estates? All of y'all are right here in the area?"

"Ha, brothers. Well, there are actually four of us. The other four do their own thing. Only one of us is married with children and he lives quite well running his own business. One is too busy just living off of what my father left him. Well, I guess he lives off of the interest his money accumulates every month which is a nice penny. One tried working a nine to five but it didn't last long because he didn't like the weekend money checks he was receiving from his hard work. So he's trying to figure out what kind of business he can start on his own but in the mean time, he works for me helping to run our father's company. The other one … let's just say, he hasn't grown up yet and he probably is talking to my mother right now asking for more millions."

Sandy looks up at him chewing her food slowly as her mouth dries up and she takes a sip of her Mimosa. *Did he just say millions? Damn! And they are not in the acting, singing, or rapping business.* "Wow! I am totally speechless. All of this wealth and no one has snatched you up yet? Your interview skills of us must be vicious." *Sandy you have a motherfucking gold mine with this man right here. Will his family like me? I'm only concerned with Mama. Brothers can kiss ... my ... yellow ass!*

Ray doesn't respond yet he leaves his seat and fix plates of food for the four dogs.

Chapter Eleven

11

Ring! Ring!

Dammit!! Who the hell is this calling me? I'm tired and drunk two bottles of wine last night by myself. Shit! Picking up the house phone, she answers with the hoarse morning voice, "Hello! You better have a good reason for calling me this early in the morning. I might still have my mask on but my body knows it is very early."

"Hey Lene. Good morning grouchy. You sound like you were still sleeping. And you actually answered the house phone. I'm surprised yet I'm glad you did. No company, huh?" Regina laughs. "I didn't know you were a late riser, but it is Saturday so I guess I should have known. I get up early all the time."

Colleen sits up in her bed. "Regina? Good morning to you too. Yea, I know you are an early riser but you ain't ever called me this early. Normally it's Sandy that you call this early, remember? But I guess you're my rooster today, huh? What's up? Is everything okay?" Colleen lifts her night mask off her eyes. The sun hits her too hard in the face and she pulls it back down over her eyes and lies partially propped up on a pillow.

"Well, yes, I'm calling you *this* morning. And how you know what time it is? I know you probably still have your damn sleeping mask on. Maybe you should invest in some of those shades that keep the sun out." Regina giggles. "You mind getting up for your friend?"

"I'm half sleep but I am sitting up, barely. And yea, my mask is still on. Hunh, you better know it." Colleen sleepily giggles. "So what's going on Gee Gee? Did something happen that I need to know about right away? I will say it is about six in the morning."

"Well, it's actually seven thirty. So rise and shine honey. I was wondering if you would like to come over for breakfast. Or do you want to meet me out somewhere for breakfast? I need to speak with you about something and if I don't say anything soon, Stan is gonna explode. And I don't feel like dealing with all of that."

Fuck! I knew something was going on with all of her church mouse antics every time I saw her ass. "Before he explodes? About what?" Colleen abruptly sits up in her bed. "So Stan told you to call me? This goddamn early?! Or this is the time you chose to call me? Did he say why he wanted you to call me and not Sandy or Bee?" *I'm not in the mood to be getting mixed up in your bullshit Stan!*

"No, I chose this time. I wanted us to talk over breakfast. I didn't want to wait until later. I have already waited. Stan wants me to talk to all of you but he suggested that I talk to you first. I don't know why but I am just doing as he asked me to so that I won't have to hear his mouth later." Colleen doesn't respond. Regina wonders if she has hung up on her since she hasn't answered to her name twice.

"Yea, yea, yea, stop calling my name Gee Gee. I am here. I do hear you. Just gathering my thoughts as to what this could be about." Yawning, she asks, "So what do you want to do? Since Stan wanted you to call me, that means I need to know about some serious shit so, let me know what you wanna do. It doesn't matter to me. We can eat at your place or out somewhere. The ball is in your court."

Regina is confused from what Colleen just said. She was already confused as to why Stan suggested that she speaks with Colleen first if she hadn't spoken to everyone at the same time. "Sooo, because this is some serious shit, he wants me to talk to you first? Why is that? It sounds strange to me yet you seem to know what it all means."

Playing it off, Colleen replies, "Hey, that's your husband and I'm just your friend. Maybe he feels I'm the one that won't freak out once I hear whatever it is." Colleen plays that off very well. "So, where are we eating at Gee Gee? I *am* kind of hungry. I ate dinner sort of early yesterday. But even if I'm not, this sounds like one of those drinking conversations and I'ma need food on my stomach for both."

"Okay, so let's go out somewhere then. I don't want any disruptions or snooping around while we are talking. Stan and Maria are both wandering around the house this morning like they are bored. It's been shockingly quiet around here this morning, I can tell you that. I don't want Stan popping in on us pretending to be attentive but actually being nosy."

"True, true. I gotchoo. So, I will pick you up then. What time will you be ready to go? That'll let me know what kind of time I'm working with." Colleen yawns, takes off her mask looking at the clock on her nightstand.

"Lene, you don't have to pick me up. I can meet you. I'm already dressed for the day. Do you wanna go to IHOP out in Clinton? Or do you want to go somewhere else? Like to a buffet? Or maybe you would like to go to Mimi's Café?"

"First, you are not driving to meet me anywhere. If there is some bullshit going on, I have no problem coming to get you. And apparently there is some bullshit going on. Regina called Colleen at seven-thirty. And second, hell no I don't want to eat at IHOP or a buffet. I like Mimi's but not for today. All of those places are too far and out of the way. More than likely, all of them are going to be crowded and since you are worrying about ears .... We will go to Bistro Français. Is that okay?"

"Oh, girl, please. You are full of it." Regina laughs out loud. "How about you just say that you prefer to go where the white and hosidity folks hang out because the Bistro Français place is no closer than the other places. As a matter of fact, I do believe it is the furthest." They both have to laugh.

"Oh shut up. Ay, I figured since you woke me up this early on a rest day and Stan wanted to make sure I heard about whatever it is, I have a choice to pick a bougie and hosidity place. So you just be ready Regina. I'm getting up now. I'll be there within the hour. Make-up free and sweats."

What the fuck is really going on? And Stan wants her to talk to me first. I swear Stan better not be on no bullshit. We all made it out of the hood and I am not trying to go back there. Regina's head is so high in the cloud that she sees nothing happening around her or just brushing shit off when she should be paying attention. I'm glad he wants me to be informed but if this is more than me being made aware, we're gonna have an issue. Stan needs to take care of this all by his damn self.

Regina and Colleen arrive at the restaurant and they are seated quickly. Looking around admiring the restaurant Regina says, "Wow, this is nice Lene. Very, very nice. Yeap, this is definitely right up your alley. Fancy-Shmancy and it's in the heart of Georgetown. How many times have you been up here? And when you answer that, make sure you say who you came here with." Regina picks up her menu looking through it. "Oh and before you answer, I like how my breakfast invite turned into a brunch for you."

"Whateva Girlie. I had to get ready. It ain't my fault that you get up at the crack of dawn every day. I was still in the bed and I had to wake up in order to get up. And what you mean 'right up my alley'? I really like the atmosphere here and the food is great. I've only been here a few times with Byron."

"Ah, the infamous unseen VJ. So when am I going to meet him? You have only talked about him for the past few years … off and on that is. He has really made an impression on my Girl."

"What?" Colleen laughs leaning back in her chair away from the table over the menu looking at Regina. "What in the world is an unseen VJ? Where did you get that term from and what does it stand for?"

"Well, it used to stand for Video Jockey back in the day on WHUR but for you, it stands for Vagina Jacker. He has no problem sneaking up on you taking it and from your stories, he takes it quite well." They both laugh out loud in the restaurant without a care in the world. The waiter approaches with their waters and take their drink orders leaving in a hurry, giving them a few more minutes to decide on entrées.

"Whew! Vagina Jacker? Girl you are on one this morning. What do you do all day when you're at home? Create shit in your head?" Colleen and Regina laugh softly. "But you got that right. That man is the real deal. Has my toes curling … *TIGHT* too." Colleen blushes looking down at her menu but not really reading it.

Looking down at the menu again, Regina decides, "Well, since it is later than I had expected, I am going to go with the lunch menu. I want to try the avocado stuffed with crabmeat. Then I will get the steak Caesar salad." Regina looks over at Colleen waiting to hear what she is going to order.

"Oh okay. That's all you're gonna get? Then that says you don't like the menu. Especially since you went from brunch to lunch." Colleen props her face up on her hand looking at the menu. "I'm gonna start off with the homemade liver mousse and then get the omelet."

Regina snatches the menu down from her face. "Excuse me? You're gonna start off with what? The woman that never even liked scrapple when we were growing up and now you're eating liver mousse? I can't even imagine what the hell that tastes like. But, that's *your* appetizer, so enjoy."

"Yes, I like it … and? Byron ordered it one time and I tasted his. It was really delicious. I didn't think I was gonna like it either. Hell, I ended up ordering one for myself." Picking up her glass of water with slices of lemon and lime, she says, "But … you didn't get me up out of my bed early this morning to meet up and talk about Byron or liver mousse. So what's up with you? Start talking Mrs. Wooten." Colleen takes a sip then a swallow.

"Well, you know I've been having a problem with seeing that black Charger everywhere I go, right? I don't like it and you have seen the car for yourself. I am not sure how you were feeling about it but I'm really uncomfortable …"

Colleen frowns at Regina, slowly placing her glass down on the table and interrupts. "Wait a minute. Everywhere? As in, what? Where else have you seen this damn car? I'm not liking the sound of this already myself Gee Gee. Do I need to order something a little stiffer than this damn Kir? Or do I have to down a few of these to get in the right frame of mind for your dilemma?"

"Well, before I saw it in the parking lot at the class, I also saw one sitting outside of the house. The driver's window was cracked and there were flashes like the person was taking pictures of the house. I never mentioned it to Stan." Colleen swallows half of her drink listening. "Then I saw it at class as you know and when we pulled off, I thought it was just my imagination because it wasn't behind me. But when I got home that night, right before Maria opened the door for me, a black Charger drove past the house. It wasn't on a creep type of thing so I thought it was just a coincidence. Now, I am not so sure that it was."

Colleen is heated, swallowing the rest of her drink motioning for the waiter to give her another one. "And you never thought to mention any of this to anyone?" Regina doesn't respond. "You've only mentioned the car in the parking lot to me?" Regina gives her a "yes" head nod putting a straw into her water. "What else Regina? I'm sure that is not it."

"Lately, when we are in class, there seems to be a shadow at the door as if someone is watching. It only seems to move away when I would look at the door. At first, I wasn't sure if it was my imagination because the instructor walked into the class. Then it started feeling like the 'shadow' was there but just didn't want to be seen by anyone. As time went on, it made me think that they were watching me. I am sure I am not the only one that would have been looking back at the door with the stuff we do in those classes. I don't know. It's just weird." Regina runs her left pointer finger across her left eyebrow.

Nothing is being said right now. Colleen looks out the window at the couples, families, and people walking. She is staring into space like she is thinking while she is waiting for the waiter to bring her another Kir. Looking over at Regina, she leans onto the table with her arms clasping her fingers together asking, "Sooo, who in the hell have you or Stan pissed the fuck off Gee Gee? This is some bullshit and I don't know how deep Stan expects me to get with this."

Regina jumps back a little because she doesn't know this "Colleen" sitting in front of her. The eyes are cold and the posture is on alert.

"Okay, lately, you have been a little different since I showed you that car in the parking lot. Do you have some hidden secrets Colleen?" Regina tilts her head to the side with a speculative look. Colleen softens her posture slightly but still keeps her stern attitude. She is already in the fuck-something-up mode.

"Regina, you're my friend. I don't tolerate anyone bothering my friends or my family and it's apparent someone thinks they have a vendetta against you … or Stan … or both. But I can tell you one motherfuckin' thing, it's a vendetta that they won't see through. I promise you that." The waiter places Colleen's drink on the table. She smiles at him as he walks away and continues, "They're creating a war they won't be able to win. Now, what did Stan have to say?

Did he give you a plan? Or is he expecting me to put one in place?" Colleen has hardened eyes and Regina swears that Colleen's eyes look like they belong to Satan.

"A plan for what? Wait a minute … what is this? Some type of gangsta type of bullshit? Why would I need a plan?" Shaking her head Regina continues. "I don't want the old Stan to come to surface Lene. And how in the hell are you involved with that? I mean Stan just told me to continue on with my routine as normal." Regina is confused yet getting angry.

Colleen just shakes her head at Regina. "I don't have anything to do with the old Stan." Colleen looks in her eyes to see if she is believable to Regina. She can't read the expression on Regina's face. "You can't be that naïve Gee Gee. Or are you? Look, someone in a fucking black Charger with illegal tinted windows is following your silly ass *and* taking pictures of your house. Really? In this day and time? Someone is clocking your moves and knows where you live? What the fuck!" She leans back in her chair, folding her arms, crossing her legs and just looks out the window. "Now, I only have what you have told me and it doesn't sound all that fabulous. But, I can tell you one thing, it is something that you should have mentioned to your Girls from day one. So get your head out of the cloud and wake the fuck up!!" Colleen yells and Regina jumps. They look around to see if anyone heard Colleen raise her voice. Colleen uncross her legs, scooting her chair closer to the table.

"Stan has two businesses that could lead to disgruntle clients and you need to look deep into your current past to figure out if someone might be after you. For the woman that you are and my other two friends are, I don't know what the fuck any of you could do to piss anyone off. This is crazy. But you better start thinking." Regina thinks about it for a few minutes before Colleen continues. "It's time to get serious about this shit. All of this following you around crap and basically letting it be known that they are there makes the hairs on my arms stand up. That's not a good thing Gee Gee." Colleen leans back in her chair looking at Regina. Putting her hands on the table with her fingers intertwined, she says, "But, ok, he wants you to act and look like nothing is wrong. He wants you to act oblivious to your surroundings. I guess he wants whoever it is to think you still don't know so they can be caught off guard."

The waiter comes over with their food setting their plates down in front of them. They smile and thank the waiter watching him as he walks away. They prepare their food to eat getting back to the conversation. Regina is feeling real uncomfortable sitting at the table across from the new "Colleen."

"I don't know who could be after me. Then again, you did ask me if Stan has pissed anyone off. He has been in the office yelling a lot at somebody. Something about they want to change around the contract after it has been signed. As for me, my circle knows I don't work, only come in contact with my friends, husband, and maid … ." Regina pauses and thinks about the maid. *That envelope in her Maid Quarters. Have I been mean to her? Have we mistreated her in some way? Could this all be related?* Regina can't think of any one. That's because she isn't thinking hard enough.

"What's wrong Regina? Tell me what's spinning around in your head. Stan didn't suggest you talk to me first for nothing." Colleen is dead serious and Regina notices it. She is not sure if she is liking the "unfamiliar" woman sitting across from her sharing lunch time. She prefers to talk about Colleen's hidden secrets but she sees that it is not up for discussion.

"Well, we are gonna eat our food and enjoy this time out but you have some serious thinking to do. You have plenty of time on your hands so you got your homework cut out for you. And you need to tell *all* your friends what the fuck is going on. Hell, you might even need to tell your family." Regina raises her head to look at Colleen's cold eyes. "Just to be on the safe side. I'm just saying. The last thing you, Stan, or me need is for one of them to get caught up being associated with you and they are uninformed. You don't know who it is, or why. Nor do you know what they know about you. We know that Stan's family is the streets. I doubt whoever it is wants to go 'there' with Stan. I can tell you one thing, whoever it is, doesn't know who your husband really is. That says an amateur to me."

Regina looks at Colleen shaking her head agreeing with her. But her friend is acting so strange, she wonders what has gone on in her childhood or her adulthood that makes her look so cold right now. *When this is all over, I will ask Colleen about this demeanor she has never shown to me before.* Little does Regina know, she will find out long before the pandemonium is over who Colleen Jeffries is.

Fuck!! I'm not gonna call Stan about this shit. His ass will have to call on me if he needs me. He has to understand that I'm a normal person now. I'm a normal person. Goddammit ... I am a motherfuckin' normal person. A woman, with a business, friends, and options. I no longer do that anymore. I will just guide her through these fucked up troubles. Colleen doesn't notice Regina observing her. Once she looks up, she sees the perplexed look on her friend's face.

"Do you have something to tell me Colleen? A few seconds ago, you weren't here in this restaurant at this table with me. What is going on with you?"

"Nothing that you need to know right now and hopefully, I can keep it to myself. Just know that your husband had good intention when he suggested that you talk to me. I don't play with those close to my heart being fucked with." Colleen stuffs food in her mouth motioning for Regina to eat up as well. Nothing else is said while they are eating their breakfast and enjoying their drinks. After they eat their food, they order more drinks.

"So, let me ask you this. Do you carry with you any type of weapon? In your handbag? Your car? Gym bag? You know, like mace, a knife … a gun perhaps?" Colleen stares at Regina waiting for her answer, even though she already knows her response.

"No, I don't Lene. Who would I have been protecting myself from? You … Sandy … Bee? Do *you* carry a weapon?" Regina tries to look into Colleen eyes, but Colleen is avoiding hers.

"How about from the damn shadow at the door that you think is watching you? Has Stan given you any basic lessons on how to protect yourself?" Colleen finishes her liver mousse, moving the plate to the side.

Regina looks at her friend and starts sweating lightly. "I can't say that he has. Well, he has shown me how to use my keys as a weapon though. But me carrying a knife? A gun? Colleen, you really think I need to know how to handle those things?!" Regina lifts her drink in her trembling hand. Colleen notices the tremble.

"Yea, I do naïve ass. Okay, now keys are okay but … has Stan never taught you how to handle a knife … or a gun?" Regina nods "no." Are you sure?"

"I'm sure I would remember something like that Lene. Why would he need to do that anyway? Especially if I never had a need to carry them. Nothing before now had been happening."

Colleen smiles at her friend saying to herself, *Wow! You are really this green Gee Gee?! So green that you didn't think to learn certain things so that you can ward off any possible crazy motherfuckas?*

"Gee Gee, you are making me want to slap you right now. But I'm gonna keep my hands to myself. You just going on with your life, with your husband, your friends, the Spa, grocery store … our private motherfucking classes - which don't seem too private right now - and the world around you doesn't exist, huh? I envy you but at the same time I'm angry with you. You have been this way since I met you in high school and I don't know who fault it is. But right here … right now … I really need you to come out of your Ms. I'm So Green cloud."

"Explain yourself, please." Regina is seeing another side of her friend and she wants her to reveal as much as she can. She can't put her finger on it but something about Colleen's demeanor points to dangerous.

"You are in this cloud that really doesn't exist in our world. We grew up in the hood Boo Boo. That means, we have a story of struggle to tell. You, maybe not so much. But Sandy, with six siblings has a story that says, fight and kill if you have to. Bee, with her two siblings says protect, fight, and maybe not kill but if it comes down to it, do what you must. And then there is me … I had to survive like your other friends and that means plenty."

"What makes you think I didn't have to fight to survive? Sandy lived in the same apartment building. My family struggled too."

"Your word 'fight' is a little different. No offense, but your mother chose to live where y'all lived. She didn't have to. There was no real struggle for you. Y'all could've been in a nice suburban community with none of our worries and concerns and we would have never met. But all of this is beside the point. We're getting off topic here. What I need you to do is think about who could be after you … or Stan. Get him to help you with some moves with the knife and take you to the shooting range. Hell, take your ass out into the backyard and shoot some fucking bottles, at least. You need to be trained to handle those pieces and then get you a little cute pink piece to carry around with you.

"So you think this situation is to that point?"

Colleen looks at her as if she is crazy. Shaking her head again, rubbing her hands over her hair, she responds. "You are really delusional, huh? Damn Gee Gee. How much more do I have to say about this mess? I thought I laid it all out to you a few minutes ago. I'm sitting here getting a pot belly from all these champagne types of drinks and you sitting across from me saying that 'life is good' and it ain't."

"I never said any of that. Someone in a black Charger has been following me around, watching what I am doing …. "

"And if you ask me, you are leaving something out of this conversation. Stan wouldn't have suggested that you tell all of your friends what is going on but then suggests that you talk to me first. What you have said is enough to put me on alarm but not enough for me to be involved. Stan can handle this himself, I'm sure."

"So what is it Wonder Woman? You know how to handle a knife? You know how to shoot a gun? What kind of tricks you got? Why can't you teach me what you know? I'm certain that what you know is more feminine and less painful than what Stan would be showing."

"Yea, I do but it was all in surviving my dear. But I suggest that you let your man help you with all that. He is concerned and as your husband, he needs to show you how to protect yourself. Hey, I've not done that in years. But I do make sure I have a few things on hand with me at all times. As a woman, we never know."

Colleen thinks about her last encounter and does not want to go back to that episode. She wants it to forever be buried in her past.

"Oh really? I am learning a lot about my friend that is sitting across from me at this table. You know how to use weapons and shit to protect yourself? What the fuck was going on in your household that you needed to know these things?"

"Nothing has to go on in the household Regina Wooten. We lived in the hood. How many people did you know that got caught slipping? And we are females. How many of them did we know that was snatched up by the Dirty Dozen? Them grimy niggas did gang bangs on a woman all night long and some of them women died of AIDS. That wasn't gonna be me or anyone in my family. You damn well know two of them niggas were brothers and lived in my building. I was on watch every day for me, my mother, and my sisters."

Regina had forgotten all about that. *This conversation has taken a turn to the left. I ain't think about that. My mother never had us thinking that way. You are right. And I can say that you and Bee did live in the worse part of our hood. A lot of shit went down in y'all neck of the woods. So yea, I can see you wanting to be prepared.* Regina is saying this in her mind. Every so often, she looks over at Colleen who seems to be in her own world.

"Well, let Stan show you a few things. He needs to, seriously. You know he was in that life and in order for him to still be here today as your husband, he needed to know how to survive out there in them damn streets. Stop knocking what he did. It was survival."

"I don't knock what he did. It made me nervous. Many of them went to jail or got killed. Some got killed in jail by rivals. I didn't want that for him. I didn't plan on visiting him in jail or burying my man then and I don't plan on doing that now. So you can't knock my feelings."

Colleen compassionately grabs both of Regina's hands saying, "You're right and I'm sorry. Those things did happen to a lot of the guys and Stan made it out of there. He had a strong woman behind and beside him back then and he married her. So we're gonna just act normal but with our antennas up and radars working, okay?" Regina looks at her with a faint smile with watery eyes. "We're going to go to class Monday as normal as we can. But don't piss me off with that quietness and you need to tell Bee and Sandy Monday after class, all right?"

"Good evening Maria. Is Stan in his office?"

"Good evening Senora Wooten. No he is upstairs. I'm not sure where though. But he's been going back and forth between the bedroom, the theatre, and the Winter Room. He has been talking on the phone since you left this morning."

"The Winter Room? And he's been on the phone?"

"Yes, but no yelling. He has been calm. He asked me to take the sheets off everything, dust and vacuum in the Winter Room. It is winter Senora so he must think it was time to start using it for the season."

"Nothing wrong with that. Thank you Maria, I will go hunt him down." Regina smiles at Maria as she walks off towards the stairs to find Stan.

She checks the Winter Room first since that is the least utilized of the three rooms Maria mentioned. Approaching the door, she hears him talking. Knocking, she twists the doorknob to enter. Peeping her head in first, he looks at her smiling, motioning for her to come in.

"Ay, let me call you back. Regina just walked in. Yea, we'll catch up later and do that. Thanks bruh, I appreciate it." Stan hangs up the phone.

"Good evening Mr. Wooten how are you?" Regina gives him a hug and soft peck on the lips. "Who were you talking to?"

"Hey babe. I'm great, how are you? Oh, I was just talking to one of the fellas. How did your meeting go with Colleen?"

"Oh, so the fella doesn't have a name? Or it's none of my business who you were talking to?" Regina smirks at Stan.

"Of course he does but it's one you don't need to know." He smiles and pops her on the butt. "Now how did it go with Colleen?"

"It went okay. She didn't seem too happy. I was seeing another side of Lene. I'm not sure if I like it. It was almost as if she is dangerous or something."

Stan sits on the couch propping his feet up on the coffee table folding his arms across his chest. "Oh really? Dangerous huh? How was she acting?" Stan laughs lightly.

"Well, she tells me that you need to teach me how to handle a knife and a gun and you need to buy me a nice pink one. And what's so funny? She was making me uncomfortable."

Stan removes his feet from the coffee table, unfolding his arms and leans forward placing his arms on his thighs. He gives Regina a look she knows all too well. "So whatever the fuck you told her says there's more to this than just a damn note in the bushes. You haven't told me everything, have you Regina?"

Chapter Twelve

12

Here we go with this shit again. I am not in the mood for this evening. One night she had my arms feeling like bricks. I couldn't lift a damn thing. Another night in this damn class, she had my legs and thighs feeling like cement blocks were attached to my feet. The pain shot all the way up my ass and I thought I had logs for legs. And here we are again looking at these damn poles. I guess my abs will be screaming when we finish tonight. Sigh! Sometimes I wonder why I signed up for these classes. Probably so I wouldn't be the outcast amongst my Girls. Sometimes I wonder why I even care.

BeLynda walks in with Colleen concentrating on her thoughts. Sandy's and Regina's greetings go unheard a few times. She continues over to the chairs and mats taking off her coat and sitting down her bag, walking over to the Ladies. Smiling she speaks.

"Good evening Ladies. How is everybody doing," she asks giving them half hugs and light pecks on the cheeks.

"Where is your mind Bee? Do you care to share your thoughts with us? Sandy and I spoke to you a few times and you kept on walking across the room." Regina returns the greeting with the normal intensity, noticing that BeLynda is a little weak with hers.

"Yea, you didn't hear a thing. We could've been standing here naked and you wouldn't have even seen us. Something has that mind of yours in a tizzy. We got a few minutes before Candice arrives. Tell us a little bit." Sandy has her hands on her hips looking concerned.

"Oh, nothing is the matter. My mind is clear. I thought y'all were talking to Colleen. Sorry if you thought I was being rude." BeLynda smiles for her Girls but it is too hard and appearing to be forced, so they don't buy it.

"Well, I don't know how you thought they were talking to me. My name is Colleen and they don't call me Bee. Bee is short for BeLynda, remember. But I think I know what the problem is." The ladies look at Colleen thinking that maybe BeLynda told her something in the car on the way to class.

"Oh yea? What is the problem? Let me hear what you think you know about me." *I can't be that transparent but maybe I am when it comes to these damn 'open up and free yourself to be sensual' classes.*

"The problem is every time we come in this room and there are poles up, you get uncomfortable. You acted the same way all of the other times and was relieved when we were basically just working on strength training. But today my dear … guess what? The time has come. You will be using all of those classes to do some swinging on this thing right here." Colleen says rubbing her hands up and down one of the poles. "I'm glad you dressed appropriately today. I wouldn't want you to burst any of the seams in those ass hugging jeans you wear. Do you get them tailor made somewhere?" Sandy, Colleen, and Regina all laugh. BeLynda gives her a wicked smirk.

"Oh, I know you ain't talking. I rather have my jeans hugging in the right places than to have them sending me to the gynecologist. You're the one walking around with the camel toe thinking that shit looks good. Only in your bedroom my dear … your bedroom." Colleen's mouth is open wide yet trying to hide a smile that is forming. Regina and Sandy smile looking at each other. Regina gives Sandy a wink.

"Way to go Bee. That's one point for Team Giles." Sandy says holding up the pointer finger.

Colleen looks at BeLynda grabbing her crotch saying, "I can't help if it is fat and juicy. So fuck yoooou."

"No thank you. I'm strictly dickly. Now put the hoof away. Really, we don't want to see it. And no descriptions please. Keep the vulgarity to your stories." Sandy covers her mouth in astonishment.

"Hmmp, it looks like two more points for Team Giles. She slipped one of those bougie country club terms in there on you. Team Jeffries still has zero. You slipping Colleen." Regina grins.

"Yea, you were all mouth at the Spa. What happened? You talked too much the other day?" Sandy whispers in Colleen's ear but loud enough so that BeLynda and Regina can hear.

"Whateva. I am not worried about her feeling herself this evening. That is only temporary. Let me hear her talk shit when she has to climb that damn pole."

Other classmates enter into the room taking off their outer garments sitting down their bags and mingling while waiting on the instructor. In the meantime, Regina still looks back at the door to see if there is a shadow there tonight. It's not every night that the silhouette is there but she still feels uneasy every Monday. However, since she had the breakfast meeting with Colleen, her friend has been making sure she gets home safely. There hasn't been a black Charger in the parking lot after class most nights. One night, Colleen walked over to the car but no one was in it. Regina thought that was bold but Colleen thought it was worth a chance to go see what she could see. She did write down the tag number though.

Fifteen minutes later, Candice walks into the room. She walks across the room to sit her bag down like everyone has done, smiling at the Ladies. She has on a purple workout top that shows her well-developed eight pack abs. Over that is a sheer black flowing top. She has on yoga shorts and flip flops on her feet. Her hair is long and flowing today.

"Damn, that woman is built. Small but built. You see the definition in her thighs? And look at how her ass just sits up in them damn shorts like she has spanx underneath them. Colleen didn't you say you go to her cardio class?" Regina is now looking at Colleen.

"Yea, I do. And she kills me every time. She has to work out every day. Then again, she does teach cardio three days a week. She is toned the fuck up though. What the hell is a spanx?" All three of her friends look at her like she must've been under a rock to not be informed.

"What is a spanx? Girl, shut up. I can't believe you just asked that."

"Well, I did. Now, what the hell is it?" Colleen looks at her friends realizing she is the only one clueless.

"Ms. Fashion Queen herself has no clue as to what the latest craze is. Well, let me be the first to inform you. Ooh, I'm loving this." Sandy says excited. "Spanx are undergarments that snatch everything up. You now, get rid of the bulges, rolls, and flab. Make your clothes look and fit better. It gives you a slimmer and shapely look."

"Oh, really? That's interesting. I had never heard about those."

"How, you didn't? They been out over three years now. I'm surprised you don't own a few pieces," Regina says surprised.

"Damn, they been out since two thousand? Yea, I had no idea. Do y'all have any?" Colleen is looking at her friends ready for an answer.

"I don't," say Sandy.

"Me neither," BeLynda says looking at Regina and Sandy.

"Well, I am guilty of having a few pieces. However, when I tried to wear them, I almost passed out. That is too much snatching up. I don't need to look that slim and shapely for all that misery. I bet you anybody that wears them can't wait to get back home to take those shits off." They laugh out loud at Regina.

"Well, I guess I don't have any because I don't need any. And if I am going to be feeling like that, I wouldn't waste my time buying them. I bet you a white woman invented it and we are not shaped like them."

"*We* are not but there are many of us that are."

Candice has been talking for about five minutes. She notices the Fantastic Four are holding a conversation that is more than likely about something else. Interrupting them, as usual, she says, "Good evening Ladies. I'm talking to my Fantastic Four over there huddled up in another private conversation." The four Ladies all turn to look at Candice slightly embarrassed that they have been called out.

"Oh, hello Candice. How are you this evening? I'm sorry, did we miss something? I thought you were just saying 'hello' and telling us what we are going to be doing this evening. I already said 'hello' and I have an idea what we are going to be doing."

Candice looks at Colleen smiling yet saying to herself, *She is such a bitch. I am surprised she has any friends.* "Well, why don't you tell us what you think we are going to be doing this evening? Come on up here and take the floor Ms. Jeffries."

Colleen squints at her rolling her eyes as hard as she can walking up to the front of the class. Some of the other Ladies snicker at Colleen's reaction to the teacher. Sashaying up to the front of the class throwing much ass at the teacher, she stands before her friends, teacher, and classmates and begins to speak.

"Well, I figured since we have already had enough Sexercise classes with this pole to have us going home with a new body part aching from here to Timbuktu that we would actually be using those techniques to properly mount these things this evening." The instructor giggles at Colleen's introduction to the class.

Is she really this crass? Or is this a front to have people thinking she is hard? It comes off as a woman in the suburbs that forgot to leave her ghetto roots in the damn ghetto, Candice says in her mind while smiling at Colleen. "Okay, that is good Colleen. You are right. Oh, and I'm glad you didn't curse me out after the sexercise classes. The intentions were good, trust me." Colleen looks at Candice as if to say, *Bitch please*, and sashays back to her crew.

"Okay Ladies, find a pole please. Spread out. There will be no talking during class, unless you want to lose concentration and find yourself on the floor with something broken or sprain. Remember now, all of you did sign waivers. So no trying to sue." Candice smiles but they know she is serious.

Walking over to her gym bag, Candice unzips it and reaches in pulling out sets of gloves for the classmates. She hands a set to each Lady. They all begin to put the gloves on preparing for the lesson.

"I have given everyone a pair of gloves to use with these exercises. The hands sometimes get sweaty making it hard to grip the pole. So we will use gloves. I would have brought some chalk powder but this is not gymnastics. Now, just in case you forgot, you will be in five private classes with this pole. The sexercise class was geared towards providing you the fundamentals to help with the correct form. Is there anyone here that doesn't think they are up for the task just yet?" Candice looks at each Lady in the class to see who says "yes," "no," and "maybe." Everyone says "yes" even though they may have wanted to say "no."

"All right … I'm gonna talk for a few minutes to let everyone get prepared for this evening's lesson." Candice is walking around the class talking. "Now, pole dancing isn't just about the strip club. It can be what you want it to be. It can be for your man, for you, or both separately or at the same time. Doing it for you help to increase your self-confidence and self-esteem while toning and strengthening your problem areas."

And how the hell am I supposed to increase those swinging around on a damn pole with my legs wide open? They kill me talking this bullshit, says BeLynda to herself.

Candice continues to talk. "This is a bare feet class. The floor has been mopped twice so it is clean other than when you walked in here with your outside shoes on. So take off your little cutesy and designer shoes. They won't be admired this evening," she says winking her eye at a few including Colleen and Regina. Colleen rolls her eyes. "I hope you made sure your feet are nicely hygiene. No funkiness please." Everyone begins to come out of their shoes laughing at Candice. "I'm just kidding … no I'm not, but I'm sure you know what I am talking about. This room ain't big enough for funk."

Taking off her flip flops, Candice claps her hands and gets started. "Okay, now we are going to try some simple basic moves. Just a few that will get you used to the feel of having a pole in your grasp. When you decide to use it and want to feel sexy, or trying to entice your mate, or for whatever reason, you want to be confident. Now I want each of you to stand to the left of your pole holding it with your right hand. Make sure there is a comfortable space between you and the pole." The Ladies follow the instruction.

"Slowly walk forward around the pole making sure you grip it enough, not to let it go but loose enough so that your hand can move." Watching the Ladies, Candice is pleased so far. She just stands there watching them go around and around.

Sandy and BeLynda are smiling sort of enjoying what they are doing. Colleen is rolling her eyes from boredom. Regina looks more like she is spinning around in a meadow. She is lost in her mind.

After going around about ten times, Candice speaks up. "All right Ladies, I am going to add a move on to this. I want you to raise your heels off the floor continue to walk around the pole but on the balls of your feet. Do this five times around, making sure you always end up at the same starting point." Looking at their hands and feet, she smiles, "Good. You're doing good Ladies. Okay, we're adding on Ladies. You ready?" The Ladies are smiling enjoying the moves and respond with a "yes" nod.

"What you're going to do next is raise your right hand higher on the pole putting your left hand at the same level and continue to walk around the pole. That's it Ladies, you're doing great!" Candice walks around making sure everyone has their hands up high enough. "I want you to relax. Some of you look a little tense. This is supposed to be fun, erotic, and sexy. We're quickly adding on. Oh, before we move on, if this position is slightly uncomfortable, then you may move your left hand straight across your chest and hold on to the pole there." A few of the Ladies made the adjustment.

"Okay, I want you to stand in place for a minute. Now, what you gonna do with this move is hook the back of your right leg - behind the knee - around the front of the pole, using your hands to hold on." Candice points to the part of the knee that is supposed to wrap around the pole. Walking around the class, she observes making sure she was clear with her instructions. "How does that feel to you? Is it okay? Weird? Uncomfortable? Let me see you hook your leg a little tighter."

Sandy smiles excitedly, saying, "Uh-oh, we about to do it!" Candice and the classmates laugh out loud and this lightens the intensity in the room. However, BeLynda gets nervous instead.

"Calm down Ladies," Candice says while laughing. "Make sure you don't lose your position. Okay, what you gonna do with this move is hook the back of your right leg - behind the knee - around the front of the pole, using your hands to hold on and swing your body forward around the pole with both legs lifted."

"Oh, hell you had me up until just now. What the hell you want us to do again," asks Colleen. Regina finds Colleen funny and gets a case of the giggles. The other Ladies begin to laugh at Regina laughing.

"Let me demonstrate for everyone." The Ladies all agree waiting to see their instructor perform.

"Yes, please do that. You were doing good until you started talking the Impossible Language."

"The Impossible Language? What is that?" Candice puts her right hand on her right hip and looks at Colleen. *What is it now?*

"Yea, the language that let's others know what's impossible for me to do."

"All right here we go Ladies. Watch closely." Candice walks around the pole slowly with one hand, then walking on the balls of her feet adding the other hand at the same time. Everyone is observing just as Candice requested … closely. Lightly and with no effort, Candice embraces the front of the pole with the back of her knee and swings around the pole like a feather floating in the air, gently landing back on her feet. "Who wants to try it?" No one responds. "Okaaay let me show you a few more times. What we are doing is in slow motion. I broke the move down in steps for you. Here we go. Again, watch so you will be able to imitate what I am doing." Candice repeats the visual instructions of the moves three more times for the class. "Now can y'all try it together as a class now?" There are plenty of doubtful faces. "Okay, we can do it one by one, then. Let's start over here to my left and we can go around the room. It's ten of you so it won't take that long."

Plenty of apprehension can be heard and felt all around the class. Each Lady did the exercise with great hesitation. However, to each of their surprise, they did very well. Candice smiles at each of them and claps her hands before the next Lady took to her pole. A few of them wanted to keep doing it. BeLynda was one of those Ladies. They were just flying around on the pole like this is a class review.

"Very good Ladies. I am surprised and I see that many of you are surprised too. You see? All y'all thought that you couldn't do it. Don't doubt yourselves Ladies. If you were doing this for your mate, they would be able to tell that you were unsure. When we finish with these classes, you will be renting out the strip club for a private dance and dinner for your mate. Wait and see." They smile and giggle at the thought.

"Now, we are going to step it up a notch, all right? We are going to do all of the moves in one motion. Putting all of the moves together and twirl around the pole we will lock our left ankle with the right ankle for a few second and land back on our feet. It looks like this." Candice demonstrates interlocking her ankles. "Now, let me see each of you do it just like you did it the first time. We are going to start from the right of the room this time."

Each Lady did the exercise with the new added move. They all did good again. Then she had them to do it together like it was a performance. Candice is tickled. Regina was into it. Colleen was quietly concentrating but she had it down. Sandy is excited looking around at everyone do their thing. For some reason, she feels someone is watching them. Turning around to the door, there is a shadow and she frowns because the silhouette looks familiar but she brushes it off. BeLynda looks over at Colleen saying, "Oh yea heifer, I am gonna talk shit. I got this." Colleen gets a big laugh out of it and they give each other high-fives.

Candice smiles at each of them saying, "You know what? I am overjoyed. Let's give ourselves and each other a big clap." The Ladies clap and root each other patting themselves on the back for a job well done. “Okay, now, the next step we’ll be adding on is to twirl down to the floor on our knees.” A few eyebrows rise. “Aww, it’s not that hard. You are doing so well. Here is a little demonstration for you.” Candice show them how it is done and a few can be heard saying, “Oh, that’s all?” She laughs with a response of, “Well, let me see it. Let’s go.”

The same as before the Ladies all showed her individually and then together. “Okay, okay, I see y’all. I like when we catch on fast. Now, that y’all know the basics, is anyone willing to try doing this adding a little … or a lot of sensual and sexiness to it?” Mouths open wide in shock and nervousness.

“What you mean by that? OH! Like we are performing for our man,” Regina asks.

“That’s right Mrs. Wooten.” Candice smiles wide giving Regina a wink.

“I don’t mind trying but can you give us a demonstration of how you would do it,” one of the classmates asks.

“Sure. I can do that.” Looking up into the small window in the top of the left wall, Colleen raises her hands and gives two claps. All of a sudden, the lights dim and Teena Marie blares through the room. Everyone is looking around in amazement.

“Aww shit now. We ‘bout to get busy up in here,” says Colleen ready to get started.

The Ladies move out of the way for Candice as she walks seductively towards the pole that is directly in the center of the room. She is up on the balls of her feet prancing around the pole mixing jazz moves with the grace of a ballerina. Her arms are extended and her finger tips are lightly fluttering up and down the pole as she goes around it. Every now and again, she bends her leg lifting her hip with it as if she is going to grab the pole but she doesn't. She is teasing the pole and looking away from it at times as if she is looking at a man sitting in a chair watching her.

Finally, she does the entire move so graceful, yet it is sexy and sensual. The Ladies have their mouths open smiling, shaking their heads as if to say they like what they see. When Candice ends up on the floor on her knees, she toots her butt out, make a few circles then bends all the way back so her back in on the floor and her arms are above her head. Seductively releasing her legs from the bend rubbing her right inner thigh on the pole ending with her entire leg propped up on the pole. She repeats this with her left inner thigh and it ends up beside the right leg. Arching her back, she raises her upper back off the floor and spreads her legs wide, planting her feet on the floor, grabbing the pole and winds her body off the floor until she is standing again.

She turns around suddenly to see her students. They are floored by what Candice just showed them. Candice raises her hands again clapping twice and the music stops and the lights brightens. Smiling, she says, "Now, do you think that you can do the moves you learn today and add your own taste, style and sensuality filled with sex with it? The Ladies are just still stunned.

"Instructor!! Now, that was a show!! I mean, you were into character for sure. You were making love to that pole! Acting like there was a man in here sitting in a chair and shit. That was all right. I like that. Hell, I really wanna see you do it again. Damn! But um … you want us to do all of that?!" Colleen was excited, surprised, turned on, yet weary all at the same time.

"Yea, Ms. Candice, I must admit. You took those little steps you showed us and added your own stuff to it and went to work. I mean when you said to add our own sexiness, I had no idea what you wanted us to do but I got you," says BeLynda.

Oh you got her? We'll see about that. Mmm-hmmm, you might wanna let your Girls critique your shit first with your frigid ass, Colleen says to herself looking at BeLynda.

"You got that right. I can just do that one move and add my shit to it all night and he wouldn't know the difference," says Regina and the entire class laughs out loud hard.

"Do you sell these poles? If so how much do they cost," Sandy asks and all of her friends smile looking at her.

"Yes, I do sell them but there are also plenty of places that sell a variety of colors. Or you can get one permanently put up … professionally of course. We don't want you pulling down your ceiling. That would be hazardous." Everyone laughs. "I've seen it happen too many times. The pole and plaster come down right along with the body. Casts are not welcome in my classes." The Ladies roar in laugher.

"Is there anyone in here that want to try it all by yourself to the music? You might as well get practice now. This is just the first basic move. There are a few others that will be taught but one move at a time and then we bring them all together."

"Oh Lord. As a performance, huh?" BeLynda asks.

"Yeap, a performance, as a final. I can't let you go out thinking you got it and the technique is wrong and you end up with something sprain, broken, or dislocated. But remember, all of you signed waivers." Candice winks at the Ladies pointing at each of them.

"I think I want to try it," Kemira says and all the Ladies turn to see who volunteered.

"Okay, then let's see what you got …" Candice pauses so the lady can tell her name.

"Kemira … but you can all me Kemira." Everyone has a good laugh.

"Okay, Kemirea. Let me know when you are ready and I will set the stage for you." Kemira shakes her head and walks to over the pole she has chosen for the night. Nodding her head nervously at the instructor, Candice did her claps and the stage is set.

Kemira starts on the balls of her feet prancing around the pole seductively, feeling on her neck up to running her hands through her hair. Candice is smiling. Kemira changes positions and goes in the other direction doing the same thing. She starts rubbing her hands up and down the like she was one of the girls from the Price is Right Game show. She shimmies slowly down the pole and back up, continuing on around the pole. Grabbing the pole with the back of her leg looking like she is about the make the move, she puts her finger in her mouth, then leads the finger down to between her legs. She arches her back closes her eyes, pokes out her butt, doing a spin similar to Flash Dance and does the move they learned this evening. Her spin seems a little high and she twirls around the pole a little longer with her head back, ending on her knees. Spreading her legs, she is in a Chinese split, laying down on her back grabbing the poles with her thighs, opening her legs again, simulating she is rubbing the pole between her legs feeling good from the friction. All of the Ladies in the room are enjoying watching her. Kemira lifts both legs to put her heels on the pole, turning over slowly so that her hands are on the floor and now her toes are gripping the pole for support. Slowly, she puts one leg down at a time, arching her back outwards slowly and seductively rising until her back is up against the pole. She grabs the pole above her head and ends with a sexy pose. She smiles letting Candice know she is done. Candice gives the signal and the class is back to normal.

Everyone is still quiet just watching Kemira admiring the performance she just gave. Some are saying in their minds, "I can do that," others are saying, "that was great," while Colleen is saying, "that is a pro."

Candice gives Kemira a big wide smile and begins to clap. Everyone else except for Colleen joins in. Kemira is cheesing, glad that she did a good job.

"That was beautiful Kemira. Have you had lessons before?" Candice asks smiling very pleased at the performance.

Of course the bitch has. She probably works at Barnone downtown, Colleen says to herself with a smug look on her face. *Yo ass is fakin' here. Why are you even here with yo Pro ass? This class ain't for you.*

"No, I have not had any classes before but the move you taught us was simple and once you said to add our moves, that part was easy. Hell, we all know how to be sexy and enticing, right?" Looking at the females in the class for approval, no one responds. "Especially when it comes to doing this for your man, right?" Kemira looks around the room at the Ladies. Some of the Ladies smile and agree.

"That was really great. I can't even imagine getting in front of my man doing that for him. I'm gonna have to work on my sexy moves to do what you and Candice did. This will become a workout for sure. That's why I need to purchase one of those from you Candice," Sandy says.

"I know that's right!! Get your swinging and twirling on Girl," says Regina. They are laughing and in the midst of it, Sandy sees that shadow at the door and it slowly walks away. *Damn! Who the hell is that? Somebody is watching one of us or all of us. But that slow walk with the slumped shoulders says they are disappointed. I guess we're not the only ones in here taking private classes.*

"One thing you need to remember is this is a dance. A sexy and sensual dance. Your goal is to look sexual starting with your outfit with or without stilettos. Then you need to be sensual with your moves and how you handle the pole. Give him the simulation that you are handling his third leg. You want to tease, entice, seduce, and make him unloosen his tie, take off his shirt, and make his nature rise …"

Busting that damn zipper beyond repair," Sandy says to herself smiling.

"The last thing you want to give off is the look of uncertainty. If you give him that look, he will stop you before you get started. Be confident, be sure of yourself … be a prowess. Look like you know what you're doing or the special night can come crashing down fast. Don't doubt yourself. Many of us do that enough in other areas including sex. Take control of that pole and the position showing him what you plan to do to him when you're done. He may think he lays pipe but always remember, it's all about your moves that determines how he lays it." Candice winks when she says that. She gave the Ladies something to think about.

That is one helluva speech. I'ma have to remember that when I am with Khalil. He thinks he's gonna be teaching me, but I have enough knowledge right now to have him stalking me. BeLynda folds her arms underneath her chest, thinking.

"All right Ladies, I will see you next week. Anyone that wants to get a pole tonight, meet me upstairs in my office in ten minutes. This was a good class this evening Ladies. I plan on us having more fun. Enjoy the rest of your week." Looking at Colleen she says to herself, *Oh I've not forgotten that you took my potato Ms. Jeffries. I will wait until you think I have forgotten.*

Chapter Thirteen

13

"Ooh, how did y'all like class tonight? I had fun. I can say that out of all of the classes, this was the most fun. I can do without all that mouth and tongue action and licking on fucking food. Her sister's classes get on my nerves." BeLynda says gathering her things.

"Well, did you like the hip and belly rolling class? That is movement and gets things stirred up. It was like dancing, don't you think? I take it that you are not for all of that mouth action, huh? Hey, everyone has their preference. You are entitled." Sandy says in response to BeLynda.

"Yea, that's true but it will create some frustration for him. And for some men, it creates arguments and straying. You over there with that young boy, I'm sure he has had a few mouths on that stick. So get ready because he is going to be expecting it." Colleen comments.

"Do you do it to every man you are with Colleen? I don't know how many there are but hell, let me know. I may need to pay attention to letting you taste my drinks." Sandy says smiling and frowning.

"Heifer go fuck yourself. As far as I know, my 'options' are in to *me* and waiting for *me* to make them mine exclusively. So I don't mind and I am sure they are clean. I don't play the dirty dick game. I let the crack heads take care of them." Colleen laughs blowing a kiss at Sandy.

"Oh they are waiting for *you*, hunh? Okay. Now *who* is being naïve," Regina asks. Colleen's turns around fast to look at Regina with narrowed eyes. "Yea, it doesn't sound good when someone is saying that word to *you*, does it?"

"Okay, moving on. What are we doing tonight? Are we going home? Or are we going over Regina's? What we doing Ladies? I don't feel like going straight home tonight," says Sandy.

"Hmm, that's a good question. Let's ask Regina what she feels up to. She might have something to tell us," says Colleen and Regina rolls her eyes.

"Fuck it, y'all can come over and we can sit in the movie theatre and talk." She just wishes that Stan and Colleen let her do things on her own time. Colleen smiles at her and winks.

"Is that right? The movie room? What's going on? The only time we go in there is when we need to speak on something. What's up Gee Gee?" BeLynda is concerned.

"We'll talk about that when we get to my house. However, we will be talking about quite a few things. Just continuing our Sista Day, you know?

"Okay, if you say so. Lead the way Gee Gee. You know I'm riding with you. Y'all ready," Sandy asks BeLynda and Colleen.

"Yeap," they say in unison heading towards the door.

****

"Whew! I need to just chill and relax. I'm tired as hell." Sandy says dragging her feet.

"Oh well, you want to sit in the Sauna Room for about an hour?" Regina asks trying to stall the talking.

"Girl, I gotta go to work tomorrow, unlike y'all winches." Sandy scrunches up her face and playfully rolls her eyes at the Ladies.

"Just call in tomorrow," Regina offers. For some reason she has a feeling it is going to be a long night.

"What? Call in? Now, that's different coming from you. Gee Gee is suggesting that I call in tomorrow. Normally you are begging me to go to work. I tell you one thing, I need to find me a business too. Gee Gee you have any ideas? I can tell Ms. Winston to kiss my ass and you can have something to do." They laugh at Sandy thinking she isn't serious.

Maria comes down the hall greeting the Ladies. Regina asks, "Maria may you bring us a few bottles of chilled wine and a platter, please?" Maria smiles and nods walking towards the kitchen.

Looking at the Girls, Regina asks, "So what are we gonna do? Are we gonna go in the Sauna and then into the theatre? Or are we gonna do one or the other?"

"That's a hard question. Actually it isn't because I have no clients to meet with tomorrow. So it is actually up to Sandy at this point since she is the only one that needs to punch the clock." Colleen says placing her gym bag on the floor.

"And my shipment doesn't come in until Thursday. So I'm game for whatever y'all decide." BeLynda takes off her jacket.

"Well, it's on you Sandy. You haven't said anything. You're just standing there looking lost. What, you trying to decide?" Colleen asks.

"Okay, okay, damn!! I will call in tomorrow. Y'all gonna have to hire me if I keep missing work. Which ain't a bad idea. So I suggest y'all get to thinking on where I can be used in your businesses." Sandy laughs and they laugh with her.

"Colleen, did you do that thing for me," Regina asks. She really wants to put a name to the owner of the black Charger.

"Yea, I gotchoo. Girl, I don't play around. I am about my shit." Colleen gives her a wink. "So are we just gonna stand here in this big ass foyer? I'm tired of hearing our echoes in here. All this damn furniture and decoration and it still sounds empty." They laugh out loud.

"Okay, let me go get our robes. Y'all get comfortable. Stop acting like this is new to you." Regina begins to walk off.

Just then Stan walks down the stairs smiling at the Ladies. "Hello beautiful Ladies. I haven't seen the three of you in a few weeks. Glad to see you. Other than me, y'all put a smile on my baby's face." Stan greets each with a genuine hug and a kiss on the cheek. He gives Regina a kiss on the lips. "What y'all up to this evening," he says looking at Regina waiting to see if he will hear what he wants to.

"We are gonna do some chillin' in the sauna and then we are off to the movie room," Regina says knowing what he is really asking.

"Ah, the movie room. Okay. What movie will be the feature tonight?" Stan winks at Regina saying with his eyes, *this is the best thing to do babe. Don't leave them in the dark.* Stan doesn't realize that they all are in the dark on certain aspects of the situation. "All right then, let me leave so you Ladies can get started. Do I need to have Maria make up the Guest Quarters? Y'all might be here longer than you planned." Stan looks at Regina. She doesn't meet his eyes. Instead she walks off to get their robes. Sandy and BeLynda look at Stan shocked then at Regina. Colleen is observing all of the body signals and the unspoken words between her friend and her husband.

Maria pushes the cart down the hall with the wine and munchies on it, parking it outside of the sauna room. Regina comes back with the plush monogram robes and matching flip flops, handing them the robe with their initials on it and a pair of flip flops. They go into the large Powder Room to change.

"It's a good thing we agreed that we would always bring a change of clothing with us just in case we decide to not go home on Mondays." Sandy says while removing her gym clothes.

"I'll be right back." Regina goes down the hall to the music room to grab some music for them to enjoy while they are in the sauna. While her Girls are settling in the sauna, she puts the CDs in the six-CD changer and pushes "play." Walking into the sauna the music comes through the speakers. It is Luther Vandross oozing through the speakers.

"Ooh that is my *song*. Can we put that on repeat? I haven't heard that in a while. I want to hear it a few times." BeLynda says moving slowly to the music.

"Girl, we are not gonna be in here long enough to give you special requests. Just enjoy it right now. How you know we want to hear that again? Hell, we might want to hear some of the other songs on the CD." Colleen says, knowing she rather be in the theatre room listening to Regina.

The lyrics start and BeLynda starts singing along with Luther:

♪ I can only speak for

The things that I've been through

So when it comes to our love

I'll talk the whole night through

About the lovin' I've been missing

Lately baby, I ain't had no kissin'

Do you love me

Can we stay together

Like when we used to be in love

But now you've got your head on another cloud

Girl, we had a good thing

But now you've turned around

Don't you even care how this love

We've had turns out

Promise me you leave me never

That we'll be in love forever

Promise me you'll leave me never

That we'll be in love forever ♪

"Bee, who the hell you singing to? What are you remembering? Surely not Steve." Sandy asks laughing at BeLynda being lost in another world singing.

"Yea, and it's too damn early to be singing about a 'boy' man." Colleen says laughing. However, she is loving seeing her girl being in the world of her memories.

"What?! How about I just like Luther and the damn song. That song goes way back before there was a fuckin' Steve. And let's make this clear, Ms. Giles won't be singing about Stephan Giles at any time. Did I love him, yes!! Do I still love him? Hell no! Do I miss being married? Yes! Do I miss being married to Steve? Hell no! So I will say it again. I am a Luther fan and this is *my* song."

"All right Mother Giles. I hear you. Loud and clear. I won't make that mistake again. I won't be hitting anymore nerves tonight." Colleen says closing her eyes relaxing on the bench with her head up against the wall.

BeLynda gets back to singing the song with Luther but she is now standing up.

♪ *Forever, ever, promise me you'll leave me never*

Won't you promise me (that you'll leave me never)

Promise me, forever and ever, and ever ♪

"Girl, you better sit your ass down. We are in a sauna, remember? I'm sure Maria has it set for like eighty-five motherfuckin degrees in here. You be done passed out in here. I do not know CPR. So please. Sit down, okay." Colleen laughs at BeLynda.

"See?! You made me miss most of the damn song Colleen. I need to hear it again. Please, Gee Gee, push repeat on the system." Regina gets up to go outside of the sauna door and pushes repeat for BeLynda. She remembers the cart is outside the door and rolls it inside of the Sauna Room. "Thank you babeee." She looks over at Colleen and winks while she is standing up, waiting for Luther to sing.

Sitting down, Regina begins talking. "Sooo, what's been up Ladies? What have y'all been up to? How have y'all been? I can say for me, I have had some strange things happening." This statement catches the attention of BeLynda and Sandy.

"Some strange things? Like what? Strange as in the Poconos strange?" Sandy asks. Colleen just waits to see how the conversation unfolds.

"It's a good thing I am sporting a ponytail. My hair would be all jacked up if I had curls. It is hot … up … in … here. What temp did Maria put the room on?" BeLynda asks.

"Fuck the damn temp. Gee Gee is talking. I said it's about eighty-five degrees in here. I think that's the normal temp for Gee Gee." Colleen says lifting her left arm wiping her face with the back of the arm of the robe.

"Oh, I will go adjust the temp." Regina stands to approach the door. Colleen is furious. She wants Regina to get on with the conversation.

Adjusting the temp, Regina enters back into the room and tries to change the subject hoping it will work. "I turned it down to seventy-five. If it is any cooler, then it won't be doing its job. Now, Colleen you said that Byron is having a holiday party. You never gave us any information. You know, no dress code, date, and time … if we need to bring something, just no information at all. You know, the logistics we need in order to actually show up."

Colleen looks at her raising her right eyebrow saying verbally, "Are you serious right now Gee Gee?! That is not what you were talking about a few minutes ago. So how you jump to another topic?"

"Yes, I am serious. As a heart attack. I want to make sure I can make it and that me and Stan are dressed appropriately. I refuse for us to be standing out like a sore thumb and shit. Everybody looking at us like we have an eye in the middle of our forehead. And you know Stan doesn't go anywhere and not be fly as a motherfucka. Now, let us know what we need to know."

Sandy notices something odd. "What is going on with you two? Y'all been acting like you know something that we don't know but we need to know yet no one is talking." Sandy looks back and forth at Regina and Colleen, expecting one of them to respond.

"Exactly!!" Colleen looks at Regina like her eyes are shooting daggers. Regina says nothing else other than, "Let's just enjoy the sauna and we can talk in the theatre. How's that?" She leans back and closes her eyes. Colleen looks at her like she could smack her. *Really bitch?*

At that moment, Peabo Bryson starts singing *I'm So Into You* and BeLynda jumps up again, singing all through the sauna. The Girls are laughing at her. "She can sing and she is singing the hell out of Peabo too."

"Go 'head Bee. Serenade us Girl. That was my song back in the day too." Sandy is smiling moving to the song watching BeLynda. By the time the song and BeLynda finishes, the Ladies are in a funk. The lyrics seem to mean something to all of them and they're wondering so many things about the love, the men in their life, and if it is real. Regina is not exempted from these type of thoughts.

Ninety minutes later, they are in the movie theatre chilling lounging around in the theatre design navy leather seats. Regina has chosen one of their all-time favorites to watch, *Love Jones*. The movie has reached the scene where Larenz Tate's character is reciting his poem. All eyes are locked on smiling and listening. When it is over, they start talking.

"Okay, Colleen what's the deal with Bryon's party? I can't believe we are actually going to meet the man behind the name and joys of ecstasies." BeLynda says smiling popping a grape in her mouth.

"Yea, tell us what we need to know. How are we supposed to dress? I mean, what type of man is he?" Sandy says tucking her feet under her thighs in the chair.

"What you mean what type of man is he?" Colleen asks confused as what Sandy means.

"Just what I said. You know, is he a casual man? Or is he a flashy type of man? That lets me know how I should be looking when I into his house. I don't want to be under or overdressed. Or as Regina said. I surely do not have a third eye in the middle of my head. I will leave that bitch early." Sandy says grabbing a piece of gruyere cheese.

"Oh, well he dresses casual *and* business yet very, very expensive. Like Farragamo, Louboutin, McQueen, you know, the shit we ain't introduced to our closet yet." They laugh. "When it comes to his clothes, he is out of my league but he always seems to like how I look when he sees me."

"Well damn!! He rolls like that," Sandy asks. Colleen shakes her head "yes." "All the goddamn time?" Colleen shakes her head "yes" again. "Shit, well, I don't have a clue as to how I am supposed to look then. Hell out of the four of us, I am the cheapest dressed." BeLynda, Colleen, and Regina look at her like she just said something stupid.

"The cheapest dressed? What the hell are you talking about? Just look like 'Sandy Robertson' when you walk up in there," says BeLynda. "I mean, you ain't going up in there as his guest. You're going up in there as Colleen's friend. Or are you thinking about bringing Larry with you? If so, then you look like yourself with your date as an invite from Byron through Colleen." They shake their heads in agreement.

"Or look like 'Sandra Robertson.' You know, put your good shit or best shit on to make the announcement that you have *arrived* honey." They get a good laugh out of what Regina said.

"But Sandy has a point though. This man dresses like that and all the time? He got a nice place, doesn't he Lene? He probably has one of those expensive ass condos or something, right?" BeLynda asks.

"He does but his sister and her two children live in that. He lives in a three bedroom house. Nothing big but it is laid. Very nice and expensively laid. Glass, leather, professional clean only, and plush everywhere. The only time he allows shoes to be worn in his house is when he is having something. Afterwards, the carpet is professionally cleaned and it's back to bare feet. Well, of course you can wear socks and shit like that." Colleen says taking a sip of her wine.

"Okay, enough about that because you're starting to make me not wanna go. I feel clumsy around that type of environment. I would be one to drop, spill, or knock something over," BeLynda says and they all laugh.

"Are we going together? Or are we going separate with dates? Regina you bringing Stan," Sandy asks. Colleen looks at Regina awaiting for her response saying to herself, "*She would want to bring him just in case some bullshit pops off.*

"I haven't decided yet. I hadn't mentioned it to him yet. We just now have actually talked about it a little more. He needs to know everything in one conversation so that's why I said we needed to talk about it. He doesn't do the back and forth on an event. More than likely, he will go. It's at a single man's house, which means, there will be other single men, or at least without their woman. So I know he isn't going to say he will stay home."

"You got that right. You are *Mrs*. Wooten. You dropped the last name 'Cross' a long time ago. So that means, you attend parties with your husband … along with your girlfriends," says BeLynda. Sandy and Colleen smile at the statement.

"Well, it will be on December thirty-first at seven. That's a Wednesday Ladies so don't tell me you forgot. So be ready with or without your date. Hell, I will be y'all's date if it's that important. You want me to wear a pants suit and a tie?" They giggle.

Good, then I can ask Ray to come with me. He can meet Regina and we can bring in the New Year together. I hope he says "yes." Sandy is thinking while taking a sip of her wine.

Just then, the door opens and Stan peeps his head in asking, "Y'all all right in here? Do y'all need me to send Maria in? Or is there anything I can do for you?" He really wanted to check out their body actions. That will let him know if Regina has said anything to them yet. Looking at Regina to see what kind of signal she gives, he knows she hasn't said anything yet. However, looking at Colleen she is eyeing him hard and that says she knows and she is pissed at him. He winks at her rubbing two of his fingers down his lips. This was one of their hood gestures that says, "We'll talk later." She rolls her eyes at him and he smiles wide. Regina catches the entire scene and she knew that Stan gave Colleen some type of signal.

"Oh, hey Stan. I'm fine, thanks for asking. Then again, the wine is almost gone. Do y'all have any more wine?" BeLynda asks looking at Regina to see if it is all right to get another bottle.

"Yea, we are almost out. Girl, this house is never without wine." Regina laughs but really wants to cry. "Babe, can you bring us two more bottles, please? Thank you." Regina smiles but she is actually fuming. Stan shuts the door to go get their drinks.

"Okay, look, we have enjoyed the sauna, sung songs, let a movie watch us, and talked about Byron and his party. Regina has something to tell y'all." Regina looks at Colleen with squinted eyes and pursed lips, trying to hold her tongue. "Sorry Gee Gee, but I was getting irritated by your hemming and hawing around the situation. Start talking, please."

BeLynda and Sandy get quiet listening to Colleen. Then they place their focus on Regina waiting for her to speak. Silence is all around the theatre. BeLynda speaks up, "Hey, what's wrong Gee

Gee? What is going on? I'm not blind. Lene has been trying to get you to tell us something all night. Stop procrastinating."

"Why you gotta be pessimistic? How you know something is wrong? She just probably hiding the fact that she is pregnant or something." Sandy says.

"Now, you're not being observant. Look at Colleen's face. Does that look like the face of optimism?" BeLynda points at Colleen. "Now turn your face towards your friend that is supposed to be talking right now. Does that look like she has something wonderful to tell us?" Sandy follows BeLynda's advice and looks at both Colleen and Regina. Her voice drops a little because it appears that something serious is really going on.

"Hey, where is Stan with that damn wine? Bee, I'm glad you asked him to get us two more bottles. Hell, I guess that's why he asked if we are spending the night, hunh Gee Gee? Are we waiting for our wine to get here first? Or can you tell us a little bit first?" Regina doesn't respond. She gets up and starts the movie over.

"Leave that damn movie alone and start talking Gee Gee!! Stop acting like you are in the bathroom combing your damn brush!" Colleen yells and everyone in the room jumps.

Stan knocks then enters with the bottles of wine. They are quiet. He looks at their faces and becomes concerned. "Everything all right in here? Colleen I heard you yelling. Do I need to sit in here and referee?"

"Nah, we fine Stan." Looking at him, Colleen rubs both of her hands across her neck with the thumbs in front to throw the girls off. This is another hood signal that says, "I could choke you." He gives her a head nod and leaves but not before looking back at her winking.

Pouring everyone a fresh drink, Sandy sits down a little closer to Regina to see better while she is listening. "All right, my ears are fully open for your words."

Regina runs her fingers through her ponytail and across her forehead with her eyes closed. She looks at her friends, clearing her throat, she begins. "Okay, okay, fuck! Well, there have been some strange things happening around me and they have me on edge."

BeLynda gasps and puts her hand up to her chest. "On edge? Like what Regina? What the hell has been going on? I have noticed you've been a little more quiet than normal." She uses her full name because this sounds serious.

"Well, I've been noticing a black Charger everywhere I go and it's been creeping me out." Sandy and BeLynda blink hard looking at Regina then at each other taking big gulps of their wine.

"So you don't think that it's a coincidence that this car is always there? I mean, it is a popular car, right?" BeLynda's heart is beating hard. She can almost hear it. Regina shakes her head "no." "So where have you been seeing this car that has you so perturbed?"

"I've seen it outside the house and I think they were taking pictures of it. Then I've seen it at the grocery store a few times. I started thinking that maybe the shit that went on at the Poconos might be related. One time after class I saw it drive by the house. But I mean, around here just about everybody has at least a three-car garage so I thought that it was maybe a neighbor." Sandy and BeLynda are looking at her weary, listening. Colleen is frowning because Regina left out an important piece of information. Regina catches the look but she isn't finish talking. She wanted to lighten the blow a little. "The night the car drove past the house, was the same night I had seen it sitting in the parking lot after class. It was idling with the lights off. Like they were watching me. Watching us. I don't know."

"What?!" Sandy yells and drops her drink out of her hand. They all jump up to get something to wipe it up. "Damn, I'm sorry Regina. My hand gave out. Let me get this up. I'm so sorry." Sandy runs over to the bar and grabs a handful of paper towels running back over to the spot to blot it. The other Ladies sit back down and Regina continues.

"Before that night, I had been seeing a shadow or a silhouette or something at the door while we were in class like we were being watched. I started thinking they were watching me because every time I would look at the door, it would jump back. I thought I was imagining it. Now, I am not so sure."

"Wait … did you say you were seeing a shadow at the door while we were in class?" BeLynda tuned in to that part precisely.

"Yea, I'm sorry I didn't mention this earlier. I wanted to wait until I knew for sure. But Stan has been pressing me to tell y'all now." Regina looks at her friends with watery eyes.

Colleen noticed how BeLynda asked her question. She leans in, placing her elbows on her knees and responds. "What's the matter Bee? You asked that as if you have something to share. What you got? We talking and we need to know everything. What you know?"

"Well, during the class we had on the breathing, when I threw up," she pauses as if to say, *Yea it was me*, as if they didn't know, "I saw a shadow at the door. I thought my eyes were playing tricks on me since I was all in the zone. And that is the only reason why I didn't jump up and leave out. I didn't know what was going on. And now Regina, you tell me that you had been seeing this all the damn time?!" BeLynda's voice raises an octave and she is getting nervous. Colleen looks at her with a tilted head saying to herself, *Bitch are you serious?*

"So you've seen this shit too and you didn't say anything either," Colleen asks smugly. Looking at BeLynda and then at Regina, she asks, "What … y'all walking around on stupid? Like a deer in headlights? What the fuck?!"

Slowly raising her hand as if she is in elementary school, not sure she should answer, Sandy says, "Well, okay … I guess you can get mad at me too because I saw it the other day while we were in the pole dancing class. It was there, I looked, it jumped back to not be noticed. I saw it a few times that night. Then it walked away like it was disappointed or something. It was almost as if the body build was familiar though." Colleen turns to look at her with her mouth open. *What the fuck am I doing when all of this is going on? I guess I never thought to look back at the fucking door.*

Rubbing her forehead out of frustration Colleen speaks a few octaves higher than normal but not necessarily yelling. "You've got to be fuckin' kidding me! The two of you have seen this motherfuckin' thing too and NO ONE said anything? Just going around saying it is all in your fuckin' freakin' mind? What is wrong with y'all?" She looks at her friends waiting to see if someone is going to provide a smart logical answer but no one says anything.

Colleen stands up putting her hands on her hips pacing the carpeted floor. Sandy bends down to check on the wet spot on the carpet, switching out the wet paper towels for more. Colleen looks at her yelling with her eyes closed, "Leave the fuckin' spot alone! I'm fucking pissed at all of you right now. What is the matter with y'all? We are women and shit like that shouldn't go ignored or brushed off! Regina you do have a man living with you." Looking at Sandy and BeLynda she says, "But *you* two bitches and *me* do not. We go home every night solo … alone … by our damn motherfuckin selves. Am I the only sane one here? Fuck we don't smoke no more but right now … I need a hit of some bomb ass cess dealing with y'all asses. Stan got some in his office Regina?" They look at Colleen.

They have no idea Stan is at the door eavesdropping. He was walking past the door when he heard Colleen yell again. He is leaning up against the wall listening and agreeing with Colleen and shaking his head at how the actions just sounds so idiotic. He sees Maria coming in his direction which is towards the Maid Quarters. He gets off the wall and proceeds to walk back to his office smiling at Maria in passing. Maria smiles as they pass each other but looks inquisitive as she gets closer to the theatre door wondering why Stan was listening. She keeps going because she knows he might be watching her.

In the theatre, the conversation continues. "No, you're not the only sane one here. At least not right now. What has gotten into you Colleen?" Colleen tries to regroup but she is too gone to snap back that fast. Her mannerism shows she is back in her old stomping grounds … the hood. She is in protect mode. "And no he doesn't have any of that shit in his office. He better not."

Colleen looks at her saying out loud, "Aww, you don't know your husband. That's cute." She starts pacing the floor again swinging her arms as if she just got finished lifting heavy weights. She is ready to fight somebody. Her hands are itching to be around a nigga's neck. *These bitches got this damn game twisted. They must've been under a rock for the past ten years.*

Regina looks at the back of Colleen shocked. Her friend is sounding just like her husband. She jumps up asking Colleen, "What the fuck did you just say?"

Colleen turns around looking at her. "What you mean? I just said a lot!!" Colleen gives her a look that says, *You better sit your dumb ass down! You really ain't gonna go there with me! You are my friend but your husband will be taking your ass to the emergency room tonight!*

Regina is no punk. They were some rumbling ass sistas back in the day but this is her friend so she sits down. She just doesn't know how making that choice was the best for her. Colleen sits down too squeezing her eyes shut tight letting out a big sigh.

"Look, I'm just real passionate about this right now. We may have gotten out of the hood but I'm sure all of you saw when a nigga was on the creep to do some damage. And y'all just dismiss that shit? Shadows … black cars with illegal tint?" Looking at her friends she continues, "I don't take shit like that lightly! Whoever it is could've caught any of us slippin'!"

"Hmmp, that's an understatement," says BeLynda gulping down the rest of her wine getting up to pour another glass. Colleen just looks at her.

"Lene, you talking like you could've done something about the damn shadow at the fuckin' door! All that aggressive ass bullshit you talking. What were you gonna do?" Colleen just looks at her and Sandy feels a chill come over her. She turns away from Colleen's glare lifting her glass up to her mouth trying not to spill it on herself. Her hand is shaking. She has never seen that look in Colleen's eyes before.

Regina looks at Colleen asking, "So you gonna curse us out some more? Damn Lene, we didn't know. How you not see it? I guess we're not the only ones that don't want anyone seeing us doing our *private classes.*" Looking at BeLynda and Sandy she says, "But Stan told me to just go about my normal routine as if nothing is wrong."

"Oh damn, Stan knows about this?! Oh, Regina, I'm so sorry. I know how hard you worked to get him in a better place.

What did that do to him?" BeLynda thinks about it for a minute and says, "Oh! That's why he has been coming in here checking on us? He wanted to see how we were taking the news?" Regina shakes her head "yes."

"Why do you say that Bee? What did you know about Stan back then?" Regina asks waiting for an answer. She doesn't receive one. Looking over at Sandy, her eyes are wide open as if she knows something too. *What the hell was my then boyfriend, now husband in to back then?* "Well, one thing for sure, he is not too happy about it and yes he is pissed. He already took into the west wing."

Colleen straightens up listening. "The west wing?" Colleen asks with wide eyes. Regina looks at her. "Why the hell did he go there Gee Gee? What did he do in there?"

"Yea, he did. And you know about the west wing Colleen?" Regina notices her alert appearance.

"Oh nah. I mean nothing other than you saying that he has an office down there and no one is allowed in there. That says to me that he has his other shit down there. So I figured if he went down there, that means this is some serious shit … just as I thought." She looks at Regina shaking her head.

"The west wing? What is that? Damn, we ain't been all over this house yet? I thought we covered the entire house." Sandy asks looking back and forth at Regina and Colleen.

"You've seen the house. It's down there by the guest quarters. When you went in there, nothing had been done to it yet. Once he finished putting his boxes, new furniture, and his gold phone in, he had a lock put on the door. I told him I wanted to see how he decorated it, and he said, 'It's good babe,' gave me a kiss and kept going." They did find laughter in that.

"So what do y'all plan for us to do now? Lord knows I don't feel like walking around looking like walking paranoia. So are we all just supposed to continue on with our normal routines like Stan suggests?" BeLynda takes three sips of her wine.

"Yea, why not? Right now, they seem to have a liking to Regina. But I wanted her to tell y'all so everyone will know to be on alert for anything out of the ordinary. There are many things that are out of the ordinary that we take for granted but once you are aware of some shit, you start paying attention a little closer."

"Yea, like me in the damn grocery store buying fuckin' fruit for a private sexual enhancement class. I couldn't stop looking at what the women were picking up in the produce section." They all laugh out loud giving each other high fives.

"Ain't that a trip how you tend to zoom into things that may not have looked strange at first? So that's why y'all need to pay attention to your surroundings. From here on out, until this shit is over and after it is over, if anything appears weird, tell your girls about it. Aiight?" They shake their heads agreeing with Colleen.

"So Monday class is a continuation of the pole dancing right?" Sandy says yawning trying to change and lighten the subject.

"Yeap. I see everyone was having fun this evening. I did really like class. Especially when Candice got up there and performed for us. I was too through. Girlfriend worked that pole and body like she was ready to strip for her man." Colleen says and they laugh. "And then that Kemira chic got up there and did her thing saying she has never done that before. That bitch was lying. I bet you right now, we can see her as the 'special of the night' on somebody's damn stage."

"Oh you thought she lied about having done that before," BeLynda asks Colleen.

"Girl, will you cut it out? You take everybody's word for the truth, huh?" Colleen just looks at BeLynda with no expression.

"Oh, absolutely not but I mean if she would be a 'special of the night' why would she be in those damn classes with us? I'd expect her to be teaching it?" BeLynda says getting up to stretch.

"Maybe she wants to see what she can learn and incorporate it into her routine. Who knows? Honestly speaking though, I believed her too," says Regina.

"Yea, I can see that. Sandy, did you believe her too?

She smiles scratching her head showing that she is guilty of believing the Lady too. "Sort of, kind of. Yea, I did. I didn't look all into her response like that Colleen."

"Sure you didn't. Just like none of y'all asses thought it was important enough to tell me or each other about the damn shadow at the door." They all look at her and say nothing.

"Colleen, you took the tag number down to that Charger. Did you find out anything yet?"

"Yeah, it comes back to a Traylando Daniels. I don't have an address yet. I will let you know when I get that." *I just might have to pay his ass a fuckin' visit. He done fucked with the wrong district.*

Chapter Fourteen

14

"Aww fuck! Shit! That's right, suck that dick girl! Damn how old are you again?!" She smiles looking up at him with half of his dick in her mouth slurping loud and sloppy. "Slow it down for me. I ain't tryin' to buss yet. I want to enjoy everything. The look, feel, and sounds. Nurse it for me." She slows down and his toes curl in his shoes while he massages his balls. She moves his hand and picks up where he leaves off.

Ring! Ring!

Now who in the fuck is calling me while I'm getting some muhfuckin' bomb ass head? Picking up his phone, flipping it open, he looks at the name and number, pressing "talk" on the phone. He doesn't say anything, too much of being in a trance watching the young woman slob him down. She's making wet slurping sounds. They can be heard through the phone.

"Hello?!" Silence. "Rennie! Are you there?!" He hears low moaning and sounds that more slurping sounds heard when eating a popsicle. "Ay! Look, I ain't call to hear that shit man. Tell the trick to take a break!" The voice is heated from the disrespect.

"Yea, what's up my nigga? I started not to answer but I figured if you were calling, I needed to see what was up. Now … what can I do for you at this inconvenient time?" Rennie grunts into the phone.

"I called to tell you that I have been watching our brotha for a few days and you wouldn't believe what I saw this weekend."

With that statement, Rennie immediately stopped enjoying the young woman's mouth motioning for her to stop and go do something else. She gets up off her knees and walks over to the bar to fix her a drink. She licks the rim of the glass and Rennie's dick jerks a few times knowing the pleasure it was just giving him. "Now, this is Monday night. If you saw it this weekend, why the fuck are you calling me now?"

"Man, look I called you didn't I? Don't be on no damn crazy shit. I'm not with the short man syndrome so shut the fuck up with your short ass."

"Yea, well I might be short but the dick goes a long way nigga." Rennie didn't like that remark. He knows he is the shortest of all of his brothers and he didn't need Rick to be pointing that out right now. "So what did you see that was important enough to call me yet it wasn't urgent enough to call me as soon as you saw it?"

"Well, I know you told me that Ray had dinner dates set up with that chick for Tuesdays, Wednesdays, and Saturdays but he did something a little different this time."

"A little different like what? Keep talkin'." Rennie takes off his shoes and pants getting up to walk over to the bar half naked. He pours Gin in a glass taking a sip watching the woman bend over to give him a look of her hairy pouty lips from behind.

"Ray had a car pick her up for breakfast Saturday morning."

"For breakfast? At his muhfuckin' house? Oh yea?!" He was heated but he was busy concentrating on the bushy mound peaking from under the woman's butt cheeks. "Maybe he decided to switch it up a little bit to throw her off."

"Nigga, we talkin' about Ray. The brotha that hasn't had any female company in a minute. If he is following one of your plans, he isn't going to take a detour dumb ass. Ay! Look! I already told you that I didn't call to hear no shit you doing with Ol Girl, so I don't want you to be lost in whatever the fuck she is doing over there while I am talking to you. Focus!"

"I'm focus! Fuck! It's been a minute aiight?! Hell, I got all this ass and pussy over here teasing me and shit while I'm on this fuckin' phone. She bending over showing me shit."

"Yea, well sorry that most women ain't into short guys. I guess you gotta walk around advertising what you packin' then little nigga." Rick thinks it is funny and gets a good laugh out what he just said. "But, yea, she came over for breakfast in her regular getup. That says to me that it was a comfortable 'let's get to know each other better' invite. You know Ray ain't invited no other woman over to his house. They were in there for a while too. Then they left together in the evening."

"Maybe he hit it this morning. But, okay, they left for dinner, right? The normal plan? I mean, his ass got the money and time to do that type of shit but right now, I am still stuck on the morning shit. I know Ray. We all know Ray. That muhfucka cooked her ass a big fuckin' breakfast. That might be good. He is reeling her in."

"You don't know Ray well then. If he cooked her breakfast, then that means, he is diggin' her bruh. He ain't reeling her in for *you*. He is reeling her in for *self*. You might need to take another course or something. What you think?"

Damn! I knew that nigga was liking her ass. I could tell how all of a sudden he wanted to defend that bitch Regina and tried to get out of seeing her friend. I wasn't trying to go with the other bitch that I had Rufus on. Maybe I should have put him to the other bitch. He probably wouldn't have gotten so fuckin' caught up. Shit!!

"Well, you must've seen something else that made you think what you're thinkin'. What was it?"

"Well, yea they did go to dinner as they normally do on Saturday evenings but … they made a stop first."

"Wait, first, how do you know all what you told me already?"

"I went to see Mama and I noticed there was someone with Ray walking around in the Grand Dining-Room. I asked Mama who was Ray's company to see if she knew. She didn't know he had company so she called him. He told her Sandy was over for breakfast. He must've told Mama about her Rennie."

"Oh word?! How you know Mama knows about her?" Rennie swallows the rest of the gin and pours more in his glass. The woman is doing all kinds of stunts to get him off the phone but he is not paying any attention to her splits and numerous "six o'clock" in the air. He is very much into what Rick is saying.

"When she got off the phone, she was excited. She said that Ray had invited the girl he likes over for breakfast. He told her he had to go because he wanted to give her all of his attention and he would call her later. She waved at him from the porch and I saw both of them wave back. Thank goodness I had parked around the back because I know if he knew I was there, he wouldn't have said all of that. I made the mistake of frowning and Mama threw a shoe at me saying that if some bullshit was going on, she was going to end it."

"Fuck!! That nigga played his hand with his fuckin' emotions written all over his damn face. I should've known he was gonna be the one to fuck up everythang! Ay, we need to regroup *NOW*! I need to call Ray like *ASAP* bruh! He is about to really fuck up!"

"Nah, no we don't. Because YOU are about to get fucked up! By the hands of Mama Rachel!" Rick laughs out loud again. "I bet anything she is about to call a meeting with us and you will be sitting in the hot seat. That's why I don't be fuckin' with you and your crazy ass schemes. I don't know why you keep tryin' when you know Mama is gonna find out and shut your short ass down! I got enough woman troubles and I don't need to add Mama to it. I love my life and millions. Apparently you don't and you're going about it all wrong."

Think Rennie think! I don't feel like no meetings with Mama. I don't feel like hearing her fuckin' mouth. If she knows, she is going to put more than her two cents in and I don't feel like getting no visits from her or that detective friend of hers. But I need to get that bitch back! After I get some of that pussy and a few dances out of her uppity ass.

"Say bruh, what you over there thinking about? Or has Ol Girl got back to her mouth action. Then again, it is mighty quiet over there." Rick's phone vibrates and he looks at the screen to see who it is. "Aww shit! Yea buddy! It's on now! Rennie you better get ready because you are about to be hit with a mutha … fuckin' … EARTHQUAKE!!"

"Oh, I'm good. What you talkin' 'bout Rick? What fuckin' earthquake? Ain't nobody 'bout to fuck with me! They must don't know who they fuckin' wit if they try it!"

Rick laughs smugly. "Oh yea? Well, you can talk that shit all you want. But the earthquake I'm talkin' 'bout starts with an 'M' and ends with an 'a'. Our Mama just called me." Rick's phone beeps twice letting him know she left a message. "She just left a message bruh. That can only mean two things."

Fuck! Dammit! "And what are those two damn things Rick? You seem to be enjoying this shit! I'm about to explode! That bitch needs to feel my wrath! She slapped me and I ain't with the hittin' shit unless it's when I am fuckin'. And I'm the one doing the muhfuckin' hittin' then. She and her husband will feel my muhfuckin' wrath. Believe that … on our Daddy's grave, they will feel it!!"

There is silence on both ends of the phone.

"Hey you said they made a stop before they went to dinner? Where did they go?"

Rick snickers saying, "Oh yes, I said that. Bruh, they stopped at a boutique and when they came out, Rick had a shopping bag but 'Ol Girl had on a nice sexy ass dress. That means he had her outfit in the bag and that he spent money on what she was wearing." Rick then scratches his curly mane and frowns like the sun is in his eyes yet it is seven o'clock in the evening on a December winter night. "Wait … wait … hole-up bruh. Let me make sure I heard you right. Did you just say the word 'husband'? *'Husband'*?! This bitch that you are scheming on is a 'Mrs.'? Huh, Rennie?! She's *married*?! The bitch is *married*?! Have you lost your damn mind!!!! Nigga! Are you listening to yourself?! Do Ray and Rufus know this shit? Oh, my … GOD!! Man, you got me cursing all loud around my kids and shit!! Rennie Daniels! What the fuck, man?!" Rick is furious and extremely disappointed.

"Oh, you heard me right. Yea, she is married. *MARRIED* with a capital M! Ray knows it. Rufus doesn't though. But that doesn't exempt her from revenge. She slapped me! Like I disgust her and shit. She ain't better than me! I am fine, got money, and got it going on just like her square ass husband! She is gonna pay and her husband will pay for what I plan to do to her ass. When I get finished with her beautiful uppity ass, he will be divorcing her. Every time he looks at her, he will see my face and what I did to her. NO BITCH! And I do mean NO BITCH slaps me without me wanting her to and get away with it!

"Aww, man. Ay bruh, listen to me. Let it go! She got a husband man. What do you know about him? If she said 'No" then take it at that. Stop thinking that because you got money that every woman you want is gonna kiss the ground you walk on. Rennie … this ain't good man. You going after a man's WIFE?! And you don't know anything about him?! What the fuck! You trippin'. You're on some real bullshit with this one. Hell, did you do your homework before your fuckin' ego kicked in?"

"Homework? I don't need to do no damn homework. I'm grown. School and play time is over! I don't need to know who her husband is. He is the one that hired me to be her fuckin' trainer. It ain't hard to find out who he is. He is just a nigga with businesses and money, living high on the hog and probably no streets smarts whatsoever. I'll beat her ass, fuck her, make her strip and dance for me showing what she learns in those sex classes, and he will pay to get her back … and then divorce her because she will be all used up when she comes home, in a few months. He probably was her first which means she ain't had no other dick but his. He looks like one of those arrogant ass type of muhfuckin niggas that walk around bragging on his woman being pure and shit when he got with her. I'll teach her to keep her hands to herself."

"Damn! Bruh, you are gone off of this shit! If Mama knows that your plans are to do harm to a female, you are in for it. If she knows she is married, she is gonna check her husband out first. Either way, if she knows Rennie …."

"Yea you said it … *IF* she knows and I doubt she does. She would've called me by now about fifty times a day laying into my ass. As a matter of fact, she would have been knocking on my damn door,"

"Ay, look, why don't I take a look at some of the other female clients you have to see who you should be checking for? Okay? I'm telling you, this isn't feeling right to me. Damn … she is married, bruh? What is his name? Maybe I can check on some things for you."

"Man, I'm Rennie Daniels. I don't need you to be checking on no damn female's husband. Especially not his ass. Have I ever needed your damn help in the 'woman' department? This is not a charity case and don't try to pacify me. I created my plan, I have set it in motion, and right now, you don't need to be on no feeling sorry for your brotha type of shit. I'm aiight. She didn't want me on her own. I will make her want me, for two damn months. He'll lose money – while he is gathering up money to get her back - worrying about her safety."

"*Man*, what is her husband's name? At least tell me that. And I know who the hell you are and the Rennie Daniels I know to be my brotha ain't that desperate. Crazy, but not desperate."

"The punk nigga's name is Stan Wooten. I ain't like that nigga when he first stepped to me talking about his wife wanted to work out but she didn't wanna take gym classes. He stepped to me in his thousands of dollars suit and shoes and shit then rolled out by his chauffer. I got the same type of money. Fuck him."

"Stan Wooten? Wooten … Wooten … damn that name sounds familiar. I'm not sure where I might've heard that name but I will definitely find out." Rick's phone vibrates again. "Damn, this is Mama calling me back. She is serious about something and I really don't feel like being bothered with *yo* shit. Let me talk to her and I will call you back. Okay, fuck, she is gonna have to leave a message again because I wanna ask you something."

"Damn, she calling you again? Fuck *man*! She must know something. What did you wanna ask me?" Rennie is so pissed and turned off, he tells the young woman to go up to his bedroom. He would've told her to go home but after this phone call, he is going to need to pound in some tight wet pussy.

"You said something about her going to sex classes. What you mean by that and how do you know what kind of classes they are? Who you have following her around Rennie?"

"Yea, she and her friends take these classes on Mondays and they are some type of sex classes. Some enrichment shit, I assume. Ray has been following her for me. He say the classes aren't bad though. He said that they just do things to enhance their techniques. I guess to blow their man's mind or some shit. So, I plan on her showing me several moves before I'm done."

"Wow! Are you serious?! Sex classes?!" Rick laughs out loud. "And you expect to win her over, while she is trying to make sure her husband doesn't have the need to fall into some other pussy? You expect that after all of the mean shit you got planned for her, she is going to look at you as the love of her life. You are a piece of work. Where did you get your imagination from? The Wonderful World of Disney? Nigga wake up!" Rick snaps his fingers in the phone three times so Rennie can hear them. "This ain't gonna turn out like Lady and Tramp. You ain't gonna win this race. Mama is gonna take your ass down and your brothas will not be there to fix you."

"This has absolutely nothing to do with my goddamn imagination. I know my mouth was talkin' to her. I know my lips were ready for that damn kiss. My hands were touching that body. And my muhfuckin' face felt the sting of that slap she landed on my damn face. She will find out what my reality is real soon."

"You were touching her body through spotting her during fuckin' training Rennie! You spittin' a lot of shit bruh and I know you believe what you are sayin' but I'm tellin' you … if Mama knows or finds out …" Rennie sighs, "I am so glad I have no parts in this other than seeing what I saw this weekend. You've always been hard-headed but I believe you need to listen to me on this. You too old for this shit. But hey, I got his name and I need to call Mama back before she is knocking on my damn door. I always love to see my Mama but not when the topic is you."

"Yea, well, you call her back and see what she is talkin' 'bout. Call me back when you get off the phone with her and not a minute later. Kiss the kids for me. Tell them Uncle Rennie says, 'I love you.' Felicia already knows how I feel about her so there is no need to tell her shit. I got some pussy to dig into."

"I will call you when I finish talking to her. I will tell the kids what you said and as for my woman, keep your thoughts to yourself. At least she is mine and not some other nigga's wife … nigga." Rick laughs rubbing it in.

"Oh you really claim her as your woman now? Y'all got three kids and the oldest is … ten, right? Yet she doesn't bare the 'Daniels' name? Please. Like I said before …."

"Whateva Rennie. I'll let you get back to your low self-esteem trick. I wouldn't want her to miss her curfew. I'm sure tomorrow is a school day for her." Rick was pissed. "Fuck, I will propose when I am ready. She is the mother of my three children and she lives here with me. She doesn't have to carry my last name. She has everything she needs and wants. Marriage doesn't have to be in the near future for me."

"Oh, okay. We hittin' below the belt now? Felicia slept with how many of your brothas before she ended up with you? Hell, your kids just might be your nephews my nigga. So don't feel yourself too fuckin' hard aiight?"

"Fuck you! That's the story *you* tell. Ain't no one else said anything like that. What's the matter Rennie? She was another one that turned your ass down? Does it hurt that she didn't want you? That she wanted me? Your snide remarks are getting old. Just like you said, it's been ten years … I won't ignore it anymore without an ass beatin'."

"Oooh, I gotta go. She done wrapped her lips around me again. She couldn't wait for this King Kong any longer. That's it baby. Daddy will be real good to ya. Aiight bruh, go see what Felicia got lined up for ya." Rennie laughs and growls at the woman's deep throating action and closes his cellphone.

Rick looks at his phone saying out loud, "You sorry ass mutha - …" and the kids yell at him, "Daddy, you not supposed to be using those words!"

Ring! Ring!

"Hello? It's about time! What were you doing that you couldn't answer your mother's calls? Were you playing with the kids? I know you weren't in there making no more babies with that damn Felicia! I know she has three of my grandchildren but if you ain't gonna marry her, let her go. There must be something about her that prevents you from proposing." *Hmmp, your Mama already knows what type of woman she is, so no need to sugar coat it for me.*

"Hey, Mama. Give me one of those kisses that I didn't get when I was with you Saturday." Rachel blows Rick a big kiss through the phone. "Mmm, thank you Mama, I needed that. I wasn't ignoring you. I was on the phone with one of your other sons and what he was telling me was just blowing me. But, you have my full attention now. What's up?"

"Oh really? That good … or that bad, hunh? Who were you talking to? That damn trouble-maker son of mine? I tell you, the older he gets the more moronic he acts. Mmmp, mmmp, mmmp."

"Now, none of your sons are saints, I'm sure you know that," Rick laughs. "So which one would you be referring to when you ask the question like that?" Rick asks his mother facetiously.

"Don't play games with me boy. Only one of my sons would carry around that adjective. So you know I'm talking about Rennie's simple ass. Were you talking about him or not?"

"First, let's get this out of the way. Mother Dear, what were you doing before you called me and before I called you back? Let me make sure my mother is all right. Did you eat all three meals today? Did you do anything interesting today? Don't be stressing out over there about Rennie. Yes, I was talking to him." Rick wanted to feel his mother out to see if she had in fact done some research on anyone today.

"Yea, I had breakfast, lunch, and dinner. I could stand a little snack right now though. I will get one when I get off the phone with you. Sooo, you were talking to Rennie while I was calling you? I could've been over here having a heart attack and apparently, what he was saying was either more important or juicier."

"Yes, I was talking to him and it was both important and juicy as well as crazy. He done gave me a headache with his disrespectful crap."

"Ah, just as I thought, you were talking to him. What was important, juicy, and crazy? Oh I know his ass can be disrespectful. That's why he's always in some damn mess. Who called who? If you called him, that means you know something and you were checking in with his ass."

Dammit! She don't miss a beat! "I called him Mama and I wasn't ready for all that he had to say."

"Oh, is that right? Rennie, who always seems to have some type of pandemonium going on in his life, and you weren't ready for what he had to say, huh? Well, you know I don't play clue and we aren't face-to-face for me to be playing charades, so get to speaking Rickie."

"How about you tell me what you called me for first? It had to be urgent since you called twice and I think you left me a voicemail the first time. All I can say is that he is on one this time and I am glad he didn't call me to be a part of it. Sooo, what do you know Mama?"

"I too know that he is on some bullshit. I know that his plot involves him getting back at that woman that slapped him and she should've slapped his ass because he deserved it. When I see him, I'm gonna slap him my damn self. He recruited Ray and Rufus to get next to two of her other friends to help his ass with easier access to her. And Ray really doesn't want to be involved because he likes the woman he was to get next to. I also know that Rennie's vendetta is against a damn married woman, which of course he didn't do any damn homework."

"Damn, is that all you know Mama," Rick asks sarcastically. "That is a lot of info you have acquired. Who told you all of that? Surely you didn't get any of that from the horse's mouth."

"Don't worry about who told me. I know the woman's name is Regina and her husband's name is Stan. I also ran both of their names and her friends' names by my friend. He hasn't gotten back to me yet but he did say the name sounded familiar."

"No shit?! Ooh, I'm sorry … I mean word?! When Rennie told me, I said to him that the name sounded familiar to me too. I told him to let it go. But he is adamant about going through with this shi- … I mean stuff. I don't like it and I told him that I was gonna check up on who her husband is too. He didn't seem to be too concerned thinking that her husband is a nerd or wuss with money. He ain't hearing me and maybe when I do find out something by putting my ear to the streets, I find out enough for him to go sit in a corner."

"Boy, stop all that cursing while you're talking to me. I know you just got off the phone with Rennie, so it's hard to not show the frustration. But yea, the corner is right because if my friend says the name sounds familiar, her husband is nothing to play with. This man has a big ass house, expensive ass cars, and he also has a driver. That's says old money, new money or both. Hold on a minute, I gotta stir my cabbage."

"Hmmp, sounds like her husband can be one of Ray's friends … or on the same level as Ray. I heard that Ray told Rennie he couldn't compete. But I'm gonna check him out too. Your friends may can get you the basic information you are looking for but I can find out deeper shit. I don't even know why you still call them when you need to know something. I won't take as long as they do. And contacting them can start something that you might not want to be finished Mama. But … if they say his name sounds familiar, then he may be 'connected' in some way. Or may have been connected in some way. This can create chaos for others that had no idea they were potential targets of Rennie. Do you understand what I am saying?"

"Yea, it does sound like he is in the same league as Ray and that's probably why he told Rennie's immature ass that she is out of his league. I hear you, I hear you! I didn't think about it like that. I was just trying to stop Rennie. But, okay, I know y'all have your street terms but what do you mean he may be connected?"

"Connected as in, he may have money but it may have started out as street money and he used it to get out of the streets turning legit. I'm pissed that Rennie didn't do his homework first. Maybe if he had, he wouldn't have started this crap and we won't be alarmed. If this man is connected somehow to the streets, and if Rennie's plan goes into fruition more than it is … all of our lives will be in jeopardy. This man apparently has been living his life way under the radar and you can be opening a can of worms because of Rennie. He won't discriminate to get his wife back and if anyone decides to go after you … Mama, I'm tellin' you!"

"Calm down Ricardo. Calm down. Ain't no one gonna be doing anything to me. Whatever you find out, you better tell me first. If I find out before you, I will call a meeting. I am hoping that I do find out first so that all of us know who we are dealing with and we can all persuade your simple ass brother … my dumb ass son … that he needs to stop this bullshit before it gets worse. So just calm down. I am going to be all right and I am not going to be burying any of my sons behind Rennie. Rennie will be buried first, I promise you that even if I have to be the one to create his funeral." Both Rick and Rachel both shook from chills at the thought of that happening.

"Nah, you calm down Mama. Once we find out who this cat is, I am sure it will be one or the other. He is either no one we need to be concerned with, and we can work on talking Rennie out of his dumb master plan. Or … he is someone well connected that we need to be concerned about, and you can talk Rennie into aborting his plan. Either way, he needs to just forget about her and all the mess he has planned for her."

"Oh, so you know some of the logistics? What does your beloved brother have planned for this woman? Please, let me hear it."

"Well, I'm not sure about everything but he said something about beating her up, sleeping with her, and then making her show what she does in those classes, and then when he is done with her, he figures the man will divorce her because he will see his face every time he looks at her … oh and um … he will pay to get her back."

"I see. So this man-boy of mine plans to beat, rape, ridicule, and ransom her out hunh? And with his mother still living, he thinks that is going to happen? I'm trying to figure out how after all of that, his mind tells him that she is going to want him. If I have dismantled all of his dirty schemes against the men he wanted to get back at, what makes him think after knowing what I know that I am going to just go on living allowing him to do anything to that woman? Hell, to any woman?"

"Ay, Mama, I'm just telling you what he said to me. He was hot under the collar when he said all that stuff too. So the only one that will be able to get through to him will be you. Ray doesn't want to be bothered and he has the attention of the main friend. And from the shoe you threw at me, I take it that you want him to be happy … with her." Rick laughs.

"Oh, he can be hot under the collar and when I finish with him, he can be boiling under his damn collar. When I threaten to take his money, the nigga can be on *fire* under his collar. He can be in jail because I will turn his ass in. Or … he can be six feet under. Those will be his only choices. He's my son and I love him with all my heart but I will not stand by and watch him destroy that woman. He can be completely broke and disowned if he thinks he is going to abuse this 'Regina' woman. He knows his father wouldn't have allowed this and I won't either. He keeps forgetting that I was the power behind his father."

"Yea, I know Mama. I know. I was the quiet one, and I watched y'all. That's why I don't mess around when it comes to you." He laughs. "I enjoy living … well-off and comfortable. Thanks for my millions Mother Rachel." They both laugh at what he said.

"Boy, you are so silly. You are welcome and I hope you are being wise about your money. I expect my grandchildren to be comfortable when they finish college. As for Felicia … she wasn't my choice for you but you chose her. You had your reasons and I will respect them. Just don't let her live up in there off of you as your girlfriend … or the mother of your children. Make her your wife or let her go. You have more than enough to put them up in a nice size house and live comfortable."

"I know that Mama. I know. As they say, it is cheaper to keep her, right? I'm not with that child support stuff. Plus, she makes me happy and I have no problems making her happy." He realizes the children are playing in the room where he is. "Ay, y'all go somewhere with all that playing. I'm talking to Grandma. She says, 'hello.'"

"Oh, they are in there with you while we are talking? Were they really playing? Or were they being inquisitive? You know better than to be talking like that around those children. Then they go tell their lazy ass Mama. I already had to check her once on running her mouth."

"They're gone now Mama. And I do believe they were playing. You heard all that noise. What were they gonna hear over all that racket? They have nothing to tell Felicia. They weren't being inquisitive, as you said. Using those big words. Why not just say 'nosy'? You are a trip woman."

"Ok, good. Yea I heard all that noise but they may have mastered the talent of multi-tasking. With her insecurities, she may have taught them how to do that while they are in the room with you. You just be careful, I still don't trust her. And if you are mentioning child support when talking about her, then it must've already come up in a conversation. Well, she can forget about that. You take good care of those children and her ass. She won't be getting four thousand dollars a month. So I suggest you start talking about helping her start a business or something."

"Huh? Four thousand dollars a month? In child support? How do you know how much it would be? Who the hell pays that kind of money?"

"I did my homework my dear. And remember she has three. I know exactly who and what she is. Opportunist whores don't get to live like that off our hard earned money. The children didn't ask to be here. But her … HELL NO!! So you stop forgetting who your mother is. Now you go see what the children are up to. I have a few calls to make."

Chapter Fifteen

15

"Hello, hello, hello Ladies. How is everyone doing? How has your week been going so far? I haven't been doing too much. Just staying close to home. So close that I had my stylist come do my hair on Tuesday and the nail tech came over this morning to do my hands and feet." Regina gave BeLynda and Regina the normal greeting.

"Hey Girlie. I'm doing just fine. I can't complain about anything today. It wouldn't change anything if I did, right?" BeLynda responds back. She notices that Colleen and Regina came in together, which is odd. "Oh, Colleen you went to pick up Gee Gee? That's a new one. Sandy, what, you had something to do after work?"

"Nah, I came straight from work. Lene told me that she was gonna get Regina, and I said okay. Hell, it saved me some gas." Sandy looks at Regina saying, "No offense Gee Gee. I'm just saying."

"Oh none taken Girlie. I understand. Especially since most of the time we are driving our own cars, regardless of you coming by the house to change. Maybe we can take turns driving. How's that?"

"Oh, nah I'm cool with driving separate cars. That way I can go straight home after my massage. I be way too relaxed when it's time go."

"Well, I'm glad that everyone seems to be acting normal. Particularly since we had that conversation Monday night. How is everyone really feeling? Or is the fact that the car is following Regina around and not you?" Colleen looks at Sandy and BeLynda's expressions to see if she can read them.

Waving her off, BeLynda says, "Oh, I'm fine chile. It has nothing to do with me not being the target. We were told to act normal, right? And that's what I'm doing. I keep busy, have company, and I make sure that I watch my surroundings. So don't start nothing, you hear? I don't need to start being paranoid."

"Hey, I'm just asking. You of all people, I thought would be jumpy and walking in here with shades, a wig, and a hat on." Colleen laughs. "Better yet, I thought you would pull up in her business van instead of your car. But, okay. I see you. You got the nerves under control. What about you Sandy? How are you doing?"

"Girl, please. I am doing fine too. As a matter of fact, I am doing great!! Yea, we had that conversation Monday night but I am still living high off of my weekend. So I can't complain about anything. I don't like the shit that is going on with my girl but I am here and ready for the bullshit." Sandy smiles nervously. Colleen notices.

Regina smiles at both BeLynda and Sandy appreciating that they have gone on with their week as normal and haven't allowed her issue to consume them. She gives them both another hug and kiss on both cheeks, grabbing their hands squeezing them tightly showing strong love in her eyes.

"Oh okay," Colleen says approvingly shaking her head at their responses. "Well, then give me some love too. I don't recall getting my hugs and kisses when I walked in. You know I'm serious about that shit, for real." They all laugh. BeLynda and Sandy give Colleen what she asks for.

"They sort of crowded in here today. I hope there won't be any delays in us going upstairs to change. I'm ready to get into my robe, chill, and play catch-up. Hell, this has been a day for me at work. One of these days, I am gonna be able to walk into that office and pack my shit and walk right back out saying nothing. Well, I may jump up on my desk and say, 'Kiss my ass motherfuckas!'" They all laugh out loud at Sandy. Everyone at the receptionist's desk look over at the crew and smile continuing what they were doing.

"Damn, that bad hunh? I can't relate or imagine and sometimes I wish that I could but … not today." They all laugh at Regina. "I'm serious. I try to understand Sandy's plight but I don't. One minute she talks about how her supervisor is so sweet and then the next she talks about how she wants to slap a co-worker. That is not a good balance but I guess since she likes her supervisor, it makes the day a little better."

"Yea, I can see where Sandy is coming from. Granted I only worked in an office for a hot minute before I resigned. Those co-workers can get on your last nerve. I can recall going home a few times frustrated with my work day. But Sandy maybe …"

Lyla walks up to them interrupting their conversation. They speak and follow her upstairs to the lockers. Once entering the locker room, she smiles at them and leaves them to change.

"What were you saying Bee before Lyla came to get us? I want to hear the rest of what you were going to say. It sounded like you had an option for me." Sandy takes off her pumps and knee-highs getting ready to unzip her maxi-skirt.

"Oh I was getting ready to say that maybe you can sign up for working from home. You know, telework. I am not sure if they offer that at your agency or in your position, but it's just a suggestion. I know my brother works from home about two days a week. Quite a few of my cousins work from home some days too. Hell, my sister in-law works from home four days a week. Does anyone in your office do that? Maybe you can speak to her supervisor about it and apply for it too. I mean, it's worth a try. That will cut down on how many days you have to deal with the bullshit. It's cuts down on gas too."

"Hey, that's not a bad idea. I never thought about that even though quite a few people in the office do it. I will check it out. Maybe working from home will cut down on my frustration. Yea, that's a great idea! Not to mention, I can probably start developing a business plan to leave the bump and grind of the workforce."

"I feel you. I'm with Regina on not experiencing that but I saw enough from my mother to know that I didn't want any parts of it." Colleen says as she slips her arms into her robe and slides her feet into her flip-flops wiggling her toes.

They all walk out of the locker room passing by a few employees smiling and speaking as they enter into the Tranquil

Room. Sitting in their normal spots, they begin talking about something new.

"Sooo, how many of us enjoyed class Monday night? I can say that I really did. Out of all of the classes, I will say that was the best. I will also admit that the sexercise classes that her scrawny ass damn near killed us in were worth it because I know I wouldn't have been able to do those simple moves she gave us without them." Colleen says smiling like she is excited to talk about class. "Hell, all this ass, hips, and thighs weren't going to be swinging nowhere."

"You know what? I can say that I really enjoyed the class too. Y'all know I was apprehensive, if no one else was. I had all kinds of dirty visions floating around in my head but she kept it simple, sweet, and doable. I wanted to keep doing it. I really had fun. I surprised myself." BeLynda says in response to Colleen.

"Yea, I had fun too. I wasn't sure what we were going to do in class that night but she made it so easy. I know I don't have much upper body strength but I guess all of those sexercise classes gave me enough strength to swing this ass around that damn pole too. I ain't gonna say I felt light as a feather flying around that pole but it wasn't as hard as I thought. I can do away with all the other classes and just do this one." Regina smiles getting up to grab a handful of sunflower seeds.

"Well, I can say that I have been flying around my pole. You know, perfecting my craft." Sandy laughs. "I had my brothers come over to help me put it up." All eyes are on her shocked. "Yeap, I sure did. And you should have seen their faces when they came over and saw what I needed help with. Of course Miles was quiet. Just no expression at all. But Garvin was all talk. Wanting to know what I needed it for and where can he get one for his basement." They all laugh out loud.

"I bet he did ask all kinds of questions. With his old freak ass. That nigga stay horny. I'm glad you ain't had no events lately. He swears he is the Daddy of all Mac Daddies. Does he still walk with that pinky behind his damn thigh?" Colleen ask swinging her feet. All the Ladies laugh out loud again.

"And you know it! He ain't gonna change. That walk was achieved in junior high school. Right when his brain got *stuck* in junior high?" Sandy says laughing along with her friends.

"I'll be damn. He still thinks he's the man, huh?" BeLynda asks getting up to get a glass of lemon water. "How did he do that walk?" BeLynda tries to emulate how he walks. Sandy and Colleen bursts into laughter.

"Hell yea, and I can't say that he ain't. You know women still fall for those eyes. When Mint Condition came out with Pretty Brown Eyes that is all we heard him playing throughout the damn apartment. You know my father told him he was going to break that damn CD if he didn't stop playing it." They laugh screamingly.

"Yea, every time we were at your place, all we would hear him say is 'Quit Breaking My Heart' and 'Pretty Brown Eyes' just smiling all the time brushing his damn hair. But you know your brother was breaking those hearts Sandy." BeLynda giggles. "I'm mean he was cute and he grew up to be a fine ass man."

"Yea, well now his ass is getting his heart broke. Right along with his pockets. Keep trying to go after them young girls instead of finding him a woman his age or older." Sandy says, shaking her head.

"Or in his damn league. He has no children and no woman?" Colleen asks and Sandy shakes her head "no." "That raises quite a few red flags for any woman. But hell, enough about Garvin. Let's get to the conversation. Now, other than Sandy has anyone bought a pole since class Monday night?"

"Hell no I haven't. I've just been enjoying Khalil and him staying over the entire night. I cooked him breakfast for the first time last weekend. I think I overdid it though. But he ate some of everything with no problem." BeLynda says and all eyes are on her waiting for her to finish.

"Oh really? Now, we know how you get down when you get in that kitchen. You fixed his ass a big ass buffet didn't you? He probably didn't know where to start." Regina smiles putting some seeds in her mouth.

"Damn you said 'buffet' too. I didn't think I was fixing him a buffet but that's what he said when saw the spread. It caught me off guard too when he asked me about the eggs with American cheese and the microwavable sausage. I didn't know how to respond. But I was careful not to embarrass him."

"*American cheese*," Sandy, Colleen, and Regina all say in unison. "Oh, he still in the hood, huh? Well, if that's all his Mama introduced him to, you can't fault him for asking. But it's a good thing he met you. Introduce that man to some things Girlie," Regina says.

"Yea, all you can do is introduce him to the better shit. Tell him you eat real fuckin' cheese. Not the processed shit clogging up your damn arteries and shit before he reaches thirty. Tell him he has graduated in more ways than one," Sandy says. They all laugh shaking their heads in agreement.

"I know. That's what I was thinking but I didn't say it. And check this out. Right before we were getting ready to eat, guess who the hell calls? Steve!!" All their mouths are open wide and time seems to stop.

"Steve?! Well, don't you still talk to him like every other damn day? So what was the surprise?" Colleen asks.

"Yea, I do but this was Saturday morning and he has never called that early. And he called several times back-to-back. I started to answer it the first time but I didn't. Then he called while I was saying grace. I kept right on blessing the food. I know Khalil probably looked at the caller ID when he was in the kitchen but he didn't say anything."

"Damn, several times? Back-to-back? That sounds like he might've had an inkling that you weren't alone. Did he leave a message? You know? One of those 'I know you in there with a nigga' type of messages?" Colleen really wants to know.

"Nah, he didn't leave any messages but I do know that he knew I had company. I think he was trying to piss my company off." BeLynda gets up to get a few vanilla wafers.

"And how is that? What made you think that he knew?" Regina questions.

"After about five minutes, I heard a vehicle speed off like whoever was pissed. I know that 'fuckin' up the gears' sound anywhere. It was none other than Steve's ass."

"What?! Steve was sitting outside your damn house? What the fuck is going on with men these days? How long y'all been divorced? Did he not think you would move on from his cheating disrespectful ass? Hell, maybe you should've answered the phone to see what his crazy ass had to say. I sure would've loved to know what he was feeling." Colleen was shocked and pissed at Stan's stalker actions.

"Okay? And y'all haven't gone out nor have you had him spend the night over OR had sex with him since the divorce. Yet now he's making creep rides to your street and calling trying to start some shit?" BeLynda laughs saying, "He better chill. I ain't seen Khalil but I am sure if you are messing with him, he's a big stocky nigga too and much younger." They all laugh at BeLynda's observation of BeLynda's type."

"Stan said he is feeling guilty and that is why he calls you all the time. But if he was trying to make a move, it's been five damn years and …"

"And he waits until now. Men! I'm not gonna say he didn't want you when he had you because I think he did and you fucked that up. But hell, after five years and never saying or suggesting or …" Colleen says but is interrupted.

"Or implying anything about y'all getting back together, how he gonna speed off pissed? He thought you were waiting around for him? Women need to hear words, see signs, and feel the vibe … and apparently he gave you none of that. Or maybe he did and we didn't know. Hell, if you didn't want to be bothered with him anymore, that isn't hard to understand." Sandy sounds off heated.

"Yea he did a lot of cruddy shit but we not gonna get on that. We would still be talking about it come Monday. So, how was your weekend and breakfast with Khalil?" Regina tries to lighten the mood in the room.

"It was great! Other than a few hiccups I can't say that it wasn't a beautiful memory. We had a beautiful Friday evening that lasted until Sunday. I really enjoyed him, us, and the weekend." BeLynda smiles as if she is remembering the entire two and a half days.

"A few hiccups," Colleen says wanting to know what else could've gone wrong. "What else happened Girl? Don't be stalling. Inquiring minds want to know!"

"Well, he tried to be slick and slide in a question about what I do on Monday evenings. It got a little heated but I made sure I shut it down before it got out of hand. That is my time with my friends and how I spend it is none of his business."

"Oh so he asking about our *private classes*, huh? How he know about Monday evenings anyway?" Colleen looking at BeLynda side-ways wondering if she hinted around to it.

"I thought I told you that one of his friends be at the gym across the street on Mondays. So when he showed them a picture of me, that friend mentioned that he sees me coming out of the building across from the gym."

"Damn! Oh yea?! So we have eyes on us from a few people huh? Hell before we know it, our classes may not be private anymore. People keep seeing us or watching us and shit. Then people want to ask questions. You did right Bee. Shut that nigga down. All he needs to do right now is enjoy what you have learned. That's what it is supposed to be anyway. We learned and then show." Colleen says and they all laugh giving each other high-fives.

"You got that right. But Bee, what I wanna know is … since you have been kicking it with Khalil, have you forgotten about Marcus? I haven't seen that look in your eyes lately. Does it matter anymore whether or not Marcus works on you anymore?" Sandy asks getting up to get some crackers spreading port wine cheese on them.

"Oh, I still have my eyes on Marcus but right now, I am going to enjoy Khalil. That is until he does something to fuck it up. Right now, he tells me that he is all mine if I want him. I'm fine with that. He is making the moves and Marcus has kept it professional. That is cool beans with me."

"Wow, I can't believe that Bee has been holding down the conversation this evening. Bee actually has some juicy and I like it. Is that all of the hiccups in your weekend with Khalil? What else you got to tell us?" Regina smiles asking.

"Nothing really. Other than I didn't know that his Mama had seven children. However, there are only five of them living. He said that he had twin siblings, who were the oldest and they died in a fire with his father. I didn't know how to respond to that. But he wanted to change the subject and I had no problem with that."

"Wow! That's heart wrenching. It sounds like that wound is still fresh. That had to be hard to deal with it. It's one thing to lose one family member. But three at a time? I can't imagine. It's seven of us too," Sandy says.

Colleen sits straight up in the chair and places her feet on the floor. Her hearts sinks deep into her chest. "He had twin siblings that died in a fire with his father? How did the fire start? Did he say how old they were? He lives in the hood, right? Where? What is Khalil's last name? Did his father have a nickname," Colleen asks. She starts sweating a little. It sounds all too familiar.

"He didn't go into any details. I'm glad he didn't. I didn't want to be crying while eating. I would have lost my appetite. Why you ask all of that Lene? You heard something like this before?"

"Um, I was just wondering. I mean, if it happened a while ago, we may have heard something about it. Plus, it is a small world you know. We may have known his father by his nickname. Where does Khalil live now?" Colleen is very concerned.

Regina is looking at Colleen very closely. She notices Colleen's demeanor has changed. She can't put her finger on it but she has noticed strange changes in Colleen's behavior lately. Colleen feels Regina looking at her behavior. She pretends that she doesn't notice she is being watched. Getting up, she grabs sunflower seeds and a glass of lemon and lime water walking over to one of the benches to sit down.

"You all right Lene? I'm surprised you are sitting over there instead of in your favorite chair. What's the matter? You look like you have seen a ghost." Regina gives her the narrow eyes and pursed lips look letting Colleen know, she is going to have to tell what is what wrong.

"Oh, I'm alright Girl. I just don't like to hear things like that happening to families. Especially when children are involved. And Khalil is a man that Bee is involved with. I'm sure he is going to be around for a long minute and I just feel for him, that's all." She avoids Regina's eyes. *Stop looking at me Gee Gee. You're making me uncomfortable and now is not the time. I'm not in the mood and you wouldn't understand. So don't think you're going be asking me about my behavior later. The topic is closed.*

"That's sad Bee. I have never experienced that or came across anyone that has. But um, not to appear that your discussion is not important but I wanna change the subject. That's if it is all right with y'all. Bee were you finished talking?" Sandy asks not wanting to be rude and uncaring because she is not. She just wants to talk about something else.

"Oh yea. I'm done Girl. Go right ahead and talk about something else. I'm ready for your juicy if everyone else is." BeLynda says looking at Regina and Colleen.

"Oh, nah, I'm cool. Go ahead and tell us what you have been waiting to tell us. You have been very patient." Colleen says smiling ready to hear what Sandy has to say.

Regina looks at Colleen rolling her eyes. "Yea, I'm ready. What you got to tell us Dee Dee?" She puts her focus on Sandy.

"Well, none of you knew that I had finally hooked up with Mr. Ray Daniels. Well, Bee knew the first time we had dinner together." Regina looks at her confused. Colleen looks at her surprised and wanting to hear more. "We have been meeting for dinner three days a week. Okay, okay, let me back up. Our first dinner date was really nice. He was a gentleman and he was dressed casual but expensive. But not 'Byron' expensive. We found out we have a lot in common. He is very sweet which accentuates his handsomeness." Sandy smiles. BeLynda and Colleen also smile. Regina is still confused about hearing the new name.

"Okay, before you go any further, who is Ray Daniels? How did Bee know you went to dinner with him but Colleen and I didn't? Where did you meet him? You leaving out a lot of details." Regina says popping a few seeds in her mouth.

"Oh, sorry Gee Gee. I met him when we went to the Zanzibar and you were in the Poconos. We didn't talk to each other right away. He said he had been busy but I went ahead and left him a message and he finally called me inviting me to dinner. We met at the Old Ebbitt Grille. He let me order whatever I wanted. He even walked me to my car afterwards. But that was after we arranged to have dinner three nights a week and he paid for the dinner with a white card. Have you heard of that card Gee Gee?"

Regina's eyes pop open wide. "A white card? Really?" Regina smiles. "What does this Mr. Daniels do for a living? It sounds like he has big money."

"He is a video game creator … or something like that," says Colleen. "He was a gentleman the night we all met him. He came over to the table to ask Sandy for a dance. You know how Sandy dances … that man was confused," she and BeLynda laughs. "He didn't know what to do with his hands, his feet, and his eyes and then all of a sudden the front of his pants popped out like a bag of microwave popcorn. You know what that means. Old Boy was ready for some of that ass twirling around in his face." All the Ladies laugh running around the room.

"What?! Damn and I missed all of that being in the Poconos? And none of y'all told me? Now that is not fair. You don't leave out that type of juicy. I told y'all how my weekend was and you held back. Sandy you are over my house twice a week and you kept a secret like that? You know better than that." Regina throws a few seeds at Sandy. Sandy laughs and ducks.

"Okay, okay, I'm sorry Gee Gee. So, now Colleen has told you. So as I was saying, we had been meeting three nights a week. We meet on Tuesdays, Wednesdays and Saturdays for dinner. But this weekend was different." The Ladies get comfortable and sit with full attention on Sandy. "He switched it up on us a little bit. He invited me over for breakfast!! I was too through and excited at the same time. I almost didn't go. I got a little uncomfortable."

"So he asked you over for breakfast instead of taking you out for breakfast? That didn't mean you got some dick does it? I know how men can be with that invite over shit. It ain't been sixty or ninety days yet. You know the grown woman rule." Regina says winking her eye at Sandy. "But why were you uncomfortable?"

"Oh when I say he was a gentleman, I meant that. He cooked for me and everything. I felt like I was in a dream. I can't lie, he had a Sista on cloud nine. I did bring a change of clothes for dinner just in case he still wanted to go to dinner too."

"Well, did he still want to go to dinner? Or did he change up the plans because he had something else to do?" Colleen said hoping that Sandy didn't go out of dinner with Ray.

"Oh no we went out to dinner but let me get to the in between stuff first. This is the reason why I was uncomfortable. So, the first night we went out, I called him on my way home to thank him for such a nice evening. He said he was in the Billiards Room and I thought he had made a stop off somewhere but he actually has a Billiards Room in his house and it is not in the basement." All eyes are on Sandy listening closely excited by her story. Colleen is feeling some type of way though.

"Oh, so this Ray guy has a nice size house then, huh?" BeLynda asks. "Hell, a Billiards Room? That is not small at all. And for it to not be in his basement? Damn Girl!"

"Yeap, as a matter of fact, when he invited me over for breakfast, he sent a car for me while he finished up breakfast. At first, I didn't how to take that. I had never had that type of treatment. It was a Rolls Royce Phantom!"

"What?! Nooo!! He rolling in money like that?" BeLynda's eyes almost popped out of their sockets.

Colleen is looking and listening somewhat jealous. She was attracted to Ray and a little disappointed that Sandy was the one that caught his eye at the club.

"Yes ma'am. He sent a car for me, I almost told him no. He caught that I didn't know how to react and he told me that if I wanted to go out for breakfast instead, that was fine. He also offered to come get me if that was better. But I toughened up and told him that the car was okay. A butler opened up the door for me to come in, took my things, and escorted me through the house. I wanted so bad to take pictures and you know my phone doesn't do all of that. Colleen I thought about what you said. This weekend, I am going to upgrade my phone." They all laugh. Colleen winks.

"Well, go on Girl. Keep talking, this sounds real good. I want to know all you know about Mr. Ray," Regina says excitedly.

"Girl, I don't know how much money he makes or have but the driver had to punch in a code for the gates to open. He lives in an estate type of house and there are other houses on his property for his workers …"

"His workers?! Oh he has it like that? Hell, all we can afford is for the workers to live inside the house and that is the maid." Regina says and they all laugh.

"He has one townhouse looking home on the land and his mother lives in that. He did say that one of his brothers live on the premises too. And he has four beautiful Rottweilers. They were all dressed in their scarves and bows. They are trained too. But look, when it came time to go out to dinner, when he said where we were going, my outfit didn't fit the atmosphere. Do you know we drove to a quaint little boutique and he bought me an outfit to wear to dinner? I felt like I was dreaming for real. The whole experience seem like it was straight out of a Harlequin Romance novel." Sandy looks like she is on cloud nine talking about her experience.

There is silence and smiles. The smiles are from BeLynda and Regina. They are happy for Sandy and her experience. Colleen on the other hand is not all that thrilled. It is hard for her to hide her irritation, or maybe it is jealousy. Regina notices the look saying to herself, *Oh okay, you are attracted to him too? You have more than enough "options" so sit back and let her have her moment.*

"So he has a brother that lives in one of his houses inside the gates, huh? Have you met him? Does Ray have other siblings? Preferably brothers?" Colleen asks and the Ladies laugh. "Hell, if he is rolling in the money like that, maybe his entire family is. I'm just asking."

"I've not asked him about his family but the way he talks, there are other siblings. It seems as if they are all boys. I didn't hear anything that might've said there were sisters. I just had a good time and wanted to make sure that I told y'all. Especially since it seems like I will be spending more time with him."

"Oh, so you know this already Ms. Robertson? How is that? What did he say that gave you that impression?" BeLynda asks smiling.

"Well, for one, he asked if we had to stick to the three nights a week dinner dates. Before that, he said that he is free after three in the evening Monday through Friday. I even spent the night, in one of the guest rooms and his butler was very attentive to my needs. When it came time for me to go home, he didn't want me to go. He said that he hears my frustration with my job and told me to say the word and I don't have to work anymore." Regina's, Colleen's, and BeLynda's mouth drop to the floor stunned.

"What?! It's like that? This man is into you like that Sandy?! Damn! Did you call your supervisor and tell her you quit," BeLynda asks and they all laugh. "Or are you gonna be nice and give her a two weeks' notice and stick it out for another ten days? Hell, you've been patient on what you've been asking for and it seems as if it has paid off." Regina shakes her head up and down implying "Yeap."

"I didn't do any of that. I heard him and that's all. We've not upgraded our titles as of yet. He has been so good to me but right now, I am just pinching myself to make sure I haven't been sleep when all of this happened. He seems so forward and knows what he wants. And he is making clear that he wants me. And I'm liking that fact."

"Well, what is the problem then? He is fine, a gentleman, got money, and he is into Sandra Robertson. I mean, what more can you ask for you? Really? You've been looking for your man with six-figure salary and it's obvious that he has more than that. Yet you are hesitant. What's wrong?" BeLynda is waiting for the response.

"Nothing is wrong. It's perfect. Too perfect. Something is missing. Or at least it seems that there is. I'm not a gold digger and I know that he knows that by now but … we're just getting to know each other. I'm not his woman, and he is not my man. Who ups and quits their job like that off of what a man they are getting to know says and offers? I gotta really know he is serious and I do have bills."

"Well, it sounds to me like the ball is in your court. He said say the word, right? Titles may not have been upgraded, like you said, but I bet if you called him right now and said that you wanted to be exclusive with him as his woman, he wouldn't tell you 'no' or that you are moving too fast. So you have what you want right in your face, and you are questioning it?" Regina looks at Sandy with questioning eyes.

"Hmmp, I wouldn't question it. I would jump at the chance. Especially if I were in your shoes. But I have a business and I like my business so I wouldn't have the problem. You on the other hand are being made an offer by a man that apparently has no other woman or women and is into you and you're stalling. That's some bullshit Sandy." Colleen says shocked that she actually said that. *Hell I can't be upset. He likes her, and here is her chance.*

"Maybe, maybe not but I haven't even slept with him yet. Sex is important to me and I know he has been out of the dating game for a minute. I don't know why but I'm sure I will find out. And to have all of that land and house … correction, houses … yet there are no women or children hanging around? I don't know what that means."

"I can spot a good catch and I can guarantee you that he has told you why and you haven't been listening. He has money. A man with money either has too many gold-diggers and whores around him or he's a family man and wants to choose wisely. I will say he is the latter and he has chosen you to be that woman in his life. As Colleen said, you are stalling. Don't back down now from your wish. It has come true Girl!" Regina says happy for Sandy.

"Yeap, it sure has. So tell Larry it was good while it lasted but now it is time for you to move on. Meet his mother, and his siblings and work on being happy with all he may be trying to offer you, quit your stressful job and start your own business if you don't want to sit around the house." BeLynda says taking a few sips of her water.

"Exactly. All women don't get that perfect 'chance' meeting. Most women are just happy to have a man. Hell, look at Bee. She has a college degree man that has no money." BeLynda looks at Colleen with a frown. "Shit, Sandy take his offer, move in and live lavishly, and throw your thoughts away. I'm sure he has nothing to hide. And if he does, what the fuck could it be? Probably something small, right? I mean, what else could there be?" They all look at Sandy.

"Oh, y'all expect me to answer that right now? Well you ain't gone get an answer, not tonight anyway. Now, continue on."

Chapter Sixteen

16

Now ... stand to the left of the pole holding it with my right hand. Make sure there is a comfortable space between me and the pole.

Slowly walk forward, walking around the pole. Make sure I grip it enough ... not to let it go but loose enough so that my hand can move.

Raise my heels off the floor and keep walking around the pole on the balls of my feet. Make sure I always end up at the same starting point.

Okay, next, raise my right hand higher on the pole putting my left hand at the same level and continue to walk around the pole.

Stand in place, hooking the back of my right leg - behind the knee - around the front of the pole ... using my hands to hold on.

Okay, now swing my body forward around the pole with both legs lifted. C'mon, you did it in class in front of everybody ... do it right here in the basement alone with no other sets of eyes and judgments.

BeLynda is going over the steps – in her mind - the instructor taught her in pole dancing class Monday. Surprisingly she really enjoyed herself. Not in a million years did BeLynda think she would perceive the instrument in a manner different from what she always had. In all of her teenage and adult years, she has continually associated the pole with something or someone of the trashy or strumpet category. The dark smoky, hole in the wall businesses that reeked of alcohol and stale ass. Even though BeLynda is an educated woman, certain things she stuck to believing in her ignorance originating from her street and hood destructive education.

However, after Monday evening, she has been having numerous pleasurable moments with the pole she secretly purchased online. So much she hasn't thought about work, orders, or customers. She can take a few days off from all of the hustle and bustle surrounding ringing phones, boxes, receipts, packages, and deliveries. Colleen is always saying that she works too much. BeLynda is taking Colleen's advice for a change and spending some time away from work getting in touch with her confidence, sensuality, and enticing abilities. She is ready to give some jaw dropping, mouth open stunts that'll shut up her friends as well as make Khalil's dick burst the zipper and front seams of his pants.

BeLynda and the crew are well aware that Sandy unrepentantly purchased her pole right after class directly from the instructor. She let it be known in class in front of everyone that she was to see Candice in her office when class was over. There was no shame in her game. BeLynda loves that about all of her friends. They are free spirited and embrace their sexuality with a passion. The last thing BeLynda wanted was to be teased, made fun of, or be the brunt end of Colleen's joke. So first thing Tuesday morning – still in her pajamas and bonnet - she ordered her shiny brass pole paying the additional money for two-day shipping.

Surprisingly, it arrived a day early and she spent the entire Wednesday morning putting the pole up by herself. She would have asked Steve to put it up for her since she was on the phone with him when UPS knocked on the door with her sexy secret in a box but that would have given him the wrong idea. She was not about to show him any of her sexy twirls on the pole. That would have pissed him off to know that he installed it for her to perform for another man. That other man drives the white Honda Accord. She is somewhat of a handy-woman, so she pulled out her tools and connected her secret to the basement's ceiling beams.

Thursday evening when BeLynda left the house to meet up with her friends at the Spa, she smiled at the soreness in her arms and abs benefitting from the surreptitious workouts. Her evening at the Spa was worth it and needed. Marcus massaged, kneaded, rubbed, and stroked all of the aching muscles and joints of her body concentrating on her arms, neck, shoulders, back and feet like she requested. If he had slipped either of his hands in between her thighs that were hiding her heated moisture, that would have been the icing on the cake.

This Saturday morning, BeLynda is practicing what she learned in class this week. Prior to executing the moves, she did a little warm-up, using the sexercise lessons. She figures now that she is a secret proud owner of a pole, why not use it to the fullest toning and tightening while increasing her endurance. The song that is on repeat to help give her the same speed of movement through her practice is Black Rain by Teena Marie. It has been at least an hour and she is on her fortieth time performing what is known as the Front Hook Spin.

I want to feel sexy, enticing and confident. Candice said so. This is supposed to be fun, erotic, and sexy. Make sure you remember this Bee. How does this feel to you Bee? Not too bad. Is it okay? It's better than okay. Weird? Not at all. Uncomfortable? Nope. BeLynda is going over the statements and questions Candice said and asked in Monday's class. This is her pep talk. She needs to remind herself throughout her practices each time that she should be feeling sexy and confident while she is enticingly using the pole. To keep from regressing in her thoughts of this being a forbidden instrument for the trashy and vulgar, she repeats inwardly between moves that this is to be fun, erotic, and again … sexy. For some reason, she can go "there" in her fantasy world but clam up when it comes to expressing it in the world of the real.

Thirty minutes later, BeLynda takes the song off of repeat so that other songs on the CD can play. She is sitting on the floor drinking bottled water and dabbing perspiration from her forehead and neck with her hand towel. She is truly exhausted yet proudly grinning at herself. However her body is feeling like she just got beat up by a boot camp instructor. Today, she is that instructor. Outside of the pole dancing private classes, it has been a minute since BeLynda has worked out. All of her The Firm, Yoga, and Belly Dance VHSs, and DVDs have been collecting dust for the past year.

Looking up and down at the brass object in front of her, it seems to glow. BeLynda is admiring her handy work and how it hasn't come down yet. She is proud of her handy-woman skills as always. She has heard stories of how the incorrectly installed poles have brought down many ceilings at adult toy parties or intimate shows for mates. She laughs imagining the look of embarrassment that comes with that happening. Placing the towel around her neck, she moves down to massaging the balls of her feet, they are red. BeLynda closes her eyes at the soothing feeling and pressure she is applying to her sore feet knowing that it will be another six days before Marcus can get to them. *Maybe I will have Khalil massage them for me when I see him.*

Baby, I'm Your Fiend by Teena Marie begins to play throughout the basement. BeLynda smiles with her eyes closed grooving to the sultry deep smoky jazzy tune. Suddenly, BeLynda is thrown deep into her imaginative world. The world that stays hidden until she is alone with nothing to do. It seems all too real.

All right fellas, are you ready for the main attraction? Are you ready for a treat? Get ready fellas. She is approaching the stage. I want y'all help me welcome Blush to the stage. Give her all you got! Opening her eyes, the room is dark with two spotlights shining on her and the pole. She is now in a room full of men that are smiling and drooling at her. With her hands on her hips, she stands before the room of hungry men with rhinestone pasties on her nipples yet covering one-third of her voluptuous breasts. She has on a matching rhinestone thong adorned with a pair of red lips hanging from a chain across her right exposed butt cheek. Topping off the outfit is a black rhinestone mask, red lipstick, and Christian Louboutin black patent leather stilettos with a rhinestone heel.

The men are whistling and throwing money at her feet waiting for BeLynda to make her move. Teena is sounding so sexy in the background of all of the loud deep voices.

♪ *Yeah, everybody got one, huh*

And you're mine

Baby I'm your fiend

Baby I'm your fiend

Baby I'm your fiend

For your love, I've been saving

I've been paving the low road to you ♪

Giving the men a mischievous grin, seductively spreading her deep bright red lips across her pearly teeth exposing a small gap between the top front two, adding a little mystery to the woman behind the mask, BeLynda begins to sway her hips. Then she bends her left knee seductively extending her right leg out, with her arms raised, bringing it back towards her body, snaking it down to the floor and back to a standing position.

Touching her hair, rubbing down her breasts, stopping to outline them with her hands meeting at the top center of her stomach, slowly moving them down to her rhinestone crotch. She drops down, almost hit the floor with her ass, spreading her thighs rubbing her hands on her studded mound. Hypnotically closing her thighs, she turns her body slightly to the left grabbing the pole, moving sexually to the music tooting her ass out as she returns to a standing position. Simultaneously, she makes both cheeks shake, lift up and down with the red lips on the chain bouncing every time her ass smacks it. There are whistles heard throughout the room.

Grabbing the pole, BeLynda goes into her Front Hook Spin landing with her back to the men. She rest the pole in between her butt cheeks looking like a straw in between voluptuous lips. One of the men holler, *"Damn!! Shit!! That ass is eatin' that motherfucka up! Let me swipe my credit card down it Blush."* She turns towards the voice that is coming from her right, giving her profile to the crowd and seductively smiles, turning her face away again, turning to the left to give them the left profile pouting her lips into a kiss. Spreading her legs a little bending over with the pole still between her cheeks while she gyrates to the song, acting out the lyrics.

The men are on the edge of their seats. Some are moaning, "Aww, baby", a few are licking their lips with their focus between her thighs and on her ass when she turns to the side. Some have full erections resting down their thigh watching her ass gyrating imagining she is performing this dance on their dicks. When BeLynda turns to face her horny bystanders, a light seems to be shining on a handsome face out in the crowd. He is sitting in the third row resting his right arm on the table playing with a lighter. He is looking at her serious and ready.

The music changes to Aaliyah's version of At Your Best by the Isley Brothers. BeLynda gracefully saunters towards the admirable stranger watching her. She gives him an inviting smile as he scans across her lips, breasts, back up to her eyes, and then down to her swaying hips. Giving her a slight grin, he winks at her as she continues in his direction. Men can be heard yelling, "Nah, come over here baby," "I got what you need Blush," and "Marry me."

The man BeLynda has her eyes glued on is soaking it all in. He is feeling his superego crowd his head. As she nears him, he stops playing with the lighter placing it on the table slowly. The smirk leaves his mouth and all that is heard is the music. The onlookers are waiting with anticipation to see what Blush will do to, with, and for him. Blush stands in front of him just looking at him giving him permission to look at her too. He is a tall man. With her stilettos still on her feet her breasts are eye level to him. He lets out a snicker and lowers his gaze trying not to appear to be hungry. He is too smooth and suave to act like the other vultures in the room yet he really wants to take them in his mouth. Blush knows this is what he wants to do.

Abruptly touching his chin, she lifts it so that he is looking up into her eyes deeply. This makes her breast give him a jiggle. He clears his throat, looking down at them and sighs closing his eyes. She smiles because he is losing the battle. Lifting her left leg up and over his right thigh, she is standing in front of him gyrating. He gets a whiff of her Almond Cookie Butter by Carol's Daughter and it sends him into a world of jubilation. Moving close enough so that her breast brush against his lips and cheek, he closes his eyes and runs his hands through the brown curls on his head. BeLynda lets out a gasp and he looks up at her suddenly wondering what happened. He grabs her around her waist slowly lowering her down onto his lap. Her breast firmly rub against his face, shoulders, and chest. There is a force that takes over both of them. He is rubbing up and down her back moving his hips against her rubbing her ass against his brick hard dick looking in her eyes as if he is asking, "Do you wanna stop?"

He lifts her right leg up and over kissing the back of her thigh as he brings it across his body. "Mmm, flexible." BeLynda watches him. She ends up with her back to him still sitting on his lap. She feels his hard dick jerk. There are a few whistles as the scene full of beautiful raunchiness materializes. Grinding against her ass, he whispers against her neck, "Dance for me baby." She thought this was supposed to be her show but the handsome man screaming sex has taken control.

BeLynda snaps out of her world of imagination. The world of her hidden thoughts where she can do anything she wants. The place where inhibition is not allowed. The island of eroticism where she can give a hellafide show and receive one in return.

Ring! Ring! …

Ring! Ring!

The phone has been ringing for the past five minutes back-to-back. Her mind finally heard it and brings her back to her basement. She blinks a few times, looking around the room. There are no men there with her, she is still dressed in her yoga shorts and tank with bare feet and her face is uncovered. The Teena Marie's CD is still the music playing throughout the room. She is confused a little. Shaking her head a few times to snap completely out of the private performance she was giving the eyes in her mind.

The phone begins to ring again. Looking around the unfamiliar room in her very familiar home for the phone, she spots it over by the pile of fluffy colorful pillows on the floor. Sitting down on the pillow, she waits for the phone to ring again, not really caring to return the call to whomever has been repetitively calling her. She wants to get back to the dark room with just two lights where she was surrounded by men who wanted her and she felt exceptional in her sexy "fuck me" attire dancing on and around the pole and squirming around on the fine ass man's lap with his hard dick rubbing against her swollen clitoris.

I know I wasn't actually doing what I was doing but it always seem so real. If only I can do that consciously. But I'm working on it. And that man in the chair ... damn, his face looked so familiar. Who the hell am I fantasizing about in my mental escapades?

The doorbell is ringing now. BeLynda jumps up startled running up the two flights of stairs leading to the front door, she slows down walking quietly to look through the peep hole. As usual, it is Colleen. BeLynda is trying to figure out why is she here on a damn Saturday morning. The Queen of weekend sleep is up bright and early ringing her doorbell and primping in the glass screen door.

Goddammit! Every time I am enjoying my mind, she pops up. She must have ESP or something and know when I am in here having some mental personal time. Oh! She is talking to someone.

BeLynda's front door is so thick that the sound of the other voice is muffled and curiosity is killing her. *Who the fuck did she bring over to my house this morning?* Just then, Colleen rings the doorbell again knocking on the door followed by a bang on the door by the other person. BeLynda unlocks the door and snatches it open wide with a growl on her face looking at Colleen.

"Hey Girlie. Good morning! What the hell are you doing up in here? I done called about fifty times from your driveway. Then we decided to get out the car." Colleen sashays into the house past BeLynda. "What were you in here doing?" Colleen turns around with wide eyes and a smile asking, "Oh shit! You got company don't you? Where is he? Let us meet him. Don't keep us in suspense."

Looking Colleen up and down noticing she is dressed all the way down for Colleen, BeLynda is wondering what she is up to. "Good morning. I was minding my business in my house, I hope you didn't mind. And who is 'we'? Who were you talking to on my porch? I now the neighbors aren't socializing with your ass. It's too early for them."

BeLynda never attempts to look out on the porch to see who else is out there. *Maybe she was talking to herself. She does that sometimes,* she thought. At that moment, Sandy appears in front of the doorway smiling with open arms. BeLynda jumps from being surprised.

"Good morning Ms. Giles. How are you? Give me my hug and kiss. I see Colleen didn't want hers this morning. Are you surprised to see me?" BeLynda smiles at Sandy and gives her a deep hug and kisses on both cheeks.

"Hey! Good morning sassy. What a wonderful surprise to see you … and here with Colleen. Where y'all coming from? Or where were y'all on your way to? Or are y'all coming to pick me up? Come on in here, after scaring me half to death. I thought Colleen was out there talking to herself like she does sometimes." Colleen looks at BeLynda and rolls her eyes.

"Oh, nah, she was talking to me. I stood to the side waiting for the opportune time to grace you with my presence. She said that you never step out on the porch or look out. And you did just what she said you would do." Walking into BeLynda's home Sandy smiles looking around like this is her first time being here. "Oooh, girl, it seems like ages since I've been in your place. I see you've been busy. I love the color of your walls. Thanks for the ideas Bee." Sandy and BeLynda laugh.

"Well, is he here? Do you have company?" Colleen asks walking into the kitchen. "Damn, I thought sure 'nough you would be in here throwing down. I was ready to eat. Were you gonna cook?"

"For who? I was the only one here at first. No man or pets. I did feed the plants. They are satisfied."

"Oh, so you don't eat when it is just you here? But now, you have two guests. So what you gonna do? Your sister is hungry as a motherfucka." Colleen rubs her stomach then takes off her shearling jacket.

"Guests? Who? Where are they?" BeLynda looks around as if she doesn't see anyone. "You and Sandy are not guests. So sit down and relax. As a matter of fact … I do believe you are the one that provide a catering business for people, right? So, why didn't you bring the buffet with you?" BeLynda asks while Sandy is smiling at Colleen agreeing with BeLynda.

"You said it when you said 'clients.' That is not you Missy. So when we are at your home, you are supposed to be the hostess with the mostess, right? So I will take some buttermilk pancakes, a veggie frittata … you do know how to make a frittata, right? Oh and some fruit to start off will be nice. You got Mimosa ingredients? Or do we need to go to the store?" BeLynda looks at Colleen as if she has completely lost her mind, even though the menu did sound good. After being in her imaginary world for what seemed like forever, she did work up an appetite.

"So what were you in here doing Bee? Just because we didn't see an additional car in your driveway, doesn't mean you don't have company. Is he hiding in the closet somewhere? Or you have him freezing his balls off on one of the balconies?" Sandy asks and Colleen laughs with her. BeLynda smiles and waves them off.

"Go 'head with that Dee Dee. Khalil is not here. He hung out with his friends last night and I told him that I would be sleep when he was done hanging out. I am not the woman for the late night creep."

"Oooh, I get the nickname for my nickname on those questions, huh? Sooo, you not the woman for the late night creep … but he can creep early? Remember he wasn't staying over until the sun was up at first. That is what you said. I distinctly remember you …"

"Who the hell said anything about Khalil? Why couldn't it have been Steve's ass over here digging that pussy out? You and Khalil ain't exclusive, right? That college graduate can't pay any of your bills. Or can he?" Colleen looks BeLynda side-eyed. "He got a job Bee? A *legit* job? Or is he slinging? What does he do for a living? Colleen is looking straight at BeLynda to see what her facial expression is before she responds. It tells her BeLynda has no idea what her boy toy does to provide the three necessities for himself.

BeLynda tilts her head at Colleen with her hands on her hips saying, "I know you didn't come over here to meet Khalil or to quiz me on how much I know about him. So I won't spend any precious time answering your nosy questions. And what is it with you anyway Ms. Jeffries? Evidently Byron or whoever is the main attraction this week didn't do any 'digging' last night either."

Colleen just looks at her. After dealing with Regina's mess, she hasn't had any thought about a warm muscular body with a humongous dick attached to it. She is going to have to get it in a few times to relieve some stress. She knows Stan is going to be calling upon her for some bullshit. If it wasn't for her friend, she would ignore his ass. But she knows it is coming.

"Okay, what you got in here Bee? I can cook for us. The way you cook, I know you are fully stocked with everything I can imagine to use to make us an impressive spread. Sandy, make us some Mimosas please. I want to sit and chit chat a bit before I get to cooking in a strange kitchen." Colleen says wrapping the left side of her hair around the back of her head towards the right.

"Oh my! Y'all should come over here more often *expectantly* on a Saturday morning. I can get used to being cooked for and pampered in my own home. Yea, Sandy, the champagne is in the wine fridge underneath the sink and the orange juice is in the regular fridge." BeLynda smiles, sits down and tucks her feet underneath her in the oversized chair in her living room.

"Yea, whateva heifer. Some hostess you are in your own home. You just make sure you add coming to my house to cook to your two thousand and four New Year's Resolution. I will have the menu and grocery list all prepared for you." Colleen smiles and winks at BeLynda tucking her feet underneath her on the loveseat.

Yelling from the kitchen, Sandy asks, "Damn Bee, you done stepped your game up in the drinks department, hunh? Oh shit, who is this low budget crap in here for? You got Cold Duck? That young ass nigga drink this shit? Who the hell he been hangin' out with? His Grandmamma?" The Ladies laugh out loud.

"Girl, just fix us some drinks, please. I got something I want to talk to y'all about." Colleen smiles still laughing but her stomach is bubbling like she needs to throw up and shit at the same time. *I don't know how they are gonna take this but I need to let them know what we are gonna do.*

Sandy comes out the kitchen with drinks in flutes for Colleen and BeLynda. They look at it and take a sip. "Girl what is this you made us? This is pretty and taste good? Oh, your ass been over at your house making romantic drinks for Larry, hunh?" Colleen takes another sip admiring the appearance of the drink.

"Girl, shut up and drink. That is a Bellini with a splash of grenadine to give it a Tequila Sunrise look. And no I've not made any of these for Larry. He drinks wine … with me. I don't know if he drinks any of the hard shit. I don't stock that so he drinks what I have." Sandy comes back into the living-room with her drink sitting on the couch in the same position as her friends. She takes a sip of her morning drink saying, "Oh I made this perfect. Maybe I should start a bartender business. What y'all think?"

BeLynda and Colleen look at her and burst into laughter. "Girl, will you stop? Please? Everything you hear, see, and do sparks a business idea with you. Decide on what you really want to do and get started. I told you what to do. Get in good with Ray and let him help you. Hell, living like that … he won't miss the money at all. The way he sounds to be into you … he would be happy to help you." Colleen says taking another sip of her drink.

"I'm not using him for his money. That's not me. My body is not offered for that. I go to sleep every night with a clear conscious." Sandy says taking a few sips of her Bellini.

Oh really? "Okay, well use him for the dick. I know you ain't slept with him yet. I've seen the man. See what he is working with. Incorporating your private classes into y'all sex-apades and that nigga will be begging you to take his money and start your own business. Hell, get something out of the dick deal. Stop giving it up for free." Sandy and BeLynda look at Colleen crazy.

"Oh, I'm sorry that I've been doing it wrong all this time. Forgive me that I don't attach monetary gifts to the coochie. I had no idea I should be prostituting my body out to a man with money. I guess I missed the comprehension of the Gold Digging Ho memo. I didn't realize I was selling myself short all this time. Thanks, Colleen." Sandy says sarcastically.

"That's not what I meant Sandy. You been crying about your job and complaining that you want a business like Bee and me. Right now, the 'Zanzibar' man you had breakfast with just seems like the answer to all of your complaints. You have drained us enough with your wishes and desires. Let his ass help you bring your dream into fruition. That's all I'm sayin'. You think if I didn't have the money to start my own business, I wouldn't have allowed Byron to step in and assist? *Shiit* … "

"Speaking of that … how were you able to afford to start your own business? You have never had a job to save money. At least not one I can remember. Your family didn't have any money. You damn sure didn't have any established credit and your address would have made the bank laugh. Who gave it to you back then Lene? Did you do what you are suggesting to Sandy? You surely don't have a husband or a steady man that has been hanging around for a minute. So what was your secret? Tell it so Sandy will know. For as long as she has been talking about starting her business to work for herself, she should have heard something from you a long time ago." BeLynda really wants Colleen to explain and show Sandy how to get started.

Hmmp, listen to this bitch right here. Trying to pry into my shit. She surely ain't sounding like a fuckin' friend with that bullshit. More like a jealous bitch. She's lucky I know she is not that bitch. This ain't going the way I planned it last night in my bed. Too many questions I can't answer right now are being asked. I'ma give her ass a pass since she is my friend and I love her ... and I am at her house.

"Don't worry about me and how I got ahead. I don't recall you telling her any damn thing. You have your own business too that seems to be paying your ass quite well. So what do you have to offer to the conversation Bee? Don't make this one-sided." Colleen rolls her eyes finishing off her drink handing her glass to Sandy. "Here bartender, I need a refill, thank you. The non-hostess is blowing me."

"Lene, I have an Avon business, and yes it does pay well for me to not have to be stressed like Sandy going to a job she dislikes but have to continue because she needs to house, clothe, and feed herself. I've been where she is and I thank the Lord every day before my feet touch the floor for me not having to want to curse out co-workers. On the other hand, you have a business that you created. Your copyrighted name, and business plans mapped out for what you provide and offer. But if you don't really want to see your friend excel, then keep the shit to yourself."

Colleen looks at BeLynda shocked that she just said what she said. "Oh yea? Hmmp, okay Bee. I see you. Somewhere in between Monday's class, Khalil, and now, you have grown some oversized ovaries. What they hell were you doing before we called? You seem to be exuberating some unforeseen confidence. You must've have had a self-inflicted orgasm or something. I know how those can be make a woman a little mouthier."

BeLynda shakes her head and laughs at Colleen. Colleen speaks. "Anyway, I wanted to talk to both of you regarding Regina's situation. We need to put our heads together and help protect our friend. That shit just sounds like something out of a fuckin' movie, seriously." Sandy comes out the kitchen with fresh drinks.

"Yea, I know. I don't know what we can do though other than pay attention to our surroundings when are with her. What were you thinking?"

"Do either of you carry any type of weapons?" Both sets of eyes damn near pop out of their sockets stunned at what Colleen asked them.

"Weapons? Like what? Why would you think we need weapons? I ain't never ever … *EVER* carried a weapon." Sandy is sipping on her drink waiting for Colleen to respond.

"We can't take too lightly that she is being followed. We can't take too lightly that they might decide to go after one of us. I say all three of us need to be packing. We don't want to be caught off guard and then beat ourselves up if something does happen on our watch knowing there was a possibility that we probably could have done something."

"Do you carry around a weapon Lene? What kind? And why would you need to?" BeLynda raises her brow shocked at the conversation.

"Hell yea, I do. Don't worry about what I carry around. A sista can't be too comfortable with her surroundings. Now that Regina got some shit going on, I might need to carry a backup. So weapon shopping, we will do. Sandy, you look like a .45 carrier. Bee, you look like you could be a .38 special." Sandy's and BeLynda's mouth drop open like a candy machine."

Damn, I was doing just fine with my pole and lap dancing in the damn basement. I need to get back there because Colleen's ass tries to put me in a paranoid box. I haven't ever been there and that invitation is going to be declined.

Chapter Seventeen

17

"Well, well, well here we are again. Hello Ladies. How is everyone doing? I hope everyone had a nice week and weekend. I know I did. Remember now, if any of you ever need to talk, my door is always open and it is confidential. I'm a licensed psychologist so I can lose my license if I started blabbing your business."

"Damn, she is a jack of all trades hunh? Hell, her sisters too. They cover all kinds of areas of profession. Ain't nothing wrong with that, I guess. If one side hustle doesn't bring in the money or work out, they have many things to fall back on." BeLynda says admiring Candice as she walks and talks around the room. She loves seeing her Sistas doing their thing and making their way. Business and professionalism always looked beautiful on her Sistas.

"Yea, and you know what? I remember Kelly telling us in that breathing class … or one of them classes that if we ever needed to talk to someone, she can help too. I wonder if all three of them have degrees in therapy. But, I can say their mother taught them well. Never be broke and never depend on a man. One thing for sure, none of them can say they are a jack of all trades and …"

"And a master of none." Sandy finishes Regina's sentence. "You got that right. They made sure that they mastered all of their talents. I like that. That is impressive. Especially being sisters who are Sistas, you know what I'm sayin'? They didn't mess around in the business department." *I need to talk to one of them or all of them. I need to get my business shit going and I think they will be a good place to start asking questions*, Sandy says to herself.

"Yea, they are very business oriented. But hell, how in the hell do they have time for anything else? Just working all the damn time. They teach all kinds of classes including cardio and aerobics. They sell shit for these classes as well as purchase props for these classes. They must make out all right in the money department. Those damn dildos ain't cheap. Then they sit and listen to people's issues and problems? *Shiit*, I wonder how many times they have fallen asleep on a client. Giving them the bobble head, snores, and slobbers." The Ladies snicker at Colleen. "Y'all laughing but I'm serious." She finally snickers with them because she is imagining the visual.

Candice is walking around the room talking. As usual, the crew have their own discussion going on and of course Candice notices. She doesn't say anything this time. Mainly because she notices they are looking at her while they are talking. So whatever they are talking about, she knows she is the main topic. So she continues. *They must be talking about the class.*

"The last time we met, quite a few of you purchased poles. That let me know that you enjoyed yourselves. Hey, I'm here to teach and please. Well, please through teaching that is." The Ladies laugh and Candice winks smiling. "I will admit, I was very surprised at some of you. The others that purchased a pole, I was not surprised at all but I am glad that you decided to practice at home. Were any of you sore from our last visit? That was eight days ago." No one responds. They allow her to keep talking. "I sort of thought that quite a few if not all would be. But the joy of it all is that by the time you return to class, all the soreness would be gone, right? No one is still sore from last week, right?" The majority finally responded with a "no" head nod.

"Okay, well at least most of the class is back to normal. The rest of you that didn't respond, you must have been on the pole practicing throughout the week – or showing your new move to someone - ready to show us some of your sensual moves this evening." The Ladies start giggling. Some are giving classmates high five and smiling. Candice observes and smiles.

"Now, I am not going to ask for the show of hands but I am glad that everyone has dressed appropriately for class. If you are not dressed for class and you are on your cycle this evening – as well as you don't use tampons – you might feel a little uncomfortable. You might instantly feel a little uncomfortable this evening. So I suggest that you take it a little easy this evening." There is instant silence in the room.

"Is there something wrong? What's wrong? Looking around the room, I will say that we all still have cycles, right? I may be your instructor but I am a woman first and I am going to keep it real with you at all times. Is that all right with you? I don't like sugar-coating."

"Ay, you are all right with me Candice. Keep it real. I like that. There is no other way to go. It's good to know that some of these stunts aren't to be performed when Mother Nature is visiting. Hell, I wouldn't be doing none of this when she is in town anyway." The class laughs at Colleen. Candice just looks at her smiling shaking her head with her hands on her hips.

"Ok, I'm glad you want me to keep it real with you. Girl, you are a mess." Candice laughs out loud. "Now, what we are going to do today is still simple but as a woman myself, you might not want to have your legs extended too wide." Some of the Ladies frown. "Ay, I'm just pointing out the obvious. I've taught this class enough to know that some of us in here may not want to do certain moves on their cycle. It's okay."

Hell, we come to these classes every week which means at some point, she has a cycle yet she still comes in here dressed as if her cycle doesn't exist. I guess when you're small like that, you can handle it. BeLynda says to herself watching the instructor talk after she saunters across the room with barely nothing on showing off her toned physique.

"Okay, now I would like for everyone to show me that they remembered the move that I showed last week. We're not going to add on to that. We are going to do something new but I want to make sure that all of you still have the simple technique intact. At the end of the class, you will be putting all of these together. Now, let's get started. Take position and let me see it." Everyone did the move for Candice and she is pleased. She shows the Ladies by smiling. She gives BeLynda a head nod. *Great, she is into this class and not feeling uncomfortable or showing her inhibited side. If I didn't know any better, I'd say she has been practicing something. She didn't buy a pole from me though. Between me and my sisters, those walls will be all the way crumbled.*

"All right … good Ladies. I have nothing negative to say. Not that I do anyway." She smiles and winks at the Ladies. "I'm impressed with all of you. I see some of you that have poles have added your own sexy stunts in there. Very good. I like that. Always make it your own. When you are performing this outside of class, it will definitely be your own. The move I showed you won't entice him or her on its own. You are gonna have to add something to it. That includes the outfit and shoes. We will get to that later."

Sandy raises her hand to ask a question. "Yes, Ms. Robertson? You have a question?"

"Yes, I do. I was wondering if all of the moves you will be showing us in the entire class will be your own technique. In other words, will there be other ways to execute the moves?"

"Execute? Look at you. You're serious, hunh? Don't scare Mr. Daniels now. Remember he wants a relationship. Flipping and swinging around too soon might have him running … away from your hot ass. You want to keep him running to you, remember?" Colleen says and the crew laughs. Sandy smiles and waves her off trying to see what the instructor is going to say to her question.

Candice is smiling with her hands intertwined behind her back looking down at the floor trying not to laugh. "Ah, Ms. Robertson wants to know if she can do her own thing. Well, I will say this, I will only be showing beginners moves in this class. Of course there will be other ways to do what I am going to show you. But with all your seductive moves, twists, rubbing, and tongue action, he won't know anything different."

"Twists, rubbing, and tongue action? We gonna be doing that today? We're going to be incorporating other classes today?" BeLynda asks with her eyes as big as golf balls. The class laughs out loud at BeLynda. "What? I mean, she already got us up on the pole, now we are gonna make it …"

"Make it, what? It's all a part of the routine. You don't want to do that BeLynda? Why not? I think it will show us how to do it sexy without looking like … slutty." The red head classmate interrupts BeLynda asking the questions.

Colleen looks at the woman and then at her Girls. "See? I told y'all that bitch was a damn pro. Listen to her ass. After class, I'm gonna ask her ass where she work. I bet you she will say some damn strip club. Is Clancy's still open? That's the only damn place that would hire her rank ass." Regina bursts into laughter. BeLynda tries to hold her laugh in and stay serious but she can't. She grabs her stomach and laughs just as loud as Regina. The red hair woman squints her eyes at Colleen knowing she said something about her. Colleen looks back at her as if to say, *You really don't want none.*

"All right, all right … calm down Ladies. Let's get back on track. Now as I was getting ready to say, Sandy, that would be an advanced class. Now, if you or you and your crew want to learn intermediate moves, there is no better time than now to sign up for them. However, if any of you think I am a harder instructor, sorry … but my sisters do not teach any of the pole dancing classes. Just in case some of you don't know, I used to be an exotic dancer. So any and all pole lessons will be taught by me."

"Hmmp, listen to her still trying to be all professional. She said she was gonna keep it real with us. So why not just say she used to be a damn stripper. Hell, that's what she told me in cardio class. I guess the legit 'keepin' it real' is only for private conversations." Colleen says to her friends.

BeLynda looks at Colleen and rolls her eyes. "Girl, shut … the … fuck … up. Stop all of that. You're being messy and judgmental. If that's what she wanted to call it right now, let her. That has nothing to do with 'keepin' it real.'" Colleen looks at

BeLynda and says nothing. She turns her head to focus on the instructor but not before giving her the side-eye.

Everyone is listening to the instructor and understands what she is saying. They have taken off their outer clothing and are ready for class to begin. In the meantime, the Fantastic Four seem to be taking turns looking back at the door to see if they see the infamous shadow prowling. Nothing so far and they seem to be relieved. All except Colleen. She is waiting for the shadow to appear at the door, ready to run out the door and bust a cap in the shadow's ass. Regina catches Colleen's look and demeanor and knows that she is on one tonight. Looking serious at Colleen, she says, "Put the unfamiliar Lene back in her place please." Colleen gives Regina a scowl.

"Okay, now that everyone has removed their coats and outer clothing, we will be doing four very simple steps and at the end, I want everyone to show me what they can do with the steps … combining with what we learned last week. Is that too much to ask?" The Ladies shake their heads "no." However, Candice observes that many aren't too sure but she is hoping that they all will give it a try.

"Okay, great. Now tonight, we are gonna do the hang tough, the high kick hold, the standing snake pose, and sumo squat. Are you ready?" No responds. They are collecting their thoughts imagining what each of these moves entail and look like. "It's not gonna be that hard Ladies. These are very easy. If Mother Nature is visiting you this week, the only move you might be apprehensive about is the high kick hold. Now …"

Sandy interrupts. "The sumo squat? What in the world is that? I know what that looks like on the real sumo … and ain't nothing sexy about that at all." The entire class including Candice bursts into extremely loud laughter.

The door to the class opens suddenly. All eyes are on the door because they know everyone due in the class are already there. Regina and Colleen especially give sharp turns towards the door to see who has entered. That makes BeLynda and Sandy look extremely hard at the door. In walks an expensive dressed older lady accompanied by a younger woman walking behind her into the class. Everyone focuses on the duo that sways into their class. Candice smiles addressing the Ladies. "Hello. How may I help you Ladies? Have you just signed up for this class?" Candice walks over to the Ladies.

"Hello, I am just fine." The older woman holds out her hand to give Candice a handshake. They shake hands. Candice shakes the younger woman's hand as well. "Oh, I won't be signing up for this class. I came to see what y'all do in here." Pointing at the younger woman, she says, "My daughter-in-law might be interested. She is thinking about my son's private birthday party. Is it okay for us to sit and watch? I'm sure she will probably be signing up when the class is over." The younger woman looks at her mother-in-law devilishly smiling at her. Candice caught the look.

"Oh okay. Normally we do not have spectators in class but since you are females and she is thinking about signing up to give her husband a nice surprise, I have no problem with you watching. Welcome. Take your coats off and get comfortable. We were right in the middle of trying a new move. Now, if you decide to sign up after class, we can meet in my office. By the way, I am Candice, the instructor. And you are?" She asks looking at both women smiling.

"Oh, I'm sorry. I am just so excited coming in here with my daughter-in-law. At least one of us can join and I can live through her." The older woman almost got sick off of her exaggerated speech. She knows damn well that she would have never stepped foot in one of these classes for self. But this is important. "My name is Rachel and this here is my daughter-in-law Felicia. She begged me to come here with her." They shake hands with Candice.

Felicia smiles saying to herself, *Oh Mama Rachel is laying it on thick. Too damn thick if you ask me. I hope Rone doesn't ask what we did today. I don't need any stares, questions, or arguments. His ass doesn't even like the idea of toys in the bedroom. I know he isn't gonna want me up in here.*

"Oh no problem. I understand. I do not discriminate. Age is nothing here. I have had many women in my class … and of all ages. So you are more than welcome to join too Ms. Rachel. It's great exercise. Go ahead and have a seat and enjoy the show. Enjoy it enough to sign up tonight." Colleen smiles giving them a wink and glides back over to the front of the class. She had to add that sensuous effect for them to want to be more than curious about the class.

Rachel smiles while she is observing all of the women. She is too excited. When Rone told her about these classes, she couldn't imagine, but here she is sitting in one of them. Rachel is trying to figure out which Lady is Regina and who is the lady that has caught Ray's interest.

"All right Ladies, don't be uncomfortable now that we have two extra set of eyes in the room. We will continue as planned. Let's make it so they both sign up for the class." Everyone laughs. Regina looks over at the women and smile. Sandy smiles at them thinking that the older woman looks a little familiar.

"Now, the move we will do first is the hang tough. This is how it is performed." Candice goes to the pole in the center of the class. She stands at the one inch tape on the floor and begins. She delicately grabs the pole and with all of her upper strength, she lifts her feet off the floor bending at the knees making sure her toes are pointed and acts as if she is going to touch her butt with her heels.

She does it again so that the Ladies catch on to what she does. This time, she tilts her head to the left. She does it again tilting her head to the right giving a libidinous look and feel to the movement. Everyone in the class is quiet yet admiring how she performs the easy move.

"Now, did everyone catch that? Did you see how simple it is?" The Ladies smile and give her a "yes" nod. "Now, let me see you do it. Be poised and sensual with it Ladies. Always think about being sexy. No one wants to see a woman attack the pole or being sloppy. Especially me since I am teaching this class. I have your standing point marked on the floor with tape. Let's begin."

The Ladies begin. Many of them do it with no struggle. A few slide down on the pole almost landing on their knees. Rachel and Felicia smile hard trying not to laugh. "Okay, wait. Wait a minute. Some of you still do not have enough upper body strength that is why you are sliding down the pole. Unlike the first move I taught you, you will have to grab the pole a little firmer … or tighter I guess I should say. The move is very simple. You should not be sliding down on the pole. All you're doing is grabbing the pole and lifting your feet off the floor. If your palms are sweaty, wipe them off. Now, let's try it again. From the top Ladies." Candice is sounding like she is instructing a dance class.

Felicia is enjoying watching the Ladies. She is sort of excited. *Maybe I can sign up for this class. Even if I don't use it for Rone, I can have fun and it gives me an outlet. Sitting up in that damn house got boring three years ago.* She is glad that Mama Rachel text her about meeting up. She would have never thought that they would end up at a class like this. Maybe she can also make a few friends. But she needs to know first why her mother-in-law wanted to come here.

While they are practicing, Rachel is enjoying herself as well. It excites her to see women trying to come into their own as well as thinking about being sexy for their man. All of her children may be grown and most of them may be fathers but she is still a woman. The feeling and tingle down there is still very much present. In the midst of her thoughts, Rachel is trying to figure out which two women, or three women are her son's targets. Since she is not sure what Rennie's type of woman is, she is having a hard time figuring this out. Perhaps, the woman that he chose is not his type at all which attracted him to her in the first place. It's just hard to decide which one would be his intended victim. Just then, the instructor let's her know which one is Regina.

"Ah, good Regina. Yes, baby!!" Candice says in her Monique voice and the class roars in laughter. "That is it. You got it Girl!! Nice and graceful with a whole lot of sexy. Yes, be sensual for your husband Girl. I see you. Think of him while you are in class in order to get the moves right. How about you show the class real quick. Pay attention Ladies. Mrs. Wooten is gonna show us what she just did. Some of you might wanna take notes. Now Regina, take a hold of the pole in the center of the room for me so everyone can see."

Rachel is all eyes waiting to see which lady is going to walk towards the center of the room to work the center pole. Regina walks towards the center pole and takes position. *Well, there can't be two of them with husbands in here so let me pay attention to who she is talking to.* Rachel zooms in on the Lady - who is Regina - whom everyone is watching. *Oh my goodness. She is beautiful! Her face, her body, and her poise. I see why Rennie is attracted to her.* Rachel can't take her eyes off of Regina. She is watching her every move. From her walk to her smile. From her rubbing her hand across her long hair to grabbing the pole. *Damn she is gorgeous. But she definitely looks like her husband takes care of her. She looks like money. She looks like she is out of Rennie's league. He hasn't ever brought a woman of her caliber around any of us.*

All the while, Felicia has been talking to Rachel and she doesn't hear anything she has said. Felicia has been watching Regina too. When Mama Rachel doesn't respond to anything she has said, she turns to look at her. She notices that Mama Rachel appears to be in a trance, watching Regina. Looking back at Regina, Felicia wonders what is going on. Now she is looking back and forth between Mama Rachel and the Lady at the pole. Hunching her mother-in-law, she asks, "Is everything okay? I've been talking and you haven't heard anything I have said. Are you okay?" Looking back at Regina, Felicia asks, "Do you know her? Is she why we are here Mama?"

Rachel just smiles at Regina then looks at Felicia. "She is beautiful. Do you agree?" Felicia is not bad looking herself so she is not about to give props to Regina. She just shrugs her shoulders. "Oh, Girl please. Stop. She is gorgeous in every aspect. At least from where I am sitting she is. I see why Rennie wanted …" Rachel catches herself but not fast enough.

"Rennie? What does Rennie have to do with anything? What does he have to do with us sitting here in this sexual class? Hell, Mama … Mama, what does he have to do with her?" I heard that teacher say something about a husband. I know you heard it too. What is going on?" Felicia looks to her in-law for answers.

"Oh Girl hush. I'm trying to see what the beautiful woman is about to do. Look, watch her. Let's see." Rachel is all smiles and remembering her sensual days with her husband.

"I *am* watching her but you said Rennie's name. What kind of mess is he on now Mama? This is about that night you text me ain't it? What did Rone tell you? I didn't hear anything about this.

You left a lot out of our conversation earlier today. Tell me what is going on." Felicia is demanding answers in a respectful way. Rennie gets on all of her nerves, just by walking into the room.

"I said hush Fe-Fe. Be quiet and let's watch her. If I don't watch her, I will be prone to go over Rennie's house tonight and smack his ass early. She's about to do her thing." Rachel is tuned into Regina watching her take the pole in her hands and do the move the instructor just asked them to do.

"Smack him?" Felicia eyes bug out and then they get small. "What has he done for you to want to do that? Is that his girlfriend? She's having an affair with Rennie? *Rennie*?!" Felicia looks at the woman and then decides to recant her question. There is no way in hell Regina is Rennie's girlfriend. Fineness doesn't help an asshole.

"Hell, no. You heard that teacher say she is married. He just wished she was his girlfriend and I'm about to shut his shit down. Now, can we get back to watching the pretty woman?" Rachel gives Felicia a look that would have killed her instantly if that is possible.

The class claps for Regina. She smiles and proceeds to walk back to where she was standing. Candice stops her. "Oh no Miss Thang. Hold up a minute. Do you mind putting that move with what we learned last week?" Regina gives her a "yes" nod. "How about to music?" Candice smiles and before Regina could respond, she claps her hands. The lights dim and the music starts playing.

Rachel and Felicia look around the room then at each other smiling. "Oh she has this class set up right. I need something like this at home. Now *that* was sexy. They are about business up in here." Felicia says to Rachel.

"Aww shit, that's my song. Go 'head Gee Gee and work that pole." The class laughs. Rachel tunes into Colleen saying to herself, *She must be one of the friends. She is pretty too but something is different about her. She gives me a feeling of dangerous. I need to research her fast.*

Coming out her thoughts, Rachel closes her eyes and sways to the sound of L.T.D. with Leslie Wilson from New Birth crooning through the speakers singing April Love. She watches Regina combine something that looks like a forward swirl on the pole with some other moves she is not aware of, ending in the move she learned tonight. Candice claps her hands to stop the music and make the lights go back to normal brightness. Squinting a little from the drastic change from dimness to bright, Rachel smiles at Regina. *Now which one of these is Ray's pick? I can't remember if he told me her name. Damn, if he did, what the hell is it?*

"That was nice. Don't you think Mama? I wished I could do that. I had no intentions at first. Now, I'm not too sure if my intentions are the same. I think I will have fun in this class." Felicia smiles shaking her head amped up ready to join.

"Oh, they're not the same," Rachel tells her as a matter of factly. "You will be signing up for this class. I need to get close to that woman. Don't you worry about Rone. I know you're his wife but I'm his mother. You leave him to me. So you start getting your workout gear together. We will be here next week." *That's if I don't find out from her what I want to know tonight. My son is trying to step it up in the woman department. That right there is all woman, and my son's dumb ass had the nerve to go after you ... Miss Married Woman.* Rachel says to herself still smiling and ignoring the stares Felicia is giving her.

"Oh really? I'm being told what my part is going to be in this 'Save Rennie From Himself' mess, huh? They might not even be open next week. The holidays are upon us, you know?" Felicia smirks popping her gum. Rachel looks at her and Felicia stops popping.

"Okay, that was so beautiful Regina." Looking at the class, Candice asks, "Don't y'all think so?" They smile and shake heads "yes." Looking at Regina she says, "Now, I know you didn't purchase a pole last week. You must have one in that big old house already."

Regina looks around at everyone a little uncomfortable from what Candice says to the class. Rachel is listening attentively. "How you know what I live in? I don't recall us having that conversation. You following me around?" Silence fills the room.

Laughing, Candice responds. "Whoa, nope, I sure am not. I need to know who is in my classes. So it is a precautionary practice. We have to make sure there are no lunatics with ulterior motives signing up for these classes." Rachel's heart sinks hearing that. "I know where *everyone* in here lives. Let's just say it is a background check."

Regina is put on alarm. She eyes Candice closely walking over to her. She is not liking how that sounds coming out of Candice's mouth. Her friends look on trying to figure out what is on Regina's mind. Colleen grabs her arm looking at her. Regina looks down at her arm where Colleen has grabbed her, then looks up at Colleen to see if she can read her eyes. Rachel is watching what looks like a mess about to unfold all because of her son. "Don't do it Gee Gee. Slow your role baby. It's just part of her job … her business. Don't do nothing stupid. That's my job. Stay put." Colleen pleads with her eyes.

Regina doesn't move further with her feet but she is still looking at Colleen, she can't let it go. She asks Candice, "What kind of car do you drive?"

Rachel eyes open wide. "Dammit! She knows someone has been watching her and following her every move." Rachel continues to watch and listen. Felicia is looking at Rachel like she is crazy.

She wants to respond but she doesn't want to be overheard by the other woman.

"Oh, this is getting good Mama. It looks like your *pretty woman* is about to let the instructor experience a butt whipping. I might be able to say that we chose the right night to be here. The only thing missing is the damn popcorn and soda. Hell this is better than that cigarette after sex." Rachel looks at her and rolls her eyes shaking her head. Felicia is on the edge of her seat waiting for mayhem to happen.

Candice looks at Regina trying to figure out what is happening. She wants to know what she has said that offset Regina. "Did I say something wrong Regina? Or did I say something you didn't like?"

"She's all right. She's just been having a rough week. Don't worry about her. I got her. Keep the class going Candice. I'ma take her out in the hall so she can regroup." Colleen says, leading Regina out of the class. BeLynda and Sandy follow. They are a nervous wreck.

Candice smiles irresolutely and continues. "All right class. Sorry about the mishap. Let's gain control of the class and move on to the next move. Next, we will be learning the high kick hold move. Are you ready? Here is a demonstration." Before Candice shows the move, she eyes the Fantastic Four walking out of the class to help Regina calm down. She grips the pole in her hands and spreads her legs wide holding the position. The entire time she is thinking in her head. *What the hell was that all about? I have never seen her like that before. I'd expect that behavior out of Colleen, but Regina. I wonder if I need to speak with her in private. Maybe I can help in some way.* Candice is not aware of how long she was holding the position. She slowly lowers her legs placing her feet on the floor.

Rachel and Felicia look on in utter shock. Rachel gets up and walks out of the classroom. Felicia follows wondering what she is about to do. Existing the class, she hears some of the conversation.

"Girl, what is going on? What was that all about? How you snap on the instructor like that?" BeLynda asks with so much concern in her voice and face.

"Gee Gee, she has nothing to do with what has been going on. Why would she be following you? I know you want it to be nothing but it really is something. Don't start freaking out. We know you are being followed now and that is not a coincidence. It ain't Candice." Colleen says to a flushed face Regina.

"Oh, you think that she drives the black Charger? She doesn't look like the type. But we are your girls. We got you. Your triple protection when you are out with us." Sandy gives her a smile of assurance.

Regina is sweating profusely and holding back tears. She snatches away from Colleen while Sandy and BeLynda look on. "Just leave me alone. I need a minute by myself. Damn! I didn't mean to snap on her like that. But her words … She said …"

Rachel speaks up. "Excuse, I'm not trying to be nosy. Is everything all right? You seemed upset in there about something. And I couldn't help but to hear something about a black Charger following you around. Who would want to harm you beautiful?" Colleen looks at the poised woman wondering why she is interfering.

Sandy is looking at the woman closely and can't figure out where she knows the woman from. *Damn she looks vaguely familiar. I can't figure out where I might know her from though. And I can say is that she was paying close attention to us like she was trying to figure out something.* “Excuse me, you look somewhat familiar. I just can’t put my finger on it. Have we met before?”

Rachel gets a little uneasy. She knows they have never met but Sandy may have seen her sitting on her porch when she was having breakfast with Ray. “Hello pretty lady. I can’t say that I have met you before. I would have remembered such a beautiful face such as yours.” Felicia rolls her eyes up in her head thinking that Mama Rachel is laying it on too damn thick. Colleen catches it and squints her eyes at both the Ladies. “What is your name?”

“My name is Sandy. Sandy Robertson. How are you? You look so familiar. I swear I’ve seen you somewhere before.” *Whoever she is and whatever her presence is about will come to me soon enough.*

“Your name doesn’t sound familiar. Well, it is nice to meet you Sandy Robertson. All right beautiful Ladies. I see I have sparked up other curiosities instead of what I came out here to do. We will leave now. I apologize for the interference.” Rachel reaches into her purse for a pen and notepad, writing her number on one of the sheets of paper, she hands it to Regina. “If you ever need anything, do not hesitate to use the number. I’m in the business to make bullshit disappear.” Colleen raises her eyebrows. “It was really nice meeting you Ladies. I’m sure I will be seeing you around.” The Ladies watch Rachel and Felicia walk away down the hall.

She is in the business of making bullshit disappear, hunh? If Regina doesn’t use the number, I definitely might ... Miss Rachel. Her skin is flawless and reeks of money and connections. Her approach was about something other than what occurred in this damn room.

Regina is watching Colleen closely trying to psychoanalyze her behavior. “I need to go in here and apologize to Candice and the class.”

Chapter Eighteen

18

"Hey baby! What were you doing? You in your office chilling? Or you taking a break from working?" Regina sees Stan turn the corner coming from the direction of his office.

"Naw, actually, I have been waiting on you. Hey Colleen how are you?" Stan gives Regina a hug and kiss on the lips. He gives Colleen a hug and a kiss on the cheek.

"Hey Stan. What's up with you? Normally when we come over on Mondays, you are deep into some shit in your office. I'm surprised to see you out and about walking around the house. What, you were getting restless waiting on your baby?"

"Yea, well I had something else to do, so work is gonna have to wait," he says and looks at Regina sternly. She knows what that looks means. She is feeling uneasy by his look. It is all too familiar.

"Colleen go ahead and get comfortable and I will be with you in a minute. I'm gonna see what Stan wants real quick." She tries to give Colleen a smile but it doesn't form just right. Colleen looks at Regina and then Stan wondering what is going on now. Stan seems so serious and Regina seems so nervous.

Did I come over here and walk into some marital bullshit? I know damn well Stan ain't on no bullshit. He better not forgot who I am. I know she will tell me something while we are in the sauna. So I'll keep my cool until I know what the fuck is going on. Then again, I can take a little marital bullshit over the other mess she has going on. That doesn't require weapons ... then again, it can but it better not.

"Yea, Mrs. Wooten, step into my office. Oh and Colleen, you might as well come in with her. I am glad you are here. You are her friend and I know you know some of this shit, since I told her to talk to you," he looks at Regina again, and she holds her head down to prevent looking at him.

"Know what? What the fuck is going on? I'm feeling perturbed about this tension in here," Colleen says while walking behind Stan but beside Regina towards his office. Regina continues to look straight ahead. "Hey Maria. How are you tonight?"

"Hola Senora Robertson, I fine. How are you?" She gives Colleen a hug and pats her on the back.

"I'm not sure just yet, Maria. But I will let you know when I walk back out of Stan's office. Hell, the way he is looking, maybe I should just stand out here in the hall instead." Colleen gives Maria the “something-ain’t-right” look and Maria catches on quickly and walks off.

Entering Stan’s office, Colleen looks around admiring the décor and takes a seat on the leather ottoman. This is nice Stan. You picked out the furniture and decorated by yourself? There’s another office waiting for you to put your talent to work.”

Walking over to the fridge, Stan responds, “Nah, you know I didn’t do this by myself. You know damn well if I had, everything in here would be black. Gee Gee wasn’t going to allow that happen.

Pointing at the fridge while talking, he is offering both Colleen and Regina something to drink. Regina doesn’t want anything. Colleen looks at Stan asking, “I’m not sure what the fuck is going on but if this is some serious shit, do you need to give me something stronger? You keep giving Gee Gee the eye and she was extremely quiet in class tonight.” Regina snaps her head in Colleen’s direction making her ponytail slap her in the face. She removes the strands that get stuck to her lip gloss.

Stan sits down at his desk, closes his eyes and rubs his temples swinging from right to left in his chair. He looks up at Regina and asks, “Did you tell your girl or your girls what the fuck is going on? Or did you just tell me that you did when actually you didn’t? Or did you leave something out?” Stan looks at Regina frowning as if he has a headache.

“Not really. Colleen was with me when I was feeling uneasy the other night at class but I never said anything to Sandy and BeLynda. They had already pulled off. But …”

“Wait, the other night? What are you talking about?” Stan stops moving around in his chair to give Regina all of his attention. Regina’s heat is beating fast.

"Oh she is talking about the black Charger that was sitting in the parking lot idling with the lights off." Colleen looks at Regina as if she is saying, *he didn't know about that*? Regina looks away rubbing her hand across her ponytail.

Stan catches Colleen's look then returns his eyes back at Regina as if to be saying, *do you mind explaining what the hell she is talking about?* "What is she talking about Gee Gee? You ain't told me about a damn car sitting anywhere. How long has this shit been going on?" Stan is heated. He instantly appears to have turned red.

"Well, at first, I saw a black Charger outside of our house, sitting across the street and it looked like someone was taking pictures because I was seeing flashes. That was right before we went to the Poconos." Stan looks at Regina shifting around in his seat full of frustration. He pours himself a shot and swallows it in one gulp, slamming the shot glass down on the desk.

"Then when I was in class, I kept seeing a figure or something at the door but when I would look at the door, it would jump or move so I couldn't see it. I thought maybe it was my imagination and then when the teacher walked in, I didn't think anything else about it. But when the black Charger was sitting in the parking lot after class idling I wasn't sure what to think. I brought it to Colleen's attention while we were getting in our cars and she said for us to pull off together. I didn't see the car following me, so I thought I was just trippin' about nothing." Stan looks over at Colleen who is looking at him waiting for expressions. His nose is flared like a bull. Then he looks back at Regina for her to continue pissing him off with her story.

Standing with her arms folded across her chest, she continues. "When I got home that night, a black Charger drove pass the house while I was waiting for Maria to open the door but I thought maybe that it was someone in the neighborhood that might've had the same type of car. I thought it was a coincidence. Stan I really didn't think it was anything." Stan is just listening and looking at her moving his eyebrows up and down, occasionally wrinkling them as if to say, *are you really serious right now? All this shit and you told none of it to me? You told none of it to no one!*

Regina kept talking, "I never told anything else to Colleen. I told her that I would talk about it later. I just never got around to saying anything else until last Saturday. And then the crazy stuff that happened when we were in the Poconos. I wasn't sure if any, all, or none of that was related. Then it just hit too close to home when I found the note in the bushes." She holds her head down while Colleen and Stan are looking at her like she has twenty alien heads.

Stan is stunned. He is somewhat speechless and highly pissed at what he is hearing from his wife. "So the first situation was right before we went to the Poconos? How long has this really been going on Regina? What the fuck were you thinking? Why wouldn't you have said something? We all just walking around here in the blind. When were you gonna say something? After the motherfucka got next to one of us?!"

"Well, I can say that she wasn't sure what was going on. If she knew, I am sure that she would have said something to you before now, Stan." Stan looks at Colleen like she has fifty alien heads. "C'mon Stan, you know her more than any of us. Don't you think she would have said something if she thought it was really serious?" Stan looks at Regina. "But what note are you talking about? The motherfucka – whoever it is - is coming up on the premises leaving threats?! What did it say?" Colleen is completely focused.

"Yes I would have said something babe if I knew. I mean, hell, I wanted to make sure I wasn't creating something that wasn't there. I didn't want to put you or anyone on alert if it was nothing." Regina's eyes begin to water. Stan looks at her with his heart breaking.

"What damn note?! When did this happen? What the fuck did it say?! Hellooo!!" Colleen doesn't want to get off track but looking at Stan's expression, she feels like she is inside of a movie and he is about to run to Regina in slow motion. He quickly snaps out of his reverie.

Rubbing his temples with his eyes close, he says, "Ay, I don't give a fuck what you wanted to make sure. Anything you see suspicious, I need to hear about it with an urgency. It could be somebody that is pissed off with me. You never know. Hell, I don't know who you could've pissed off and wants revenge but damn, Regina think babe. Shadows at your class door? Seeing the same type of car or the same muhfuckin' car … OUTSIDE OUR HOUSE?! In the parking lot when you get out of class? Going down our street the same damn night? What the fuck?! Ay, STOP," Stan yells and hits the desk with his fist. When he says the last statement, Regina and Colleen jump. Regina sits down.

"Ay, I need a damn stiff drink. Stan what you got? What you sippin' on? I'ma need some of that. And … Regina … what … note? I done asked that I don't know how many times already." Stan pulls the note out of his desk drawer. Colleen walks over to get the note. She reads it and gets pissed off. Handing it back to Stan, she says, "Yea, Stan hurry up with my fuckin' drink, please."

"I gotchoo but I need you to do something for me?" Stan leans on the desk tapping his fingertips on his nameplate. He looks at Colleen very serious. He leans back in his chair and places his feet up on the desk with his hands folded in his lap.

Colleen looks at him and gives him the neck roll pointing at herself. "Me? What you need me to do?" Stan gives her that look.

He looks at Regina and back at Colleen tilting his head, raising his right eyebrow. *Damn he has been doing a lot of talking with his face tonight*, says Colleen to herself. She finally realizes what he is saying. She closes her eyes and sighs, pinching the bridge of her nose. "C'mon Stan … I don't have the connection anymore."

Stan looks at her hardheartedly. "Oh you don't? Since when? Or is it that you *tried* to leave that life alone? You got your business going and yea, you had to cut off a few people to do that but we don't ever lose connection Lene. And right now, there are no options with my request for you."

Regina looks at him with a pissed off look when he mentions "connection." *What the fuck is he talking about*, Regina says to herself. "Oh *'we'* don't Stan? What are you saying Stanley? What are you implying and what does this have to do with Colleen?"

Colleen holds her head down shaking her head from side-to-side not wanting Regina to know anything. She is praying Stan moves on to something else. She just thought all of that hood past shit was over and done with. Yet here it is haunting her and trying to invite itself into her present.

Stan looks at Colleen and smiles, removing his feet from the desk. He leans forward folding his hands together leaning on his desk, slightly whispering to Colleen. "Oh, so your girls never knew, huh? Really? None of them? Sorry that it had to come out like this but hey, I need your help. I need it like yesterday. And ain't nothing as urgent as this right now my Baby Girl." Colleen stands up asking for her stiff drink again. Stan quickly gets up to make her a drink. He knows she needs it in all earnestness. "Hey, can I smoke in here?" Stan gives her a yes nod saying, "Hey, help yourself. I know you need it right now."

"Will one of you tell me what the fuck is going on? It's like y'all talking in codes and shit and I'm tired of being lost. What do you need Colleen for and what kind of connections is he talking about Lene?" Regina looks back and forth between Stan and Colleen waiting for an answer. Colleen looks at Stan and rolls her eyes at him taking out a cigarette and lighter. Deciding to get comfortable, she takes off her Nikes wiggling her toes and pulling her hair putting a hair band on forming a ponytail. Colleen stands up pacing the floor moving her head from side to side like she is cracking her neck, ready for a fight.

Looking at Regina Stan says, "My baby don't know her friends, for real. Remember I said that just the other day? Well, I'm gonna sit back and let your friend tell you some things." Stan leans back folding his arms across his chest waiting for the conversation to disclose all of what Regina has been oblivious to throughout the entire friendship with Colleen.

Regina looks at Colleen. She is lighting her cigarette and takes a sip of her Hennessey. Colleen takes a long drag of her Newport, blowing some out her mouth and the rest through her nostrils. She puffs again, looking at Stan and he is waiting for her to begin speaking. She stomps her foot saying, "Okay, damn!! Regina, um … uh … remember when we met back in high school? Regina gives her a "yes" nod. "Well, I was in the drug game then but I wasn't really selling." Regina's eyes grow as big as golf balls. "I was something like … I was providing a service for many dealers, including Stan." Regina's eyes are about to pop out of the sockets. She looks over at Stan. "That's how we met and I was able to introduce him to you. But he promised me that he wouldn't tell you what I did in my spare time." She looks up at Regina and she can see shock written all over her face.

"What kind of services Lene? Were you sleeping with these damn dealers Lene … including Stan? Were they sharing you? You introduced me to one of your fuckin' *TRICKS*?!" Jumping up off the couch, she yells, "Bitch you told me that you used to date his brother

James!" Regina had heard about a few of the girls in the neighborhood that would be passed around the drug dealers, like it was something normal to do. She is extremely pissed at what she is hearing about her friend and her husband. Looking at Stan, she asks, "So what the fuck would her services do for you now? Let me hear this since you were so relentless about me finding this shit out."

Stan looks at Regina with stern eyes and his flaring his nose. Bringing his hands with fingers intertwine to his mouth, resting his elbows propped on the desk, he looks at Colleen signaling for her to finish talking before it gets messy over the wrong assumptions. He isn't liking what Regina said no more than he likes that she is lost to the hood world and she grew up in the heart of the hood. Maybe it is because Colleen is female and Regina can't envision what else she could be doing being involved in the drug world if she wasn't a dealer or a purchaser.

Colleen begins responding to Regina. "I did date his brother Gee Gee but I met Stan first … at a business meeting with Blue." Regina frowns. "Gee Gee, it wasn't those type of services. Damn, why the fuck would you go there? What part of the drug game is whoring? What I am saying is that … if they needed someone to disappear, or to be warned … severely … they would call me." Colleen is puffing hard and taking big gulps of her Hennessey frowning from the strong brown liquid burning her throat.

Regina's mouth almost hit the floor. "If they needed them to disappear or to be severely warned? Disappear as in … kill them?" Colleen shakes her head "yes" avoiding Regina's eye. She doesn't want Regina to look inside her soul. Regina laughs thinking Colleen is still not wanting to tell her why Stan needs her. Regina believes Colleen is lying. Colleen looks over at Regina to see what is funny. Then Regina sees the look in her friend's eyes. She sits down and looks over at her husband. He just stares at her waiting for it to sink in. "Oh … my … God. Oh my God! Colleen!!" Regina yells, jumps back up and starts pacing the floor.

"I'm sorry, I never wanted you to know. I wasn't proud of it but it did pay the bills in my Mom's house and that's how I was able to start my own business and never have to work for anyone anymore other than me. No one was supposed to know." Regina is just looking back and forth between her friend and husband. "Say something Gee Gee, please! I'm sorry I never told you but I was hoping that I never would have to. I shouldn't be tellin' you now!" Colleen rolls her eyes at Stan.

Regina begins to walk out of the office and Colleen calls after her. "Gee Gee, wait! Don't leave like this. Tell me you what you are feeling. Please. Curse me out if you need to. I need to know what's on your mind." Colleen starts walking behind Regina. Holding her down, she whispers, "You were never supposed to know."

Stan calls out to her. "Regina Wooten. Did you hear what your last name is? You are a 'Wooten' now and that means you need to stay right here in this room. I hate that it came to you like this but I need her. So to keep you from thinking bullshit, like you were a few minutes ago, I needed her to tell you. Babe, she is the best."

"You mean I *was* the best. I don't do that anymore Stan. I have retired. Don't talk about that shit like it is fuckin' current because it ain't. That was a long time ago. I need another goddamn drink please." She gulps down the last of what was left in her glass and holds it out to Stan.

Stan continues talking as he walks over to Colleen to get her glass, walking over to the bar to pour her another drink. "No, you *are* the best. You may be out of touch a little bit but from what Regina was telling about your demeanor at breakfast the other day, oh it's still there. It is very present so stop lying to yourself because you are not lying to me." Handing Colleen her drink, he turns to Regina and continues. "Her name sounds off alarms in the streets and she can't be fucked with."

Regina stops walking, turning around looking at Colleen and then at Stan. "Wow! You are really serious. This is not a joke? I am not being punked or dreaming this shit? My friend's name 'sounds off alarms' in the motherfuckin' streets? My friend, standing right here in my face in my husband's office … the flyest bitch I know, used to kill for a living? For the neighborhood dealers?" Silence. Stan looks at her yet says nothing.

Looking back at Colleen, Stan says, "I gotta few calls to make and they already know that you were in my life indirectly. So I need to meet up with a few people and get them ready to go."

Colleen looks at Stan invasively. "A few people? Who you talkin' 'bout? I know you are not telling me in front of Regina that you still have contact with the Good 'Ol Boys." Stan shakes his head "yes." Colleen eyes get wide, then twitch and her hand covers her mouth. "Oh shit!! Stan, you still talk to Trigga, Blade, Peanut, KO, and Dee? I thought y'all went your separate ways."

"Yea, we did … business wise, somewhat."

"Business wise?! What does that mean Stanley Wooten? What the fuck are you saying?" Regina is heated. Stan and Colleen look at her aghast. They have never seen Regina this angry. Stan is angry at how Regina is coming at him but he understands. He feels that he has let his wife down somehow but he hasn't done anything illegal since he went legit. But he always remained prepared for a war of any kind.

Responding to Colleen, he says, "Well Blade got twenty years. So he's done. Peanut died a few years back. One of his son's was killed and he got killed retaliating. He wasn't ready for the power they came with. But the rest … yea … we keep in touch." Regina looks at him hurt but glad that it's out in the open. "Ay, babe … I run two businesses. I needed them on my team, just in case any dumb shit popped off. So don't be looking at me like that. I wasn't trying to hide anything from you but I needed to protect me and mines. You have to understand that. Just sit and calm down. Please don't overreact."

"Overreact?! They are on your fuckin' payroll Stan?!" Stan shakes his head "yes." "So … let me get this straight. Colleen, you killed people for dealers, and that included my husband?" Colleen answers her this time shaking her head "yes" not happy about disclosing this to her friend of over fifteen years. "And Stan, you were that deep in that world that you needed people offed, or roughed up … and you think that you might need them damn fools you call friends now in your LEGITMATE businesses?" He shakes his head "yes" again looking at his wife not blinking standing his ground. She sits down in one of the chairs by the window to gather herself.

"Babe, and I need Colleen right now. I'm serious. No joking and no dreamin'. She is the shiznit. Trust me when I say that she is. I mean back then, her name on the streets was …"

"Naw Stan, don't do that. She doesn't need to know that. It ain't necessary. You're sayin' too much, right now. She is gonna say something to Sandy and Bee and I can't have that. None of them need to be drawn into that world. Please … Stan, don't," Colleen interrupts.

"Naw, Colleen shut the fuck up. You got my husband in here talking in Ebonics and shit … the shiznit? Really Stan? So … what did they call my *friend* on the streets? Evidently, it surely wasn't 'Colleen.' I want to know how deep she was in that world." Regina looks at Colleen with a scowl on her face letting Colleen know that she is beyond pissed right now and not to keep anymore shit from her.

Stan looks at Regina and knows she is a mixed bag of emotions right now. Cautiously, he speaks to Regina while looking at Colleen. “They called her ‘Killarette.’ At first it was like a little inside joke because she didn’t mess around. She was good at what she did but the name just sort of stuck because she delivered every time. Like a thief in the night … she was in and out. She was wanted for service amongst all dealers starting from the top of the dealer chain.” Regina is too lost for words. She sat there looking at Colleen. She realized that she didn’t know her friend as well as she thought. Colleen was puffing hard on cigarette four feeling Regina’s eyes burning a hole in the side of her face.

“Babe, it was her past but just like me, we gotta dig them up temporarily. Only temporarily, trust me. We gotta see what is going on and get it under control. I’m not gonna let someone fuck with me or my wife. That is not gonna happen and it is not up for discussion. I ain’t built for bullshit … I get rid of bullshit ... FAST!! Whomever it is got the game all fucking confused. Apparently all they know is that I’m your husband but they never did a background check on who Stan Wooten aka Wootey is for real. And I’m about to show ’em.” Stan gave his scowl with the lips turned up on the right side corner just thinking about the mess. He takes a big gulp of his drink getting up to walk over to the bar and add more to it.

Regina just sat there absorbing all that she is listening to. She doesn’t know what to think. She knows who her husband once was but evidently not completely but she doesn’t know exactly who her friend is. Looking at Colleen, she says, “I get it now. That’s why you weren’t ever too fazed about too much shit because you know what you can do, huh? Your eyes kept trying to tell me and I ignored it until recently. The other day at breakfast, talking about weapons and shit. Oh, you can handle yours, hunh? So you started working for Blue first, and then you became a household name amongst the big and small hustlers? How did Blue know you could do that? Hell when did you get any sleep? I mean, you were always with us." Colleen holds her head down avoiding her friend's eyes.

"Colleen, I need your connection to get to work and put your ear to the streets. See what you can find out. Your connection is larger than mine." Regina looks over at Colleen waiting for her to answer her question. She didn't like that Stan cut her off. Colleen is avoiding all eye contact at this point lighting another cigarette shaking her head as if to say "okay." "Do you still have your specialty weapons? If not, I have them. We can go look at them in a few."

Regina is thrown for all kinds of loops tonight. Throwing her hands up in the air, she yells laughing, "What the fuck! Am I trapped inside the movie Blue Hill Avenue?! Y'all just continuing on talking as if I'm not here." Stan looks at her then returns to his conversation with Colleen waiting for her answer to his questions.

"Naw, I got rid of most of my shit. I didn't want any memories of my dirt. I did keep a few things just in case I needed them for me. Aww man, I thought this was all behind me. I was really trying to live my life as normal as possible. I got my business to run and I have my girls. I'm not trying to bring harm in their direction Stan."

"I know, but you never know. Your girls will be fine and you can still live your life normal, it just has to be put on hold for a minute, just like mine. But first, I just want to make sure Regina is all right with hearing all of this." Looking over at Regina he asks, "Babe … Gee Gee … Regina, you all right?"

Looking up at Colleen, Regina says, "Oh, you had weapons preferences, hunh? I mean, I don't know what to say. You never at all let on that you were into this kind of business. You really hid it well Girl, I have to hand it to you."

"And that's what made her great at what she did. You weren't supposed to know. What she did was not for you to know. People who live the lives of hitman never let on what they do. They can't Gee. You can't be mad at her baby. She did what she was supposed to do or she might've been locked up or dead. Or anyone connected with her, starting with her family. Then what?" Regina says nothing to Stan's statement.

Walking over to Colleen, she says, "Give me one of those damn cigarette. Stan fix me a damn drink." He looks at her surprised about the cigarette but he says nothing. Stan jumps up quickly and fixes her a strong margarita and hands it to her. Taking two big gulps making a painful expression Regina says, "Damn, I will have hair on my chest in the morning from this damn drink." They laugh. "Are we done here? I can't take anymore. I need to get into the Sauna Room. My mind and body needs to relax from all of this." Stan shakes his head "yes." "Aight, Colleen let's go. I've had more than enough surprises right now. But we will talk in the Sauna. No one can hear us in there."

Stan gives Colleen the look that says, *you will be letting me know what is said in that room.* Colleen gives a slight head shake and follows Regina out of the office. Stan picks up the office phone making a call.

Ring! Ring!

"Speak." The deep voice on the other end of the phone says.

"Is this the secured line? Or do you need to call me back," Stan asks.

"Always. Now, are *you* secured is the question."

"And you know it," Stan laughs.

"Aiight. You know I have to check. Now, what you got for me?"

"Chinning wit button man." (Talking with the professional killa)

"Oh word?! Dropper down? (Hired killa ready)

"Yeap.

"Aiight. I'm on that. Need that call bruh."

"Done yesterday."

"Sleep." ***click***

****

"Ooh, this steam feels so good to my body. I needed this after class and damn sure needed it after being in that office. Whew!" Regina sinks down onto the bench in the Sauna Room.

"Hell, we both needed this. I'm so sorry that you had to find out like this Gee Gee. I really thought all of that mess was behind me. Please do not be upset with me. That is not something that you just sit around talking about kickin' it with the Girls." Colleen takes a sip of the brown liquid in her glass.

Damn!! I'm worried about my Girl. I know that I could take care of this for her. She getting notes 'n shit out of the fuckin' bushes? And Stan wants me to result to my old ways? Tonight is more than I bargained for coming over here. But even if I had gone home, Stan would've been calling me. That might've been the way to go. This is some fucked up shit. No joke! I'm gonna be getting a call from one of those damn goons soon.

"Don't worry about it Lene. The important thing is I know now. At least I know what was behind those dark eyes. But now that I know what I know, let me ask you something." Regina turns around to face her new friend.

"Oh Lord, Regina. What is it that you wanna know? Don't start getting too deep prying. I can't answer certain things. I'm thirty-one years old now. Not seventeen. Don't judge how I ate." Colleen rubs her temples closing her eyes squeezing them tight.

"Okay." Looking at Colleen, she asks, "The other day at the Spa, when Bee was talking … you seemed very interested in the story she was telling about Khalil's father and twin siblings. Was it really a fire that killed them?" Regina looks at Colleen to see if she will look over at her. And she doesn't.

Fuck!! "Regina, what are you doing? Don't do this," Colleen whines. "Why would you ask that? Did you just hear what I said?"

Regina closes her eyes saying, "You killed them didn't you?"

Colleen just looks at her. Regina has her answer through Colleen's silence and says, "Don't worry, your secret is safe with me. I don't even know why. I just need to know who my 'friend' is. I love you Lene. Remember that." Regina stands to take off her robe. It is getting extremely hot from the heat and the conversation.

Colleen hugs her friend. "I love you too. Thank you so much. I am not proud of the things I did but it paid well and I needed to make sure my family was okay. I needed to make sure my friends were okay too. The hood was not for us Gee Gee. I would have done anything to make sure we got out of that hell hole so many called home, life, a pot of gold, and are still there. I never understood why some were willing to stay. We weren't gonna remain in that trash. I refused to. But … you got your husband, Bee and I got our businesses, and Sandy got a government job. But you gotta promise me that you won't let Bee know that I am the reason behind Khalil not having his father around. You have to promise me that my street name doesn't come out to her and Sandy. No one knows the person behind the name other than the hood game and they know the code of the streets. Can you do that for me?" Colleen is pleading with her eyes holding Regina's hand tightly.

"You have my word. The same way Stan made you say certain things to me … I won't make you repeat those words to our friends. Your past was presented to me because of what the hell is going on with me. So unless they are presented with some bullshit, it will be our secret. I'm glad I know and I do understand even though you may not think I do. I'm not as naïve as you and Stan may think. I was disappointed that you didn't think you could confide in me. I may not have liked it, but I do understand survival. You may think that my mother had us in the hood because she was being cheap, but a lot of shit came with her choosing the hood over her bank account."

Colleen listens closely to her friend. She is sensing there is some underlying shit that Regina is not saying. Some things that her friend since eleventh grade never told her, or anyone. She is wondering what is it that prissy Regina could have been holding on to as tight as she holds onto her purse … her man … her dignity … her escape from the hood. Then Regina answers her thoughts.

"I never knew my father. I know you noticed while y'all talked about a father and some of y'all spent weekends with your biological, I had no one to claim as my 'daddy.' My birth certificate has no name by the 'father' line. I was told he died before I was born yet we all supposedly have the same father. I guess that's why we all look alike yet we don't look like no one on our mother's side of the family. There was no one there to claim me … to claim any of us. We were an outcast amongst both sides of the family. Yet, the sonofabitch that was there had no problem using his damn tongue and hands on me and my sisters once each of us reached the age of fifteen. I was the last one and my sisters never told me he was like that. Fuck, they never tried to help me and take me out of the hell-hole when they moved out. That is why to this day, I have nothing to do with what 'the world' considers 'family.' You, Bee, and Dee Dee are my sisters … Stan is my husband … all of you are my family. I had to create my own and I am not ashamed of who I ended up with. So if I had the strength, courage, and heart that you have, I would have killed that motherfucka without a fuckin' blink of the eye. But God knows what we went through and he blessed his ass with an instant death through a drive-by shooting that was meant for the man he stopped to shoot the breeze with … his damn undercover agent brotha. That made it look like he was an informant telling some shit." Regina takes a sip of the brown liquid in her glass. Colleen looks at her surprised.

The murders are clearer to Colleen now. "Damn Gee Gee, I never knew. Why didn't you ever say anything? We are close friends. Not associates. You supposed to tell shit like that. He did used to look at me lustfully but I guess, my eyes told him he was barking up the wrong tree. But had I known …"

"I know Lene. You would have ended my misery after the first lick and touch. Had you ever told me in confidence what you were up to, I may have requested your services. I guess that is what

I am mad at the most. You out there helping out the dealers, yet your friend right here needed you more. He never penetrated me but he did that to my sisters. Now one is on crack with one of his damn kids and the other can't trust herself to be in a committed relationship because of her nightmares. And they never said anything. My mother was just fuckin' clueless. She thought things were just wonderful. That nigga used her … for her daughters."

Colleen and Regina are crying through Regina's soul searching. "Damn. I don't know what to say. Am I the only one you have told this too?"

"No. But what I am about to tell you, has to stay between us too. I have your secret and then you will have mine." Colleen looks at Regina wondering what is it that she wants her to keep a secret.

"What is it Gee Gee? Tell me. I am here for you. Don't hold anything back. Apparently you have been holding on to it too long."

"I am the cause behind that motherfucka's death. It was planned that way. Stan wanted his brother and I made sure his ass went to the store to get some bread so he would run into his ass and kick it with him. Stan was the passenger in that car with his weapon of choice that ended his life, with his brother's. I'm sure everybody knew who did it. But by the grace of God, Stan never got picked up or questioned."

Colleen now vividly remembers the day. Many events she suppressed in order to live a life normal as possible. It was all clear to her now. Looking at Regina saying, "I remember that Gee Gee."

"Oh you do? Stan told you about that?" Regina is shocked. "I thought you said things like that were not supposed to be known."

"Gee Gee, the hood doesn't talk. At least not on Stan. He went deep and no one wanted to cross his path, at least not like that. That would have been as wrong as they could get if they spoke on his actions. They would have gotten more than stitches. You really didn't know who Stan was, hunh? Well, I won't tell you … he would have to do that."

"So he told you before or after it happened?" Regina really wants to know. She thought this was just their secret.

"Does it really matter when he told me?"

"I asked didn't I? What did you say when he told what he was gonna do?"

"He didn't really have to tell me anything Gee Gee. 'Killarette' was driving the car."

Chapter Nineteen

19

"Ho! Ho! Ho! Merry Christmas Lady! How are you doing? I see you got the hams on display this evening."

"Ho! Ho! Ho yourself Girlie! Where is your red Mrs. Claus' suit since you're coming in here all jolly? You're looking good too." Sandy asks greeting Regina.

"Oh, my bad. I forgot. Damn, I will remember the next time," Regina laughs. "But that outfit doesn't complement me all that well. So I chose what I do best. And that's this Tahari piece. Is that all right with you dear? I guess it does since you gave me a compliment." They give a little laugh.

"Hey, that's your husband's pocket, not mine. So, if he is fine with the outfit, then it is definitely fine with me." Sandy and

Regina giggle. "How are you otherwise? How are things going? You still looking good. I have to admit though, that plum wool double-breasted dress with the wing tip bottom backing looks sexy on you. It accentuates your ass … not that you need any accentuating. I'm just pointing out the obvious. Stan picked this out for you? If so, I'm sure he didn't expect you to be wearing it on Christmas Eve to meet up with your Girls." Sandy slightly turns Regina to the side leaning over to check her ass out.

"Well, thank you for the compliment. I think I heard one or more in what you said, right?" Regina frowns laughing and watching Sandy look at her ass. "And for the record, I chose this dress this evening, not Stan. And before you ask again, yes, he was ready for me to take it off and do some stunts real quick before I met y'all but he knows I got him when I get home." Sandy laughs with Regina.

Colleen sashays into Morton's Steakhouse dressed to the nine in her full length silver blue fox that is hiding her Lord and Taylor navy cashmere sweater dress with a plunging neckline. Her gray Enzo Angiolini knee high boots are heard clicking across the floor. Sandy and Regina hear the clicking – clacking on the floor and turns to see who is coming their way. They see Colleen has two big shopping bags full of gifts. They smile standing to greet her.

"Hey Ladies. Pre Merry Christmas! How are y'all doing this evening?" Colleen sits the bags on the floor by their table. "I thought I'd never get to this table with these damn bags. Look at my fingers all red and smashed." She receives their smiles, hugs, and kisses. "How long y'all been here? Is this our table? Why are y'all standing?"

"We haven't been here that long. We got here at the same time. Good to see you Girlie. You looking good in that fox. I see you. I'm liking those boots too." Sandy says admiring Colleen's appearance. “And your make-up is flawless. Did you have your man-girlfriend come over and hook you up? He must’ve been mad at one of his men and gossiped the entire story when he was doing it. He beat the hell out of your face.” Sandy and Regina laugh out loud. Regina looks around subconsciously to see if they are drawing attention from the other eaters.

“Thank you Lady. But no, he had a fashion show to do this evening. So I beat my own face up. Thanks for the compliment though. I took extra time to make sure I was looking right for my pre-Christmas gathering with my Girls. I do that from time-to-time, you know. It’s reassuring that I did a good enough job for you to think that Jamie did it.” The Ladies take off their outer garments hanging them on the back of their seats.

“Oh you did your face? Really? Damn girl! You were on point, not that you aren’t any other time. You took extra care for having dinner with us today. If you weren’t a one woman business, I would say that you should add make-up artist to your business. But … I know, that’s what Jamie does for you.” Regina smiles excitedly at Colleen. She loves Christmas and she can’t wait to give out her gifts.

Looking around, Colleen asks, “Where is Bee? She not here yet? This is a first. I’m surprised. She is never late for anything. Ms. Punctuality is serious about being on time. She don’t want to be waiting on you and she don’t want you to be waiting on her.” Sandy and Regina shake their heads on agreement.

“Well, I guess there is a first for everything. She probably had to break Khalil off a piece before she got here.” Sandy gives a wide smile. “She had to make sure he was thinking about her while she is with us for a few hours.” The three Ladies laugh. “They seem to be going strong. I’m happy for my Girl.”

Sitting down, they finish their conversation, waiting for BeLynda and their attendant to come with an introduction, taking their drinks.

"Both of you look nice this evening, as always. Sandy, you got the thighs on display. I just noticed they have gotten a little thicker. Thanks to those three nights a week dinners." Colleen laughs, Regina smiles looking at Sandy. Sandy blushes. "What you got planned when you leave here? Meeting Ray … or Larry afterwards?"

"Thanks Lene but I am not meeting anyone when I leave here. Hell, after that talk about getting Ray to help me start my business, I'm beginning to feel like a user. He has called a few times but I've not answered or returned his calls. Larry, I've not spoken with him since we went to the movies and he came over for a nightcap." Regina smiles and Colleen looks at her ready to hear some juicy. "I've been spending so much time with Ray but I'll tell y'all about that later."

"A user?! Ignoring his calls? For what? You didn't even agree with what I had to say so why would it be based off of my words? All I was saying was, once a woman sees a man with all the right aspects … looks, style, dress, home, car, dick, and money, they will do what it takes to be there for a little piece of that livin'. Ray is *offering*, honey. You haven't had to do anything but show up … just be present."

"I'm not a gold-digga. That has never been me. I haven't even had sex with the man and that's important to me. I'm a woman of the stages. You know such as, we meet, talk, get to know each other, spend time together, date, sex, update titles … to a possible marriage. Do you know anything about that Lene?" Sandy looks for an answer even though she is playing with her. "Hell, we haven't even kissed yet nor has my title changed from anything other the woman he is getting to know. So I don't care what he is offering. I won't be looking like a thirsty bitch. And as an independent business woman such as yourself, I am sure you can understand that, right Lene?"

"Wait ... wait one damn minute. Heifer, all this time you are spending with this man?! Three nights a week for dinner, and he ever cooked breakfast for you ... at his *house*? Got cars picking you up, and you have felt his lips on your lips?" Sandy laughs shaking her head "no." "Have you felt them on your hand, your neck ... anywhere?! Other than the kiss on the cheek he gave you at the club that night?" Sandy laughs shaking her head "no." Colleen is dumbstruck.

"Maybe he is working up to that 'kiss' Lene. He is taking his time with her. He is giving Sandy what she wants."

"Working up to swapping spit? Girl, please. All that stuff that man is doing for her? He is working up to the pussy."

"Maybe ... maybe not but I wouldn't say that he is working up to the pussy either then even though I know it would be an added bonus if he was getting it, seeing it, smelling it ... something. He is around it several nights a week and that shows he has patience and respects Sandy." Regina looks at Sandy and smiles. "This man is actually dating Sandy and I like it." Colleen looks at Regina as if she is crazy rolling her eyes.

Colleen has had enough of listening to the fairytale man. She is happy for Sandy but she gets the conversation back on track. "Now, look at Gee Gee. I see you got the ass – ets on display this evening Girl. That dress is saying something Girl. Stan must've been in his office when you got dressed and when you left. He didn't critique your outfit? All that ass is saying *'PADOW'*!" Sandy laughs at Colleen while Regina is smiling giving Colleen the "will you shut up" look.

"What?! I'm sure you saw those young ass hustlers over there at that table checking out all that ass - ets and those hips. That dress is accentuating in all the right places. I mean goddamn Gee Gee! I know those young boys over there trying to figure out how they can slip you their number without them damn hood dates causing a scene." All the Ladies softly giggle.

"Hey Ladies. Hello, hello, hello. Pre Merry Christmas to each of you. Sorry I am late. What y'all laughing at? I know y'all aren't giving up the juicy before I get here. Have y'all order drinks yet? Or were you waiting for me?" BeLynda smiles sitting her bags of gifts on the floor next to the rest of their bags.

"Hey Sexy! We haven't ordered anything. We were waiting on you. And I guess the waiter or waitress thought we were waiting on you too because no one has been over here yet. Then again, it is crowded in here though. Everyone must've had the same idea this evening." Looking at BeLynda, Regina says, "Hell, Colleen … you talking about my dress. Look at Bee!" Bee does one of Colleen's moves and turns around showing off her ensemble. She knows she is looking extra delectable in her mustard colored form fitting dress hugging her in all the right places.

Looking at everyone smiling BeLynda says, "Wow, everyone looks so nice this evening. Everybody decided to wear a dress today, huh? I have such beautiful friends. Where are my huggy-hugs? I need them today!" The Ladies get up one more time giving BeLynda hugs and kisses. Colleen smiles over at the table of hustlers and their dates winking at them signaling that she knows they are watching Regina's ass. The not so cute honey brown complexion one smiles as his pretty gold-digging date gives Colleen a scowl. *The game hasn't change, but the playas have.*

Just then, their waitress for the evening approaches the table as they finish with properly greeting BeLynda and are beginning to sit down. She asks for their drinks order. Sandy speaks up, "Hello, yes Eliza. May you bring four glasses of water with lemons and limes in each, please? And we will be ordering drinks from the bar but um … we are going to try something different this evening." The Ladies' eyes take a detour from the waitress and towards Sandy. She smiles at them looking up at the waitress. "Yes, we all will have the Baltimore Zoo. Can the bartender make that for us?" The waitress went to go check with the bartenders. The Ladies all howl in laughter.

"Girl!! No you didn't! Oooh, now you know I haven't had one of those since the eighties. Damn!! That brings back some good fun memories." BeLynda says with a wide grin.

"Yea, I knew ordering that drink would get y'all's attention. I figured after the month we have been having – especially Regina - it would be nice to bring some sweet innocence back in it, you know?" Sandy mentions. They all nod in agreement. *The sweet innocence that we had back then even though we were too young to realize it. Back to a time when we had fun, pajamas parties, dressing alike, getting into fights with jealous girls, going to the go-go's and house parties, and making sure we kept at least a 3.0 GPA. We were inseparable, we still are though with the exception of having the need for some male company.* Sandy inwardly smiles. *Yeap, a helluva time.*

"I know, right? We all would get the Baltimore Zoo and the fried clams basket. Yea, those were some fun times. That's when Stan was planning to wife me up while Steve was begging Stan to hook him up with Bee." Regina laughs pointing at herself and BeLynda. *Yea, good times. But they were stressful at times. The stress of worrying about your boyfriend's safety. I made sure Stan called me every night by twelve midnight to assure he was home and safe. That was the only way I could go to sleep. He had to be home. But thinking back on that time, being young it just never crossed my mind that there could've been a home invasion. It hurt me to my heart that I had to have an abortion back then. He never knew but I was determined that I was going to college to get my ass out of that damn hell hole we called home. My baby made it out of the hood and loved me enough to take me with him. I never made it to college. That might be something that I think about now.*

"Well, I can say, even though my spirits were pretty high when I walked in here, you did lift them more. Thank you Sandy-Dandy. I appreciate it and you. That was really sweet." BeLynda. *Those were the time, I tell ya. Me and my Girls hung tight, and still do. Steve was so cute running behind me. That man loved me down to my dirty drawers. Probably would have worn them on his head walking down the street professing his love for me.* BeLynda lets out a chuckle. Then she sadly remembers. *It is amazing how pussy can change things. He knew I had only been one other boy, yet as soon as we said "I do," he thought I was supposed to turn into a freak machine. All because he had been out there getting licked, fucked, and sucked before me. I dealt with so much disrespect from him. I took so much shit off of him all for the sake of our vows. Now he wants to sit outside my house and spy. Had he acted right, he wouldn't have had to do all of that.*

Colleen smiles taking her down deep into her memories. *There are so many things I would like to change about my memories but I can't. I love that these three Ladies became my friends. They accepted me in that cafeteria without falter. However, by that time, I already new Stan and was square to the street game. Stan was so deep in the street life that he requested my services to be a protector of Regina. She had no idea. This woman sitting across from me at this table accepted me back then with loving and caring open arms. Stan loved that shit too.* She smiles holding back tears. *We've been going strong ever since. Sandy lived on the floor under Regina so I would see her just as much and so was mad cool. I learned a lot from them about being a female. I was caught up in that male dominated street world until I started to act like a damn boy in fucking girlie clothes. I was sooo tired then. Whew, Colleen you have come a long way.*

Looking up at her friends, Colleen finally says, "Yea, me too. When you said 'we were gonna try something different,' I had no idea what you were about to say. But … that was a pleasant surprise Dee Dee." Colleen smiles at her friend then looks away from her eyes playing tug of war with the tears that were trying to fall.

"Aww, listen to Ms. Mushy this evening. Are you getting sentimental on me?" Regina pauses and looks at Colleen. "Unh – unh, GIRL!! Don't do it Colleen. You gonna make me mess up my make-up. Don't have me in here crying. Stop it! Dammit Lene! We just got here!" Regina whines and smiles fighting to prevent any tears from falling that will make a domino effect around the table.

Colleen smiles, looking at all three of her friends through eyes that begin to fill with tears while somewhat stuck in her heartfelt memories. She says nothing with her mouth yet her eyes tell everything. She places her hands in the center of the table reaching for the hands of her friends. Sandy, BeLynda, and Regina all reach for Colleen's hands squeezing tightly. All four Ladies are smiling with watery eyes looking at each other, sharing a loving, emotional moment of bonding that is full of so many memories. The good, bad, and ugly. The happy, unhappy, and sad. The fun, boring, and pandemonium.

"I just love y'all. Thank you for being my friends. You know I was an outcast in school. People saying I was strange. Thank you so much." Colleen's tears run down her face and she shakes their hands as she squeezes them, trying to smile but she can't. She gets up excusing herself to the bathroom. The Ladies take napkins, patting underneath their eyes to catch any mascara from running down their face.

"Colleen is really in a different mood this evening. That drink really brought back memories for her that she must've packed away. I don't think she has ever showed us that much love. Now, that was a pleasant surprise for me. Colleen crying? Making us cry too?! My friend is actually human." Sandy says pulling out her compact checking her face. She looks around the restaurant to see if anyone has been watching them.

"True. And did you notice that her mascara didn't run? She did the damn thing on her face this evening, for real. Girlfriend went all in on looking nice for our pre-Christmas dinner. She must have on the waterproof kind." BeLynda says reaching for Sandy's mirror to check her own face.

"Bee, you silly. Right … but silly. Her face is saying something. The make-up *and* the expression." Regina sighs. "Maybe she knew she was going to get emotional this evening and she wanted to make sure she didn't look a hot mess when the tears fell." Sandy and BeLynda look at Regina with tilted heads. "Hey, she is Colleen, I'm just saying. She thinks of everything when it comes to staying on point. I don't think I have ever been that prepared to remain put together." Sandy and BeLynda shakes their heads in agreeance.

Meanwhile in the bathroom, Colleen is in the mirror checking out her face titivating her make-up. Making sure the mascara remained on her lashes and the eyeliner remained on her inner bottom eyelids. It is confounding that she literally got emotional. She is flummoxed that her emotions spilled over in front of her friends. What really is irksome to her is the fact that she could have continued to cry. Cry long and hard enough to fill up four twenty ounce glasses. Colleen cannot remember a day that she has ever cried. Her pre-teenage years are a blur from change of life experience she went through upon meeting Blue. Unfeeling and tenacious is what she had to be once she turned fifteen and started working for Blue. Feelings and emotions would have created sloppiness, which would have created jail time … and possibly her death. Nonetheless, over the past few years, she has worked conscientiously on connecting with her emotions. She had to in contemplation of administering a business that emphasizes engaging with humans as a requisite. Plus the last thing she wanted was to appear automated to her friends. However, she is aware that robotic can be a description of her.

Colleen smiles at her reflection. She feels lighter. The tears she cried seemed to have each dropped a pound allowing her emotions to begin to take their rightful place and shine rambunctiously. The oppressiveness that has always harassed her seems to be losing this battle. Ironically, she has never lost a battle or been unable to rid herself of anything other than the dankness of this cloud only visible to her. She doesn't feel awkward, powerless, or like a bitch-ass nigga. She is human. A business owner, a daughter, a friend, a sister, a woman, and a neighbor, all of which requires different facets of emotions from her. Colleen feels much better about the woman staring back at her in the mirror in this bathroom of the restaurant.

Realizing she has spent more than enough time in the bathroom, she releases a big sigh, rubbing her hands down the front of her dress across her thighs, approving of her appearance and departs, heading for the table her friends occupy. Regina sees her first and smiles. Sandy and BeLynda follow the casting of Regina's smile that has Colleen hooked to the end of it. They smile at her watching her approach the table. Colleen sits down at the square table across from Sandy but beside BeLynda.

"Okay, well, where were we before I decided to go for an Academy Award nomination?" They laugh at her words. "I better have won too. I done gave myself a damn headache. Thank goodness I decided to go with the waterproof extender lash shit this evening. Whew!" Batting her eyes are few times, Colleen picks up her shot of beer pouring it in the rest of her drink. "I see the bartender knew what you were talking about Sandy" she says taking a sip. "Mmmp, now that's what I remember! But you know we can't have too many of these. We are ten years older and Stan and Steve ain't driving tonight." They laugh remembering that's how their nights ended after having a few of the drinks. "You know with or without the beer, this shit is just as strong as a Long Island. We need to stay focused."

"Some things still just don't change hunh Lene? You finally have a moment of emotion and you are right back to business as usual. Relaxation is never an option for you hunh?" Sandy asks surprised – not really – at how Colleen can snap back to her normalcy so fast.

"Correction." Colleen takes another sip of her drink, looking at Sandy. "I am right back to paying attention to my surroundings. I am a woman honey and I can't be too careful. Nothing business about that. And there is always room for relaxation. That's what I normally do on Thursdays at the Spa with y'all, which is tomorrow. But … tomorrow is Christmas, they won't be open, and so I am relaxing with y'all as we speak. What's the matter Sandy? I'm not relaxing according to your definition? Tell me what is it that I should be doing?"

Sandy smiles and throws a crumb of bread at Colleen. "Oooh, don't let me have to read you in here heifer. You are sooo lucky that you showed me tears about fifteen minutes ago. At least I now know your ass is really human. For a very long time, I wondered." Sandy smiles as Regina and BeLynda watch the show.

"But I was just saying relax completely. Clear your mind, ease into the mood … let your brain rest. Paying attention to your surroundings requires some form of concentration." BeLynda agrees with Sandy.

Regina doesn't have a mental opinion regarding Colleen's behavior. In the beginning, she was in the same boat with Sandy and BeLynda in relation to her thoughts of her friend. Consistently thinking that Colleen was detached from everything and everybody. This is a new day and Regina understands Colleen more than she has before and more than their other friends do.

After having the conversation within her husband's office with him and Colleen, many things, including her actions began to make sense to Regina. She now understands why Colleen would take naps at her house before she went home. Regina realizes, Colleen wasn't going home, she was going to work for Blue and the streets once the streets were quiet. More than likely, being alert to do what Colleen was doing was a must. Even though the majority thought Colleen was a fly yet weird beautiful girl, she understands why the hustlers had mad respect for her friend. She understands why Colleen wouldn't ever sit with her back to the door. She needed to see what is happening or about to happen to prepare to be prepared. Just like a male in that life. She understands why Colleen was almost drag queen-ish with her style back then. She was trying hard to be and look like a girl because of her boy stance.

For the next hour, the Ladies laugh, reminisce, get emotional, eat, share their food, and order more drinks through their Christmas Eve conversation. They were really having a wonderful time. The love was felt and shown all around the table.

Sandy started feeling her mouth get watery. Then her stomach starts feeling like a simmering volcano. She knew exactly what this means. Trying to ignore it, she sits listening for a few more minutes. Trying to talk would have been a no-no. Finally, she excuses herself from the table.

"Hey, I'm going to go to the bathroom. Watch me walk to make sure I'm not doing anything stupid." Even though they have heard this statement before, Colleen and BeLynda look at Sandy confused. However, Regina jumps into action.

"No, I will go with you Dee Dee. Lene, order black coffee, a sprite, and hot water please." Walking together, Regina holds Sandy's hand. "Are you all right Dee Dee?" Sandy doesn't respond. Instead she speeds up her walk and Regina is in tow matching her steps. She looks back at Colleen and BeLynda and see they are watching.

Reaching the bathroom, Sandy enters a stall and see the bowl is full of toilet paper and piss. She hurriedly exists to enter another stall. As soon as she turns around to the bowl, it didn't matter whether it was full of waste because the volcano in her stomach erupts. She immediately vomits in, on, and around the bowl. As she continues, Regina pulls her hair back out of the way. When there is a pause, Regina gathers toilet paper off the roll to pat the perspiration off Sandy's face. Sandy continues with her purge. When she is done, she stands up, takes a few deep breaths and walks over to the sink not looking at Regina. Regina sees tears but not sure if it is from the episode or something else.

"Aww, Sandy, what is wrong? Are you all right? Are you crying?" Sandy looks at Regina smiling with sadness in her eyes. "What's the matter? Was it the memories that have you emotional? Of course I'm not talking about what you did in that stall. I know that was the drink." They laugh and Sandy gargles and rinses out her mouth several times before speaking.

"Regina … it's just that. I'm falling for him," she says pouting.

"Falling for who? Larry or Ray? It doesn't matter which one because it is ultimately your choice but what is the issue? Is it wrong for you to be falling for either of them?"

"I'm falling for Ray. He is so sweet, treats me the way that I want to be treated and I love it. I just don't want Colleen or anyone to think that I chose him over Larry because of his bank account or what I can get out of him."

Regina gives a warm smile. "Okay, well I don't think anyone would think that about you. As long as you know that is not true, don't worry about the others. And Colleen? Please, she is our friend and we know damn well that her word are more about her hatin' that he didn't choose her that night. You can't miss your happiness over assumptions or speculations. But what else? I don't think that's where you're ending this."

"There is something there but I can't put my finger on it. We have a good time together and he shows that he is feeling me. Then something enters the room with us and he seems to leave the room just leaving me with his shell. He can be smiling one minute then looking either sad or frustrated. He will say nothing is wrong but something is definitely wrong. Like he's feeling guilty or something. That is one of the main reasons why I have not answered his calls or texts in the past few days. I don't want to give him my heart and then get smacked in the face with some bullshit story about he needs to take a break … and that break never ends."

"Have you ever told him how you feel?" Sandy shakes her head "no." "Then tell him. He may be acting like that because he is into you and you aren't responding the way he wants you to. Maybe you are scaring him and his mood changes because you're being closed. It seems that both of you may have a little pain there from a lost love. So let him know your feelings. Let him in Sandy and this may change things."

"You think I should say something? I don't want to come off as if we have an updated title and then he shoots me with the he's just getting to know me bullshit."

"Listen to you. This man is offering you shit that many men in his position would arrogantly expect a whole lot of degrading shit from a woman in order to just buy her a damn quarter pounder with cheese meal. I'm getting ready to go back to the table to keep Lene and Bee from worrying. You get yourself together and call that man before you leave this bathroom. Did he call you today?" Sandy shakes her head "yes." "Well then, I'm on the outside looking in but if you had to ask me, I would say that he is trying to spend some holiday time with you. You are considered new pussy … and 'that' doesn't get the holidays the first time around. Call him Sandy." Regina turns to leave.

Sandy pulls out her cell, flips it open and stares at it. Taking a deep breath, she dials Ray's number. It rings a few times and she thinks she is going to get his voicemail. *He must've found something else to do.* Just when she was about to close her phone, he answers.

"Hello? Sandy? Where have you been? I've been calling you. Is everything all right? What's going on babe? Where are you?" Ray sounds too anxious.

"Hey Ray. I've been around. Everything is fine, calm down." She chuckles. "Nothing is going on. Right now, I am at Morton's in DC with my friends. We normally meet up on Thursdays but since tomorrow is Christmas, the spa will be closed. So we decided to meet up on Christmas Eve for dinner and exchange our gifts."

"Is that right? Oh okay. You and your friends hang tough, huh? That's beautiful to have friends like that. But why do I hear like an echo instead of people talking in the background? What's wrong? You sound so dry. Where are you exactly right now?"

"Well, I'm in the bathroom right now. I had this bright idea to order one of my famous drinks from back in the day … the Baltimore Zoo, and I just got finished blessing the porcelain god."

"OH! I see. The Baltimore Zoo, hunh?" Ray laughs. "Yea, you went way back for that. So that was y'all drink of choice back then? Y'all were going hard weren't you … all those white liquors will mess your stomach up every time." They laugh. Sandy feels so much better hearing his voice. "What are you doing later? I wanna see you."

"I was hoping to see you." Ray perks up. "Will you come get me from restaurant? I'm not gonna be able to drive. I can come back later to get it."

"Are you sure? I won't be imposing? I'm over one of my brothers' house. He can drop me off and I can drive your car back here. I can be there in fifteen minutes. Is that all right?" Ray is motioning for his brother Rick to get up and get ready. "Sandy are you there?"

"Ray, I need to see you. I need to talk to you."

"Babe, hold tight. Go back to the table and relax. They know me there. I'm already in the car. I'll be there before you know it." **click**

Sandy returns to the table with all eyes on her. She looks at Regina who gives her a wink and Sandy smiles. Regina smiles back at her knowing that she made the call.

"You all right Girl?!" Colleen asks with so much concern. "I thought I was gonna have to come in there and check on you. I didn't know what happened."

"Yea, me neither until I repeated her words in my head. That was our cue back in the day to say that we had a little too much to drink and we didn't want to catch the eye of some grimy up to no good ass nigga preying on the tipsy or drunk girl at the club. Then I knew what was up. Hey, blame yourself Girlie for having the bright idea to order the Baltimore Zoo." BeLynda smiles and swats her hand at Sandy. Everybody laughs out loud.

The table of hustlers and their dates get up to leave. Passing their table, the mocha complexion one with the tattoos on his neck and diamonds in his ear approaches the table with his thirsty gold-digger behind him. He places four business cards on the table looking at Regina saying, "If you ever get tired of your husband and want to have a real good time, do not hesitate to call the number." There's silence at the table watching the scene. He looks at all the Ladies, bends his head saying, "Merry Christmas Ladies and I hope you have a Happy New Year."

As he disappears out of their sight, Colleen smiles looking at Regina saying, "What did I tell you? And the look on that young whippersnapper's face that's with his ass was priceless." The Ladies burst into loud laughter.

****

That man is fine. Nice build, sexy jawline, fresh cut. That shearling he is wearing nice. He looks just like money. Damn, it looks like he is walking this way. Oh shit, he is looking at us. That's a smooth walking brotha right there. But he looks sort of familiar. Where might have I seen him before? Colleen is checking out the handsome man walking in their direction. She straightens up in her seat, ready to see if he is actually coming to their table.

The Ladies are busy eating their dessert. Sandy is drinking black coffee. As the man approaches the table, he places his big hand in the upper middle of Sandy's back. She looks up and see that it is Ray.

"Hey, Ray. You really came. And in fifteen minutes." BeLynda and Regina stop talking to see the tall dark shadow that seems to hide the lighting from their table. BeLynda smiles and speaks. Colleen waves and sips her water. Regina's mouth is hanging to the floor. This is her first time seeing Ray.

Frowning with a smile, Ray asks, "Did you think I wasn't going to come? I told I would and that I was fifteen minutes away." Looking at the other Ladies, he speak, "Good evening Ladies. It's nice to see you two again. I haven't met you. Hi, I'm Ray." He extends his big masculine hand to Regina. She smiles, extending her hand in attempt to shake his but is stunned by the kiss he places on the back of hers.

Regina's mouth is still on the floor. "Hello Ray. I am Regina. It's nice to meet you. I've heard so much about you." Colleen and BeLynda look at Regina lost in Ray's world.

Of course, I know exactly who you are. My dumb ass brotha has the hots for you. I do see why but he needs to let it go. Ray is saying to himself while smiling at Regina. Letting her hand go, he says, "I really hope I'm not intruding on your plans. Is it all right if I take Sandy with me? Or would you like for me to stay until you're done."

"Oh, where are y'all going Ray? By the way, you look and smell good. I love your coat." BeLynda is all smiles and Colleen wants to slap her a few times.

"Nowhere special. I haven't seen or spoken to this beautiful Lady in a while. Just playing catch up." Looking down at Sandy with loving eyes, he says, "I do believe we both need that." Sandy blushes yet returns a loving gaze of her own. BeLynda and Regina watch them interact and smile like, "*Girl go get your MAN*!"

Sandy stands to put on her coat. Ray reaches for it and helps her put it on. Looking up at him since she stands over a foot taller than her, she asks, "Are you ready?" He winks and grabs her hand. Regina is watching the love scene.

"Hey, let's exchange gifts real quick. They all pass out their gifts, give Sandy and Ray a hug and the Ladies watch them walk out of eye sight. Silence feels the table. Regina looks at Colleen and BeLynda puzzled yet excited.

"Well, I be damn! Did y'all see that gorgeous hunk of specimen that just came in here to get our Girl? The man that look like he was dressed for a Bachrach photo shoot that Sandy just walked out of here with? So that is Ray, hunh? No one told me he was that beautiful. It was like having an outer body experience. I swear I was watching me and Stan walk out of here." Regina and BeLynda laugh and give each other high fives.

"Did you know he was coming? She was in the bathroom for a minute with and without you." Colleen inquires.

"I didn't know he was coming but I told her to call him. She is feeling him just as much as he is feeling her. So apparently they are going to talk this out. I love seeing love. Maybe she will get that kiss and a new title." Regina smiles as she puts a spoonful her dessert in her mouth. Colleen rolls her eyes.

"Oh really? You think they are really going to talk … with their mouths? That man wanted to sop her up with himself." BeLynda laughs.

"Hey, that handsome big piece of a man came in fifteen minutes … on Christmas Eve to get her. Whether they do anything with other body parts, they are definitely going to talk before she leaves him. You can rest assure *that*." Regina says.

"Yea, probably so. But, something was weird about his demeanor when he was introduced to you. As if he was saying something in his mind about you with that fake smile plastered on his face. Yea, y'all want me to not pay attention to my surroundings. That fine ass motherfucka is up to something. And I don't like my girl being tied up in it." Collen frowns, saying to *herself I got both my eyes on you Ray. Something ain't right.*

"Colleen what's wrong with you? Why you quiet? Do I sense a little bit of envy at this table?" Regina devilishly smirks.

"Oh, the man is fine. No doubt in that. I surely can't deny that he is heaven to a woman's eyes. I can't and won't play down his sex appeal. Walking up in here looking like fresh crisp money, and he ain't even trying to give a show but he gave one. His suaveness and disposition demands attention … from EVERYBODY. I can guarantee you every woman in here that has watched him saunter over to our table have creamed in their panties." Regina looks on in astonishment. "Did you see how the people that work here was speaking to him as he and Sandy left? Oh yea, the brotha has it going on. But something ain't right. Maybe that's why Sandy hasn't gotten that kiss or dick. Maybe that's why he's been off the dating scene for a minute. That man has secrets."

BeLynda and Regina look at Colleen. BeLynda is confused but Regina has sense to realized Colleen's intuitions. Women have one type of intuition but Colleen has two. It is shocking to Regina that there are similarities in Colleen's and Sandy's feelings and observations. *Damn she sounds almost like Sandy. This woman is good but for Sandy's sake, I hope she is wrong.*

Chapter Twenty

20

"Go 'head in baby while I get your bags out the car. Take your coat and shoes off. Make yourself comfortable." Sandy looks at Ray wondering if she should wait for him instead. She didn't want to just walk in his house and help herself, even if he has given her the permission. Ray can feel her hesitance. Looking at her as he pulls the second gift out of the car putting it in the bag with the first gift he pulled out, he smiles, saying, "Sandy, it's okay. Really. I'm right behind you."

Turning around smiling at the gentle old man that is standing at the door, Sandy walks into the house, feeling as she if she has just been swallowed up by the Grand Foyer. This is only her second time being in Ray's house and she doesn't know how she should behave. Taking twenty-one steps through the foyer, she doesn't know whether to go left or right. About fourteen steps to her right, the hallway starts to bend the corner. Eleven steps to her left, there is a double entryway to a beautifully decorated room. To prevent from getting lost or being labeled nosy, she decides on the entryway to the left.

Walking inside the room, her heart slightly palpitates as she looks around the room. Sandy warmly smiles at the room. In the center of the room, there is a dark chocolate fluffy leather double-sided armless sofa with chestnut wood flat round legs. She rubs her hand across the supple leather. Other pieces of the sofa's family are nicely placed throughout and around the huge room. Against the short wall, there are matching loveseats diagonally positioned in each corner with twenty-five inch round leather pillows in shades of mustard and milk chocolate randomly placed on them. On the wall between the loveseats is the biggest fireplace Sandy has ever seen. The ledge is two inches above her head and a fire has already been started.

Hmmm, this must be the room he expected me to enter. Why else would he have started this cozy fire? Damn, it feels good because I was freezing with all these thighs out. I feel so much better now that I have gotten rid of that drink. It was good but I think I should have decreased my limit from three to two. Sandy laughs to herself. *I can't believe I actually threw up in the damn bathroom. It's a good thing we weren't at Club Love. They would have taken my ass to the detox center. And I would have been the damn joke for the next year.*

Sandy removes her black cashmere belted coat and Narciso Rodriguez burgundy thigh high boots. She is fantasizing that she lives here and she just came home from an excursion with her rich friends, waiting on her butler to bring her a glass of Don Julio. She is looking sexy, beautiful, and well-off. However, she knows that the coat and boots have set her back a few pay checks to pay down her credit card. *Hey, it was worth it because I look good*, she says to herself as she admires the look and quality of the coat laying across the other loveseat and her boots sitting beside her on the floor. She tucks her feet underneath her but and sinks into the loveseat giving permission to the heat from the fire to warm her body. She closes her eyes smiling, feeling as if she is floating.

Ray stands in the entryway with the bag of gifts he retrieved from the car, watching her. She is beautiful to him. The glow on her face from the fire makes him melt. Everything about her sends electric waves through his body. He is really into her. Something happened between them and he is not quite sure exactly what. Why did she avoid him the last few days knowing that they had a dinner date? He had not spoken with or seen her since Saturday. She canceled Tuesday's dinner and she had already told him ahead of time about this evening. He thought he wasn't going to see her this evening as well but is very appreciative that she called. She said she needed and wanted to see him. She needed and wanted to talk to him. The feeling is mutual but he has a feeling that their wants and needs don't match. Their topics of conversation will be polar opposites. Something is wrong and he needs to fix it. He wants to see how far this goes with Sandy. He is not going to worry about Rennie and his ridiculous plans. He knows they won't advance more than where they are now.

"Enjoying the fire?" Sandy eyes pop open fast to see Ray walk in with the gifts from her friends. He smiles and she untucks her feet sitting up straight. "Is it warm enough for you? Or do I need to add a few more logs? I had it right for me but if you need it warmer, let me know." Ray walks over to the nine feet pre-lit Christmas tree in the corner to the right of the door and sits Sandy's gifts under it. Sandy smiles. Just then, the butler comes in the room with five beautifully expensively wrapped gift boxes.

"Hey, Ray. Oh my goodness. That is a beautiful tree. Is it real? It looks like one of those trees they have in the department stores. Wow! I don't know how I missed that coming in here. I need to get my peripheral checked out. The first time it was the four big dogs. I don't know how I missed the overgrown tree." They both laugh.

"No, it is not real. I have never had a real tree before. I've heard enough stories about the watering, dry bristles all over the place and fires. I'm aiight with the pre-lit ones." They laugh. "I used to have a smaller narrow tree but my mother said that it was too small for the room. Once I got that one, I realized she was right." He smiles looking up at the tree. "I take it you are pleased with the tree?"

"Oh yes, it is very pretty." *A little too expensive for my pockets but I do love it*, she says to herself. "This is such a beautiful room Ray. You have great taste. Did you decorate this yourself? Or did you have help?"

"Nah, I didn't decorate it. Well, it was my ideas and concepts but the interior decorator did all the work. How did you know to come in here?" She smiles at him turning away from his observation. "I'm glad you like the tree too. If you didn't, I would have made sure I took notes for next Christmas." Ray smiles and Sandy tilts her head returning a perplexed smile. Trying to avoid his last statement, she continues.

"And yes, this room is nice and warm. It feels so good in here. The temperature sure did drop outside. I couldn't get in here fast enough. I'm still a little chilly but if I sit here long enough, I will be just the way I like it ... nice and toasty." Sandy smiles bashfully at Ray. *Damn he is fine. Man, you need to stop looking at me like that.*

Looking down at her exposed thighs and legs that are covered by opaque tights, Ray responds, "Hold that thought. I will be right back. I have something for you. I don't know why I didn't think about it earlier." Ray exits the room.

Sandy leans to the right watching the GQ model glide on the catwalk. Studying his walk she disappears into a daze. The wool slacks tailor made for the perfect fit around his waist, and on his ass, brushing against his thick athletic thighs. Watching closely each foot lifting from the floor and landing back on the floor in their black lizard skin tie-ups, making his walk sound sexy. *Damn, I wonder what designer made his shoes,* Sandy says not realizing she says it out loud. She swears she sees his biceps flex as the swing of his muscular arms in the light grey silk shirt goes back and forth. Ray continues down the hall and bends the corner. Out of her eyesight, Sandy scoots over to the corner of the loveseat using it as a shield to be more comfy. The fire has warmed up the piece of leather furniture perfectly. She closes her eyes again while waiting for Ray to return.

Ten minutes later, Ray reenters the room with folded red fleece material in his arms. Walking over to her, handing the material to Sandy, Ray speaks. "Here you are. It's just a sweat suit and a pair of socks. I bought a small. Will that fit? I did buy a medium as well as an extra small just in case." His hands are still extended waiting for Sandy to take the outfit. He has been around her enough to know what her hesitation is about. "Sandy, it's just a sweat suit. Nothing more. I bought it because you are always cold. I wanted to make sure that you were warm when you are here."

Sandy looks at the outfit then up to Ray's face observing the loving gesture. His thoughtfulness is blowing her but melting her like chocolate at the same time. Slowly lifting her hands, she accepts the clothing from him standing. She smiles like she wants to cry but instead, she toughens saying, "Thank you Ray. This is really sweet. I'm sure the small will fit but make sure to keep the medium one too. Colleen has already made comments about my thicker thighs." She blushes.

Ray's brow rises in surprise. "Oh really? Your thicker thighs? She actually said that? Well, I hadn't noticed," he says playfully. Sandy swats him on his arm. "But they still looks good. Real nice. I like it when you give me those love taps. I like when you touch me." The room gets still as if time has stopped. "Hey, I'm just saying. So go change, please. There is a bathroom five steps to your left outside of this room. I will be right in here." *Now it's my turn to watch you walk out of the room. I know you were watching my butt and thighs. Ray snickers to himself. Now let me watch yours. Damn she has a hellafide walk!!*

Ray watches Sandy stroll towards the exit of the room. Her petite shoulders, toned back, and slim waist. He smiles as her ass looks like it follows its own rules. Just hard-headed, misbehaving, doing what it wants to do in her dress while her hips try to gain some type of control over the situation. It's a fight going on and her thighs are about business giving the swishing sound as they rub together in her tights. Ray smiles at the vision. For the first time since they have been keeping it with each other company, a twinge is felt deep in his groins. Immediately, grabbing the waist of his pants, shaking his left leg, he readjusts his dick, rubbing down the shaft to calm it down. Ray softly says, "Damn! What the fuck." Repeating his motions, he says, "Calm down, not tonight. This ain't the time. She and I have some things to talk about."

Walking to the bathroom made her feel as if she wasn't quite done vomiting. But the feeling cease as fast as it began. Entering the bathroom, turning on the light Sandy is in awe. She has seen the powder room before but it just amazes her that Ray actually lives like this. The crown molding, built-in shelves, French closet doors, Verona marble floors, double sink with six shelves base. This is the biggest powder room she has ever seen. Sandy begins to change into the sweat suit. *He lives as like he has twenty children. Everything is just big. Then again, he is not a small man and he would need room to maneuver around. In my powder room, he would soon find out whether or not he is claustrophobic or not.* Sandy silently giggles to herself.

Walking over to the intercom, pushing the button, Ray requests for a cart of beverages and glasses. He is not sure what she would like to drink – after throwing up - so the decision is to have a variety for her. He sits on the same loveseat Sandy has been sitting on and takes his shoes off. Walking over to the fireplace, he picks up the wrought iron poker and pushing the logs around and adding another log. He stands there daydreaming at the burning logs deep in thought. He is falling in love with Sandy.

He hears the cart being rolled into the room. Turning to see the butler pushing the cart to the normal spot in the room, Ray smiles. He puts his hands in his pockets and turns back to the fireplace, where he left his thoughts. "Thank you John."

The butler nods his head asking Ray, "I brought you one bottle of champagne, two waters, four sodas, and two bottles of white wine. You also have baguette slices with dipping oil." Ray winks, smiling. "Will there be anything else sir?"

"Thank you again John. For the next two hours, Ms. Robertson and I do not want to be disturbed. There shouldn't be anyone calling or stopping by anyway. It is Christmas Eve. But just in case … I will not be available for any other conversations or visitors. Well, unless it is my mother."

The butler nods again saying, "Will do sir," and turns to walk out of the room. On his way out, he notices the powder room door beginning to open. Nodding at Sandy, he continues to walk down the hall, disappearing around the wall.

Sandy watches him. I wonder what is around that corner. *He led me straight passed this intersection when I was here Saturday.* Sandy walks back in the room observing Ray staring at the fire. She is feeling a little nervous. He looks so serious on top of his handsomeness. She knows that she told him she needs to see and talk to him, taking Regina's advice. She is regretting listening to Regina. Now, she is not so sure that she wants to give him a little peak into her heart. Not tonight. Not this month. But she is here and she is going to be a big girl and just flow with the events of the evening.

Ray senses her presence at the same she clears her throat to get his attention. "You're back. Good. That sweat suits fits perfect. I kind of figured you are a size small. I have some drinks for us. Which one would you like? John has brought us champagne, water, sodas, and wine. I'm going to pour me a glass of Chardonnay. There's also munchies to coat your stomach. No vomiting for the rest of the night." Ray laughs showing off his beautiful white teeth. Sandy giggles.

"Yes, the sweat suit fits. But um … Ray … this is not *just* a sweat suit as you said. You didn't go into Target or Wal-Mart for this." Ray looks at her puzzled. "This is Ralph Lauren … and you brought *three* … to see which size I would need? Ray?!"

"C'mon Sandy. What's wrong with the sweat suit? Did you want it to come from those stores? You don't look like you shop there. I ain't ever been in those stores. I don't know what kind of boots you have on tonight but I can guarantee you they don't sell Via Spiga or cashmere." He smiles and Sandy lowers her eyes. "Did you want me to lower you standards via a sweat suit. It's a sweat suit. Now what would you like to drink?"

Damn he has a point. "Okay Ray. You're right. I do not shop at those stores. I just thought that's where you'd go for a sweat suit for me to wear when I'm here just to keep warm." He laughs at her corrective statement and thought. "I will take a glass of Chardonnay too." Stan pours her a half of glass of the wine and hands it to her. They both walk over to the loveseat. Sandy sits on the floor directly in front of the fireplace.

Ray's get wide. "Oh, I will be right back again. I see I need to change too. Give me five minutes. I won't be long. Enjoy your champagne. Don't go nowhere sexy." Ray jogs towards the entryway, turning around jogging back to get his shoes. Then he disappears out of the room.

Sandy sips on her champagne enjoying her drink and waiting on Ray's return. He comes back in exactly five minutes with red sweat bottoms and a white wife beater on. Sandy tries to notice his biceps and big ass chest.

"Now where were we before you got upset about a sweat suit?" He smiles teasingly and she melts in his smile.

Sandy wastes no time getting to the point. "Ray, I just want to say that I have not been ignoring you. It just seems as if since I met you, I've been in a dream. With that feeling, I didn't want to wake up and be in the same place I was before I met you. I don't know if you are understanding me or not but that is how I've been feeling. I know you said that you are just as ordinary as me … but you're not. The ordinary men I know or have come across cannot afford this big ass estate with several other houses on the land, or have cars, drivers, or are able to offer me what you have. It frightens me a little bit. I'm not a gold-digger nor do I want to be labeled as such. You were throwing so much at me so fast. I decided to take a break from the dream." She looks at him deeply and he can see her soul. He loves it.

Looking back into her eyes, it's his turn. "I'm glad you said that you weren't ignoring me because I really thought you were. I thought I did something wrong. I am only being me Sandy. It is not a dream, it is real. Just me being me. As far as feelings, I am really feeling you and I do apologize if I offered and showed too much too soon. I know you are not a gold-digger. You have shown that in so many ways." He smiles and continues. "So many ways that I wanted to show you more. But I will slow down and not overwhelm you. It's only been a little over a month but I can say that I am falling for you. Trust when I say that I am not weak soft nigga but I go after I want … and I want you. NO need to take a break from the dream … what do you want me to do? Pinch you to let you know that it is real? That I am here? That I want you? That I want to share with you all of me?"

Damn, he is on for real. "Ray, how come you don't have a woman? Women? No children? You have so much to offer and yet you have kept it all to yourself."

"I had a woman. She was killed and it's been about three years since her. Others I have met were out for what I can do for them. Others didn't measure up to her. But then you came along … and you surpassed everyone, include her. I am not getting any younger and I do want someone special in my life. I want that person to be you. You Sandy. No, I don't have any children. Do you want children Sandy?" Asking that question made his dick jump a few times. He jumped with it and she looks at him wondering what is going on.

"I'm a woman Ray. How many women do you know that don't want any children? So to answer your question, YES I want children. I want a house full. I just never had anyone in my life that I thought about having children with until now." Ray smiles lovingly.

"Well, then Sandy. We want the same things, it looks like. Let me love you. Show me how to love you. Be with me. I don't know what your friends want but it seems as if Regina is the only one that is married."

"How do you know that? I've never said anything about my friends."

"You didn't have to. I know a wedding ring when I see it. The other two that were there with you at the Zanzibar didn't have on rings. But tonight, I kissed Regina's left hand that had a big ass blinding wedding ring on it. I'm very observant and when it comes to the woman I am interested in, I scope out her surroundings. Your friends are your surroundings. Was I wrong for that?"

"Ray, this is not about my friends. It is about me … you … us. I wasn't sure what we were doing. I am not sure what we are doing now. Yes, Colleen and BeLynda didn't have on rings but BeLynda was married at one time. She is now divorced, so she did have a ring at one time. But Colleen was getting on me and the last thing I need is for my friends to interfere in my steps."

"Steps? What you mean? Okay, baby you lost me. What are you saying?" Ray grabs her hand caressing it. He wants to understand.

"Yes, Ray, steps. My steps are to meet, talk, get to know each other, spend time together, date, have titles updated or exchanged, sex, … . You know, the steps it takes to get to that point of … "

Ray smiles and finishes her steps. "Ah, leading up to maybe a marriage, huh? What's wrong with that? Why wouldn't you want those things? We have the same steps and the same goal. Who in the fuck want to carry the "friend" on the end of that title forever? I know I don't want to be any woman's boyfriend … walking around with grey hair and a cane. What's scaring you Sandy? Am I too forward with my wants? I'm not getting any younger. Neither of you."

Sandy looks at Ray. "Damn Ray! I feel like I am dreaming for real. Are you serious? I mean, you talk a good game and I don't want to play any games. But you do sound for real. Are you for real? You are serious?"

Ray grabs her hand. "Look at me. Look at me Sandy." She looks into his eyes and almost jumps while melting. "I don't play games. That's why there hasn't been another woman in a long time. I didn't need a user or any entrapments. It's just been me and me and my dogs. They have been my children. What you wanna do? I know you think it is soon but fuck, you can keep your place … but just be here with me."

Sandy is quiet soaking it all in. "What do you want me to do? Are you saying you want me to move in? Here, with you?" *Damn did I just say that shit to this man?*

"Stay with me … most of the time, if not all of the time. If you want to quit your job, you don't even have to go other than to get your things. Better yet, make a list of the things you have there and I will have them picked up for you. We can erase your headache now. Just say the word and it's done."

"It's done? Just like that huh? I don't know Ray. What if this doesn't work out? Then what? What am I supposed to then after that?"

"Dag, pessimistic are we? Don't worry about it Sandy. You're fine. Everything will be just fine. Trust me. I knew you were the one when we out to dinner that first night."

"What are we to each other? We haven't even kissed. We haven't seen each other naked. Not to mention, we haven't had sex.

How you know after seeing me naked and having sex that you won't regret all that you're saying right now? I'm not for having my heart broken. Not by you or any other man."

Raising his eyebrows with a wide grin, he says, "Well, if you will have me, I am your man … you are my woman. Wow, that sounds good to me. How does it sound to you? We can break the news to everyone later. There is no rush for others to get into our business asking all kinds of messy questions. I didn't want to kiss you unless you wanted it. As for sex, it comes with the territory and I have had some feelings tonight that I hadn't had in a minute. But only when you are ready. It's been some years but I promise I will be gentle and you won't be disappointed. Sandy I won't hurt you." Ray says the last statement humbly which was a signal to Sandy that he was going to tear her ass up when they do get to the nasty.

"This is a lot Ray but I promise, I will think about it … and think about it hard. No pun intended." They laugh. "I will let you know in a week. My sister can move into my house if I decide to come here." *I can't believe I am saying this shit but I am really feeling him. He doesn't seem to be the controlling type. He doesn't appear to be the abusive type either. Only time will tell with both of these.*

"Okay, then. It seems that we have made an agreement. Now, as for that kiss … ." He leans in for a peck. Then two more pecks and his manhood begins to wake up excitedly. Before he gets too hard, Ray jumps up grabs her hand and heads towards the tree. "I have a few things for you. The three additional gifts all belong to you."

"For me?! Why? I mean, really?! They are so pretty. You bought me five gifts Ray?" She looks at him with teary eyes. "Damn, I've already cried a few times tonight. You trying to make me cry again?"

"You cried yesterday. It is now Christmas day. Open them. In any order you want to. However, he hands her the Tiffany box first. "Here, it is just a little something. I'm just happy that I have someone other than my mother to buy gifts for." Handing Sandy the box, she smiles, stares at it, and then stares at Ray. "It doesn't matter that you didn't get me anything. I don't need anything. I don't want anything but you. That's gift enough." Ray kisses Sandy softly on the lips.

Unwrapping the flat long rectangular box, Sandy assumes she is about to become face to face with a piece of jewelry. Removing the top of the box, there is an envelope inside. She can't imagine what it is. Ray is smiling looking at her as if she is taking too long to open the gift. Peeking inside the envelope, Sandy's mouth opens into an "O" and she hesitates a few seconds before pulling them out of the envelope. "Ray! Oh my God! You are so sweet! Thank you! Thank you! Thank you!" The gift certificates to her favorite Spa for the next year made Sandy jump up and give Ray a big hug. Her arms barely wrapping around his muscular back. Ray laughs at her excitement. Loving that something this small gives her this much joy. Sandy has already estimated that he spent fifty-two hundred. That's not a drop in the bucket for her.

Handing her another gift, it smaller than the one she just opened. The assumption is this is a pair of earrings. But she realizes that she was wrong about the first gift. Removing the wrapping paper, she waste no time opening the box. Her mouth opens into an "O" again. She looks at the contents and then up at Ray. "Are you serious? This is for me? I don't know Ray. A Visa gift card with five hundred dollars on it? Oh … wait, I'm sorry. There are SIX of these in this box! Three thousand dollars Ray?! "

He smiles saying, "I'm not taking them back Sandy. Give one to each of your friends, then if you feel it is too much. That will leave you with fifteen hundred. Would that be better?" He laughs teasing her. "You're lucky I changed my mind from getting it put on a debit card. That would have had your name on it." She just smiles at him and rubs her face, then his. *I swear I must be dreaming.*

"*Damn!* Okay, Ray I'm done. Don't hand me anything else." Sandy fumbles through the two types of gift cards in awe and speechless. "This is beautiful Ray. All of this is really too much for a Sista all at once. I mean, save some for my birthday … Valentine's Day … achievements … anniversary … those 'just because.'" Sandy and Ray burst into laughter. "The first gift will cover - on average - gifts for Christmas, Birthday, and Valentine gifts for the past five years."

Ray is surprised at how frugal Sandy appears. "Really? Okay. I understand. I will just hold on to the last box then. How's that?" Ray can tell by Sandy's facial expression that even though she said what she said, it didn't literally mean that she didn't want to continue opening the gifts. He laughs at her expression as he hands her the third box.

Sandy is not sure if she can take much more. Releasing soft blows from her mouth, she accepts the gift from Ray's hand checking out his manicured nails and his watch. It is a classic Rolex DateJust. Sandy smiles as she opens the gift. She knows what kind of watch he is wearing. The big time hustlers would sport the watch.

Deep in her thoughts, she opens the box a little too rough and a yellow canary diamond tennis bracelet falls out heading for the floor. Ray catches it in time. He never looks at her face. Ray already knows the expression is priceless. Opening the clasp, he asks, "Which wrist would like for me to put it on?" Sandy's words are caught in her throat. She extends her right wrist to him, raising her wrist to her eyes admiring the beauty afterwards. She dares not ask how many carats it is weighing down her wrist. *Maybe I am really sleep and in a few minutes, I am going to wake up over there on that loveseat where I must have been for real.*

"Earth to Sandy." Ray snaps his fingers to get her attention. She blinks looking at him. "This is from me, of course. Was that hard?"

"I'm here. I thank you so much and I'm embarrassed. I had no idea you were going to have anything for me. Hell, you know how the saying goes. New pussy don't get the holidays and gifts." Ray chokes on his champagne ejecting from his mouth. He leans over to prevent permanent damage to his shirt, laughing uncontrollably.

"What?! Is that what women have been subjected to? Is that really what they say? Who says that, the broke disrespectful niggas?" Ray is still laughing. "How it go again Sandy?" Laughing she repeats it. "Ah, that is too funny. You are a trip."

"No, I'm not, I'm just saying. That's what they say and that's what they do." She picks up her glass of wine asking for a refill. Ray walks over to the cart with her glass.

"Well, you have the gifts from your friends left. Are gonna open them? Or is that private? Do I need to leave the room?" Ray hands her refilled wine glass. She thanks him.

"I can open them right there. Nothing to hide." Sandy walks over to the tree and pick up Regina's gift first. Reading the gift tag, she smiles and begins to rip into the paper. She sees it is three boxes of LaMer moisturizing cream. This is Regina's favorite cream and Sandy always finds a reason to use some of it when she is at her house. Regina had taped them together making it easier to wrap as one gift. *Only Regina would have thought of that.*

"Hmmm, La Mer, that's nice. Who gave you that? That was very generous of them to give you three of that."

"Regina gave me this." Sandy smiles at the cream. "That's my girl. I guess she got tired of me using up hers every time I am over there." Ray and Sandy laugh. Putting her hands on her hip, she asks, "And what you know about LaMer Mr Daniels?"

Ray smiles. "Oh I know a lot about it. My mother uses it. As a matter of fact, she won't use anything else. For as long as I can remember, that right there in your hands has been a part of her life." Ray snickers. "And you had the nerve to be uncomfortable with my gifts? Why is this different? Because that's from your girl?" Sandy looks puzzled. "You must don't know how much that cream cost, huh? I've bought plenty of it for my mother. And you say you use it every time you go over her house? Every time? I can see why she bought you your own." Ray teases Sandy. Sandy is still holding the cream realizing that she never thought about how much it costs. *I've been over Gee Gee's house just using up her shit like it's priced like Bath & Body Works.* Looking at the cream in her hands, Sandy smiles uncomfortable and says nothing. "Well, I won't be the one to tell you. You can go to their website and price it. Okay baby, next gift."

Picking up BeLynda's gift, Sandy shakes it and giggles. "I don't know what she got me. Bee is always original with her gifts."

"Open it so we both can see. Regina giving expensive gifts and all, I'm sure BeLynda's gift is just as expensive."

When he says that, Sandy realizes even though she is into fashion, her friends are on another level. They have been exchanging gifts all of their adult life. The thought of the price of her gifts compared to what her friends' prices may have been is making her feel weird. "All right, here it goes." Removing the wrapping paper, she immediately knows BeLynda gave her clothes.

Her smile widens. Opening the box, Sandy screams in laughter, "Bee! No you didn't!" BeLynda gave Sandy a black label cashmere slim fit crewneck sweater.

Ray smiles approvingly. "Oh that is gonna look real nice on you. Your friend has good taste. Cashmere huh?" Sandy shakes her head agreeing with him. "All right, it's getting late. Last but not least. Let's see what your other friend has given you." Ray picks up the gift. It is a little heavy. He is wondering what could be in this gift. He hands it to Sandy.

Sandy frowns at the heaviness of the gift. "Damn, what the hell did Colleen buy me? Hell, what did she buy us? I know she gave us the same thing." Sitting the gift on her lap, she unwraps it. It is a cute black case with her name engraved on a metal tag. Flipping the locks on the case, there is silence and anticipation.

Ray immediately knows what it is. He had to think about it a few seconds because the case has been upgraded. Grabbing Sandy's hand, Ray asks, "Are you sure you want to see what is in this case right now? You're stalling. You can't wait until you're alone if you want to."

Looking at him Sandy opens the case and almost dropped all of the contents on the floor. Once again, Ray catches it. Sandy is shaking worse than a leaf. She can't believe that Colleen would give this as a gift. She tries to stand but trembling too much she falls back on the seat.

"Babe. Is this really from Colleen?" Sandy shakes her head "yes." "She meant to give this to you? This isn't a mistake?" She shakes her head "no." Looking at the gift, Ray says, "I have to admit, it is cute. But why would your friend feel the need to give you … well all of y'all a damn gun? And as a Christmas gift? What happened?" He knew something was up with Colleen when he saw her in the parking lot that night.

"Shaking her head, Sandy responds, "Nothing. She just likes for us to be prepared to protect ourselves at all times."

"Protect WHO?! Why you need to protect yourselves? What's going on? Talk to me!" Ray is trying to hide his franticness.

Sandy covers her face saying, "Someone has been following Regina and after she told us everything, Colleen believes we need to carry a weapon. She talked about us going to the shooting range. I mean, I didn't think she was *this* serious. I thought we had some time to think on it."

Ray stands up immediately running his hands over his eyes and down his mouth and landing them on his waist, then to the back of his head pacing the floor. He can't stop moving his hands. He has forgotten that Sandy is in the room. *So Regina knows she is being followed. Her husband probably knows too. Colleen purchased motherfuckin' guns for all of them? Did the husband tell her to do that? Oh there needs to be a meeting ASAP. They not bullshitting. Rennie will get the whole fuckin' family caught up in this shit!!*

Private Classes 3 coming soon!!

Before you get started on the next book, it would greatly be appreciated if you write a review/comment on Amazon about this second installment to the *Private Classes* serial novel.

Thank you for reading!

Dear Reader:

I hope you enjoyed ***Private Classes 2***. I admit, I really love all of the characters from the main women to the introduction of Mama Rachel and Felicia. I love many of the male characters too. Many readers wrote me asking, "Where is Devin," and "Is anything going to develop between Devin and Colleen?" Well, stay tuned because the chronicle of publishing urban drama filled with erotic scenes isn't over. Devin will be back in book three. Will he hook up with Colleen or get a chance with Sandy? I sure hope so.

When I wrote the first book of the ***Private Classes*** series, I received so many letters from fans thanking me for the book. I had no idea I had any fans and I am very thankful for those who decided to write me. Some had opinions about Sandy, Regina and Colleen, and others rooted for BeLynda. As an author, I love feedback. Candidly, you are the reason that I will explore Devin's future. So tell me what you loved, what you liked, even what you hated. I'd really love to hear from you at: authornatljohns@gmail.com.

Finally, as a favor please, if you're so inclined, I'd love a review of ***Private Classes 2***. Loved, liked, or hated it – I'd just enjoy your feedback. Reviews can be tough to come by these days. Many read and enjoy yet forget the review. You, the reader, have the power to make or break a book. Here is a link to my author page on Amazon, where you will find both books: http://amzn.to/1tHeUZN

Thank you so much for reading the second installment of Private Classes and for spending time with me.

In gratitude,

Nat L Johns

Erotic and Urban Author

www.ingramcontent.com/pod-product-compliance
Lightning Source LLC
Chambersburg PA
CBHW021431240626
47153CB00001B/104

* 9 7 8 0 6 9 2 5 9 4 0 5 6 *